Night Drive

Modern German Short Stories

Night Drive

Modern German Short Stories

Edited by Klaus Humann

This book was published with assistance from the Arts Council of England

Library of Congress Catalog Card Number: 95–68390

A catalogue record for this book is available from the British Library on request

First published 1996 by Serpent's Tail,
4 Blackstock Mews, London N4, and
180 Varick Street, 10th floor, New York, NY 10014

Typeset in 10pt Times by Intype, London
Printed in Great Britain by Cox & Wyman Ltd., of Reading, Berkshire

Contents

Introduction

Breaks and Break-outs

I f one were to believe the German critics, then the literature of their country is nothing but mediocre. This complaint is not new, not in Germany or anywhere else. Apart from this lament, however, which has almost the inevitability of a natural law, there are a number of breaks, or ruptures, which make it hard for readers, as well as critics, to buy, praise, enjoy German literature.

With the passing of the formative figures of postwar German writing in both East and West, the old fixed points are missing. The new Böll, the new Grass, the new Fühmann, the new Andersch, the new Hermlin, new books by Lenz or Johnson—the glory of former years has faded. The big subjects—German war-guilt, pacifism, anti-fascism—belong to yesterday, have no equivalents in the work of younger German authors. The single discourse dominating all the literary reviews, the figures who overshadowed everyone and everything, are no longer there.

German writers have taken their leave of politics—at least for the time being. Grass at SPD party conferences, Böll at demonstrations against US missile bases—that was the 60s and 70s. Commitment was superseded by reports on the state of mind of individuals, good ones as well as embarrassing ones, by the record of experiences in marginal zones—drugs, therapy culture and the rest—and by a melancholy kind of ethno-poetry.

When, in November 1989, the Wall fell in Berlin and

elsewhere, a great deal more fell with it, in the West as much as the East. The laboriously rehearsed view of a world consisting of opposing power blocks was no longer in demand. The literature of the GDR, so often in opposition to the regime, had suddenly lost its aura—and from now on had to allow itself to be judged by literary criteria. East and West German authors became reunited authors with eastern and western characteristics and colouring. Hence the decision to include authors from both Germanies was a logical one. My bet, however, is that it will take some time before there is something like an all-German literature.

Even if the majority of authors have turned to more private concerns—Auschwitz or the ozone hole are no longer dominant themes—a number of writers were, nevertheless, already describing and analysing German-German sensitivities well before 1989. Martin Walser, Botho Strauss, Hans Magnus Enzensberger, Günter Grass, Christoph Hein, Christa Wolf—they all disprove the myth of the withdrawal of writers into privacy and introspection. Whether Botho Strauss, one of the most important contemporary dramatists and writers of prose, flirts with the New Right or Christa Wolf defends the good old GDR—they are certain of a hearing far beyond the books pages of the press. And no one, certainly no German politician, is more attentively followed, interviewed and reviewed by intellectuals abroad than Günter Grass. In any case, as explicitly political as Grass or as reticent as Sarah Kirsch, authors continue to function as seismographs of the state of health of the new Germany.

This anthology, like every anthology, makes choices. It presents texts written exclusively by German authors. Authors from Switzerland, Austria and Romanian-German authors are not included. With four exceptions, the texts are self-contained. The majority of writers are being presented to English-speaking readers for the first time. The selection presents a Germany a long way from (or beyond) Wagner–wurst–Hitler–Volkswagen. This selection, my selection is, I hope, a controversial, entertaining snapshot of a country, which in the fifty years since the end of the Second World War has not yet learned to be adult.

Klaus Humann
Frankfurt am Main, July 1995

Rainald Goetz

What is a Classic

What is a classic?

Stupid question, man! Any clown knows that. I'm the only one who doesn't know, poor bastard. So every evening, every night, I have to go on patrol, everything is meticulously checked, each new haircut, each one of the countless faces on the scene already mutely looked at a hundred and sixty four thousand times, all well known to me, thank god only by sight, each new little moustache on each upper lip, classic? Each new coupling, oh yeah him with him since just last week, each drunken binge by someone somewhere, every bit of Schumann, every disagreement, a classic? Everything is steadfastly scrutinised and registered, stored up and the next day early in the morning as the blood alcohol level unhurriedly falls, the whole lot is boosted with Schiller's letters from the hot Weimar summer of 1787, with encyclopedia articles about Arcimboldo, Trieste, I'm already at Winckelmann, then quickly there's the tabloids and Julie Burchill's latest column in *The Face*, boost, boost, boost with Goethe's Winckelmann essay, which has such nice solid thick headings, Friends, World, Unrest, at the same time morning TV with the sound turned down, because in the evening I never get round to watching TV, because I always have to drink so much, because it's always so hot, and the sound from the speakers as well, You gotta say Yes to another Excess, logical man, logical, boost it up even higher, Hans Henny Jahnn on Lessing, Lessing on Hamburg, Nick Rydenback on Foucault, Kaiser on Wagner, Names

Names Names, Thinking Thinking Thinking, looking at *Abart* magazine photos by Miron Zownir, total madness, and then, now it's eight minutes past four, and at last I'm sober, now WHOOSH short circuit everything with WHOOSH everything else.

That's why it's obvious that Andreas Dorau is a classic. Anyone who doesn't know that gets junked. Because Andreas Dorau was in Munich recently, completely surrounded by neat stupid little pill-popping teenies and even neater even more stupid Film School students, simply charming. Another definitive classic was also in Munich the week before, and his name is Stephan Oettermann.

But I had to go to Marbach, to the Archive of German Literature, because I simply don't know whether Friedrich Schiller is a classic or an arsehole. In *Minima Moralia* Adorno often has harsh words for Schiller, which is something I recently discussed with my long-haired Adorno-freak philosopher brother, and it's logical, it was immediately obvious, that Adorno isn't really fighting Schiller, but some old Gauleiter or other or some Nazi Party guardian of the literary heritage, or some SA or SS officer, perhaps he was also thinking of some idealistic BDM girls' troop, reading Schiller for edification, because the *Völkischer Beobachter* newspaper says: Schiller is the Eternal German, the Prophet of Our Age. Today no one needs to be against Schiller, but against Adorno, with whom the thinking of every normal person begins, but that's just it, it only begins. But I'll run through these strategic questions in another sermon, or even better— I'll keep quiet about them, so as to hoodwink spies.

Let's rather go to Marbach, because there's an exhibition on there: *Classic Writers in Dark Times 1933–1945*. And as we all know dark times cast this odd light on things, a kind of bright slanting light. But instead of discovering in Marbach whether Schiller is a classic, I find myself standing in sweltering heat in the obligatory Marbach pedestrian precinct. In the 70s every last dump with ten thousand and one inhabitants acquired a pedestrian precinct, just as in the 60s every miserable middling town urgently needed a television tower, perhaps the repulsively tasteful steel and glass arcades will be the planning epidemic of the present decade, anyway in the 70s pedestrian precincts, and not a soul knows why? what for? against what? pedestrian precincts burst upon the German provinces, and at the edge of the deserted pedestrian precinct stand these delightful cute half-timbered houses, and in the shops the people talk in their delightful cute half-witted retarded dialect, all of it completely harmless, all of it one big depression, the structural depression of the German provinces. Quickly back to my beloved concrete desert, away from this landscape, whose delightfulness, I notice every time I raise my eyes, every time I look, is nothing but a merciless kick in the balls.

The best thing about classics, or so I realised the next day while looking through the voluminous informative exhibition catalogue, is that they are far too well known to far too many people and that any clown can do what he likes with them. That's why a classic is a pop phenomenon. It can be used for the most contradictory ends, a rich store of quotes to be plundered, and the undisguised affirmation it is granted by a Nazi imbecile or by worthy responsible democratic imbeciles, who are valiantly responsibly and democratically overcoming the darkness above all, over there in Marbach, is truly subversive. Is anything anywhere clearer afterwards? in anyone's head? that is very much the question, but so what. At its best a classic is, what pop too is at its best: that is, a hit, it's logical. Hits are so good that they never get boring, quite the opposite, the better you know them, the better you want to know them. Apart from that hits are splendidly short-lived, one hit overthrows the next hit, which overall leads to complete full throttle speed, at every moment, and the speed would not be there if there were no hits. And, you always come back to them, especially at times of weakness and discouragement. Is a Peter Huchel poem any good? or Babylon is Burning? or Grace Jones, or Motown Alltimegreatests, or Bacon on Love, or Charlotte von Kalb's memoirs of Goethe and Schiller, or Frieda Grafe on film, or is not yet again today the best cure the collected essays, conscientiously collected by me, of the classic cultural critic B. B. Blackmon, I need some old hit or other in times of weakness, so I go to the Megalomania Dance Hall, where no one who thinks they're hip goes any more, which is why I constantly go to that very place and drink my beer there, because I'm so hip that I don't need to be hip. So the Megalomania is clearly a classic classic like Goethe. The letters of Schiller, however, which I'm reading at the moment, encourage the suspicion that he must have been a pretty dumb, overexcitable, timid wretch. I can't read too much of it, because it discourages me. Therefore Schiller is not a classic. Because a chief characteristic, virtually a cardinal symptom of the hit as of the classic is in the end that it is encouraging, gives one new heart, new strength, new new and new anger for the next newest attack.

Glossary
Andreas Dorau: Pop singer who achieved a degree of success in the early 80s and enjoyed a revival in fortunes in the mid-90s. He combines classically simple pop tunes with mock naive lyrics.
Stephan Oettermann: Critic and writer on culture and art.
BDM = Bund Deutscher Mädel: Section of the Hitler Youth which enrolled girls aged between 14 and 18.

Adolf Endler

Exemplary Expectorant

*S*mog *alert in West Berlin! Second day running, too!*—But must the poisonous clouds of another world mar our *own* creative temper? The *perpetual state of non-alert* in the matter of smog, which distinguishes our capital city so favourably from yonder mere fragment of Berlin, the Berlin of the Senate, ensures, at least with regard to this point, that we may fall asleep in peace ... *They're going down like flies on the KuDamm!* ... Hardly skin off our noses, madam! Our *own folk* give us *quite enough to chew over* as it is; O yes, we have other fish to fry!—e.g. the fact that late autumn 1982 finds our author liable to spend days on end embroiled in repeatedly vain attempts to complete even a single sentence; it ought to be possible to come up with two or three sentences in twenty-four hours that actually do make it to a full stop, an exclamation or question mark—the very minimum I require to maintain self-respect, as well as the necessary, optimistic outlook ... Petering out with three dots in the middle of nowhere is simply not enough! Not by any stretch! Smog alert in West Berlin!? Simply not our funeral, my dearest postwoman! For as you will no doubt be aware yourself, the so-called WALL, separating us from capitalism and its disruptive deformities, is barely two hundred and fifty yards west of here. *My* problem is not at all ecologically determined; what bothers me, dearest Frau Kippenberg— and excruciatingly so!—is the *vital issue* of whether my writer's block, which only yesterday seemed to have settled in for good, has now deigned to lift once and for all, or whether I must expect it back soon. (Admittedly, unlike the inability to string two words together which was granted to me as an additional torment in my puberty, admittedly, this time I also feel it physically: a borderless pain, defying definition, a pain that won't be pinned down; crawling, sometimes hurrying between one bodily zone and another, putting some sixty to seventy kilometres behind it every twenty-four hours, unless, that is, it decides to stop over for a while in my head.) Today I'm glad to report that it's *coming on smoothly* (as Judith K. would describe the act of writing), though the horrors of yesterday evening still haunt me like a potato-schnapps hangover . . . Whatever, the whole caboodle, writer's block and all, is unlikely to strike us as new; although in this case, i.e. our own case, there can be little doubt that we are talking about something *special*:

Oh, but how curiously obstinate, how inordinately gooey for the time of year were the festering fumes that brought viscous, but *exemplary expectorant* to the denizens of Lychener Straße, to the lower, Pappelallee-end of Raumerstraße, and also, if in somewhat dilute consistency, to Gneiststraße; and fascinating, too, if only for the unusually muted colours of their swirling wreaths, tormenting each other like lachrymose creatures: the ground colour, beyond a shimmer of a doubt, was intent on a malicious mouse-grey tinged with Bavarian blue—but what words could be adequate to the task (and it's more than tempting as the subject of an essay!) of turning all this into something palpable, something for the reader to get his hands on; what adjectives, for example, could render the metamorphosis of the blood-red neon sign ZUM SCHUSTERJUNGEN, which, drowned in swampy, metallic-tasting fumes, took on the specific tint of tired and fretfully mumbling propane gas? (How much more difficult to describe the logo of that usually so accommodating public house ZUM LANGEN ARM: neon letters, normally azure, now blackened, degenerate, not unlike the nicotine-stained ruins of rotting teeth which, for all their evident lack of charm, are exposed in beery laughter . . .) Stationed most advantageously half-way up Lychener Straße, and armed as I was with my ever-ready investigator's *ROTBUCH* diary, I did not this time have to face the usual disapproving-distrustful looks and remarks, such as: 'You betta wochit!' and 'Get lost mate, pissoff!' (the deportment of yesterday's passers-by seemed to convey: We have other fish to fry!)—and yet not one sentence!—no, not a single, finished sentence!—or none, at least, that could be said to do justice to the length it was embryonically predisposed to. Instead, a soulless gobbet of ugly-looking phlegm was expectorated into my poor note-book, no doubt providing a means of recalling this depressing state of affairs for some time to come . . .

Later that afternoon I took refuge in my work as a publisher's reader, a job pitying hearts had put me in the way of—'put me in the way of': another phrase that bears some thinking about!—along with a list of questions, devised in the late 70s by the managing board of a leading GDR publisher, to be kept forever in mind—and never too far from scribbling hands—by internal and external readers compiling their 'critical' reports: '1.1 Did you find the manuscript interesting? (Is it thrilling, *captivating*, humorous, informative, educative?) / 1.2 Is the subject matter interesting? / 1.3 Is the author on top of his subject? Refer to deficiencies and errors! (Is the subject matter *excessive*?) / 1.4 Does the manuscript contain details of an *implausible*, tasteless or *generally dubious* nature? // 2.1 Assess the *value of the theme*. / 2.2 What is the author's aim, what is his *fundamental concern*? / 2.3 What is the standpoint? Is it external to the plot or does it emerge as an organic component of the plot itself? / 2.4 Is there a discrepancy between the author's intention and the execution of the latter? / 2.5 Is the *educative effect* achieved by didactic or *artistic-political* means (exemplary effect, *deterrence*, enlightenment, *stimulus to thought*)? 2.6 What picture of reality and human beings is provided (*glorification*, one-sidedness, idealisation, romanticisation, over-simplification of issues, a *realistic* picture)? // 3.1 Is there a central figure (main character trait)? *Is it possible to identify with it*? / 3.2 Does the *manuscript contain a pivotal conflict*? (Motive? *Is the conflict resolved? If so, how*?) / 3.3

Is there a *balanced* and *well-integrated* cast of characters? *How do the major and minor characters relate*? 3.4 Are there places where the main character's behaviour is *hard to understand*? 3.5 Do any of the other characters act *gratuitously*? // 4.1 Is the story easy to follow and clearly structured? Is the story *rounded off*? / 4.2 Does the plot have one or more strands? Episodic structure? / 4.3 Is the composition *clear* and *logical*? / 4.4 Are there longueurs? (Indicate passages that could be cut.) / 4.5 Does the manuscript place more emphasis on action or reflection? // 5.1 Which person does the narrator use (I/he)? / 5.2 *Assess the relationship between narrative perspective and authorial standpoint.* // 6.1 Characterise language and style/register (hackneyed, vivid, affected, superficial, slap-dash, antiquated, jargonising). / 6.2 *Fundamental* strengths, weaknesses or idiosyncrasies of style. / 6.3 Where could stylistic improvements be made? // 7.1 *Assess the tradition* to which the author, consciously or not, adheres. // 8.1 For which reader group is the. . . .'

Now, it was in bringing that day (something I should also like to record here) 'to a close' that I suddenly realised—by dint of one of those rare, pre-alcoholic illuminations—where to look for the *true culprits* for my writer's block (which was quite favourably received in some places, as it happens): in the punctuation marks . . . Yes, my growing, manic aversion to some of the more extremist punctuation marks is precisely what has led to the increasingly frequent paralysis of my innocent writer's hand; for although they are deployed sparingly by the present writer, as everyone knows, there are still too many by far.—Do you always eat cheese in class, Schramm? Why don't you have the Mongolian Festive Maggots for once?—For some time now I have felt an insuperable repugnance when I see one after another of those ridiculous exclamation marks come stomping, or rather staggering, out of the misty void to form unattractive cordons of three, four, or five—like stewards sent by the Free German Youth to keep the peace. Recently, I have felt equally disgusted by question marks: tiny curling, rootless tapeworms, caricatures of sea-horses with shameless little dots of turd under them. As far as semi-colons are concerned, however, I have finally—and fortunately, though I've taken my time, I'm not too late for Xmas—succeeded in grasping the fact that a demi-semi-colon is, at best, a comma or, rather worse, a full stop (i.e. *mass products par excellence*!). What half-baked hybrids! But also: how vain! What airs they've given themselves in prose—in poetry too—during the last seven or eight decades! ... One might as well write without any punctuation marks at all, like one of those so-called 'modernists'!— *Smog alert in West Berlin*!? Don't make me laugh! Honestly, I feel moved by sterner stuff, and by one question in particular whose tone grows shriller by the hour: how on earth am I going to master the plague of punctuation marks, vast swarms of which already darken the heavens, or at least *my* heavens? Back to Sardanapalus!!!—I've heard that certain other writers are not all that much better off! Driven to distraction by excessive toing and froing, they seem to be searching for a kind of back door, or emergency exit—even at the expense of ending up abroad in a capitalist country ... (It's worth noting that our *temporary loss* of the promising young writer Günter 'Pussy-cat' Kunert, now resident in Kitzbühel or Cuxhaven, derives from the same sense of failure as that suffered by the present writer—or to cite words that Kunert himself frequently repeated before his hasty departure: 'I shall never get another line of lasting value down on paper under these circumstances!' Is it coming on again smoothly now he's in Itzehoe or Iserlohn, I wonder ...?) But what an incriminating, what a thoroughly enervating panorama: *one lot*, retiring into their shells like snails, have become practically inaccessible, whatever format they once had blurring in the eyes of 'normal people', the man-in-the-street; the *next lot* leave the hive like a swarm of disorientated bees, ending up in distant centres of the international white slave and joss-stick trade, up to their eyeballs in the hanky-panky and high-jinks of Hollywood swimming-pool parties (see under: Heiner Müller), implicated in the magic rites of Polynesian aborigines etc. etc.; the *third lot* ... , the third lot ... , the third. ...

Could it be that we are about to witness a Great Age of the Socialist Fairy Tale? (If only that could come out of it; at least it would all have had some purpose, whatever one might think of it at the end of the day.)

'My little horse must think it queer/ To stop without a farmhouse near/ Between the woods and frozen lake/ The darkest evening of the year . . .'—And it is before a red traffic-light that I finally come to a standstill, pondering those New England rhymes by Robert Frost, the favourite poem of Robert F. Kennedy, daring to hope for amber and then, perhaps, though it would be almost too good to be true, for green: that is the situation as it stands! Nor could it be described any better *at the present moment in time*!—Three minutes later, certain nuances will have altered, with individuals and smallish groups to the left and right 'going down like flies'—which is *only natural*, as Peter Altenberg would have said; the present writer appears to be an exception; the present writer is still standing, still tiptoeing in expectation along with three other men of roughly his own age (curious one should notice that!), or rather with *two* (the third, without twitching a muscle, having this instant flopped on to his lopsided, bearded face); but I'm still standing, and somehow I seem to keep standing, or, to take it one step further, I seem to want to fly! Heavens above! A maybug in November? Must be going batty! I ascend vertically, wings a-flutter . . .

a) Elke Erb: 'Reality has failed . . .'—Well delivered! b) But then, what about Bert Papenfuss-Gorek: 'between you and me, the superstructure's going under . . .'—But what's it supposed to *mean*??? (Three question marks that could easily straighten up into three exclamation marks! Don't you think?)
(1982/1986)

Ludwig Fels

One of the Family

The moon had a cloud in tow. I wanted to be a missionary. The teacher who took us for Scripture lived nearby. I loved her in spite of her rolls of blubbery fat, or maybe it was because of them. I wanted to convert heathen savages. The journey there was the most beautiful thing I could imagine.

I'm not going to let you starve, said my mother.

She kept her word and lost weight.

You'll get knee-socks for Christmas and a pair of long, thick, warm underpants. I went to church for her. When I slept beside her, on the other side of the big bed, an angel stood there playing with a hairy tube right next to my face. In the musty cavern of her wardrobe, which smelled of clammy sponges, hung her wedding-dress of midnight blue.

If she went out to dig in the garden, I'd catch the worms and cut them in half, if I hadn't already torn them in two pulling them out of the earth. I flattened the ants with a cobbler's hammer, or threw them into spiders' webs. I trickled water down the carpet-rail till the earwigs were flushed out. I'd have tickled an elephant if I could. It hurt me deep down inside to see rats, baby ones, impaled on the prongs of pitchforks; or the way the hens would thrash about in tied-up sacks every Christmas, gabbling and squawking till their heads flew off. Worst of all was when I had to go and fetch a brick for tiny kittens that were still wet from their mothers. I wouldn't touch the water they were drowned in.

If I held my ear to the bucket, I heard them scratching for ages after.

Let them stay alive!

Who's going to feed them?

There were unnatural goings-on in that landscape. The pets were kicked about the house, the children were beaten. But then it was their owners, the parents, who wept. I loved the birds, for they knew the world. They didn't make me feel dangerous. With them I felt helpless.

What I liked best in the Bible were the passages about slaves and warriors. I read the prayers in the catechism, read the songbook and the *Parish News*. Poisonous snakes recoiled at the sight of the Cross, the Son of God had been seen walking in no man's land between the trenches. Everything was exactly the way it wasn't in real life: an edifying good deed. For a while, I sang before coffins, my face white as chalk above my black habit, till it all got too sad and I couldn't help crying myself. Begging with an almsbag wasn't as bad since the alms were going to poor people who didn't have white skin.

I considered myself one of God's children. He was better than my stepfather; he didn't drink and never came home.

During the early days, when the grown-ups were picking potatoes, we were allowed to look after the cows. So we tried being cowboys, slinging string lassos round the animals' horns. If the cows started to buck and snort and run after us, we'd fire our cap-guns at them. We saddled them with mattresses, poked sticks into their shiny wet, ruby-red orifices, did secret things. Our games sorted the cowards from the heroes. We haunted ruins, old air-raid shelters, the cellars of new buildings, sandstone caves. We were drawn to darkness, to the dead, and the girls' fear made enemies of us. We went into the forest and bombarded the trees with rusty shells and moss-covered boulders. The sun was like gun-fire, and in our deep, deep loneliness we were lords over all the world.

When the fists rained down I never let out a squeak. I

laughed in defiance and to numb the pain. I couldn't bear the thought of becoming even more earnest.

The first years of my life were good, for I don't remember a thing about them. I learned to walk in a house which I was supposed to inherit one day. I had a garden to sleep in and a street in which to play.

Shortly after my arrival in the world, my grandmother died. My grandfather died when my sister was born. When my little brother came along, my relations, tired of being leant on, made themselves scarce. Still, we children survived. My mother, weak from childbirth, sat in a wheelchair, my grandfather lay on the bier, the baptismal water was like the sweat of the dead. So I read out fairy-tales to myself, giving myself goose-pimples and the shivers with severed horses' heads that talked, crowned serpents that sucked at the udders of cows. The shepherd is blowing his horn in the hills, all aboard the dream ship of love, I yelled, walking through the forest, and saw a bicycle with tinsel wrapped around its spokes under every fir-tree. On the farm where my mother occasionally got work as a labourer was a large orchard with apples, pears, plums, beehives, and colonies of wasps in holes in the ground. Branches poked in between the pales of the fence at the forest edge, where wild pigs sometimes came out in the gloaming. There was a pigsty on the ground floor of the retired farmer's house. At home, as it was called, my mattress froze to the springs of my bed. Winter decorated the walls with hoar-frost. When the frost melted, the undercoat peeled off underneath. I survived floods and downpours, up to my neck in liquid manure with drowned piglets disappearing under floating haystacks. The dominant colours at school were those of blood and ink. I was quick to learn I was a nobody. It was the kind of place where fleas and lice were forced to share the same school bench.

A bearskin over one shoulder, I creep through ferns between the rough-hewn palisades of the Roman fortifications and the refuges of the Celts. The Romans eat long noodles. Grinning robber barons swing on the gallows, or stick long tongues into jugs of wine, their dark beards in flames, blazing like bonfires. Plague and executioners, crusaders and hordes of Huns, mercenaries, Swedish punch, Schrammhans's castle, Florian Geyer against the bishop's castle at Würzburg, Old Fritz's tall guards, the English and French versus the Red Indians, Bavaria versus Prussia, the German colonies in East Africa, the Wilhelms, the Ludwigs . . . school was out before we got to Hitler. 'That used to be the Jews' street. They wheeled all their stuff to the station on barrows. People smashed up their synagogue and set it on fire. Willi Bredel wrote a poem about the Altmühl once. Trouble is we lost the war.'

The workshop for the disabled at first took on people who were not so very disabled. Then industry came to the area: excavators mowed the meadows, cranes lined the horizons, the combined activity of bulldozers and tanks cut paths through the cornfields. The turnips drooped their heads, hops no longer climbed their poles. Soon, the women too were in employment, before their work at home.

Fatherless with a prick,
I had to be manly
the woman, then
my mother, hard
on herself. It fell on me
and stayed.

My friends' fathers, redundant members of the Wehrmacht, drank regularly at the pub. They chewed over the French women they'd fucked, sucked bloody intestines, took the arses of Russian and Polish women in their powder-black mouths. At the children's service, Jesus Christ was waiting in the offertory box. I was particularly taken with the Papuans. They waged war against spirits in the rain forests of New Guinea. The only blond thing about me was my parting.

The old folk would look after us when our mothers were pregnant. That was great because they were too ancient to hit us and hadn't the strength to tell us off for very long.

They just had to be good to us and leave us in peace. In the evening the mothers would be too weak to stand up. Mine had no husband and didn't smell the same. She lay in bed unsmiling and wouldn't say anything nice to me. I bawled my head off. But eventually, I lost interest in cuddling.

What's your father's job? asked the teachers.

I cried.

Behind the fence at the bottom of the garden lay piles of rags, animal bones, clattering heaps of rust, men's corpses, whose trousers dripped, whose eyes had squirted out, stammering, grunting creatures who grabbed at women's breasts. The women screeched and bickered and bent over to complain of the holes in their stockings, through which you could see their awful bruises. The ghost town that conjured me weighs on me now like a gravestone.

Nothing but insinuation
forgiveness, habit.
Dirt between your toes
rain in your hair
men shaving with bulging
underpants, at the knees too
women wringing hands, spreading legs
with wailing and choking
thighs and aprons.
Keep your tears
for better years!
And as if you weren't enough
another's on the way.

My childhood was merely a kind of practice for what was to come; later I stilled my hunger by drinking, and stuffed my skull. The only thing I can do with the past is write it down. There are images that rumble like an empty stomach: yoked-up cows steaming in the morning mist, the plough slicing through white clods of earth, potatoes that were balls of ice. The old women, among whom my mother barely stood out, looked as if they were digging their graves. We had to say a prayer before every crust of bread.

To me the ruined buildings were castles after an Indian attack. Me Bomba, I said, because I couldn't climb like Tarzan. I was in every gang. The spy.

I was hardly given a chance not to feel what work was. Work determined what I did with my time before and after I went to bed. Work got to me when I was reading, when I was dreaming, when I was ill. I tried to escape from it; work punished me when I returned. It was like a person. It upset me. Whenever the grown-ups took a break, I became their servant. I ate less, drank less, pished and shat more. I wanted to romp when I was supposed to be behaving like these grown-ups who did their duty so mercilessly, who got tough, suddenly got nasty and threatened me with the future.

When I drank from the well at the cemetery, where most of my family lay, it tasted to me of corpses, as if it were pumped straight up from the bellies of the dead. I poured water on the gravestone in order to read the name more easily and watered the wooden cross as if it could still grow.

The first street I lived in was one in which only bicycles and carts were allowed. When I heard that one of our neighbours had suddenly passed away, I joined the others and stood on the staircase. I waited for the coffin-bearers, but there were just two men who came down the stairs carrying a shiny wooden box that looked like a trunk. I went on waiting for the dead woman to appear. Afterwards, I found it difficult to believe that she had been carried past me so secretly, so well hidden. When I was lying in bed at night the dead woman returned to her flat, and I felt relieved to think that she was in bed, too.

My mother was having a bad time, and it seemed her children were destined for no better. Without a father I was her disgrace; without a husband she was just a woman, not really a mother, and certainly not a wife. It cost my stepfather little more than a hundred drinking sessions until our house belonged to somebody else. For some reason this seemed to be the end of things to come. We loaded our things on a

wheelbarrow and went to live in lodgings. After that, my
mother went crawling after a cloth on other people's floors.
On Saturdays we all went to visit one of my school-friends
who had lots of brothers and sisters. His parents had been
living in a barrack hut and had saved enough to move into
a flat in some new terraced housing. Their flat had a bath,
and I was put in it along with my friend. Then we were
allowed to watch television, and there were sometimes more
people sitting in front of that television than there were in
the cinema on a Sunday afternoon. I sat down and watched
black-and-white adventure stories, dreamt of steel hooks and
eye patches, until some kid suddenly said something about
fucking, and repeated it as if you were supposed to know
what it meant. I had no idea. Our imaginations ran riot, little
secrets were blown up out of all proportion. We tried to
solve the puzzle, but since none of us could speak from
experience, everybody fibbed. If you pish in their stomachs
it makes them have babies. They've got these hollow plugs
in their belly-buttons where you put your cock. One day I
had my hands in my lap under a book in which a doctor had
written about love. I had to muster all the powers of my
imagination for the bit about a lady riding on a gentleman.
But soon I heard the echoes of sounds that had once been
so very strange to me.

At some point or other someone said: You're grown up now!
But the clouds still waved to me like tiny hankies. My mother
hit me because her work couldn't keep the wolf from the
door. Then she turned on the gas and nearly died of shame
when she was accused of putting our lives at risk. I know
now that she was really trying to rescue all of us. The gas
tasted of sweets, like chocolate at the back of my throat, like
perfume in my nostrils. My mother breathed so heavily it
sounded like sugar-lumps crumbling between her teeth. Then
there was light, air, my godmother in the kitchen, people
shouting at the open window. Our landlord threatened to
chuck us out and I hid a knife behind my back, prayed blind
rage would make me strong, wept and screamed when he

attacked me and my mother darted between us with wide, staring eyes.

My heart is flown
my head wants no return.
It wants to remind me of my wish to forget
of good old days in a scrotum
or a mother's belly
of Abraham's cauldron
from which my begetters scooped me
like a funeral repast
and of the first beer drunk with old men
cradled on hard knees
in soft laps.
People tell me of the old days
but they're never my days
an interim called the past.
Am I just a memory picked
to shreds and mended
a lonely dream that's sleeping rough?
The fact is I was there
and it went on and on.
I was hungry
but so what, today
I've something to eat
and tomorrow I'll get paralytic
and it won't hurt a soul.

The laughing-stock of farmers and cattle dealers I climb into the piglets' pen to play with the soft, snorting beasts which squeal as tough, horny hands haul them into the air to wriggle at the end of their uncurled tails. Then my mother yanks me out by the hair and the howling onlookers make me go red because I think they've mistaken me for a porker.

Behind the kindergarten was a river with a weir. It had usually been pouring with rain when I went there and lay down on the slimy, green concrete slabs to listen to the dirty brown floodwater rattle the iron grates. I went with it, too,

meandering along the edge of forests and back through meadows that were turning into marshes. I saw floating horns
and the roofs of a nearby village, and the blows of the
woman who found me fell like rain. The molehills were my
mountains.

Rübezahl was my favourite giant. I stared and froze as the
Indians died like brutes. I ducked the first time I found
myself looking down the barrel of a gun in a cinema. I
screwed up my eyes, put my hands up to hide my face, hardly
dared peek between my fingers as daggers pierced coats and
doublets like knifeblades sinking into melting butter. In my
wildest dreams I was a pirate on horseback wearing a loin-
cloth and pith helmet, but even at carnival time I was forced
to wear a pullover and gloves.

I had my grandfather for all of six years. Sometimes I would
steal his stick when we were out for a walk in the park; he
just stood there and couldn't move. He liked his beer more
than his food. He had worked till he was a little old man
with a stoop, and had drunk until he was skinny. His shuffling
figure seemed almost transparent.

I weighed a lot. I could get a lot down me in those days.
I wasn't much of a hero at school, though; I cried when I
was beaten by grown-ups I didn't know. They didn't realise
where I came from, or were incapable of wanting to know.

The Wild West lay somewhere between the meadows and
the edge of the forest. If I closed my eyes I could picture it
clearly, with the castles where the Martians lived rising above
the horizon. There was a different world under the ground.
It was as if the darkness was light, and you could breathe
the stones like air. But up on the surface I was a great fan
of the stars; they looked so warm, and often I would roam
the seas on the moon. These were all things which I had
got to know so much better than the real world. The only
globetrotting we ever did was the odd trip to the nearest
larger town.

Wherever you looked there were people absorbed by their
work. They would gaze so absently at the ground that you

hardly recognised them. Only during lunchbreaks would they lie down on their backs and stare vacantly up at the sky.

I got along
with thin legs, a fat belly.
Every morning cocoa and white bread, a lot
and mealy-tasting eggs and bacon and fried potatoes.
Then I shat in my bed.
Recuperation, they said.
We were healthy
when their blows
stopped hurting our bones.

My godmother was my only relation. Today she's somewhere between seventy and eighty and has cancer of the womb. She gave me a watch when I was confirmed, but it wasn't luminous and soon stopped working. She stripped tree trunks at the loading station, working outside in all weathers and powdering her frostbitten nose with soot. Once, over a quarter of a century ago, when her dog was asleep in my pram, I darted under the cooking range and ate its bowl of bread.

The elephant sits on a tricycle, its broad backside completely hiding the saddle. It has a turban-like cap stuck to its head between its soldered-on ears, a striped ball spinning on the tip of its raised trunk. When I became older, I sent my armoured scout car into battle against a police car which had a siren and a blue, flashing light. I preferred the elephant. I thought it was a clown in disguise and, with all my strength, screwed the ball from its trunk and the head from its body. But there was no dwarf hidden inside. Once, my drunken stepfather gave me a tractor with a driver sitting on it. The toy made me forget how hungry I was until my mother kicked it and smashed it against the wall. The driver broke and his head went rolling down the corridor like a red berry. My hunger was back. Then my stepfather laid into my mother, and I helped him when he was too drunk to stand. That was Christmas Eve.

Flocki belonged to Herr Bähr who would be seen trudging around in his great big garden while the dog went mad, howling behind the wire fence of its kennel. Occasionally I'd abduct Flocki from his prison and we'd run away together. The forest upset him deeply because he was incapable of besprinkling every tree. Sometimes my penis went hard and I couldn't understand why, but I took it out and let the sun shine on it, and flies would come buzzing round and land on it and tickle me with their legs, and then the dog would snap at them and lick the places they'd been.

One of the boys in our neighbourhood was allowed into the shed on his parents' allotment where there were deck-chairs, mattresses and a workbench. I remember laughing at his white bum; I didn't show him my cheeks.

When I began to feel with my cock, I would hang around older women who thought I was just a child. They bent over with their arses in the air when they were doing the housework, and I envied their husbands. I was simply jealous and fondled myself miserably behind their backs. I was harmless. I couldn't do anything. I didn't come, and didn't know what else to do.

Because I had no father, I couldn't get used to men. They were inscrutable figures: either they were cold and loud, or else flushed from drinking and on the verge of tears. I wanted my unknown parent to come from a far away place, in which case he wouldn't be German, but the colour of my skin didn't change. Only, in my mind I could speak in tongues that didn't exist, but they didn't explain anything either.

I was on my own; all of us were. We longed to be part of a horde, started up gangs, thought of ourselves as lone warriors of a lost tribe of red-skinned, slit-eyed pygmies. We let out blood-curdling screams at the mere sight of our enemies, which was often enough to send them packing. When the grown-ups attacked us separately, however, we swore to each other afterwards that we'd given nothing away and had suffered in silence, even when blood had flowed like warpaint in our dreary families, in which our only development consisted of our self-defence. Today, I feel that workers often tend to see new 'bosses' in their children, and that they do their best to ensure the latters' demands are nipped in the bud.

I had a savings bank, but no key. A bank clerk came to our class once a year, unlocked everybody's tin and counted the money. Counting my savings took him the longest and always produced the smallest amount. He examined the paint on the tin for scratch marks, closely investigated the slit and exact intermeshing of serrated teeth between which the coins were pushed. He accused me in front of the whole class of excessive greed, instead of testifying that saving made the poor poorer.

Such humiliations were far from uncommon. I had no idea how to respond to the piercing looks of my chance companions. They were all the sons of craftsmen and farmers, but also of men who wore shit-caked rubber boots when they poked their heads out of gulley-holes. It wasn't long before I began to understand the pride of kids they contemptuously referred to as Mohammeds, Polacks, hut-dwellers and bin-people, who didn't suffer as much as I did because they were smart at stealing and swore misplaced vengeance against their parents. Because they spoke Russian, Czech or Ukrainian, they were put in remedial schools where the numerals from nought to X were drummed into them by special teachers who ruled with the cane and the rod, the strap and the birch.

YOU'LL SEE, YOU'LL EARN ALL RIGHT: EITHER YOUR JUST DESERTS OR ENOUGH TO KEEP YOURSELF IN BEER AND YOUR WIFE AND CHILDREN IN FOOD AND CLOTHING. WHAT ARE YOU GOING TO BE? EVERYBODY'S GOT TO BE SOMETHING! THERE'S A FUTURE TO BE HAD IN EVERY TRADE. WHEREVER YOU GO YOU'LL HAVE TO WORK. NOTHING IN LIFE IS FREE. LOOK AT ME, LOOK AT ALL OF US, IT HASN'T KILLED US, HAS IT? AT LEAST YOU'LL NEVER STARVE. THE MAN WITH NO MONEY NEVER GETS THE GIRL.

I spent most of my time out of doors, even at home. During heavy rainfall, water from the drains would pour through the corridor. Sometimes my shoes would float out into the garden like leaky boats, soon to be washed back in by floodwater from the river. The engines of haulage trucks roared outside our loo. When it froze we did it in buckets and our wormlike turds all looked the same. In the meadow behind the fence was a tall apple tree. The river washed its roots, there was foam among the reeds. Life didn't seem so bad when you could sit cross-legged and undisturbed on the topmost rocks of the sandstone cliffs, spying on labourers in the surrounding fields as if they were enemy invaders. Every fencepost was a sword, the twigs on every bush were daggers.

All these years are at the back of my head, dragging and pushing at me like a boil that moves. They weren't a game, and I can neither accept them, nor put them behind me. It was life that bent me low, and I sometimes think that only my dreams, a ballast without memory, have a history.

It is as if I floated through the murderous repose of this small town whose roofs lay under the criss-crossed shadows of church spires. There was no place for me there, and yet the edge of the world was always further away than it seemed. So I got my world out of books, only to find that that was not where I lived.

One day they blew up the air-raid shelters and flattened the barracks. Rubbish-tips spewed out over the meadows. My old haunts had gone, and I didn't look for new ones. The boxlike shells of houses appeared, row after row of cement-coloured dice on every hillside in sight. Concrete covered the grass and stones, the animals perished. The people I had known as long as I could remember became expressionless faces on the other side of a glass panel at the funeral parlour. The heroes of my boyhood stories were tortured at the stake. But they didn't talk, and I grew silent with them. I listened to the complaints of the grown-ups when they confessed jokes. And gradually I grasped why I'd become what I was, why I didn't want to stay, wanted to be different: penitent, rebellious, less certain.

Grown stronger by a couple
of years, I was made my mother's
right-hand man, hit
brother and sister at her behest
when she was too weak
to do it. Thus I took on
the role of my own father.

I wept and sweated blood when the final school holidays began. Puffed up with pride, my mother bought me two pairs of white overalls at the outfitters. I didn't look at myself in the mirror as I cocked the peak of my stiff new cap. I was fairly sure that I hadn't heard the end of the story.

For the first time in my life, I managed to present a completely different face.

Karin Reschke

'Cold Kiss'

Marie awakes.
This time it's serious. On the corner they're playing war in the shadow of the mountain of rubble. English soldiers in camouflage gear are running in bunches across the street. The enemy must be there somewhere, in some house in the field of ruins opposite the Lime Tree, hidden somewhere, invisible.

The enemy isn't the Germans any more, the private, the buffoon in the final victory, the enemy is the arch-enemy from the East, the Russians. The joke is that the hunt for the enemy has nothing to do with real Russians. So the only people watching are Mr Nobody, who is actually making the shorter trip from his house to his car, and the longer journey to work, and next door's children. Mr Nobody stands on the kerb, arms crossed behind his back, a grey hat in his hands. But it could also be a little cap like the ones the soldiers are wearing, a beret, a steel helmet, the Field Marshal says hello, says Gary, look at the fat bloke, he's pleased about that.

Actually things are taking a dramatic turn. They're taking a prisoner. Twisting his arms behind his back, disarming him, humiliating him by pulling his belt out of his trousers, sticking their boots in his rump, their rifle-butts, shouting, falling silent, five of them taking him away, rattling their weapons, jumping into a jeep with the prisoner and roaring off, through the line of onlookers. Mr Nobody goes on smiling, rotates his hat, the children think this is war in peace-time. Preliminary exercises, says Gary, it's just preliminary exercises.

The iron curtain falls to the ground with a loud crash. It wakes the city.

In all probability the sea begins behind the Stössensee Bridge. The sea is another battleground that has to be defended in peace-time. The huge steamers with coke on board under which weapons are said to be hidden, pass through the inland canals of the city and beneath the bridge.

The journey to the sea leads through the Havel. The Havel stops the sea from flowing to Berlin. Imagine Berlin having high and low tides. The Berliners can imagine that, they take quicksand from Travemünde and strew it by the shores of the Wannsee and say Berlin's right next to the sea.

The British landing-craft, laden with tanks and jeeps, anchors between yachts, rowing boats and smaller paddle steamers. A new troop storms the jetty, the boys and girls are shoved together, the teachers hold protecting arms around them, the tommies jump from the jetty, each with a huge leap, on to the landing-craft. It casts off in no time, an engine starts up and leaves a black stripe behind it on this bright, sunny morning.

No one gets over-excited about the sudden breakthrough of an army on the west. Preliminary exercises, that's all. The children, on the school's orders, are taking a trip from the Stössensee. Marie almost goes flying into the water when the tommies dash across the jetty, tear free the rope, practically run across the water, in battledress with full pack, ready to swim if need be.

Slowly the steamer sets off, toots, leaves the bridge in the direction of Schildhorn, the waves settle, the landing-craft has withdrawn from reality long since, friend and foe doze peacefully in the sun. If the city wakes up it won't die. No.

Puntil stands on deck and counts everything, blinks in the sun, immediately starts telling some story about the origin of the Havel basin, the foundation of the towns of Schildhorn, Kladow, Gatow, the Wendish times, pagan and pre-Holy Roman Empire. The big stretch of sand on the Havel-chaussee gleams, the sand-dumpers drive ceaselessly into this desert, the forest rises above them, they travel back out of the desert, sand-laden, into the city, the forest recedes. Tourist pubs pop up, boathouses, sandpipers, in the middle the marching English, the city seems surrounded, who cares as long as the enemy is lying in wait behind the iron curtain, refusing to show. The steamer slowly sails round the large Wannsee.

Marie and Biggi look, like everyone else, into the water, across the water to the smooth-rubbed coast, the sand whipping back on the bathing beach. *Blue moon* says Biggi and reaches her hand out to the clouds and the white shadow of the daytime moon. Marie smiles at herself in the water, hey Biggi, show us your teeth, show us your face. They look at each other and can't help laughing.

Your lip's turned right up to your nose, Marie. Then they nod to their reflection that comes in waves and vanishes again. They look like one another in their black studded jeans, black jumpers, white socks and black gym-shoes. Around their necks on a silver chain the coin of friendship and above it the neckerchief, Marie's turquoise, Biggi's pink. Outwardly one heart and one soul, identically dressed, down to the black edges under their nails that they hold to the light, hand to hand, pleased with their image.

Marie calls it a self-portrait that she has to remake every day, the quarter of an hour in the bathroom at the mirror all to herself, so as not to look the way mother and grandmother would like her to. The nice open forehead for all to see, hair brushed to the side and held with grips, respectable, clean and innocent, so that even the wind can't mess up that hair, that forehead. Every morning she combs her hair up a storm because everything at home smells of order and respectability, and because that smell tickles her nose so provocatively.

They aren't listening to what Puntil is saying. Tousled thoughts, she hears her mother saying, behind the covered brow indelibly change a girl's character. Tousled thinking is out of the question from the word go. Of course Biggi and Marie see this trip as something less than a compulsory exercise, and smile indulgently at Puntil, let him talk about Schildhorn and Wannsee, Kladow and Gatow, the catfish on its way to the Antarctic via the upper and the lower Havel, dabbling in mysteries, heavy, good-natured and peace-loving. The elephant fish, the mudfish with its human characteristics. But it never reaches the Antarctic, what nonsense, the ice floats on the top, the mudfish down below on the warm, soft bottom. He'd be finished in the ice, only people have that really thick skin and dabble everywhere, if Puntil's to be believed, even in the Antarctic Ocean.

I think he's talking about the Ice Age, says Biggi.

Marie lets the words melt on her tongue. The Ice Age still, the Wannsee a huge flat wing, clear right down to the bottom. The Ice Age, antediluvial age, war age, the bone age, the specs age, dividing oneself up and fitting oneself into invisible spaces of time, feeling nothing of it but knowing they were there. The silent age, because the grown-ups are silent and full of self-importance about their secrets.

Did you see the mountains of specs in the paper, Biggi? I can't understand that. Nobody talks about it and nobody's worried that the English are always making enemies here.

Biggi laughs. You're exaggerating.

It's true though. You're reading something, you just have to read it out loud and grandma's clapping her hands above her head and mother's washing hers in innocence like Pontius Pilate and Puntil still hasn't wasted a single word on the thousand-year Reich after Christ. The world has never seen so many specs in a pile, and the Ice Age over so long ago. Can you imagine that, Biggi?

No.

We're landing, calls Puntil, line up in pairs.

The English are even in Moorlake, emerging from the forest, running into the bay. Ice-cream men stand at the jetty shouting *Kalter Kuss*—'cold kiss', choc-ice, twenty pfennigs. They all dash over in twos and lick their vanilla choc-ices.

Lovely war on a warm summer's day, whispers Marie.

You're lovesick, says Biggi.

If only.

Marie relaces her gym-shoe.

I don't like the way things are going, I'd rather just clear off somewhere.

Oh, come on.

Close up, calls Puntil, go on there.

The schoolboys and schoolgirls are in the exercise area. The Yanks are about to appear on the horizon. That's today's strategy: kindle the cold glow of armistice using the example of the defence of this city. Over in Potsdam the sabres are rattling, says Puntil by way of explanation, the chocolate cruiser over there, you see, that's them. Nobody's interested in the greyish-brown ship in the sun. Chocolate cruiser, he's making fun, that's all.

Marie is swimming in thoughts.

People, the victims of war. Wake up, resist, no more war, so keep your eyes open, Havelkette, Wannsee, Moorlake, the victims come from all over the place, you can read it in the paper, bones piled up on top of each other; could be made of marble, figures, unreal, if there hadn't been a war.

Hair, an incredible amount of hair, woven into a carpet you can fly on, hair can live longer than people, but that isn't what frightens her, it's the glasses, the incredible amount of glasses. And the eyes that go with those glasses, short-sighted, long-sighted, people and their faces. Glasses thrown on top of one another, superfluous, a photograph in a paper.

Mother stares at it. Grandmother looks away. Nobody says anything. Marie is swimming in the glasses.

The repatriated POW with his new teeth is the only one who laughs, and says we can't change history, we can't influence it, certainly not after the event, don't brood so much, kid, it'll make you ugly and then you won't get a man, concentrate on the beautiful things in life. Marie is swimming in yeah, yeah, rose-tinted glasses, yeah, yeah. Somebody took a picture of the glasses after the war, who knows . . .

They storm the sandhills, Puntil at the rear. They run off. The teacher has trouble keeping up with them. Wild activity at the top. The sand plovers fly up, all profoundly peaceful.

Breathless the schoolchildren form a big circle, Puntil suggests scouting games. He hasn't a clue about them. He is dreaming of the broad, washed-out Havel basin, Albrecht the Bear, good-temperedly growling in the sun, the city emblems in the sky, pale or bright in the kaleidoscope. Marie disarranges the bleached stars, the cut-out daytime moon, displaces the sky through the coloured glass. The earth grows further from the moon. Even on tiptoes, with your eyes turned towards the sky, the landing strip is blurred, a little pile of spangles, the wings have grown back for good.

Robbers and princesses hide in the forest. The girls easily escape the boys for the time being. Puntil looks on helplessly. What has he instigated, he can't keep track of everything, he convinces himself that youth must let off steam, sits down on a tree-stump and gives them half an hour. But the sherbet battle goes on longer than that. The English fly past overhead, the undergrowth cracks, Puntil stands up, stares through the trees, they would have manoeuvres today. The boys and girls are waving under bushes and leaves with their bright faces, sometimes he catches a laugh, sometimes the corner of a dress, or a flying arrow from a robber chief. Nothing will happen to them, don't worry, teacher, they've just caught their booty, the girls, the princesses.

Here she is Herr Puntil, the star, the dollar princess of the lower sixth, tapped on the shoulder, the rules of the game kept, her knees camouflaged with moss, her pony-tail full of forest floor, red blotches in her face, all alone in the open meadow and safe in her hiding-place until the moment when she is discovered by three robbers.

Three against one's for cowards, she cries angrily.

Shut up dollar princess, if you're caught you're caught.

She has to sit down with Puntil and wait.

What happens next?

We're swapped for liquorice, says the dollar princess. She rummages in her bag. I don't suppose you have any liquorice?

Puntil opens the treasure-chest. What's left from the outings kitty.

The dollar princess laughs, she's pleased. I'm tired anyway. She drops to the ground and closes her eyes, the trees dance, the water in the sky, the forest whirls. More and more princesses are dragged in, the robbers are fulfilling their masculine duties. Some prisoners defend themselves, break away, are caught again. The game doesn't come to an end, the dull faces disguise themselves, burrow on their bellies over and over into the forest floor, escaping the enemy. Finally Puntil blows his whistle, once, twice. Arms and legs appear, prisoners and winners drop exhausted to the ground.

Has anybody hurt themselves?

They all laugh: Nobody.

Puntil opens the treasure-chest. Countless hands reach in. Nobody is waiting for a proper end to the game. Biggi takes the kaleidoscope, holds it towards the trees. They grow red and blue, yellow and purple.

It's going to rain, she says, you can see it.

Marie, where were you the whole time?

Puntil counts off the class: two, four, six . . . he closes his eyes, it'll be right.

Anybody missing?

Marie, where are you coming from?

From the moon.

Biggi hands her the kaleidoscope. Idiot, you didn't join in.

Kids' stuff, she says.

Spoilsport, she hears.

Line up in pairs. And even that goes like clockwork. Listen everybody, now we're all going back to the steamer.

The ice-cream man has disappeared. Most of them are chewing liquorice, licking sherbet, the steamer heads back.

The enemies lie on the left and right of the shore, waiting for twilight and the order to retreat, so warlike is peace, the chocolate cruiser aims its navigation lights at its own bank. Here soldiers of the heavenly army can go on playing war in peace.

Puntil counts them all again. Fine, they're all here.

They have no eyes for the evening mood, the river sluggish

like syrup, the rain-clouds in the distance. No eyes for the warlike tribes in the forest, Yanks, English, day trippers.

It's true, Marie thinks, I'm lovesick. The unruly heart. What a stupid title, why do I have to think about something like that? She twists her silver chain up to her throat, swallows.

Stop it, says Biggi.

Yeah, yeah.

They put their arms around each other's shoulders and cease hostilities because in the end they're one heart and one soul with everything that's beginning to be in the past.

Johanna Walser

The Songbird

The family. A family, when you think about it, is not only beautiful but also useful, as long as you are very candid and approach it in the right way. How charming it is to talk to a member of a family, and what a relief it is to tell your own problems to someone so that you no longer have to bear them alone but have the strong shoulders of the family to help. At Christmas, at least, everyone tries to find a place in a family. It is not always only the sweetness of memory, but also the pain of what is lost and the pain that that festival, which was once so rich in promise, and later so magical and full of nostalgic promptings, is now merely a day or evening when you feel even more powerfully than at other times that you lack something. I should also like to look in at a pub and see if there are poor people drinking there now as well. If they only drank today they would have more of an excuse than ever. But now I have forgotten my family. I have a sister, and no one can tell how she feels. She is almost always joking, except when tears she is in a hurry to hide suddenly run down her face. You can hardly grasp that she is crying because just a second before she was still joking. A lot of people have a poor opinion of her and think that what is her sole weapon and camouflage is in fact pride. I am sorry about that, but her story would not be anywhere near as beautiful if everyone could see it immediately. There are others too, often very simple people, who do not see how she is, it's true, but do value her open ways and her wit, and perhaps even love her. She herself is very happy when she earns that kind of acceptance, and loves those people, but still she longs for someone who would see right through her, to whom she could open up fully without shocking him, who would appreciate her real, hidden, deep, sad being and value it. She loves everyone who makes the attempt to understand her. She gives herself to everyone who takes an interest in her, allows herself to be taken along, is attached to him, devoted as a dog. Unfortunately, though she thinks highly of me and I of her, I can never talk to her, because I instantly have to submit to her. I have to submit to everyone I love. Since I only appear in subordinate clauses, I at least try to fool them into thinking I am in the main clause; at times it sounds so genuine that I am almost tempted to believe it myself. It is likewise unbearable, it seems to me, if one dear person likes or loves you more than he does another dear person who for his own part loves or values that dear person very much.

Alone with Mother. Alone. Mother has no one at all but me when Father is away, which is often, since he is a sailor. My younger brother and sister are still small and make work. When she sits on her own of an evening and calls out I have to go in to her quickly. Sometimes the radio is on, low, but mostly it is completely quiet. Night presses hard against the windowpanes as if it wanted to come in. The cat raises its hackles when Mother strokes it vigorously. When Mother has held it for a while she lets it go. The cat runs off right away. Now I have to stay, how can I leave now? If I had not come she would not have let the cat go yet. There is complete silence between us, I lean against the table and cannot bring myself to sit down. Then Mother often starts talking about my big brother, who is here almost as rarely as Father and always says his studies keep him so busy—he's been allowed to study. She is almost talking to herself when she says he hasn't phoned for such a long time, but, she promptly adds, he does have so much to do. When she spoke of a professor who had called wanting to talk to my brother, she laughed and could not conceal her pride. Suddenly I found it revolting, sitting there with her. And just as I'd felt uneasy before when the cat didn't want to stay with her, that was exactly how I felt as I inched closer and closer to the door, past the table and chairs, as if I was doing it unconsciously, without meaning to. Mother called out again, but it seemed she was only talking to herself: That's Mireille Mathieu singing, what a terrific woman she is. That made it feel even more unpleasant to me, and, though it seemed more and more impossible to leave, I left. Mother behaved as if she hadn't noticed. I could still hear the voice in which she'd said: What a terrific woman she is. I found that voice inexpressibly unpleasant. Why isn't *she* a 'terrific woman'? Why can't I be one? It seems to me that she has passed it on to me, as it were, this not being able to be one. The knowledge that you can't is overpowering in itself. Many things are so uncannily overpowering. When I turn my back on the forest, it could attack me at any time, from behind. I admit that it only lies there, silent, bent as if to protect, around me like an arm, but when I turn round it comes after me, dark, and if I then look round it has moved forward with a rush. I force myself to go in. I've not been so brave in a long time. No, not brave, simply getting a grip on myself, because I was afraid, or maybe brave after all, that *is* what they call brave, isn't it? I met a young man with a sheepdog. He looked at me, and as my gaze met his he bowed his head to his chest as if stricken. But then he promptly looked up again and pulled the dog on the lead to his side. Then he turned after me and hastily snatched at the lead again, which had slipped out of his hand. I had to laugh. Two girls came past. I would have liked to talk to them, but couldn't think of anything to say, and they seemed not to notice me at all. They looked so much like each other that I could not imagine coming between them. For those two, it occurred to me, everything must look quite different from how it looked to me. I hate this perpetual not doing things. The star that peeped so tenderly from the dusk was like the eye of distance. It occurred to me that people have ways of looking that tremble with tenderness like that too. The star was like a friend to me. As it grew darker it became much stronger and surer. What hadn't changed was that its golden light proclaimed the distance we do not think of by day. And it is the stars that bring us our thoughts, the night that brings reflection.

The songbird. I have swallowed a little songbird. It flew into my mouth when I was out walking and looked up into the tops of the trees. It is so tiny. Because it is a songbird it wants to sing all the time. Sometimes it starts singing in the middle of the day, and I have to quickly puff my mouth out round so that people will think I am whistling. At times they tell me I whistle nicely, which made me think that perhaps my little singer might have his uses. I called on music teachers, so that they could listen to him and see if he had any prospects. Unfortunately it was precisely then that my little bird never wanted to sing, he always remained silent. The teachers gave me commiserating or vexed looks. 'Sorry, there's nothing to be done with that.' 'I'd appreciate it if you could be a little more serious in your dealings with me.' 'I really do not want to have anything to do with a lunatic.' 'Go to . . .' Once we had been gently but firmly shoved out, or the door had been slammed behind us, setting a breeze of air wafting across my hair like desolation itself, and we found ourselves out in the busy street again, mostly when it was already dark, and the darkness was all about us and we were out of doors for a while, then my bird began to sing again. It seemed as if he was out to tease me. When I am doing my work at school he can cause problems. Suddenly he will sing out, and whistling is not allowed, after all. So I like it best if I have a cough and can drown him out. So I try hard to keep my cough going. In music lessons, on the other hand, he seems to fall asleep. But in the evenings he seems to wake up properly, and he sings ruefully, like a sick person in springtime, like a lame person at the deer compound in the zoo, like an old woman among children. At those times I feel him beat in me like a heart, and I think he really must be a nightingale, but then, his song is not quite that sweet. By now I would prefer to take back everything I have said. The fact is that my bird cannot really sing. He is mute. Would he have hidden away in me if he weren't? When his heart, hot and aglow, pounds harder and harder, is not that his muteness singing? His imprisonment? His powerful, rosy limbs are tied up tight, and are constantly tensed to burst his bonds. I once saw a baby kicking and flailing. Its eyes were almost popping out. It just kept on gulping as it thrashed its arms and feet about in the air. But that isn't singing, it is only screaming. A scream is most terrible, though, when it is mute. I once saw a picture of a child screaming. The endless, silent scream was appalling. That is how it is with the bird that has to sing and cannot. If you're hungry, and there is nothing else to eat, do you eat shit? Do you kill the other one because he wants to kill you?

A bicycle. I have a bicycle with a small round lamp, smooth and round as a baby's head. Even if the whole bike has started to rust, the lamp remains perfectly shiny. Unfortunately, though, the little head always bows down when I ride. When I start off I raise it up so that it is pointing straight ahead, and the head is so proud atop the bike and, if it cannot *look* proud, with its gentle curves, then at least it looks plucky, peering bravely ahead and taking on any black knot the darkness puts in its way to disentangle. But once I have ridden a certain distance the head will have bowed down almost as low as the mudguard again, as if it had seen something on the ground that it wanted to take a closer look at and not lose. But it isn't that it has seen something and that time stood still and now it is collecting its thoughts on the ground: this round little head is simply too sensitive for the paths around our parts. If it bows down again this evening I shall have to have it removed tomorrow. Perhaps a worker at the factory let himself go for a moment and fashioned the lamp with all the tenderness that his feelings guided through his hands, putting in everything he felt himself. Alas, we have no use for lamps like that. Tomorrow I shall probably have a proud, irresistible, gleaming, powerful lamp. It will dispel the knotted and tangled jungles of darkness at lightning speed, like arithmetic problems.

On the threshold of life. Suddenly everything you do and say has more meaning. You are responsible for what slips out of your mouth. Everyone can tell right away, from what you say, whether you are stupid or clever, good or bad, useful and important or incapable and insignificant. I should like to be a hard nut to crack, so that they cannot fathom me. But the moment I try something, it may be the kind of thing they can form a judgement from. Probably I am then assigned to the division of stupid and insignificant people, which is what I would prefer anyway. True, Life tempts me to dive into its waves, but I am overcome with hesitancy too, a feeling I am familiar with but which I have never experienced to so strong a degree. Gladly I would live amid the mass of people found to be insignificant, all of them are like dear brothers to me, but I should like to achieve something great. I should like to work hard for it. Not that I ever want to rise into the group of the important by that means, I only want to make something that is for everyone, especially the insignificant. And apart from its being something for other people, it gives me a certain satisfaction, it mitigates my joyless and sometimes painful sense of life, or indeed it gives me for the first time a feeling of being alive at all. It may of course be that I do not have the right to do this work; there are so many people who have not succeeded in making Fortune smile. In that case I shall be one of those many and will turn my back on this cold sun. Somewhere or other I shall find a place for me. To date I am the only one who believes that it might perhaps be possible for me to embark on that work, or at least I am the only one who dares give me permission to make the attempt.

The wheel of the world mills down our feet till we are sensitive and very cautious and can only mince along on tiptoe. All the things I should like. I ask for too much, for instance your gaze, with your dream in it. Or a place at your breast.

Listening to you. Oh and you sing, so I am no longer aware that it is only song, and so I believe everything, and simply do not know, and am startled, that the song must end. It would be better if you did not let me come to you. To be rid of me you would have to lever me off. And still I think: Just one time. This thinking of you, this recollection of you, bleeding again afresh, brings its painful longing into the fabric of the many days that mean little or nothing. And so, in the whole body of time, there is this pain, and one can no longer locate the wound, that place you hurt in the beginning. At times things are in a pretty state with me. Suddenly I feel I want to cry out: Why am I expected to put up with all of this stuff that has nothing to do with me? Why do I find it so unbearable? That I know you! Perhaps, if one knows someone like you, one is no longer able to like things without you. I should like always to be as it was when you looked at me, and I looked at you, and we both knew something that blossomed afar off for us. The skin of that moment, that it should always grow about me, be taut about me, and I should not have to wear it because it would really be growing. But you no longer look at me, and whatever blossoms for you, you keep secret. That I must blow my secret, which was for you, my island, which I made for you, my flower, everything, into the wind, plucked apart, for it to save itself. Time and time again it all comes back to you.

Gerhard Köpf

Fahrenheit

Ten years on. All solace gone. Instead: misgiving! Surely I can't have come too late? Here I am, lying in the semi-darkness of this guest-room at the villa, defenceless against images that glide in and out my mind like paper kites. Karlina's face, closing cautiously, like the fronds of a sensitive fern. There were nights, I remember her saying, when she'd mull over old photos, her head propped in her hands. Later, she'd pace up and down in her room for hours in total darkness.

I can hear her quite plainly now: a soft, intermittent sobbing through the thin wall, as if someone were idly humming. Her voice rustles like tissue-paper. What villa is this anyway? Can't I hear Karlina screaming inwardly, hatching out a new darkness? Or can we bridge these crevasses, make excursions into the world? In an effort to overcome past failings, I put death behind me. The doors won't close. I'll shift mountains. Me: a trembling rabbit, all the terrors of times long past before my eyes. I can tell her about it at last.

I know where I am now. I know my place.

I see myself at home with the photos spread out before me. I'm sitting all on my own in the old vicarage just outside—or rather, above—the village. The house and yard are hedged in by hazels and surrounded by open pasture. Evening after evening I sit alone in the sewing-chair by the window and work at making myself afraid. I've no interest in reading. I prefer looking at photos of film-stars. I like this woman. I like the stubborn expression of her eyes and mouth. I wish I had lips like hers. I can be stubborn, too—but nobody takes photos of me. I am alone with my talent in this house, both farm and vicarage, though there haven't been cattle here for years—just a few hens. We live on the first floor. A huge room, living-room and bedroom in one, dominated by a big, tiled stove that doesn't heat and a long, thin kitchen and at the back a dark, narrow corridor to the water trough. To get there, I have to leave the kitchen and go past my father's big postman's capes, hanging from their coat rack like a row of mounted moths.

I've decided I'm going to tell Karlina something tomorrow that nobody else knows. My secret.

Down a steep, poky stairwell at the end of the corridor you come to the main hall, where a trapdoor in the floor leads to the cellar. Another staircase, without a banister, actually more like a ladder, goes up to the loft, a quite creepy part of the house when you're alone—stuffy, dusty, menacing. Whenever I go near these places, I whistle as loud as I can. How often have I felt some invisible hand dragging me up to the loft, or down the steps to the yawning maw of the cellar! As long as I hear the familiar sound of our neighbour banging away at his blades on the long, summer evenings, I feel safe. It's only when the bats start to flit in and out through the shaftlike skylight, which is overgrown with ivy and can no longer be closed, that fear begins again. What'll Karlina say when the dry, metallic hammering suddenly stops? And what about winter when it gets dark early and the faces you see are even more frightening? Is all that really over? The dreadful hours in bed as a child, listening to dull thuds through the wall! Isn't that the same tapping now: through the wall of the guest-room in an isolated villa, surrounded by a deserted campsite on the shores of an almost entirely frozen lake? Summer evenings are all right, I suppose. I spend as long as I can outside, roaming the meadows and fields, enjoying the smell of freshly mown grass, inhaling the fragrance of hay. I usually climb up and sit in one of my tree-houses, which I've built in the forks of the stronger hazels. They're great hiding-places! I can seesaw in them too, rocking back and forth till the creaking branches warn me I'm about to fall. Nobody knows where my tree-houses are; I haven't got any friends to play with because the boy next door, who was two years older than me, fell off the hayrick and broke his neck. I can still remember him lying there with threads of blood trickling from his mouth and ear. His eyes were glazed over by the time his parents came rushing to find him. But I'll tell Karlina what fascinated me most: it was the little white coffin they put Luis in. It was only because I was the first to find him that I knew the bright summer flowers crowning his little ginger head hid a gaping hole from which blood had flowed. Since he had foxy hair, the patch of dried blood went unnoticed. Although his father had told him again and again not to jump about in the hayrick when the grown-ups weren't there, Luis had 'felt the curse of his evil deeds', as the teacher put it. The announcement of his death in the newspaper, for which I greatly envied my friend, said: 'in the bloom of youth . . .' In the bloom! The path that led to the cemetery started just behind our house. Sometimes, in the long, warm, summer evenings, I went with my wooden scooter to Luis's grave to talk to him. As soon as it got dark though, I'd race back home, switching on the wireless and all the lights the moment I got up the stairs. Drenched with sweat, I'd fall into the chair by the window where my mother sat when she was sewing.

To distract myself, I get up and fetch a book. I read until the letters swim before my eyes and all I can see are lines of print with myself behind them speeding home past the junipers on my scooter. I see it all quite clearly: I'm looking at pictures of James Dean's car accident. My brother collects them; the actor they call the darling of the gods is his hero. I see the silver wreck of his crushed Porsche. I think I can hear not only the whimpering through the wall, but his screams mingling with the unrestrained weeping of Luis's mother. In fact, I think I can smell the blood as it oozes from mouth and ears. In the end, it's not only James Dean they drag from the wreckage, but a small, freckled boy in leather shorts, his hair stuck down with blood. The teacher has strange words for this. I only remember the beginning: *To those they favour, the gods, eternal ones, give all.* I wish I were a darling of the gods! How I envy Luis his fall from the hayrick! But most of all, I envy him the announcement of his death in the newspaper and his white child's coffin, with his great big father walking along behind it, and his mother completely veiled in black, and the children from the village in their communion clothes: the girls in starched white dresses with garlands in their hair, the boys with sprigs of myrtle in the lapels of their dark-blue suits. Luis's grave isn't very big, but it looks deep to me, deeper than our cellar. I'll describe to Piloti the sound of earth pattering on the lid of the coffin—like rain beating on the tin roof of the old coach-house on a warm day. Perhaps tears will come to my eyes as I tell her, because the white coffin's getting so dirty. Through the veil worn by my grief-stricken mother I read what it says on the grove next to Luis's. It reminds me of the teacher: *All falls in God's will.* Under the writing, a leaf falling from a twig is painted over with the silver paint people use for stovepipes. The communion children strew flowers on the coffin. I feel envious of Luis again, and I'm very angry with God. Why have these pictures come into my mind? Why now, when I'm lying here alone in this guest-room and not really reading at all? Perhaps it's because I'm aware of what's happening to us—that we keep trying to avoid something we're frightened of, but can't actually prevent, like a leavetaking. I'll take Karlina at her word; I'll remind her what she wrote to me when first we arranged to meet. Come on, she said, let's tell stories; as long as we tell our stories, we're immortal. So I'll tell her. About Brigitte, too, for whom I once pined away. Another darling of the gods! On some photos, she had thin, white bandages elegantly bound around her wrists, like a gymnast working out on the horizontal bar. The magazines said it was because she had tried to commit suicide. She had tried to cut her arteries with a razor-blade, but someone had found her before it was too late. They'd taken her to hospital immediately, preventing her from bleeding to death; she'd lost a lot of blood because she'd held the cuts under water. I'll tell Karlina how I thought of asking the teacher whether you had to draw the blade along the arteries, or across them. I'll tell her about listening to the wireless, too. Alone every evening while my parents were out cleaning the post-office in the valley, I would always turn on the wireless. We had a Löwe Opta with a bass tuner. When I turned up the bass, the cloth cover on the loudspeaker vibrated. Above the wavelength scale, right in the middle of the set, there's a magic eye, like the sanctuary lamp above the high altar. Sometimes, when I'm in the mood for faraway places, I turn the needle to names like Sofia, Hilversum or Monte Ceneri. My brother only listens to *AFN*. My favourite programme is *Music in the Air*. I can still remember the theme tune, so I'll whistle it to Karlina. We'll talk about jazz musicians whose names and biographies were in my brother's jazz-calendar. The pages of the calendar are pinned all over the wall of our bedroom along with the photos of James Dean. She'll find out what it's like when you have a high temperature and have to wait half-asleep in a stifling old postbag till your parents finish the cleaning—but then they never seem to stop, and you can see them mopping the counter room, or waxing the sorting-table, or polishing the brass. Didn't Piloti want to know where I came from, what my background is, how I grew up? Didn't she keep asking me that? I'll tell her all right. I'll tell her how I flinch when Anna Kolik, a refugee with chapped fingers and dark hair on her chin, lets the empty sub-post-office resound to her booming voice:

The German warrior's single blow/Stops the steed of his Turkish foe;/His blade is sharp, his aim is true,/He hacks the animal's forelegs through./Once the warrior's felled the horse,/ Down comes his sword with terrible force;/A fearful blow, a dreadful feat/He slices the rider from crown to seat!/Nor does his weapon end its work,/Till it cleaves the saddle under the Turk./Thus sinks down, after ill-fated ride,/Half a Turk on either side.

I'll remember the stains, too, where the blood flowed from

Luis's ear. And when Karlina strokes her dog I'll tell her how I flung our cat out of the skylight in order to prove that cats could land on their feet by steering through the air with their tails. I'll see the pictures of Brigitte again, standing there in her cool, pretty dress, surrounded by young men all looking at her. I'll walk through the flat with my new girl-friend. We'll go to the kids' room, walk past photos of James Dean's accident. We'll listen to the frogs croaking in the nearby pond where, in winter, you can play ice-hockey and go skating on a thing my Dad calls a 'footsole-render'. I'll take Karlina to the coach-house in summer; there, suspended in one of the dark corners, is a manure tank where Luis sometimes played submarines. The manure was so dry, you had to knock big, crumbly bits off the top if you wanted to open the lid and get in. In fact, people didn't really call it a coach-house at all; they called it the fire-house because it was next to a large well with a huge iron vat and hydrants standing guard in threatening, uniform black. I really ought to put this book down; I'm not reading it anyway. I'm holding on tight as if I were about to swear a solemn oath to tell Piloti my whole story tomorrow—and put the past behind me at last. I was frightened of the well, too, and our songbook had an awful picture next to one of the songs we often sang: *A man has fallen down the well*. We'll go back and look for the old fire-fighting equipment in the fire-house. But we can't find any. It's full of junk that belongs to farmer Hitzelberger, the milkman and driver of the hearse. People call him 'the blasphemer'; he's got a speech defect and swears like a trooper, uttering the most horrendous profanities. His shadow, following him everywhere, is Fedor, a Russian pris-oner. He has been on the farm since the year Hitzelberger's son was declared missing. Fedor was a labourer, then gradu-ally came to take the place of the son and wear his clothes. A big fellow with raven-black hair and a thick beard, he rarely speaks. On summer evenings he crouches at the edge of the pond, whimpering and rocking back and forth on his heels. I'll show Piloti the enormous grinding stone and take her to see the hearse: a rickety old crate with peeling paint and squashed flies on its black curtains, and tassels and fringes that once were silver. Sometimes I climb up to the driving-seat and sit there thinking about my life, and Luis, and the half Turk.

Perched on the hearse, I read the tale in my schoolbook about the fieldmouse who goes to town and gets terribly lost; then the one about the race between the hare and the hedgehog: *But the hare did not reach the end the seventy-fourth time. With blood streaming from his mouth, he fell to the ground half-way up the field; and there he remained. The hedgehog had won the piece of gold and the bottle of brandy. Fetching his wife from the furrow, he went home in the very best of moods.* I've underlined the end of the tale in my school primer. I can see the facing picture too: the hedgehog, with the brandy-bottle raised to his lips, reeling home in the moonlight, while the hare lies dead and bleeding in the field—like Luis, perhaps. The children are swallowed by the mountain, and Rumpelstiltskin tears himself in two. My only solace is Brigitte, who is stubborn and beautiful and mysterious, with things around her that are precious and lovely. But I'm at home on my own, searching the flat for something with which to drive away my fears. I pull open drawers and, in my disappointment, slam them shut again; I know exactly what's in them, having opened and closed them a thousand times before. Is there really any comfort in running my hand over the furniture as I wander restlessly through the flat, or in fiddling with the tap that sticks menacingly out of the wall? I want to hear the sound of dripping water, and to think of earth pattering on a little white coffin. I'll confess to Karlina that Luis didn't fall off the hayrick at all; I pushed him because he'd got a white coffin strewn with flowers and an announcement in the papers, and because he could hear earth falling on him and was a darling of the gods. The kitchen dresser is the north face of the Eiger— with me hanging on it like a hapless Japanese mountaineer.

Then I'll reveal my final, my greatest secret: I've managed to find something after all. Opening and closing cupboards and drawers in this empty flat, which is like an iceberg, I suddenly came upon this book. It was lying under a pile of discarded scarves and gloves; at first, I didn't even realise it was a book. Mainly because of the horrible stories in our schoolbook I've never been much of a reader. But there's something compelling about this book. Just the fact of my having found it is so thrilling that I forget to tidy the things back into the drawer and close it behind me. I take the bundle of paper to the sewing-chair by the window, tune into *Music in the Air* and, before examining my find more closely, gaze out into the dusk of a September evening, locating my tree-houses in the hazels. The book is a joy to hold; a Bible worth any oath you'd care to mention. It's about the size of a prayer-book and has no cover, or title page, or illustrations of any sort. Soon I discover that the last page can't be the end of the story, either. Perhaps it's the first book of a series. Or perhaps it's only one link in a chain of which I know neither beginning nor end. In any case it's as light as a feather. The pages are a well-thumbed, greasy yellow; I hold them to my nose at once, inhaling the smoky aroma, which grows damp and mouldy towards the middle, making me feel as if I've read at least half the book already! I weigh it first in one hand, then in the other, stroking its back, its front, turning it upside down. I caress it, running my fingers along the spine: a bleached and brittle mesh of threads, knots and encrusted glue. A miraculous book! Karlina will probably ask how it got into our flat in the first place. It can't have been my brother, since he reads cowboy comics, or those weird film magazines with their never-ending stream of previously unknown stories and pictures of James Dean. Nobody read in my family—unless you counted magazines, or serialised novels in the *Thulsener Herald*. Cleaners and country postmen just don't read. The thickest volume on the shelf of our tiled stove was leather-bound and big as the missal at church. It was called: *The Viennese Cookbook*. But who on earth could have spirited my magic book into a drawer whose contents I had gone through so often, so thoroughly, and always in vain? It can only have been one person, someone who has often guided me in the past, showing me all kinds of things I didn't know: Aunt Maria, who told me about the motorcyclist Piloti in the first place. Maria is someone who does own books. But what's this book called? I've no idea. Nor can I find a logical explanation for its sudden appearance. I shall just have to invent some! I may as well start with the author's name. I can think of several, among them my own. And what about a title? No sooner does one occur, than I immediately reject it, though I've hardly read a page. That's why the first page has taken so long. All the titles are linked to the place where I discovered the book, or to my fears. But perhaps it was Aunt Maria herself who wrote the book? Aunt Maria? An author? She can fairly spin a tale, it's true! Because of the magic book, my schoolbook grows smaller and smaller until it practically disappears altogether. I've forgotten the photos of Brigitte. This evening I don't even hear *Music in the Air* come to an end. I usually wait for them to play *Moon River*, a tune that makes me feel strong enough to go to sleep. Sitting in the sewing-chair at the window, I don't even notice it's got dark outside. All I do is read. My book starts on page 15, and I'm going to read out the first sentences to Karlina, loudly and slowly: *Perhaps it was true after all. I can't tell. In any case, she certainly dressed like an Indian. She wore a necklace of turquoise beads and such a large quantity of rouge, one felt almost blinded; her cheeks glowed like twin sanctuary-lamps.* I immediately learned these sentences off by heart, my mind a panorama of nightly blue, my eyes bright, my head full with the promise of a complex skein of plans that would never be unravelled. Effortlessly, I managed something that would never be like this again. I also learned the final paragraph of my first book. It came on page 207: *It was as if neither of us were aware of our true intentions. Filled with a quiet wonder, we surveyed the surrounding countryside from the cemetery hill, before descending arm in arm to the sum-* ... This is where my novel ends. Wrestling with her ghosts in the room next to mine, only Piloti knows of my repeated attempts to imagine new endings, spinning ever-changing narrative threads as I sit at the window or in the tops of trees, rocking back and forth and singing to myself. My magical book is mainly about a boy called Collin Fenwick who, along with two crotchety women, an old judge and a tramp who live in a tree-house, gets tipsy on bramble wine and tells stories all night long: *A twig sprang aside; the tree flooded with moonlight*. With no end to the stories I can think of, my book—such a pleasure to hold, and with so strange an odour—has become thicker and thicker as time goes by. Piloti will understand me when I tell her this: from the very first sentence, our flat in the old vicarage and farm above the village, with its crown of hazels and surrounded by green pastures, has been released from the cast-iron grip of fear and is gentle and peaceful. The loft and cellar, with their treacherous staircases, shine as if with a bright new coat of silver paint. With the book in my pocket I feel brave enough to visit Luis's grave when it's getting dark. Sometimes I sit next to Fedor in the grass at the edge of the pond and listen to his whimpering. I've even put my hand on his shoulder when he was feeling very sad. But I haven't breathed a word to anyone about my book. I read and read, and all the horrible stories in my schoolbook have vanished in a deep well. The stifling old postbags and batlike capes are ablaze in the tiled stove. While Radio Monte Ceneri plays *Moon River*, someone in the background beats a strangely soft, metallic rhythm to which a small, red-headed child gently sways. There'd be freckles in the sky, and a flying cat and jolly hare splitting their sides over a drunk hedgehog at the edge of the furrow. Anna Kolik, meanwhile, hums along happily to herself.

Even now, even tonight, whenever I think of Karlina Piloti, I read the story about the tall grass of the faraway prairie and the wind rustling in the holy-tree (a magical word!) with the tree-house perched under the canopy of its topmost branches. *The grass harp it was that held all, told all*. I manage something that nobody has ever done before:

I overcome the force of gravity, and feel a strength as I read, as if I could dig my way through—dig through to Alaska, or cause an earthquake with every page I turn.

Hanns-Josef Ortheil

The Visit

From time to time I visit her. Her house is in a lonely clearing in the woods, and not easy to find. In summer it is hidden away among mighty trees twisted into their shapes by the bluff winds, and in winter it is tucked away behind walls of snow that make it inaccessible some days.

Often I think of it as a hideaway. I drive along the narrow woodland track and stop the car close to the house. There she is: I can see her through the window, flitting about, dressed in bright clothes. She must have been waiting for this moment for the last few hours. She may have been sitting at the window, about some unimportant business or other. Maybe she opened it at some point, to hear the engine the moment it became audible, but I don't think so: the window has never been open when I arrive. Quite the contrary, I tend to notice that she hurriedly opens it shortly after I arrive. She waves, and I hear exclamations of joy breaking upon the quiet of the wood, sounds no one understands but the two of us. They are the sounds we know each other by.

I call back, and only when she has heard my response, this call of recognition, does she become more animated. She quits her place by the window, and I know she will now come towards me, leaving the house, while I put down my luggage beside the car.

That is how it has usually been. At one time this welcome struck me as odd. It has only been in the last few years that I have known more, and not till I had learnt as much as it was possible to know did I grasp that it was not me alone she welcomed, not only me she was waiting for, not only me she embraced.

This is not easy to understand, and I didn't understand it myself at first. I could see she was delighted at my arrival, but then I would be embarrassed as she drew my head down to her. We leave the luggage by the car like some foreign body, and hurry into the house; I shall bring in the case and bags later. She links her arm in mine, and, since she is distinctly smaller than I am, I walk towards the front door bent sideways as if by a weight. She tells me what has changed in the wild and rambling garden since my last visit. But she talks hastily, as if the words meant nothing, and it may be that by now she has realised that I cannot listen to it. Who can listen when he knows from the start that the conversation is only carried on for the sake of appearance?

Anyone watching us might well think we were talking to each other. But it is hardly that. We merely toss each other scraps of talk, and they don't mean very much. That too I didn't grasp for a long time. I used to listen and reply; not till later did I realise there was no point in any of it. She was not yet able to listen to me; her talk was only her way of getting through the few steps it took us to reach the door. Oddly enough, I used to feel strangely good when she opened the door. It was as if I were coming home. Now that has changed. It is as though I am entering some unknown darkness. But that, as I have remarked, is saying too much. Let me explain.

A few days after the Party came to power, she saw pictures of the Reich capital in the village cinema, for the first time. She made the connection between the torchlit procession through the Brandenburg Gate, which then turned in front of the Reich chancellery, and the bonfires in the valleys of the Sieg, where she and her parents and relations lived, which she had had a good view of.

Six years later, when as a newly-wed she followed her husband to Berlin, it seemed in her memory as if the fires had all been one single beacon summoning her to the distant city. It was back then, in the early days, that she had got to know her husband, a farmer's boy who wanted to be an engineer. At night she returned to the family home from parties in high, boisterous spirits, leaving her parents at a loss to account for her sudden changed mood.

For a time she cast all reticence to the winds. Her love heightened the thrill of the new and the hopes which drew on the newsreel images at the cinema ran wild. She wanted to be part of the movement, the energies of which she sensed excitingly all about her and which she could at first respond to only by dancing and singing. She did not want to take active part, only to see the red of the flags and run off for once to the gatherings which the loudspeaker vans had canvassed for days.

But soon she became more cautious. Her father had warned her, and she knew that it was not yet decided which was right, this new feeling that had given her a husband or the recollection of the quieter years before, when she had run the library at the village church. For the Party had quickly aroused her suspicions. When the black lists appeared, with the titles of banned books that were to be destroyed as soon as possible, she had her first clear intuition that the pleasure she had known in the last few months did not come without strings. Among the banned books were several she liked. One or two she managed to put aside. She tied them up together, and later they went along in the move to Berlin, which she saw as a new beginning, in the chest her husband's parents had given the young couple.

And so, barely a month after the war began, they moved into a new house in the suburb of Lichterfelde, and on the morning they moved into the fine corner house with its rural hipped roof a Party comrade and the vicar looked in to welcome them. Her parents, business people with a small fortune, had paid for the furniture, and the pictures, which she hung the very first day, showed the parts she had grown up in: the hilltops where the bonfires had burnt, the nearby castle, and the meadows along the banks of the Sieg.

The young engineer had become a civil servant who was

getting ahead nicely in Berlin. But she found it hard to feel at home there. The new, different noises would not let her be. Even at night she heard every thump or loud knock. Often she rode to the wrong destination, and waited patiently in the trams till the names of the stops stuck in her mind.

'In the evenings,' she wrote to her father, 'my head goes round in circles and gets out instead of me, and my legs go reeling along the curves with the tram. I can remember what the news vendors shouted in the morning for ages. Sometimes I think: if only you're not blown away by the wind, like Father's hat in the fields back home! But what's even worse is that I can't talk as I do with you. People stare the moment I open my mouth. "Say that again!" they shout, but you know I talk so softly, so softly that you, Father, once told me to speak up or else no one could hear a thing I said! People poke fun at me. Oh, if only I could talk like the men who make speeches!'

She began to improve her pronunciation, and paid attention to the way others spoke. She would murmur things aloud and practise in the evening before her husband was in the flat.

At length she decided to go to a rally outside the Reich chancellery. She stood as if on tiptoe. When the speeches were being made, the silence of thousands of people crushed her body. She kept quiet and sensed the pressure. Not that she understood what was being said: she listened to the singsong, the banging, the spitting. The pressure mounted; something in her rose, reached her throat, and found its way into her mouth whenever the voice up there resumed softly, trembling as if a stone were being moved and slowly beginning to totter. She stretched her body up as the others did whose cries of 'Heil!' melded like mountain echoes or the plash of waves, till their accumulated expectations gathered into one multiple and uncontrollable sound that broke at last upon the outstretched right arm of the man on the inaccessible balcony.

She could not shout, though she thought that it might have done her good to do so. When her voice failed her, it felt as if she were awaking, while the rest persisted in their sound, like a tree slowly drifting downriver. She was frightened and longed for the end, and later she stood at the stop, exhausted as if after a brief ascent and an endless plunge into a valley, till she realised that she could not take the tram because she no longer had the strength.

From that day on, the fear was always with her. The loud words, slogans and songs scattered by the Party were an unfailing feature of the marching columns that tramped through the streets to the parping and drumming of brass bands, their steel tipped boots staccato on the cobbles.

So she began to avoid the entertainments as far as it was possible. She took her fear to be a premonition of a terror she did not believe she would be able to cope with. When her husband was transferred to Poland, to work on the extension of the militarily essential rail network, her first feeling was that she would never see him in one piece again.

She became taciturn, as she had formerly been, and secretly read the books that had been but temporarily laid to rest in the chest, starting a soft dialogue with herself in that way. She began to grasp why these books might have been dangerous to those in power, for reading them conferred strength, a strength which bound one to the words without one having to surrender oneself.

Almost of their own accord, her trips to the city centre began to fall off; instead, she took to crossing the Gardeschützenweg more often, coming to the green, tree-lined streets of Dahlem and remembering what it had been like at home. When she became pregnant she made sure to avoid any district that was noisy. She abhorred parades and rallies, and the instinct grew more alert in her with every day that passed. Since she no longer dared to write down what she felt, she pursued her dialogue with herself all the more insistently. She listened to herself, interrupted, reproached, questioned herself. Within her there were now two people: I ask the questions and do the talking—you listen and reply. Presently she could no longer say which was in the right. Might it not be that she was lending the voice of lament to the child she was expecting, and that she was not talking to herself but with the voice of a child still inexperienced and far from any past?

In seclusion she made ready for the birth. At weekends her husband came to visit, and they would go out to the Wannsee, to Schwanenwerder or the Pfaueninsel. She was afraid to confess her fear to him. The scent of vegetation startled her whenever the tram halted and the windows were opened. She still associated silence with her home district, but that image of peace, no more than longed for, she conceived in muted grey or dark blue that would not run.

In a fit of courage she suggested to her husband that she leave the Reich capital and have the child at her parents' home. The notion left him cold; he could not understand her anxiety, and urged her not to 'run away from things'. When the air raids started, her walks were at an end as well. The big city, which she had thought of before they moved there as a vast terrain for the sheer enjoyment of life, shrank to a tiny neighbourhood where she led her life thenceforth.

The raids increased, and together with the other tenants she sat through it as the bombs fell nearby, and angelic wings came rustling earthward in the dark.

On one occasion, lacking the strength, she did not go down to shelter in the cellar. She waited in silence. For some time, nothing had been hit in the neighbourhood. Then, penned in behind the black-out blinds in the darkness, she noticed her murmuring, and it grew louder, the closer she believed the humming, whistling noises, bursting in as though through a sound barrier, to be. The murmuring sound came up from within her from a remote place that was unknown to her, and she uttered strange noises that she hoped would be some help: 'eternal light, thou whose works will never be destroyed, maker of the deep light, tiller of the earthen sod . . .' She had flung herself down on the floor. A number of bombs fell nearby. The pictures dropped from the walls; the windows shattered; incendiary bombs caught next door's roof, and when she ran out there were people blackened with smoke struggling free of the chalky rubble, wearing wet blankets. Fountains shot up from burst water mains, and glowing patches of phosphorus gleamed in the dark.

A bare half hour later her labour pains began, but when the taxi reached the hospital the child's heartbeat suddenly stopped, and she gave birth to a dead baby.

She was inconsolable when her husband came to see her. Discharged from hospital, she felt she could no longer be at ease alone. She walked warily, glancing sideways like a cat, as if to forestall the observation of others. There were houses that she imagined to be the look-outs of infanticides, hedges she took to be the quarters of warmongers, whose slogans she now understood entirely.

When she was expecting the second child, her decision was irreversible. She managed to get hold of a removal van, and her husband, who had long since been transferred from Poland to clearance duties on Tempelhof airfield, was given three days' leave to help her. They left one room as it was. She took the train and travelled home, with trains for the front going in the opposite direction.

She moved in with her parents once again. Air raids were still rare in the country. Again she went picking berries and gathering mushrooms, and collecting windfall fruit in autumn. Every few days she went out to the woods with a hand-drawn cart to fetch wood. One might have thought she had never known any other life, but she herself was undeceived. She spoke even more softly than usual, so that her father told her to speak up, they couldn't understand a word! But she made no effort, and did not show any greater pleasure till her son was born and she was able to present him to her husband, home on leave.

From the first day she spoke a different language, hard to understand, with the child. She addressed him with sounds no one had ever heard, sounds that puzzled everyone. Some believed she had gone mad—but that could not be right, because in the evenings, when she had put her son to bed, she talked as she normally did. When asked about it, she replied evasively that it was baby talk. Others noticed that she performed her daily tasks listlessly, and never looked up for long, as if for fear of meeting too many looks; only when she was talking to the child did she become more animated, but still, even with time, no one else could understand her murmuring, which often sounded like a whimper, and once her father, angered by so much that was unfamiliar to him, left the table. She took no notice. For days she would vanish into the woods with the boy, as if she had to hide him and had things to discuss that were no one else's business. 'Helper in every need and fear, tight knot that cannot be untied, true observer of all things secret and known to none . . .'

Unexpectedly, the months passed in peace and tranquillity, and the boy came on. But it had soon become clear that he would not be touched or even walked out by anyone else. He seemed irrevocably tied to his mother, snuggled up to her, and often would only stop his groaning and whining when she began the puzzling sounds. It was not till the closing months of the war that the air raids extended to the country around the Sieg as well. The Americans had crossed the bridge at Remagen. But still it would be late in the evening when she brought the boy home from the woods; darkness would be falling in the eerie hours before the raids, when the cars glided about like green, glassy coffins and the last people hurrying along wore buttons and animal badges that glowed.

In one particularly bad raid, the station and houses near it went up in flames. No one believed they would survive the next raid. So the family decided to abandon the house and head off with the bare essentials to a nearby farm; her father knew the farmers, who had had the property for generations. But when he announced that everything was fixed and they could leave for Hecke (the name of the farm), the boy took the greatest possible exception to the name. It was impossible to say it aloud when he was there, and he would put his hands over his ears if anyone said, 'to Hecke, we're going to Hecke!'

The others explained this by the boy's being used to the house he had grown up in, and related his behaviour to the peculiar sensitivity he had acquired during the years of special treatment by his mother.

But she too urged that they move quickly. The others went ahead, and she followed with a small hand-cart and the boy, since that was the only way he could be calmed.

Even on that one-day trek there were air raids. If they turned round they could see the village silhouetted against a red glare, with black lines, as if of heavenly ladders above it, trembling with the thumping roars. There were craters left by bombs along the wayside, filled with water, and yellow, poisonous flowers, and weeds of a deep green colour, and, once, fish in pools. And later, in the evening, a sulphurous yellowy-green sky far off, so they all knew the village was no more.

Late at night, talking softly, she reached the farm with the boy. After she had put him to bed, though, not a word could be got out of her at table. Only when she was repeatedly asked and badgered did she say that the language everybody used had become repellent, once and for all, a thing of ghosts, and behind every sound was the dying babble and moan of the dead.

And so she talked mainly to the boy, in the incomprehensible language that she used only with him, in which some fluid understanding seemed none the less possible, for the child had begun to return the sounds and, when the others pressed him with questions, lapsed into a bewildering stammer.

She now expressly forbade the others to speak to the child. To her father's objection that the child would never learn to talk she responded by drawing the words the boy was expected to learn on little scraps of paper.

'A big word, a rugged cliff, with little spires, a flyaway word with creepers, a laughing word. Butcher, baker, wordy-maker.'

In time the child, who was of course unable to tell what the scrawl meant, took to demanding certain words and letters, and the others even found that he would do without his mother at his side if only he had the right picture games to keep him occupied.

She had meanwhile got hold of a map on which she marked the approach of the Allies and the shifting of the front with little flags. The closer the foreign troops came, the more restless she became, not, as she told her father, because she was afraid of the enemy, but for fear that the end would not fit the beginning. There were some words, she added, that would have to be completely destroyed in good time before the victors arrived. They would have to be sorted out, so that no one would utter them unthinkingly any more.

The pieces of paper bearing the torn-up names of the Party leaders, of the SS and the SA were found in the neighbourhood, and she was given a ticking off. 'Earthquake!' she had scribbled on one little piece of paper that she always had in her bag, whereas she was forever tearing up others, keeping scraps and writing on them anew and tearing them up, so that the others had to follow her wherever she went, to burn the paper that rained from her bags, and the drizzle of writing that left its traces all around the farm.

And so in the closing days of the war, of all times, she became a source of danger. They kept her busy so that none of this language that kept on bubbling out of her should be picked up by the wrong ears. She tidied up.

The news reported that the Americans were steadily approaching. The air raids on the village had stopped. No one dared go further afield any more. They were waiting for the foreign troops to arrive; the barking of dogs faltered in the valleys all around, and the crowing of cocks split the expectant silence with such force, that it was as if a bell which had enclosed the closely packed buildings of the farm had been pulled away.

One afternoon about three o'clock the farmer of Hecke saw the khaki uniforms of the Americans above the stables. They were moving slowly through the green, and then he noticed the scout car rumbling out of the woods like a toy and slowly trundling towards the barn.

They were all together in the kitchen when he told the others the news. They sat around without a word, waiting, when suddenly the child began to cry. For the first time, as his crying grew more violent, she talked to him in the language he was unfamiliar with but which all of them could understand. With a strength that was barely credible she picked him up in her arms and ran very quickly into the bedroom. There she pulled a sheet off the mattress; they tried to stop her, but with the crying child in her arms she raced up the stairs to the roof where she made fast the sheet, hastily tying it round a wooden pole, like a flag.

Exhausted, as if she had performed the least needful deed to achieve the peace that everyone longed for, she started singing in the kitchen. She made so calm an impression that the child stopped crying and tried to wheedle something from her. Nothing had happened since she had hoisted the flag, but tanks could be heard grinding closer, seeming to follow the soldiers who ran ahead, their voices audible very close by like a squabble that had suddenly begun. She had sat down at the kitchen table and had sat the boy on her lap to spread honey on bread for him when the shells hit.

The others flung themselves to the floor, but she remained sitting. A splinter grazed her forehead and she was bleeding a little, but she was otherwise unhurt, whereas another, larger splinter struck the back of the boy's head. She sat the dead body up and failed to grasp what had happened as the lad kept falling back, sagging and finally threatening to fall off her lap altogether.

The American machine-gun volleys hammered into the woods farther down where the German artillery, firing from cover, had taken up its position.

They say that when the noise of battle was roaring at the gates, as it were, and above the roofs of the farm, sounding already as if there could be no calm till every stone of that hideaway too had been razed to the ground, the two opposing forces suddenly heard a cry such as might have come from the eternal seat of Judgement, a sound beyond all imagining, a trumpeting that went beyond human strength, that quite unexpectedly silenced the din of combat at a stroke.

They say she opened wide the kitchen door into the yard and went out with the child in her arms, into the line of fire between the warring enemies. No one, they say, dared to follow her. They all held their breath, and the silence was once and for all the silence of an ending more terrible than anyone could have imagined.

And the fact was that there was no more fighting. The German artillery apparently abandoned their position, and a large detachment of American soldiers pursued them into the valley. The rest of them settled into the farm, though without enjoying any peace, any more than the inhabitants since the mother with her dead son on her knees was crouching under the blossoming cherry tree, where she remained for hours on end without making a single sound, and all night too, motionless, and all the following day, from morning till night, till the child had to be torn from the grasp of a woman who seemed turned to stone, to be given a temporary burial nearby. But some say that at the moment she no longer felt the body of the child she fell sideways and lay for hours where she had sat for so long.

These events marked the end of the war. Later the boy was buried in the village cemetery; she did not attend the funeral. She firmly believed that her husband had fallen in the fighting in Berlin. When, however, she was told one day that he was only a few kilometres away on the homeward road, she did not set out, nor did she go to meet him when she could see the truck on which he was being brought home. Indeed, they say that when she was face to face with him she suddenly flinched from him in horror. Asked later who she thought she was, to be afraid of her own husband, she answered that she could only account for the sudden appearance of this soldier by supposing a guardian angel had intervened. But when she recognised the man in his tattered clothing she thought (so she said) that the guardian angel, who could be none other than the dead child, had drunk his fill of the festering wound of the limping returnee, to survive in the shape of the man.

Might there really be someone watching? Sometimes I think she is afraid of his scrutiny, and that is why she urges me indoors so fast. Why else should we be in such a hurry?

Ah, my questions get nowhere, and all I can really say is that we are going on. Maybe we are still arm in arm, maybe she has now let go of me to lead the way ahead. For—I have to say it—there are times when she walks almost as if someone had once got in her way out here. But she plainly does not want to register him in words; she has never talked about it. But why, then, does she not make straight for the door, but takes a crooked path instead, by which I am least of all able to follow her?

A watcher—supposing he does exist, then—might think she was dragging me through a whirlpool and I were hanging on by a short knotted lead, the tautness of which would only relax once we were finally at the door.

But I can imagine how bewildered an outsider might be if he watched her unlocking the massive lock, turning the key several times; the key would make that cracking sound I know so well, as if a stone were being kicked aside and were now flying off, unreachably far—how shall I put it?—beyond the horizon. We go in together, while she suddenly—'we have talked and we are still talking, it's time to put a stop to that'—as I was saying, suddenly—'now everything is topsy-turvy, back to front and front to back, bottom-most on top of the mountain and top-most in the valley'—suddenly her talk changes, the old language comes to the fore, and I, shoved gently into these rooms which I am so familiar with, I go under at the very first steps I take, go under in the maw of sounds, which closes at the very moment the door clicks shut and she, quite against my will, manages to turn the key from the inside and withdraw it, so that now, at the end, no observer can intrude any more between the two of us.

Brigitte Kronauer

The Woman in the Pillows

I used to visit a very old woman who was always sitting in bed. Behind the bed, which had been pushed next to the window, there stood a sideboard with black trim and a wavy wood-grain. Its many open drawers and shelves had been emptied, apart from the photograph of a man wearing a hat and smoking a pipe. I never saw her turn her head back towards it, and from where she was lying she could probably no longer do so. Above her head there was a little hole in the cupboard door. The missing handle had been replaced by a loop of wire and a hook. A little light fell from the window on the red checked eiderdown and the blue carnations on the pillow. A second, yellowish blanket was stuffed between the window-sill and the woman's body as a shield against the cold that came from outside during the night. The rest of the room was kept dark dark, and beneath the red checked quilt she often drew another thin woollen blanket up over her chest.

'Everything here is exactly the way she wants it!' said her daughter. I listened to this, and when she had left the room I said loudly, 'The Malayan bear is alone now. One of the two, the male or the female, has disappeared. The one that's left paces up and down on the concrete, not making a sound. Only two foreigners, hoeing weeds into a bucket in front of the cage, said anything.' Then I was silent for a while. I would not, in any case, have been able to continue. The words had to make contact with her, find a way into her, and finally, much later, she would reply. We were both interested in the zoo. On other days I told her that she had once been a passionate collector of stones, and got people who were going on their travels to bring back stones, most of which were valueless, but which she would inscribe precisely with details of the place where they had been found, the name of the person who had brought them and the year, and which in the course of her long life, with the burgeoning of tourism for all, became 'stones from many lands', as she called the collection, so on other days I told her about the display pieces in a lapidarist's shop, about the gleaming crystals, sunrises and sunsets over snow-covered mountain peaks, locked in vitrines, protected by Yale locks, a multitude of ways of glowing, sealed at their most gleaming moment.

There was a third thing I was able to tell her about. That was important events from the neighbourhood, a theft, the sudden marriage of flighty Frau Hoffmann, a win on the lottery, a fight between sect member Schmidt and Karl the cripple. She let all these things, delivered in a loud voice with considerable pauses, wander around in her own way: she smiled with a shake of her head, while I waited patiently, and took everything in with a slow eagerness. She wore a pale blue padded bed-jacket that didn't cover her thin, brown-flecked forearms. Her hands gripped the ends of her pillows, the individual strands of hair were almost discernible, grey, white only at the sides and combed straight into a little bun at the back, like a heavy little ball of iron pulling all her hair back to her neck. The cat, which had run like an elastic fluid through her hard, crooked fingers when I first visited, had died long since.

'The female orang utan was proudly displaying its offspring. The baby was clutching fast on to its mother's fur, and glanced out only very occasionally. But at the end, when the zookeeper was hosing down the tiled floor he was allowed to hold the little one's hand. But the parent grabbed his broom as long as he did so.' I said this sentence cheerfully, as though a conversation was going on between us, I said it louder than the first one, although she hadn't made the slightest discernible response to that. I did not know what still got through to her. She had thrown away the stones, had her daughter remove all the souvenirs and presents from the sideboard, and no longer looked at the photograph of her own husband. For the first time she didn't give me any hint whether she still understood my words. When I had talked about the zoo before, she had always given a start at appropriate intervals. I was determined that I would soon given her the next unusual feature of my visit to the zoo, which I had memorised specially for her. But for the time being I dumbly watched her hands, which were half hidden between her bedclothes today, her very wrinkled mouth, shrunk to its smallest size, her distinct but not very prominent nose, her eyes the colour of the bed-jacket almost hidden behind big, white, tissue-paper-thin lids, but most clearly the ear that was turned towards me. It was an enormous, extraordinarily finely wrought ear, the largest in relation to the rest of the face that I have ever seen on a human being. In the effort to receive the sounds of the surrounding world, it seemed to have grown larger and larger and more yearning. I had never touched her. With what simple but shrill signals could I lighten the darkness of her senses once more, how could I reach her ear, so that the pale lids would finally rise, and the pursed mouth would open for a moment while the transmitted image, after it had hit her like a short, benevolent blow, would stand motionless and burn within her for a while?

So I said, 'The mandrill,' almost shouted it, 'the oldest one, the one with the beautiful blue lines in his face, was being fed with Russian letters. But he couldn't get the B through the bars at first, while whole sparrows were flying in and out without the slightest difficulty.' I stopped speaking. She didn't move, only her heart, her pulse must have been beating quietly, a faint breath must have been passing over lips which had vanished inwards.

'In the big restaurant I had sausages and chips again. Some people had their food brought to them under domed silver covers. Seldom have I heard people coughing with so little embarrassment. It kept breaking out in some corner or other, a barking and trumpeting. After the noises of the animals outside, the people inside had lost all restraint, and, under the pretence of sneezing and throat-clearing, imitated them with pleasure.' I would gratefully have taken even a tiny tremble in the conspicuous wings of her nose as a smile. But I didn't see it, I saw the black hollows of the sideboard behind the bed, empty apart from her husband's picture, he might have been an old Tyrolean, on the middle, damaged shelf, its edge cut in several places, and I could see her eyes from the side. She wanted neither to close nor to open them properly, and I didn't know whether she was listening with the huge funnels of her thin, pale ears.

'A grown man was led past the lynx cage by a sensible, even solemn-looking child. Mentally ill, the grown-up. You could see it in his terribly sensitive skin. The man as a whole looked naked and had, probably for protection, so as not to look so bare, put a hat on, a felt hat in that heat.'

'And the lions!' I cried straight after, 'I actually caught the lions trying to mate! The lion and the lioness, the king and queen, were lying opposite one another, for a very long time, and looking steadily at one another. Then they stood up, walked a little way, they did everything together, in harmony. They walked side by side through the outdoor enclosure as if they were walking on to Noah's Ark. Then all of a sudden they tried to mate. Both roared briefly and then they didn't do it after all.

'And always, of course, the uncouth people talking smugly at the elegant animals, bawling in front of the cages and showing off with the names, read from the signs, in shiny, shapeless anoraks most of the time, that day sweating in their safari shirts.' Would she have jerked up if I'd shouted 'Fire!'? My talking raced against her silence, into the gloom, her increasingly undifferentiated senses, into their commingling I related my details like final bars, grids, brakelights in her spreading darkness. I mentioned the moments in front of the carnivores in their cages, bound fast for ever in all their savagery, hissing and menacing, but never hunting, and in front of the herbivores, the gentle ones, which were like smooth-worn stones and were never pursued. I wanted to throw her little objects again.

The light from the window fell on her face, which was turned both towards it and, at the same time, through the eiderdown, towards the floor. Her whole body was on a wordless, motionless journey, I could see it, and stopped raising my voice against it. Her back and her head were already growing out of the blankets like a three-quarter circle, and now the gap would be filled, the last piece, down to the cellar, the floorboards, the dark earth. She was an elastic fluid slipping away from all of us, with gentle obstinacy, and I sensed she was beginning to form a whirlpool, capturing, sucking in, all the solid individual images and all my events from the neighbourhood, and all fragments of memory from this room, so that everything participated in its flow. She was taking, she was taking it all with her, with her quiet, faint remainder of life, and everything solid melted away, melted into her, and, fused together, it bent with her back into the curve, along with the sideboard, the daughter in the next room, myself and the strong, silent buffaloes and the screeching monkeys on the ropes and climbing-trees. We were all set in motion, in her unstoppable flow. Without paying any attention to us she was changing us, and with her we were wheeling away, away from the brightness of dependable outlines, and we haven't forgotten it since then and we know it all the time, into the, and we're still afraid of it, not soft, warm, silent, not hard, cold, loud, but we sense, infinitely yielding depths.

Christoph Hein

Goodbye My Friend, It's Hard to Die

The conductor had noticed her as she was still standing on the platform, a young, fat woman wearing a brown suit and with a leather suitcase, which was so new that she evidently didn't dare set it down on the grey concrete.

When the conductor entered her compartment and asked if anyone had got on, he looked at her. At that her small fingers fumbled anxiously and hurriedly in her handbag. The suitcase lay beside her on the seat, on top of it the carefully folded jacket of the suit. A young man opposite her watched with equal interest as, embarrassed, she looked for the ticket, muttering something inaudible to herself with her broad lips. Amused by the flustered woman, the men's eyes met for a moment.

'You've had the ticket extended twice?'

'Yes. I wasn't able . . .'

'You don't need to explain anything, it's all right.'

The compartment door closed behind the conductor. The handbag was now in the woman's lap. Her face was furiously red, her hands gripped the strap tightly. The young man's head had disappeared behind a magazine again. The landscape sailed past the carriage window.

About midday the conductor appeared once more, he glanced through the window of the closed compartment door at the passengers and the empty seats. No one else had entered, he passed through. Beads of sweat stood on the woman's forehead and her reddish upper arms.

She got out of the train in Greifswald. She left the railway station and walked to the bus terminus with short quick steps. She didn't ask anyone what number to take, went to the waiting vehicles, circled them, in order to find out the names on the front, and then got on to one of these battered metal coaches boiling in the sun. She told the driver the name of a town. Slowly, coin by coin, he gave her the change. She sat down. On the bus there were only a few passengers, who listless and drowsy and with vacant expressions, were waiting for the departure. The woman had been studied attentively, as she got on and paid for her ticket, but now her fellow travellers seemed to have lost interest, their eyes closed again or stared despondently at the street.

After a quarter of an hour the bus suddenly shook itself and drove off: out of the town, over cobblestones and asphalt, across a plain divided up into fields and meadows, with occasional red-roofed brick houses and grey water towers. Noisy and metallic, the bus drove through the midday landscape and for a few seconds a pale blue exhaust trail was left behind in the stillness of the Saturday.

The woman had not wanted to take off the jacket of her suit for the journey. She sat breathing heavily. Her fingers crumpled a handkerchief, with which she dried her forehead at ever more frequent intervals. The creases in her skirt were now no longer to be smoothed away—bulges of material across her lap, which resisted her nervous fingers.

When the bus reached the fourth stop, the driver looked round for her. She was already standing at the door, her feet felt for the pavement. Then the bus drove on.

She breathed in the heat, which was refreshing after the oppressive closeness of the bus. She rummaged in her bag for a scrap of paper and read it, her lips moving as she did so. Then she carefully put the paper back. She picked up the suitcase and set off, slowly, then more quickly, slowly again. Finally she stopped, looked round to the bus stop and then nevertheless continued walking. Later she stopped a child in the street, told him an address and thanked him, bright red in the face, for the information received.

She found the street, the house, she read his name on the door, she rang.

'I would like to speak to Dr Bürger, Dr Peter Bürger.'

A young woman had opened the door, a very young woman, hardly more than a girl, with short black hair and brown eyes, which quickly glanced at the visitor and, surprised, took in the suitcase.

'He isn't here. If you want to wait for him . . .?' The woman dried her hands with a cloth.

'Yes. I'll wait.'

'Please come in here. Take a seat.'

The young woman excused herself, she had washing to do. Then she went out.

The visitor had evidently been shown to the waiting room. Against the walls of the room stood the most diverse assortment of chairs, kitchen stools, upholstered easy chairs, extravagantly carved show pieces of heavy wood, an armchair. In the middle of the room were two tables covered with tattered, grubby newspapers and torn magazines. Above the chairs hung animal photographs in simple white cardboard mountings; the pictures were all of the same size and presumably taken from a calendar.

The woman had sat down. She looked at the animal pictures on the walls, she inspected them intently, almost greedily. Later a two- or three-year-old child came running into the room. He stayed by the door, watched her impassively and did not respond to her smile either. When she asked the boy his name, he turned round and left the room swinging his arms.

There was silence. The woman opened the bag and pulled out a pair of fur gloves, which were made up of small remnant strips stitched together, a pair of gloves made for a man's big hands from a thousand tiny patches. She looked at them and put them back in her bag.

When the doorbell rang, she stood up and went to the window, but all she saw was a vegetable garden with a summerhouse. Quickly she went back to her chair and sat down. Through the half open door she heard someone being let into the house, then whispering, steps, a door opened, closed. After a few minutes a man came into the room, wished her a good afternoon and looked at the woman attentively and with a surprised smile. She remained sitting and said only, 'Peter.'

The man rushed over to her, pulled her up from the chair, called out her name, Karin, and swung her round. Breathless, he set her back on her feet again, kissed her cheeks and said, 'I would never have thought that you would find your way out here.'

The woman held his hand and looked at him. 'You look well.'

'Thanks. All the work in the fresh air, you know,' he hugged her, and since she said nothing, he continued. 'You haven't changed at all. You look quite gorgeous, my girl.'

She lowered her head and whispered, 'It's not true.'

'Yes, yes,' he assured her, 'you haven't changed. And the same beautiful hair.'

She took a step backwards and looked at him. Very serious now, and still in a whisper, she asked, 'Why do you say that about my hair?' He didn't understand her.

'Why do you say that about my hair?' she repeated. 'I read that one can always at least tell an ugly woman, she has beautiful hair.'

He became embarrassed and embraced her again. 'That's nonsense. Right, and now we're going to eat. You're eating with us, aren't you?'

'With . . . you?'

'Yes. You've already met my wife, and then there's my little boy as well, a philosopher, a stoic of a child. You'll like him.'

'Yes,' she said, 'I thought it must be your wife.'

He had put his arm around her shoulder, they went into the kitchen, where the vet's wife had laid the dinner table. He introduced the two women to one another. 'My wife Angela, and this is Karin, from Berlin. An old friend, you remember.'

Little Bert was supposed to shake hands with Karin, but

silently and with lowered eyes he pushed his hand between the buttons of his shirt and had to persuaded at least to pull it out to eat.

They talked about Berlin, about the four inseparable friends, the two students, Peter and Jens, Elvira, the laboratory assistant and Karin, the fur sewer. They remembered jazz concerts, a journey to the Harz Mountains together, a lecture in animal anatomy, to which the two girls had been taken and where they had felt sick. They talked about the café in Friedrichstrasse, where the waitress greeted them with a handshake, and about the visit to the synagogue, about the evenings listening to records with candles and wine in Elvira's one room apartment and about the Berlin museums, which one missed most of all out here in the provinces.

'Did you study too?' asked Karin suddenly.

The vet's wife nodded, she was a teacher, rather, she had been a teacher. The housekeeping, the child and a difficult husband took up all her time.

'And how are you getting along?' he asked.

'Well,' she replied, 'I've got a lot of work.'

'But you aren't eating anything at all,' the wife interrupted her.

She had already eaten in town, she only wanted to drop by as she was passing through, to say hello.

Now the parents had to attend to the child, who, distracted by the presence of the guest, had until now only looked at the woman with big eyes and hardly eaten a mouthful. They coaxed him gently, trying to get a spoonful of soup into his mouth. The vet turned to Karin, 'Look at him. Such a little chicken. Sits there and says nothing, but looks at everyone as if he understands it all. A little chicken, a little chicken leg.'

After the meal the child was put to bed and they sat down in the kitchen. The vet's wife brought coffee. She said that once she had been jealous of this Karin whom she didn't know, very jealous, because her husband often talked about his student days and his friends and she had been unable to imagine that it had really only been friendship, nothing more. Her husband laughed at her, God knows, it had been nothing but friendship and companionship. He wanted to hear what Karin thought, now, years later. She agreed with him. The vet's wife remarked that the other two friends, Jens and the lab assistant had married six months before. That had come as a big surprise to him, unexpected, said the man.

'I knew it,' said Karin, 'I always knew it.'

'Maybe,' admitted the vet, 'at any rate I didn't notice anything.'

Karin was astonished, 'That's impossible!'

Angela put her hand on her husband's arm. She looked at him affectionately, as she said, 'That's what men are like, the simplest things in the world and they have to be explained to them.'

'Very well,' he responded good-humouredly, 'very well, that may be so. Perhaps some things do have to be explained to me. That's the way it is: I chase after my animals all day, you're only interested in these little stories of love and pain.'

He beamed at the two women with a good-natured and patronising smile.

Karin talked about their friends' wedding, to which she had been invited as witness. The young couple had been very sorry that Peter had been unable to come because of a calf inoculation. Apart from that, the others had not known either that Peter was married and already had a child. She told how before the wedding the registrar had objected because they wanted to play an English song during the ceremony. He recommended a more serious record, but in the end they managed to have the music played that they wanted, their favourite song from their time in Berlin. He must remember.

The vet did not know. 'No,' he said, 'I can't remember. We had a favourite song? Sorry, no.'

'He forgets a lot,' his wife smiled, 'but please,' she turned to the visitor, 'what's the song called?'

Karin was embarrassed. 'I can't speak English,' she apologised, 'it was an English song, you know. Perhaps it will occur to Peter, if I hum the tune.' They asked her to do so.

Karin began to hum. She sat self-consciously in the room, staring at a shelf with kitchen utensils and herbs, so as not to have to look at her hosts. She interrupted her humming, began again, stopped again and tried to hit the tune. And suddenly she began to hum loudly, quite abruptly she filled the whole kitchen with powerful humming. Happy to have found the tune again, she still looked fixedly at the ornamented kitchen range, while her large breasts rose and fell with her heavy breathing.

The vet leant his head to the side, the situation made him feel uncomfortable. His wife stared at Karin fascinated and speechless. This strange, fat, humming woman seemed like an apparition to her. Mouth half open she sat at the table and looked at her.

When Karin fell silent, she noticed that the vet was looking out of the window in embarrassment and his wife was biting her lip hardly able to conceal her rising laughter. She started and wanted to apologise. She wanted to say that after all they had wanted to hear it, his wife had asked her to hum this song. But she said nothing and passed her hand over her damp forehead several times.

The man interrupted the silence that had arisen, as he smilingly declared, 'We were very sentimental in those days.'

'Yes,' confirmed his wife and now no longer had to suppress her laughter, 'yes, you certainly were that.'

Karin nodded vigorously, before bursting into hysterical laughter. She stood up and shook hands to take her leave of the vet and his wife, her other hand pressing a handkerchief to a face distorted by shrill laughter. The vet's wife saw her to the door.

On the train she brooded over why she had shaken hands with the couple as she left. Her face leant against the window-pane, her fingers ran along the screwed-on metal sections of the compartment, over the window crank, the bin, the wet coldness of the window-sill. Opposite her sat a little girl who pressed timidly against her mother, when Karin smiled at her. Later she heard the little girl's question, 'Why is the lady crying?' and the mother's whispered reply, 'Quiet, just be quiet.'

In her lap was the bag with the fur gloves for the mighty hands of a man, and although beads of sweat were slowly running down the reddened skin of her upper arms, from pore to pore, she had put one hand into the half open bag, into one of the gloves inside, into the warm familiar security of the fur.

When the conductor finished his round and joined his companion in the duty compartment, he muttered in an aggrieved voice, 'She was only in my train on the way up.'

The other railway man turned to him, 'What's that you're saying?'

The conductor dropped down on to the bench and waved his hand in resignation. 'There's some fat women in the world, no kidding!'

His colleague nodded and bent over the crossword. The conductor unwrapped his sandwiches, parted them a little with his thumb and looked at the filling.

Clemens Eich

Back Lighting

She had plunged to the depths. Or fallen. Now she clung to the rusty brace. She saw some sun above her. The photographer's unshaven face appeared. He was leaning out over the iron bars, trying to get her into his field of vision. She relaxed her grip marginally; tiny flakes of rust settled on her face. The photographer pressed the shutter release several times in rapid succession, then he was gone. She saw sun again. She heard voices above her.

She awoke in the twilight. She seemed to have fallen further, for her hand no longer clung to the brace. Perhaps her body was stuck. At least she could move her arms. She heard a gurgling noise below her and was startled by a sudden light in her face. A powerful spotlight was pointing at her. Although she had shut her eyes immediately, it had been a fraction of a second too late and the glaring light continued to blind her in the darkness. She pressed her eyelids and lips together tightly until the effort brought relief. Then she heard the photographer's voice. He was shouting something into the rising wind. She didn't feel the wind, only heard it. The spotlight went out.

The well of light tapered away to a small hole for the rainwater. It reminded her of a naive picture of the region between life and death which once, as a child, she had seen in a book—or was it a catalogue? Again she heard a number of voices above her, all talking at once. One of them was more distinct now—a high-pitched, shrill voice, almost like that of a small boy. The voice called: 'It's almost five!' This remark was passed on and repeated. She began to wonder what it meant. As she did so, she realised she had regained her curiosity. She looked upwards and thought she could see a star. In the dull light of a torch or some similar lamplight she could make out the face of the photographer. He seemed to be fiddling about with a light meter. For a few seconds she saw two shadowy figures come up behind him, grab him, and pull him away. The gurgling went on beneath her, but nothing else could be heard. A day's countless voices, noises from near and far that had made the day what it was, had grown silent.

A weak beam of light was shining up at her through the drainage hole below. Through no effort of her own, her position had slightly improved. She no longer felt trapped. Although she could hardly move, she again felt something like hope. Like a weak, but deep breath of air.

The gurgling near her feet had grown fainter, but was still audible. The beam of light touched her knees; it was as if it were identical with the gurgling. Words like 'sleuthnose' entered her mind, inventions that made her laugh. 'Big Chief Sleuthnose, come and get me!' she shouted, shaking with laughter. Then fear broke through the laughter. The light went out and the gurgling grew louder. She quickly tried to remember what her father had told her about the states of anxiety felt during heart attacks. She had always felt strangely reassured by the things he had told her. Her father had been a doctor.

They had often climbed the mountain together. Like almost everyone else, they had called it their local mountain; but it wasn't a mountain really, it was barely more than a high hill, and so strictly speaking, they hadn't really climbed. On one of these walks her father, in his usual calm and casual manner, had for the first time talked about death and the different states that accompanied it, about just these attacks of panic and anxiety. Later, he had talked about silence; first about 'deathly silence', then about the 'silence of death'. From then on, he had told them something different and new about death every time they had gone out for a walk. He had also told them about ways of dealing with death and dying; about how he would repeat the news of a death so often and to so many different people until he had eventually received news of it himself. His stories had reassured the two girls, who had grown in confidence, feeling stronger every time they had heard them.

She sat there quietly. Or was she somehow hanging? She could no longer exactly tell what kind of position she was in, yet she felt a sense of peace, the memory of the stories and, more so, of the walks, had calmed her. The hunted feeling which fear so likes to push one into had left her. She looked for the brace but could see nothing. The darkness was absolute. She wondered what had happened to her arms, and quickly stopped thinking about it again. She simply no longer had any.

Something like bitter dust fell on her face. Someone's breath touched her. There were whispered responses. She heard the photographer quietly say: 'I am a person who's been taken apart.' She knew then that he had a lot ahead of him. She felt water, saw her father climbing the mountain before her, and her little sister beside her, breathless, trying to keep pace with the big ones. They had emerged from oblivion solely to be forgotten, forever. Then she saw herself climbing the mountain, and the waves broke over her head.

Thomas Brasch

Flies on the Face

The shift ends at five. I'll be at the gate at quarter past. Will you meet me?

What else, he said, I'll be at the gate at five.

I should have told her. Tomorrow she'll finish her shift, and I won't be there. She'll think, I've forgotten. She'll wait till half past five and then she'll cry. She'll think, I've been with another woman. When I was out with Harry, she rang his place three times. I should have told her. Or made up some story, that I was going away, then she wouldn't need to wait tomorrow. She'll find out sometime anyway. I'll either write to her from over there or I'll be dead. Perhaps tomorrow at five I'll be dead. How odd that sounds: Perhaps tomorrow at five I'll be dead. Today I say that tomorrow I'll be at the gate at five and tomorrow at five I'm lying in the morgue. Or I'll be sitting in front of a policeman. One from here or one from over there? I should have told her. Tell your fairy stories to someone else, you don't think I believe that, what do you want over there, she would have said, looked at me and turned her back. Then I would have gone to the place anyway and made the attempt. But it would have been different from the way it is now.

Robert crossed the road to the stop and got on the tram.

I'll go somewhere. Still more than six hours left. I'll get out somewhere and sit on a bench. Perhaps I'll have a drink and then go to the place. I must think about something else now. Over there I'll study and one day I'll fetch her, and we'll live together. When it's safe, she'll come. I'll prepare everything. Or I'll be dead.

Excuse me, Hiddensee Strasse, can you tell me where I have to get off. I'm not from here.

The small man smiled at Robert.

I don't know, Hiddensee. I don't know. I'm not from here either. Perhaps you should ask the driver.

Thank you, said the small man and smiled again.

The man began to push his way through to the driver, and Robert got off.

Tomorrow she'll wait and the day after tomorrow she'll announce a long-distance call. My mother will be afraid. The first thing she'll think about is the bother she'll get at the factory. Or she'll think about father: if he were still alive, it wouldn't have happened. And perhaps I'll be dead. But if I do manage it, everything will be different. I'll phone. That's a good idea. Mother, I'll say. No, first I'll call her at the factory. Hello, I'll say. Yes, Robert, where are you? Why weren't you at the gate? You can't do. Then I'll interrupt her and say, very calmly, as if nothing had happened: I'm in the West. And nothing else. I'll wait, till she says something. Quite simply wait.

Hey, you, hey. Stand still for a moment. Yes, I mean you.

That's it. They've been watching me the whole time. They've known everything right from the start.

Robert felt his armpits turn wet with sweat. He turned round. A man was leaning out of a window in the new block of flats and pointing at the ground.

My cushion's lying down there. It fell down. The lift is broken. I'm not so steady on my legs any more. Could you bring it up to me? Fourth floor right. Werner. The door's open.

That's all right, said Robert, picked up the cushion and walked over to the entrance. Two boys were standing at the lift door, and Robert followed them into the cabin. They nudged each other. Werner, said one and they both laughed. Robert got out at the fourth floor, walked down the hallway, pushed open the door at the end of the passage and entered the apartment. He was met by the smell of old fat.

Leave the door open, he heard.

Robert went past the kitchenette into the room. The old man was sitting up on the rumpled bed, wearing only pyjama trousers and a vest.

Did you fly? Four floors in half a minute. Not bad.

The lift's working, said Robert and put the cushion on the armchair.

I should have known about that, but they just never tell you a thing.

The old man shoved his legs over the edge of the bed and looked at Robert.

Do you want tea? You can have a glass. I'll put the water on right away.

Thanks. But I've got to go. Don't put yourself out.

Put myself out.

The old man laughed. Nothing puts me out any more.

There's something I've got to do, said Robert.

I know. You're thinking: He's got a screw loose. First I have to bring up his cushion, and now I'm supposed to sit down in his dirty flat as well.

He took a deep breath after every word, and Robert thought he could hear a whistling in the man's voice.

It can't be so urgent that you can't keep an old man company for ten minutes.

Robert sat down in the armchair and looked round. The old man looked for his shoes, found one, and finally went into the kitchenette barefoot.

He had known the lift was working. What am I supposed to talk about to him? But it doesn't matter. Six hours. I'm better off sitting here than being terrified of every uniform on the street.

The old man began to cough. He stood at the sink and let the water run into the kettle. The coughing grew worse, and suddenly the old man dropped the kettle and vomited into the sink.

And now he's puking.

Robert went into the kitchenette.

It'll pass in a minute, whispered the old man, and his body trembled.

Then he vomited again, and Robert saw the red lumps in the sink. The old man pressed his head against the wall. Tears ran down his face. His trousers slipped down. He grabbed at them, but couldn't catch them in time. Robert bent down and pulled them up again. The trembling of the body grew stronger.

Now he's going to pass out.

Robert gripped him around the shoulders and under the knees, lifted him up and carried him to the bed. The old man had closed his eyes.

How light he is.

Robert pushed the pillow under his head and covered him. Then he went to the door.

I can't help him either. Why should I stay there. The damned lift must be here somewhere.

Are you looking for someone, Robert heard a voice behind him.

The grey-haired woman stood in the apartment doorway, drying her hands with a dish cloth.

I wanted Herr Werner's flat.

But you've just come from there, haven't you?

Perhaps I didn't see the name plate. Perhaps I didn't read the name properly.

The woman pushed the dish cloth under her apron.

What do you want from Herr Werner.

I've got something for him, from his sister.

She took a step towards him.

What, he's got a sister? It can't be true. Now I've heard everything. She should come here herself sometime, instead of sending somebody. Her brother won't last much longer, you can tell her that. He's not all there any more as it is. Up there, I mean. He marches up and down his room all day. Or he fetches strangers into the flat. Now he's started singing at night as well. Singing, what am I saying. It's a croak. And suddenly it turns out, he's got a sister. Just tell her, she should . . .

Robert turned round and went back.

Tell her. Her brother is dying here, and she sends somebody or other. She should be ashamed.

The old man was sleeping. Robert covered him up and looked at him. The face was wrinkled, covered with stubble, and a deep scar ran from ear to chin. The fingernails were long and dirty. Now he stirred and groaned. He pushed back the blanket and Robert saw the narrow hairy chest, which rose and fell at irregular intervals. The gym shirt was stained and torn in one place. Robert pulled the blanket up to the old man's chin and sat down in the armchair again. He pulled a cigarette out of his pocket and lit it.

And what if he dies. A doctor? The police: what are you doing in this district? How do you know this man. They won't believe a word. A cushion. Ha ha. You can't be serious. Where were you going. What is your job. Nothing at the moment. That's very interesting. Just come with us. Clearing up the facts of a case.

Robert threw the cigarette into an empty vase, stood up, went to the bookcase by the door, took out a book and read:

Far From Moscow.

He opened the book in the middle:

You will take it there yourself, Comrade Syatkov, together with Comrades Umara and Batmatev you will personally present this precious gift to Comrade Stalin, answered Pissarev. Again there was thunderous applause, the like of which Adun and the ancient Taiga had never heard before.

Robert closed the book and put it back.

That's all I needed. One of them. The classic couple: young citizen about to flee comes face to face with veteran of the working-class movement.

Robert took the picture frame from the shelf. Men in leather jackets with shouldered rifles and stars on their caps stared out at him from a newspaper photo.

Red Front, said Robert.

I was there, Robert heard and turned round.

The old man had pushed himself up against the head of the bed and was looking at him.

I was there thirty-eight years ago. In Spain. Give it to me.

Robert went to the bed and gave him the picture.

I cut it out of the newspaper.

The old man lay on his back again and held the photo in front of his face with both hands.

Thirty-eight years ago, he whispered, and I was there.

Fine. Shall I make you some tea.

You probably don't believe me. But it's true. I was there, and every time I look at the picture, I feel as I did then. Those were historic times. Other people have only got two children and three days' holiday for loyal service to show for their lives. I'm not like that.

I'll make tea. Robert went into the kitchenette.

Did I sleep long, asked the old man.

Not long, said Robert and let the water run into the kettle. Just a couple of minutes.

He looked for the matches.

I'm sorry about what happened earlier.

Robert put the kettle on the flame.

Where's the tea.

The old man had turned to the wall and was still looking at the picture.

At the bottom of the cupboard.

Robert put tea into the pot. Then he sat down on a stool in the kitchenette and waited.

Every time I see the picture, I think about it. I see the stars on the caps and right away I hear the shots and see the flies on the dead faces.

Sure, said Robert.

He saw the old man speaking, but he wasn't listening to him any more. After a few minutes he stood up and poured the boiling water into the pot. He took two glasses out of the cupboard, went into the room and sat down in the armchair again.

You can never forget something like that, said the old man and turned to face Robert.

Stop it. I know the tune. They were already playing it at kindergarten.

The old man looked straight at him.

What's wrong with you.

Nothing. There's nothing wrong with me. Only I know what comes next, and I don't want to hear it for the thousandth time.

I see, you don't want to hear it, said the old man. But your babble music, your electric doobidoobidoo, you want to hear that.

Just leave it. I know the game by heart. In a minute you're going to say that we know it all already. That we get everything stuffed into us from behind and still open our mouths for more.

That's the way it is, said the old man.

Nobody asked any of you for it. That's the answer you were waiting for, isn't it.

Look out of the window. Go on.

What's the point of that.

You'll see.

Robert went to the window.

What do you see. Just tell me what you see. Thirty years ago you would have seen nothing but ruins and dirt. And what do you see now?

Boxes, said Robert, a big prison with some green spaces.

Oh, I get it, shouted the old man, ruins are nicer, freezing is nicer.

Stop it. It's all right. I told you that I know the game. I'm going, I'll leave you to shout at your wonderful new walls.

Robert went to the door.

Wait, called the old man. It's my fault. I wanted to tell you something else. I was in Spain. We fought and we knew what we were fighting for. I saw the flies on the faces of the dead. I was a young man. But they finished us off. When there was no point any more, we went over the border. It wasn't easy, but when there was nothing more that could be done, we had to go over the border.

Fine, said Robert and sat down in the armchair again, let's

play it right to the end. So you had to cross the border and you did. What border can I cross, when there's no point any more?

What do you mean?

Don't pretend to be more stupid than you are, said Robert and looked straight at the old man. It's part of the same party game. You had your say, now I've got mine, and it goes like this: I can't do what you could. After all you built a wall round all the pretty houses as well.

If we hadn't built it, you would all be over there, where all the glitter is. The old man leant back.

Or precisely not, said Robert.

What do you want over there. What do you want from them.

Nothing at all. I don't want anything from them. But I'd rather be there than here, far from Moscow. So, and now you can go to the telephone box. Make an emergency call to the police.

The old man looked at him.

What's the matter with you. Did someone do something to you. What do you want.

Robert got up and stood in the middle of the room. It was as if he had already said these sentences a hundred times and he was listening to his own voice.

What I want, he shouted, is to cut this umbilical cord. It's choking me. Do everything differently. Without factories, without cars, without censors, without time clocks. Without fear. Without police.

He struck the bookcase with his fist, but the tiredness stayed in his voice.

Start from the beginning somewhere that isn't enclosed.

Go on, sit down, said the old man.

I know, Robert went on shouting, it's all been said before, it all sounds pathetic, none of it's new. If I knew something better, I wouldn't be standing here now.

He lowered his arms. The old man stood up, took the record player from the bookcase and put it on the table by the bed, went to the sideboard and took a record out of the drawer.

Sit down, he said, you're shaking.

Robert dropped into the armchair.

In Spain our cause seemed lost. Pushed back step by step, sang a hard metallic voice. And the Fascists were already yelling: The city of Madrid has fallen.

Madrid has fallen, Robert heard the old man sing too.

Then they came from every land. On their caps a bright red star, and at the Manzanares River they cooled down Franco's blood. Those were the days of the 11th Brigade and of their freedom flag . . .

Robert saw the old man close his eyes.

Another five hours. I'll go to the border. They'll shoot. I'll lie there with flies on my face.

It was quiet in the room again.

The old man opened his eyes.

Sometimes one thinks nothing matters any more, he said softly. One's friends are dead or no longer know you. Nothing matters, only suddenly one is afraid. Sometimes I think it would have been better if I had died in Spain. But I'll die here, in bed beside a record player.

Robert stood up and put the pick-up back on the record.

In Spain our cause seemed lost, sang the voice again.

We have nothing in common, said the old man.

Robert turned the volume up as far as it would go, and the music drowned out the old man's voice.

We do, said Robert, we're both afraid of flies on the face.

What, shouted the old man, bent forward and suddenly looked at the door.

Robert turned round. The grey-haired woman from the hallway was standing by the bookcase. She crossed the room, went to the table and tore the pick-up arm from the record.

Have you finally gone mad, she shouted at the old man, do you have to listen to that stuff at full volume? There are still people who want to have some peace and quiet when they come home from work. I'm going to have a word with your sister. You should be in an old people's home or a lunatic asylum.

The woman turned round.

Did you fall for his big stories, she said. He probably told you that he was a freedom fighter. In Russia or in Spain or with the Red Indians. Glorious past. Medals and decorations. Don't make me laugh.

The old man jumped up. His hands were trembling.

In his whole life he never got further than Oranienburg,* and now he brings young people up to his apartment every day, acts the great man and blocks the refuse chute with all his newspapers.

Robert saw the old man take a step towards the woman.

Just get out of here. Fascist, Nazi cow, women like her put Hitler in power and ruined this country and now they eat cream cakes all day.

The two stared at one another, their faces filled with hate. Robert pressed his back against the cushion and looked at his watch.

* Small town north of Berlin, location of a Nazi concentration camp from 1933 *(trans.)*.

Katja Lange-Müller

The Big Journey

The most banal story, though,
is history itself. J.S.

Margott was the only child of a level crossing keeper and his wife. Between oak sleepers she played with clinker and sharp ballast stones. Golden rue, hemlock or snow, her earliest memories were rusty brown. The shrill cries of the steam valves were greetings meant just for her.

When Margott had learnt how to put longing into words, she begged: 'I'd like to take a train ride, just once, it doesn't matter where to or how long the ride is.' 'You're not big enough yet,' her parents, who were poor, said in comforting tones.

Margott developed a large bosom early on, but her teeth were crooked and she laughed a lot. So no engine driver would have her, and only occasionally, at night, when the half past midnight train went by with a whistle, she would jam a hand between her legs and wish – just to take a train ride, just once . . .

A clothes presser married Margott. 'There's a place for everything,' the presser declared: 'a wife in the home and whoopee in bed.' And so Margott got no honeymoon. Instead, Margott with her crooked teeth had five children as time went by. For work reasons, the presser and his family lived in the heart of the city. The rattle of a Singer replaced that of trains: Margott sewed curtains. The latest child, sucking at scraps of cloth, would be jammed between her legs. There was hardly any time even to think of train rides any more.

The eldest child, a girl, died of polio. One good thing was

that at least she died before she had reached puberty. There were still six of them to look away when she was buried. Two days later, Margott discovered the wreath from German Railways on another mound of earth. She had recognised it by the three upright waxed-paper calla lilies, but since the definite proof, the red sash with 'In sorrow, signal box 9' lettered in gold, was missing, she did not carry it back.

Her two sons – yes, it's the old story – went to fight in the First World War and returned as black-bordered printed matter. Her husband, by contrast, was still there in the flesh. The interval between the First World War (drawing to a close) and the Second (beginning) he filled, as usual, with occasional work as a presser. The only difference was that now he drank away a great deal of the little money, reason and memories he had. Since there were no more children to be jammed in, Margott carried on sewing in a factory, for a few pennies more. Perhaps she could have saved a little too, for her big journey. But: 'The finest part of Woman's art is the kindness of the heart.' The motto was embroidered on a runner Margott inherited, with a Bible and preserves, from the widow of her father. The rest of her worldly possessions the priest got.

We know, you and I and all of us, how the story goes on. First the children became unemployed, then the adolescents, then the women, then the men. Then along came Adolf Nazi and the end of the Golden 20s. Then the men had work, then the women, then the adolescents. Child labour was abolished for the time being. Then the Communists, the Jews, the insane and the mentally retarded, the Social Democrats, Poles, Czechs, Russians, Belgians ... became corpses, and the men became victorious heroes. Then the adolescents and those unfit for service became soldiers, then the women, the children, and the territorial army veterans. By then forty million people had lost their lives and the rest had lost almost everything else.

All Margott had not lost was Liliane. A pale grandchild with crooked teeth and eyes that darted restlessly, ever since those nights of bombs that had rid them of Hitler and their houses she had talked only in her dreams, to a dog she had been buried with in a bombed building. Margott and the child sought refuge in the crossing keeper's cottage where her parents had lived and where a one-legged Jehovah's Witness, a former colleague of her father, had moved in right after her mother died. Soon a Singer sewing machine was rattling away again, working heavy military material, and after a while the track was patched and trains were running again and Lilli was going to school. Her sleep became less talkative, as she lay between Margott and the one-legged man.

One Sunday in nineteen forty-nine Margott presented herself at a ticket counter, in a blue woollen travel suit she had tailored herself, a white artificial silk headscarf on her head. She had no luggage, not even a handbag. She shoved her hundred mark note across the counter and bought a second class ticket for the D-521 express to Stralsund. She left the change, against the protests of the ticket clerk.

Margott found herself a window seat facing the locomotive. Beneath the damp blue wool her heart was beating fast with the excitement of travel. The train pulled out right on time. Margott sat rigid and silent. Her arms tight against her body, she stared out. Tense, ready for the happiness she had waited all those many years for, all that time: 'To take a train ride, just once, no matter where, no matter how long the ride.' Soon, any moment now, she would experience that lovely feeling, the loveliest of all, which she could scarcely imagine but which she believed in as she had never believed in a dear Lord above. 'Travel is a fine thing, a wonderful thing,' she told herself. 'Off we go, away, one yard more, away away away . . . off and away, off and away, away away, off and away,' she decided the train was saying. But in fact the train was merely rattling, rattling across some patch of ground as her Singer rattled across some scrap of cloth. Countryside flew by, flew past, flat and dull. Alders, stray willow bushes, birds on the grass. Nothing else, only a train crossing the country on its way to the place Margott came from. 'Just you wait and see,' she said to herself, almost threateningly, as if to someone else, 'you're just too worked up.' But her excitement had passed, and all the tension had long been displaced by the disappointment that seemed the sole mover of this train, taking it further and further away from Margott. How little one sees through the window, she thought. Tears and acceleration increasingly blurred the images of bushes, fields and sky into one as they raced by, into a single broad, striped ribbon. For several minutes she continued to sit staring at that ribbon, staring with a gaze that erased individual patterns as the fabric of landscape unfurled by the yard from its inexhaustible roll, and listening to the even rattle of the train's machine, sewing and sewing away. From her calm hands the white headscarf hung in capitulation.

Quietly, almost unnoticed by her fellow passengers, Margott left the compartment, opened the door, and did not wait for a train in the other direction.

Postscript: she did not die in fact, but merely broke an arm and her legs. But she said nothing as they put her fractured limbs in makeshift splints, said nothing in her plaster when the doctor asked how it had happened. Nor did she say anything to the specialist, who would have liked to note down a reason why she no longer spoke or even combed her hair.

And if she is still alive, which is unlikely, since she would now be a hundred, she will be sitting by the window in some nursing home, in silence. She made her exit thirty-two years ago.

Jochen Schimmang

Laederach
An ethnographic report

The district of Laederach, in the west of the country, inspires terror in all of us travelling salesmen. Inevitably, we're always meeting up in the hotels when we're on the road, and they're always the same hotels, the same hotel bars, the same faces. But I don't know of a single colleague who has not had resignation at least, but more often a quake, a sense of horror in his voice when he had to say: Next week it's my turn to go to Laederach.

And no one spends more than a night in Laederach, because there's no point. That is one of the reasons why the place inspires such terror in us. In Laederach, the consumption of any kind of article falls short of the levels to which we are accustomed, and which are so important for a blossoming commercial life. The inhabitants of Laederach are modest, even ascetic, from the point of view of use value, and thrifty, even miserly, considered from the vantage point of exchange value.

So hardly have we approached the businessmen in each of our branches, bearing our briefcases and order-books, than they pull a face and refer to their overstocked store rooms and a pace of business even more sluggish than it was on the occasion of the last visit. To listen to the businessmen of Laederach, it is quite extraordinary that there are still so many shops, and that they aren't closing week by week, until the range of goods on offer is reduced to the barest minimum.

But as far as we're concerned, whether we go to Laederach

or to Düsseldorf we follow one law and one alone: sell, sell, sell! As we are more likely to do this in Düsseldorf than in Laederach, it is easy to understand the terror that arises in each of us when we're told: 'Laederach next week!' And that's why people say of their former colleagues who have made it, who have put their rep work behind them, or more precisely, beneath them, and are now in charge of other reps from an office in some great metropolis, that's why they don't say of them, 'They've made a success of themselves!' or 'They're making their way up the ladder!' no, they say, 'They don't have to go to Laederach any more!'

The place isn't only consumer-hostile, it also looks rather ugly, dirty, virtually backward. Laederach is a community of about twelve thousand inhabitants, including a good five thousand in remote villages and hamlets which have been incorporated, so that only around seven thousand people live in the town. The surrounding countryside is agricultural, and the town itself is still marked by its agrarian past. If dung-heaps are now no longer piled in front of the houses, you still imagine you can smell them, and if cows and sheep are no longer driven down the main shopping street, you still think you can see their muck on the cobblestones.

The houses in the town, apart from two new housing estates in the south and east, look at once massive and crooked, an impression created by the frequent use of large grey ashlars. This material looks so mis-shapen that hardly a single building seems to have been erected with any degree of accuracy, and this image is reinforced by the fact that the houses are not whitewashed. As the people of Laederach are economical with everything, they are economical with their whitewash.

Few repairs are carried out on any damage to the houses; craftsmen too suffer from the modesty of the population's requirements. Some of the houses, although inhabited, are already half derelict. The disinclination to improve them is due in part to the location of the town on the borders of Holland and Belgium. 'Ardennes offensive' is all the old people of Laederach will say. Some of the damage really does date back to the last war, and some of the people of Laederach do not think of the past war as the last one, and individuals even say, 'Peace is a stop-gap, war's normal.' They point out that throughout the entire region they are still finding bombs that need to be de-fused. We haven't the faintest idea, they say, what lies underneath and around our houses.

The two biggest employers in Laederach are a textile factory which has gradually balanced its accounts again after a series of lean years, and a lead smelter. Large sections of the population of Laederach complain of fatigue, lack of appetite, pains in the head and limbs, and many of the children suffer from a great lack of concentration, which is reflected in school results, so that in far-away towns when they talk about somebody from Laederach they say, 'He comes from the place where the stupid people live.'

There is not a great deal of other notable industry in Laederach. The rest of the population is employed in retail business, craft trades, public service, transport and agriculture. Unemployment stands at around eight per cent. All types of school can be found in the town. There is a hospital, a swimming pool, a cinema, and for public occasions a multipurpose hall which was built five years ago and cost considerably more than anticipated. This extravagance temporarily cost the ruling party in the council a considerable number of votes, but this was soon made good again, as the people of Laederach are nothing if not persevering.

Among the people of Laederach 81.2 per cent are members of the Catholic faith, 16.4 per cent are Protestant, and the rest cannot be classified.

Clubs are keenly frequented. The voluntary fire brigade plays a major social role. The local football club is promoted to the regional league every other year, and dropped again the year after.

The travel agent in Laederach does the worst business. The people of Laederach do not travel. Sometimes they go to Aachen, or perhaps even Cologne, sometimes they go shopping in Holland or Belgium. But their lethargy stands in the way of further travel, whether this is due to their nature or the high concentration of lead in the air of Laederach.

But while they may not travel, the people of Laederach are eager for news from the whole world, which may on one occasion be about Vilshofen, on a second about Hamburg and on a third about Canada. Their bodies may be lethargic and disinclined to move, but their minds are alert and mobile. They cannot hear enough stories about how things are beyond the district boundary, and often they will listen to stories about such things until the small hours.

For this reason, we sales reps, even if nobody buys anything from us and if we always write off Laederach as a negative entry, are very welcome. We are almost received like princes or, to use a more contemporary comparison, like cabinet ministers or members of parliament. If a number of us visit Laederach on the same day, half the town gathers in the evening in the public bar of the Borderland Hotel, where we traditionally stay, they stand us wine and beer and crowd round in a circle, and that means telling stories, telling stories into the night. If we timidly point out that we have to get out of bed and into our cars early next morning, and go on to Aachen or Koblenz, or maybe even to Frankfurt, they succinctly point out that they have to get back to work early the next morning as well.

And yet each of us has something like a special subject area. Thus, for example, I am responsible for the north of our country, someone else for the Fichtelgebirge, a third has to talk about South Baden. The people of Laederach don't necessarily need new stories. They like to hear the old ones again, five times, ten times. But if you start telling an old story, you have to stick to the earlier story both in content and in narrative style. Should deviations be too great, the sequence of events be changed or a part of the story be left out entirely, their protests are vehement, and should one have difficulties in reconstructing the old story which they still have in their heads, they sometimes even adopt a threatening attitude, although actual violence has never so far occurred.

Some of my colleagues are utterly committed to the old stories. One of them must, over and over again, tell of the three years he spent in Canada, although it was more than fifteen years ago and Canada has undergone fundamental changes since that time. The people of Laederach are not so stupid as to imagine that these reports from Canada are still in some way up to the moment. But they seem to prefer out of date stories from Canada to no stories at all.

Another has to talk each time about his experiences in a Viennese brothel, which are also far from fresh. The people of Laederach listen wide-eyed to his account. And they thoroughly condemn the storyteller. They like to hear all kinds of stories, but when necessary they deliver a silent moral judgement on the content and the protagonists of the stories, and their moral standards are generally Catholic. The narrator of the brothel story, who is, of course, given the same hospitality as everyone else, they have already expressly condemned, as he does not subscribe to Laederach's majority faith and cannot hope for absolution.

At the same time, in their eagerness for good stories they are entirely willing to suppress their moral principles. In order to have a storyteller all to themselves, some families invite one or other of the salesmen to their home for dinner, forgetting their usual thriftiness. A great deal of food makes its way to the table, most of it coarse, much of it fatty, for this is the best they have to offer.

For those of us who have eaten in gourmet restaurants in Munich or Cologne, or even in a Swabian country pub, this is, of course, simply touching and, given the fat content, also a little nauseating. Out of politeness we bravely eat what is put in front of us, although never as much as we are expected to, and drink the highly alcoholic schnapps that is supposed to make the fat more easily digestible.

To have even more exclusive rights to certain storytellers, some families also invite them to spend the night. Normally these invitations are refused, as each of us prefers, after a trying day, to spend at least a few hours in the intimacy of his hotel room. But to make the allure all the greater some families are even prepared to offer the invited reps their daughters for the night. This is, of course, as a rule indignantly refused, but at least one case is recorded – before the time I had to start coming to Laederach – in which one salesman was unable to resist the temptation. This colleague continued to be welcome in Laederach, while the girl was withdrawn from circulation by her family at the age of seventeen. She is said to have been sent to a boarding-school in South Germany, later married a man from Switzerland and now lives in Zürich.

The next morning, our eyes small and red from the previous night's alcohol, we sit in the breakfast room of the Borderland Hotel, each of us already preoccupied with the day ahead, studying the addresses and the results of the last visit, maybe the road-map too, although we are very familiar with the roads that lead from Laederach to Koblenz, Aachen or Mönchengladbach. Even if there are others at table we are sparing with our words, still exhausted from storytelling. We might swap our destinations for the day, talk about the general deterioration of the economic situation, our last holidays or the ones immediately forthcoming, but always sluggishly with plenty of pauses, a long way from the artful stories with which we had swept away the inhabitants of Laederach the previous evening.

Some of them, if they have time, line the streets when we leave the town close on each other's heels, and wave to us, sometimes they actually spur us on our way, cheering as loudly as if a president were driving through their town in a flower-bedecked carriage; they applaud the fact that we are returning to the world so that we will be able to tell new stories. Then the crowd slowly dissolves, the people of Laederach go back into their houses or workplaces, slightly stooped, with slow steps, as if, for the first time since we told our stories, they can once again feel the lead above their heads and in their bodies.

But we heave a sigh of relief and step on the accelerator, and before us, in the sun of an October morning, gleam the autobahns.

Daniel Grolle

There's Something Down There

Klaus is a gardener, a man with both feet placed firmly on the ground, a man steady as a fixed star in the heavens. His family were farmers who, for an incredible sum of money, sold their centuries-old, isolated farmstead to the state.

Friesland was to have a better infrastructure, they'd said. It would bring the world to the farmers, they'd said. Today, Jeringhave Motorway Services stands exactly on the site of the Jönkes' old farm. Exactly where Klaus's bed once stood is a row of automatic, thermo-sensitive, self-flushing urinals. When triggered off they make such a loud noise that Klaus, visiting the scene of his childhood one day, pissed on his leg in fright.

Klaus doesn't like all this newfangled rubbish. He's a gardener in a small Hamburg cemetery, situated between the railway freight depot, a motorway slip road and the glass works. It's a quiet spot, except when there's an east wind and the planes lower their landing flaps about a stone's throw above his head. When he started there twenty-five years ago he had to sit on the lawnmower. But he went into such a sulk that after only three days the foreman asked him: 'Don't you like driving the lawnmower then, Klaus?' Klaus shook his head so convincingly that the subject was never raised again. Now Ebi drives the lawnmower, or Hannes. Klaus has been weeding for twenty-five years. He has a particular gift for getting out deep-rooted thistles. Whatever the weather, he'll squat over the graves and carefully, with amazing skill, pull out roots anything up to ten feet long. You can almost hear the dead groan as he draws the thistles from their eye sockets and rotting intestines.

Then he examines the little hairs at the bottom of the roots. To normal people they simply smell of decay, but to him they speak of a different world. For he is the spirit made flesh of this well-fertilised piece of earth.

And he has his suspicions.

Until quite recently he'd been living in the gardener's shed with the tools. There was nowhere he would have liked to live more; the cemetery management had had nothing against it either. But then he got caught in the web of a statistical survey conducted by the Hamburg Electricity Board, who were planning a 300 megawatt nuclear reactor. His electricity consumption during the past twenty years turned out to be lower than the survey's absolute minimum of 7.5 pfennigs. The Department for the Prevention of Contagious Diseases decided that Klaus, who had never been ill in his life, was highly vulnerable to cholera, dysentery and typhoid. The same week he was bundled out of his garden shed on to the seventh floor of a nearby tower block.

'I don't like all this newfangled stuff,' he said, pulling a face as if someone were asking him to drive a lawnmower.

But nobody from the Department for the Prevention of Contagious Diseases came to see his face, so he stayed in the tower block. The parish authorities did put a telephone in for him, however, since he was the only worker available at short notice every weekend, or on public holidays. They even forgave him for falling asleep so often now with his hands in the earth; he hadn't been able to find a place to sleep in his new flat.

His suspicions were growing. He'd said it again and again even before he was forced to move: 'There's something down there.' Each of the few people who had anything to do with him interpreted this sentence differently, for it had never occurred to any of them to ask him what he actually meant. Since he'd moved, the sentence had become more insistent. One day, having pulled yet another long thistle root from a grave, he ran about the cemetery like a madman, finally storming into the garage, where the grave-diggers were totally drunk, and giving the lawnmower a kick. He held out the root to them in his outstretched paws, giving them such a penetrating glare that they stopped laughing. They had never seen the gardener so excited. A stranger mightn't have found anything unusual in his voice, but the grave-diggers noticed the slight tremble as he spoke: 'You've got to get that lawyer out of plot 93,' he said. 'It's in there.'

First of all, they had already emptied a whole case of beer; secondly, it was evening, and there was nobody about in the cemetery; thirdly, the soil in plot 93 was still nice and loose; and fourthly, a little bit of fun doesn't do anyone any harm, and anyway, the gardener's wish was their command.

The first tangle of roots had penetrated the coffin and pierced the lawyer's jelly-like skin. Precisely above his heart was a ragged hole.

'Wow! A thistle did that!' said one of the grave-diggers to the other. To them it was like a dream. They had always imagined this when he pulled out thistles.

But the enraged gardener confidently inserted his hand deep into the hole. There was a squelching sound and a gentle snap and he pulled a piece of metal about the size of a cockroach from the infernally stinking corpse. In the imagination of the grave-diggers, the pacemaker, still ticking quietly away, was a bullet.

Klaus listened to the ticking all night. As soon as it was dawn he placed the device on a nearby railway track where the wheels of an endless train of goods wagons, loaded with heavy fibre-optic cables, indifferently ground the little piece of metal to dust.

Later, still smiling, the gardener went on muttering under his breath: 'Eat yourself, eat yourself, eat yourself . . .' But he knew his suspicions were confirmed: 'There is something down there.'

The only thing that interested him in his new flat was the telephone. He had learned how to dial the number of the cemetery management; so he tried other numbers as well and was quite astonished at the funny things the roots of the telephone led to. Full of mistrust, but also full of curiosity, he listened to the bleeps and burps, the clicks and crackles, to human sounds, too. He heard 'hello' again and again, but never said anything himself. The cemetery management was surprised at the size of his telephone bills, for the gardener naturally sometimes ended up dialling foreign numbers, but they paid up none the less. Klaus was still the cheapest gardener they'd ever had.

He couldn't get over the 'hello' in the receiver. The grave-diggers would often see him holding a thistle to his ear, as if hoping to hear it talk. Meanwhile, insomnia made him look so grim that some of the old people felt too frightened to visit the cemetery any more.

It was in this state, too, that he was dialling numbers one day in his flat on the seventh floor. Suddenly, he felt more wide-awake than he'd ever been: the 'hello' that sprang from the earpiece was so bright and cheerful that it seemed to be turning a somersault. For a second he was utterly bewildered, then a tremendous idea struck him. Overcome by enthusiasm, he was on the point of returning the 'hello' for the first time, when the dry, hollow voice of a man intervened: 'Get off the line, will you!'

His fit of courage gave way to an unprecedented attack of terror. Only the little piece of metal in the lawyer's corpse had made his heart beat so fast. Pale with fright, he threw down the receiver. 'Hello, hello . . .' The light, silvery voice tripped and tumbled from the earpiece a couple of times . . . then clicks and crackles.

Briefly, the gardener's big hands trembled; briefly, his heavy body and head vibrated, but only briefly. Then a deep rattling sound entered his hot animal breath, a muttering rumble like thunder. He knew what he had to do.

He squatted down in front of the wall where the cord disappeared into the junction box, gripped the flex in his immensely skilled hands and pulled. He pulled slowly, then harder, drew on the wire with a concentration nobody else in the world could have mustered. The plaster came away, and with it yard after yard of wire all the way to the door of his flat. Calmly, his mind fully focused on the job in hand, the gardener pulled his way forwards as surely as the moon follows its path through the night sky. He took no notice of people who stopped to look at him as he descended the stairwell. Shoving open the cellar door he traced the wire to an inconspicuous trapdoor in the floor. This seemed to be where it ended. He lifted the trapdoor. A staircase spiralled twice to a bare concrete floor below. No door, no opening, just blinding darkness.

But the gardener held on to his wire. He pulled on it gently, gave it a short yank, twisted it round a few times. There was no fooling him. He went down on his hands and knees and groped about in the dark until he found a hairline crack in the floor. He unsheathed his gardening knife, scraped and heaved; he neither ate not slept, he had taken up the struggle. He knew neither day nor night, only darkness and dust, until at last a gleam of light shone through the crack. Lifting a flagstone and pushing it aside, he found himself looking down into a bright, neon-lit aluminium tunnel as high as a man. He could see his own wire along with a lot of others which were cleverly knotted and inter-twined as they fed down the tunnel. At every knot the wires changed colour, but there was no fooling the gardener. He picked out his own wire unerringly, even when the wire suddenly took on the colour of the tunnel and discreetly merged with a ribbed section of the passage. Undeterred, the gardener tapped the wall until he found a large, hollow space behind it. The aluminium wall shattered under the gardener's fourteen stone as if it were an old barn door.

One step further, and a different world began. It was cold, very cold – the sensation of a plaster torn from the skin. The gardener's warm, heavy breath no longer evaporated, but fell frozen to the ground and lay there like footprints. There was a mildewy gleam on the walls, and in the frozen puddles through which the wire snaked lay the half-chewed cadavers of huge rats. In the distance he could make out small clusters of moon-coloured spots gleaming in the ever thicker blackness, their rays splayed like the fingers of a skeletal hand. But the gardener let nothing distract him from the rotting wire on the ground, halting not even when he saw that the skeletal hand was composed of living rats. They clung to each other in a living stalagmite, their eyes staring upwards into the daylight that shone down through the endless shaft of a drainpipe to reflect metallically in their eyes. The rats, barely moving, paid little attention to the gardener. The dots of light merely trembled as he felt his way past.

The quivering reflections on the walls resonated with a regular pulse. It was as regular as a heartbeat, as the gentle vibrations that sometimes came out of the phone. That'll be the cold; Klaus knew that, knew the beat of a heart, the quiet freezing. He followed his wire without faltering.

The passageways were becoming larger, damper, warmer. There was a suggestion of putrefaction in the air. The wire grew soft and powdery. When the gardener rubbed it between his fingers, he found there was no copper any more, only dirt, like the rings left by worms on the mud at low tide.

And still he went on into the buzzing that seemed to whisper to him from the walls; walls covered by flies with thin, quivering wings.

A hard smile flickered over the gardener's face. He had known it all along. You could hardly see it for the flies and dirt in the dark, but the walls weren't really walls at all, the ground wasn't the ground: there was nothing but wires, cables thick as pythons, crawling on and on, despite the walls that smouldered like charcoal, despite the dense tongues of white smoke that whispered and oscillated at different frequencies, blowing the occasional ring as they licked the walls: the whispering of a thousand telephone conversations. Soon the lithe squirming of the cables rubbing together their decaying plastic coats became more distinct as they drew closer and closer to a throbbing that was like the roar of distant aircraft engines, like hordes of monkeys howling at night in a rain forest, finally emerging into a huge space in which everything ended, darkly lit by the smouldering glow of scorched plastic, a place like an enormous quarry.

The gardener ground his teeth together with powerful jaw muscles, his brow and hands covered with sweat. He still grips his wire, which crawls on and on, slowly and deliberately into the sinewy throng; the wire is alive at last.

The gardener's hands are drenched with sweat as the wire slips finally out of his grip. But tendons slide out with it from his wrists, sinuous worms snaking out of his body: a wiry body, a wormy body, dissolving in crawling to earth to end.

Klaus Modick

Off-season

Once the currents of the streets lay smoothed in shadow by the dusk, the sun was no more than an afterglow on the tinted glass of the Center, and light, as if under great pressure, suddenly burst from the windows, he went back to the office once more. That way he could be sure of seeing no one but the black switchboard girl and the people in yellow overalls as, with the indifference of routine, they disposed of the rubbish of the working day. There were to be no repeats of the farewell scenes that had been acted out at his leaving party yesterday, and which he had played his part in, just as he had always obeyed the rules during his time there in the tower. Of course everyone had been tipsy on cocktails and Martinis, and he had even flirted with the woman from the acquisitions department as he had from the very first day, feeling as he did so the relief of never having gone beyond the buzz of a flirt. As it was, they were still able to give each other a farewell come-on as they looked into each other's eyes, and to enjoy the lack of commitment of that look.

He glanced at the vacant desk, the emptied wastepaper basket, the swivel chair waiting for another occupant. Then he took the envelope containing work documents and the invoice from his pigeonhole, over which the name of his successor had already been stuck (which smarted a little), waved to the switchboard girl, and left. The glass panels of the double door clicked gently shut behind him. The corridor on his floor, strangely empty at that time of day, seemed to stretch far away in the cool fluorescent light, seemed to have gone cold. The sound of his footfall, not completely muffled by the carpeting, came back in a hesitant echo off the walls.

The elevator took him in—a mechanical, rigid embrace. On the illuminated indicator the floors slid by, the height shrivelling into numbers, 57, 56, 55, no one got on anywhere, 45, 44, 43, the lift was the vein in a sleeping body, pumping used-up blood back to the heart. He felt for the ticket in his breast pocket; tomorrow he would be flying back, back to what had been, once. 38, 37, 36, yes, he was thirty-six now, and 35, 34, 33 was how old he had been when he was offered the job and took it without hesitation. Three years in New York on a good salary was a good break. It was a chance to break with boredom, with the corridors, looks and faces that were always the same. And the loneliness, too, that had had him in its grip ever since he and Lisa had separated, he wanted to leave behind him as well, like a worn-out raincoat. Here he had worn the required business suits, and here he had worked harder than ever before, 12, 11, 10 hours a day, but he accepted the demands the job made almost gratefully because it meant he scarcely had time to think about himself and Lisa, and the five, or was it six, women he had slept with here, and 3, 2, 1—three years had sped past him.

A soundless tremor, and the elevator released him. An after-hours crowd was surging through the hall, a shaded and twilit bustle which never quite ceased even at night. Suddenly a feeling of nausea overcame him, a vague giddiness that had befallen him in the first few weeks there whenever he used the elevator, only to lapse into familiarity before long. Strange, though, that the unbidden and forgotten guest should knock at his stomach once again today, on his last day.

Late summer was oppressing Manhattan; the skyscrapers looked squashed; the waves honked and stank and roared through the ravines between buildings; and all of this hit him with another shock like that of the first few weeks. His nerves were strained as he walked the seven blocks to his apartment, his ears were assaulted, the pores of his skin were beset, he was jostled and shoved by a juggernauting steamroller.

That's life, nodded the porter cheerfully, after a glance at his perspiring face, and he nodded back and, with mixed success, attempted the American permanent smile. Lying on his bed, he knew that the city was not all of life, and that life was not like that, or at least ought not to be. For a few minutes he kept his eyes closed and tried to listen within himself, to concentrate on his ebbing heartbeat, till a headache sparked up, as if from far away outside him, spiralling closer and getting bigger all the time, till he got up unsteadily and went to the bathroom to hold his head under water— the coldness felt like heat at first—and take pills. The rhythmic drilling grew duller, fell away, leaving a fine, milling jet, and then something switched it off.

He pulled up the blinds. The sky blue as ink, beneath it the yellow eyes of windows. He wondered how many people in the city lived in furnished apartments, temporarily, leaving no trace behind them, transient. It seemed to him as if a face were looking out of every one of the countless windows that together made up a shapeless shimmering ornament, and all the faces were looking at him. He pulled the blind down again and wondered how many people were now going to bed as he was.

At the door waited the cases, packed and heavy but made of lightweight material. He dreamed of a whitewashed operating theatre. Drop by drop the anaesthetic fell through the mask into his breath, his body leaden, his brain a jellyfish swept about suspended in the surge. The city had drugged him. I no longer feel a thing, he had often told himself. But he did feel still, or feel again. And everything he had experienced while drugged must have had an impact, subterranean, deep. In his dream it seemed he awoke and the things that had happened to him as he lay in the artificial sleep of bustle, of affairs that swept past, began to hurt.

He had been lying on his left arm and it had gone to sleep. He shook it, and as the blood penetrated the numbness he knew that nothing, nothing at all would have changed if he flew back today. The selfsame man would be arriving in the selfsame place he had left three years ago.

He opened the morning paper and leafed through it, bored at first but then suddenly with a sense of purpose, holiday homes, off-season prices, not too far away, New Jersey Shore, Asbury Park, Point Pleasant, Bay Head. He called the agent. The house was available, a two-hour rail journey away. He cancelled his flight, snatched up the cases. A taxi. Grand Central Station.

Refineries, rusty steel frames, warehouses with grey grass growing on the roofs, endless heaps of gravel, coal or sand, indistinguishable, chimneys spewing out cloudy smoke, semi-derelict factories, relics of better times, then more modern aluminium hangars, dockside plants with track and cranes, dumper trucks, marshalling yards, wagons as far as the eye could see, gigantic parking lots in amongst it all, cars every colour of the rainbow, hardly any people and no greenery at all, the sky low, grey and heavy, as if it were going to slit open its bellyful of showers on the television aerials. The industrial landscape between New York City and Newark, what they called 'urban sprawl' in the office, criss-crossed by six- or eight-lane highways, with bridges above and tunnels below and aircraft and helicopters flying ceaselessly overhead.

In the train it was oddly quiet. Soundlessly it glided through the mechanical rhythm of the labyrinth, across track that forked off confusingly, travelling southwards from Newark on, towards the Atlantic beaches. Beyond a bridge, the totally rusted ironwork of which looked antiquated and frail but also seemed strangely alive, a petrified spider's web, a park-like terrain appeared, lawns, old trees, which promptly vanished, before he could get a good look at them, behind soot-blackened noise protection walls.

The person sitting opposite him in the compartment, a tanned man of perhaps sixty with a grey walrus moustache and a white, grubby sailing cap, had been talking to him with unforced straightforwardness ever since Newark, or at least had been talking off his lonesomeness, while he for his part barely made any reply, not that any was expected, merely nodding occasionally, as if absent-mindedly.

For the noise protection walls, the man reported, who had just told him about having a pacemaker implanted, talking enthusiastically as if it were some tremendous, as it were, sporting achievement, the doctors and patient forming a team—for the walls they had to fell all the old trees in the district, a thousand, if not more; and he made an abrupt downward movement with the edge of his hand.

A pity, he said, and at that moment the noise protection walls ended, affording a view of New Jersey's suburbs full of villas, the 'Garden State', commuter oases for the upper crust, from which the men travelled to Manhattan every morning, did their business, visited their lovers, and returned home every evening exhausted, while the women supervised the servants and the children, played tennis at the Country Clubs, and took active part in charitable works.

That was progress, said the man, and he sounded proud; or at least there was no trace of sadness or irony in his voice.

The man got out at Asbury Park and urged him, tossing the words over his shoulder, to take it easy.

On the inland side, it was less built up, and there were solitary pines here and there that quickly gathered into groves and then small woods, the precursors of immense state forests, barely any industry any more, an occasional loosely connected scatter of places, villages or solitary houses, farms even, and animals in dark green pastures. On the side towards the sea, by contrast, was an almost unbroken front of whitewashed wooden houses, or houses with grey and brown shingles, and between their well looked after driveways the sea occasionally flashed like a mirror, or a strip of sand bulged yellow like mustard from the layers of a sandwich.

The cloud cover tore and the sun's fingers felt warily at his face. He blinked at the things shooting by and was unable to grasp them. He felt giddy, as he had before, as he had yesterday in the elevator, and in his giddiness a nebulous thought took shape, that the things were not shooting by at all but were revolving about some far distant centre, a hub or a kind of axis, and he could not say whether it was real or imaginary, and the things around that hub were a whirlpool turning ever faster and pulling everything into the centre, which was in a state—or was it not a state but a formula?—of rest. Had he not been at that hub once before? He had known it, for sure, or at least seen it from afar. That holiday with Lisa; they had been so happy that he had known it must come to an end, since it could not be sustained in such concentration and proximity. And then the end really had come, and nothing had remained of the centre, merely a feeling of hollowness and emptiness, because everything had been caught up in the whirl that was shattering him, shattering him to pieces. And, shattered as he was, he had stood in JFK airport in New York one day, wanting to reassemble himself, differently, not guessing that the city would scatter him still more asunder and drive him away. For, if there was a law or formula for that city, it was this: atomisation, the dismantling of coherence, disintegration of the single parts. He was unaware of the law as he stood crammed in with the other passengers at the baggage claim. One after the other the bags and cases came up from the depths and circled on the belt beneath the gaze of the people waiting, circled and circled, and the cases all looked the same and the travellers all looked the same as well, and he did not know which case was his, so he waited till all the others had taken their cases and his was the only one left circling before him.

Bay Head. Not a station, a halt along the track, with crossing barriers and an open shelter. Only a very few clouds in the sky now, drifting across the ocean. The sun powerful, salty air.

Noon on an early September day.

Everywhere, larger and smaller patches of white paint were flaking and cracking off the split floorboards. In places where people walked a lot, at the thresholds, the wood had been trodden bare and was a weathered grey. He wondered once how much paint had been worn off by his tread in those few days. One post by the three steps that led down from the veranda had been freshly painted and gleamed in the early light of day. The paintwork was holding the wood together. On the inside, the post must be a confusion of passageways and nests. Perhaps there was some kind of order in it too, just as the movements of crowds along the symmetrical streets of New York often seemed to him to possess an order, to obey a pattern or programme, creating random ornamental images, figures consisting of individuals, appearing briefly and then instantly dissolving again, only to regroup in ever new configurations. A line of ants hurried to and fro from the base of the post to the small garden behind the house.

Carpenter ants, said the neighbour from whom he had had to fetch the house key. It would be better to have someone in to put down the pests than go on wasting paint, she said. But what concern was it of his? In three weeks he would be gone again, and she had been in Heidelberg and on a tour of the castles on the Rhine as it happened, and then it would soon be time for the autumn storms, and the post would definitely not survive them, and the supermarket had been shut since Labour Day, only the little, expensive shop on Twilight Avenue was still open, and if he needed anything he knew where she was, too.

Between the veranda steps and the beach was only a narrow strip of marram grass, its matt green bleached by the salt in the air, pressed down flat in a landward direction by the sea wind. The sharp edges of the blades stroked his bare ankles like fine knives; they did not cut the skin, but left white lines that did not disappear till something else touched the skin. The memory of what one thought to be love never disappeared till the next illusion. Nancy after Alice, Sarah after Emily, or Alice before Sarah and Emily after—the name was already gone. These affairs were no more than training for the next, little more than a keep-fit exercise, just as the man in the train had come to terms with his heart operation by seeing it as a sporting exercise. And very far off in his memory, as if in the mists that came off the beach in the mornings, he sometimes heard Lisa's voice—rather than being able to imagine her face.

Bright yellow, almost white and dazzling, the endless sweep of sugar-fine sand running north and south and vanishing against the horizon, sand into which one's feet sank deep as if in some melting fluid. Step by step his footprints filled behind him with the unrelenting, unceasing sift of glowed-out dryness, in which summer still clung, a woman whose body warmth one can still feel even after the door has been shut, and so the whole beach lay there without a trace on it at all.

An arm's length from the waterline, the sand was dark brown and elastic from the wet breathing, in and out, of the tides; his feet squeezed frothy bubbles to the surface, the goose pimples of the sand, and the water was disappointingly colourless. He could see the sand below the surface, the ripple marks notched into it by the waves, pebbles that gleamed under water and became nondescript in the sun, shells that rarely had the living creature within, seaweed like wet pubic hair, and jellyfish whose bobbing motions revolted him. The deep blue was always there when the sun shone, but it began far off. It was always where he was not, where he was only looking. It attracted him, perhaps because it withdrew from him whenever he waded out or swam in pursuit of it. Once, when the sky was very bright and the air utterly transparent, he scrutinised the horizon intently, as if he could bring back with his gaze the two gulls that were vanishing where the sky and sea touched, and he felt disappointed that nothing resulted. But usually he managed to pull himself together and think of nothing, or at least, above all, not to think of Lisa, and at such times he was able simply to walk along the beach and look at the water without searching for anything. Nothing at all happened, and it disturbed him to find that the quiet refused to enter into him. All that grew in him was a feeling that time was up to its neck in nothingness, gasping for air like a cat held down in water, and was drawing him to it hour by hour, but was neither halting nor devouring as it had devoured the past three years. The hours were simply slipping away, slipping past, ceaselessly, like the women, the slipstream of the city had swept by him.

Silence. And suddenly a profounder silence, as the regular beat of the breaking waves faltered, as if something had put them off their rhythm.

In the evenings, when the rim of the sun was pressing down on the horizon and tracks of light were coursing across the water, looking, if he narrowed his eyes to slits, like endless blurred trails of headlights and rear lights in New York at night, he would sometimes be overwhelmed by a feeling of being revolved around the sun in slow motion, though without ever seeing the other side. Mist rose and came towards the beach like breathing veils, and he felt as if he were wading through marshes.

Then he would begin the walk back, strolling around the little town by indirect routes, the place seeming more deserted than ever in the twilight. The windows of the planking houses, whitewashed or with shingles, grey and weatherworn, were dark and shut up; the tables and chairs at the two cafés were stacked in towers and covered over with tarpaulins. Of the few people who lived all year round at Bay Head he rarely saw anyone: occasionally his neighbour, widow of a naval officer, who talked a lot and spent her days watching television with her hair in curlers, and regularly the shopkeeper, who quickly knew him well enough to have the bottle of whisky waiting for him beside the till in a brown paper bag.

Basically, night was the same everywhere. Here by the beach it was quieter than in the city, but in its depths there lay hidden the selfsame weightlessness that could suddenly tip over into gravity. The blackness, the loss of sun. It always startled him, and only after the second or third glass did a kind of unstable equilibrium establish itself. Through its old-fashioned faceted glass mosaic shade the standard lamp cast patterns on the walls and ceiling. He traced the patterns with his hand as if a writ and message were concealed in them which he could decipher if only he understood the law underlying their form. But he did not understand; for, being afraid of loneliness, he failed to find himself once he was finally alone.

Outside, in the refreshing breeze, clouds scudded across the moon, forming into streets, avenues, highways, repeating themselves like the arc'd ribs of a woman breathing in her sleep. Not so long ago he had washed the perfume and sweat of a woman from his skin, Sarah or Emily or—the name escaped him, always hoping to find love and always ready to give it the slip. Whenever he was ready to fall in love he could not find a woman to share the willingness with him. But as soon as he was with a woman, his longing, sentimentally opened, closed up again like mimosa leaves touched with a fingertip. The hope that this time it might be more, and might last longer, or even be as it was back then, evaporated in the moments after intercourse like water from a pan on a stove. At such times he would lie mute beside those bodies, the silence blossoming on his lips like a sore.

He leafed through his address book. Who could he call? Her? Or her? And which of them would come? Her? Or her? He hurled his glass at the lampshade. For a moment it seemed to hesitate, as if considering a response to the attack, and then it shattered with a sound like a sigh of disappointment. The bulb exploded with a report that startled him.

Morning was already straddling the window ledges, and he stared at the shards indifferently, feeling himself fall apart into shards and knowing that it would require a painful effort, as it always did, to restore the form that he bore with him. The form that he sometimes saw from afar, and which he perhaps wanted to be, he had never tried to construct, because he was afraid he would never achieve it. And so he remained in what was comfortable, accepting pain and deferring the possible, with its blurring outlines, ever further off.

Like the mist that rose from the beach in the morning and left no trace on the sand, so too the bodies he had spent nights with in New York had left no traces in him. He swept up the shards and went to the beach, which consoled him, but in the rising cool of morning he grasped that he had not yet even experienced the emptiness he imagined himself to be in—and so did not deserve consolation, either. For he did want to be consoled, and was capable of being consoled.

He stripped and plunged into the water. The bite of the cold on his skin cleared his head; he surrendered himself to the pain of cold, from which clarity came. The might of the ocean touched him and gave him a sense of what a sea really was. In New York he had only ever been brushed by what was unfamiliar and challenging in the other country; he had never truly opened up to the country, had remained a stranger, a tourist with a work permit, employed by an overseas branch of a German planning office. He suddenly realised that he had missed his chance of defining himself anew, perhaps even making it to the horizon, to the limits of what was possible for himself. All he had seen was the reefs, maybe an offshore island or two.

No, he was not fooling himself any more as he now ran along the beach to warm up. Lisa and he had often run side by side like that, had dropped on the sand, breathless, and laughed, and once he had almost wept for sheer happiness, and in the tears that welled up he had had the certain knowledge that the end was already near. The sun had burnt its way through the mist. He began to sweat, ran on, ran northwards, till he could make out the boardwalk at Point Pleasant as a fine black pen-line on the yellow surface. And then he lay on the sand and closed his eyes.

It had been August when he arrived in New York. The city one gigantic frying pan in which a dish of mixed and indefinable ingredients that were melting into each other was cooking away in its own heat. In the air a ceaseless roar that was merely muted at night, and the roar overlaid by the high-pitched singing of the air-conditioners. Out of doors, the slightest exertion made one break out in sweat; he changed his shirt several times a day. At weekends, half the city poured out with a groan on to the beaches. He could have afforded to go to Long Island or here, southwards, to the New Jersey shore. But that first summer he had been attracted, time and again, by Coney Island, the city's public beach—which the people at the office turned up their noses at. Much too crowded and much too dirty, they said, and what they meant was: too many blacks.

And Coney Island really was a hopelessly overcrowded beach, nor was it particularly clean there either, but to him the beach seemed a state of mind, a crucible where all the contradictions of New York were concentrated. The few miles of sand, punctuated by the wooden frameworks of piers and boardwalks, over-exposed photographs in an album the pages of which the wind was turning over. There he saw what he did not see in the white ghetto of the office or in the fleeting encounters of night-time adventures. Bodies in their various shades, colours and shapes, in their never identical attitudes of relaxation, slackness, effort and energy. In his memory, those snapshots of the uniqueness of every body, and the diversity of that uniqueness, raised echoes as if they had been a language. When he drove back in the evenings, that concentrated uniqueness dissolved in the immense, mobile mosaic of the city, blurring into unconnected points, grids and pixels on his computer when he worked at it, exhausted. But the teeming mix of bodies and sand, faces and shadows, sun and eyes, saved him from the pace he had set to escape memory. The play of shapes and shadows from which bodies and things emerged as if from clothes, or into which they disappeared once more, dancing away in the heat of the day. Coney Island meant singles, solitary people who suddenly joined into groups, playing or talking or simply standing around, without asking where they had come from or where they were going; or families and groups that came together only to fall apart again on the beach; and every colour of skin, every age, and many languages.

Once he thought, that's Lisa, but of course it wasn't her once she came closer, only the colour and cut of the hair was the same.

The sheer unfolding of a blanket, laboured or casual, hasty or easy-going, the way the old man shifted his deckchair to face the sun, the children playing ball, the black girls whose age he could never judge and whose glances at him might be either contemptuous or a come-on, he couldn't tell. On one occasion he spent a long time watching an artist who, with a breeze constantly blowing, paying no attention to either the time or the people watching, made sculptures in the sand, on the narrow space between high and low watermarks. The figures would vanish, their images surviving only in their creator's memory. I ought to write down things like this, he had thought at the time, or draw them; for he felt a sudden need to preserve this legacy that was already fading even as it was made. There was a similarity between the sculptures in the sand and himself, but back home he lacked the drive to make notes on it, just as conversely he lacked the subjects whenever he did feel the urge to write something in his notebook. Apart from a few addresses, it remained empty.

Coney Island, he now knew, as he lay on that empty beach between Bay Head and Point Pleasant, was a grand comedy. And he had played his part in it. In brief, laconic conversations, such as are easy to have in America and imply so little, he realised that he was one of them, one of the crowd, belonging with them because he was a stranger and had finally arrived in New York. That the others were not bizarre creatures one could be amused by. That they were individuals worth remembering.

The profile of the skinny, wrinkled lady, up to her ankles in the waves and undecided, her face turned enquiringly to the open water, her back to the beach and the bustle, the noise and the shade. From the smell, though, that inimitable Coney Island smell, she too could not flee either, and he liked that. He entered into that fleeting vision of vulnerability and ease, participation and renunciation, and was able to share in it because he knew that the vision was fleeting. At the time the thought had reassured him, but now he sensed that the vision had etched itself into him and nothing could be lost. And that reassured him all the more.

Or the man, thin as a rake, lying on a towel on the sand, his bones and muscles as much a part of the earth as of his body, just as he lay here on the sand, a part of the beach that stretched to Coney Island and further, further on to the beaches where he had walked with Lisa. In the contemplation of it he saw his own frailty. But at the same time he also saw the amazing capacity to go on living despite ourselves, here and now, on a beach in September.

In the black, heavy arms of its mother, striped and stroked by the light that fell from above through the boards of the walk, a child slept.

And over it all the repellent, tempting smell, impossible to reconstruct except in memory, of mustard and ketchup, hot dogs and hamburgers, French fries, candy floss and salty sea air, and far off a haze that was New York.

In the crumbling façades of Bay Head there dwelt a bright melancholy in which he felt as good as he did in his faded blue jeans and tennis shoes. Bay Head was the summer residence of old money on the east coast, living off itself; the big money, the new money that was being made now, moved a few miles further south in the summer. He drove north in a hired car, north to the boardwalk at Point Pleasant. The smell was like that of Coney Island, with an insistent undertone of shrimps and grilled lobster. With the planks below him, the beach and sea to the right, to the left the fair, he enjoyed the blend of sophistication and cheap pleasures. There were even blacks and Hispanics there, people one never saw at Bay Head unless they were gardeners or maids or delivering goods.

With a bag of shrimps in his hand he strolled aimlessly, and saw a Panama hat he liked in the window of a souvenir shop. He bought it, put it on, and was transformed. Black girls along the railings on the boardwalk. He was wondering if they were whores, whether he should talk to one of them, when a gust of wind tore the hat from his head. On the girl's face a smile of contempt flashed across her tremendously white teeth as he chased the hat with awkward steps. He was annoyed, and sat down in the ice cream parlour by the entrance of which the hat had come to rest, pretending he had been on his way there anyway. He did not need the hat.

Before one finds what one really needs, he thought, stirring the chocolate sauce into the scoops of ice cream, one is forever trying to substitute something else for it. Time and again one deceives oneself about the fact that nothing can take the place of the right thing. Thus he had fooled himself in the feeling of being forever in love, which was really no more than a willingness to experience the feeling; he had drifted about the city, from one attraction to the next, constantly exposed to temptations and new offers—and new desolation.

Only on weekends at Coney Island had he almost shed that sense of drifting. Once he played soccer there with some people; afterwards he was surprised that they had played soccer and not baseball, or American football. They had to mark the goalposts with something, and he saw a bottle bobbing in the foam where the incoming water drained from the beach, and ran over and picked it up. It was made of clear glass, streaked with seaweed, corked. When he wiped off the weed he saw the piece of paper, pulled out the cork to get at the message, but couldn't shake it out. So they played soccer, and the bottle containing the message marked a goalpost, and that evening when he went home he took it with him. He smashed it in the sink. On the paper was a poem, written by hand. The poem was about water and about love.

At the table opposite a woman, perhaps his own age. Beside her a pushchair with a sleeping baby, which she rocked to and fro. And the five- or six-year-old boy who was running about the café was with her too, since the woman called him over to her table from time to time. She looked contented, though the strain of having two children around her overshadowed her eyes. There was a rapport between the mother and the children which spread tranquillity in the café, which the liveliness of the boy only served to confirm. He wondered if he wanted what people called family life, wondered if some such feeling of tranquillity could not also have been in him if Lisa and he . . .

The boy came over to his table and reached for the Panama hat. His mother called over, telling him to leave it alone and come back, but he put the hat on the boy's head and said he could keep it. The mother gave him a smile as the boy moved on with the hat down over his eyes.

He knew that he had not thrown away the piece of paper that was in that bottle. But the harder he thought about it, the less he could remember where it was. Half a bottle of whisky on, he started to look for the paper, unpacked his cases, turned out trouser and jacket pockets, leafed through books. The longer he searched, the more nervous he became, and the less he knew why he wanted to find the paper again in the first place. Was there not a message on it, a message for him? Was it not important to read the message now, tonight, in this house, by this beach? But he could not find the paper. As he tossed sleepless in bed he tried to recall single words, but they wouldn't come back.

When it was almost morning he fell asleep, it had been about the sea, about water and love, and woke about midday. It was raining. Even so, he went to the beach, which had taken on the colour of the sea, and the sea was as grey as the rain which was falling from a very deep sky. Wet and cold he returned, and ran a bath.

Lisa and he had quarrelled, yet again. And yet again over nothing at all; two days later he had already forgotten what sparked it off. He was sitting in the bathtub, and she was standing at the mirror combing her hair. Suddenly he hated her. All he wanted was for her naked, warm body to vanish as fast as possible and leave him alone in his hot bath. From somewhere or other the thought had come to him that he ought to think about what his destiny was. Destiny: the thought had come to him in the shape of that pathetic word, and the word would not let him alone. It was ridiculous, but he wanted to dwell on that word, that word alone, and to be alone as he did so. Why did she have to be combing her hair, of all things, holding her head back with the strokes and saying something inconsequential as he sat in the bath, vain and unwashed, with no intention whatsoever of washing, wanting only to think about what his destiny could be?

Out! Clear off! he shouted, and she went without a word. Next day she stopped by one last time to collect her things, last of all her toilet bag from the bathroom.

He knew where the piece of paper was. He had folded it up and slipped it in a packet of aspirin—and the packet was in his toilet bag. He leapt out of the bath, tore the zip open greedily, opened the packet, the tablets fell out and rolled across the floor. As if in slow motion the folded piece of paper floated down and settled in a puddle on the tiles at his feet. The ink ran.

He dried it between sheets of newspaper and smoothed the creased, softened paper with his fist.

An abstract landscape of ink, run, blurred, the lines dissolving into each other, the stroke of the hand dissolved, just single words left, Go . . . brooks or books? . . . love, quite clearly, love, several times, I will . . . but what? was this rivers? fish once, and oceans, the whole thing possibly a three-stanza construction, a song or poem, no name under it, no date or place.

Sluiced along clear streams, the lit-up side-streets of the Village at night, flowing into the rivers of the great Avenues or seeping into muddy rivulets, hustled in the crowd, rubbed against, jostled by smooth bodies, schools of fish, cool, iridescent, faces of every colour, scales, eyes of every shade, shapes, spurning, dead, harassed, jiggling, fugitive, slipping through the holes in the net, curious, smiling, giving the come-on, slippery, horny, the flashes in eyes that swim by, the promise: there goes your happiness, lost in the current as you look back, gone, lost, nevermore, till the next promise, the next invitation, a neverending chain, a dragnet, hole to hole, from lure to lure, happening to catch your own skin, your scaly armour, meeting each other, falling upon each other, tasted and chewed up in just a few nights below the surface, spat out again into the waters of the city, drifting on between stone banks, channelled, conducted into the pre-scribed current, regulated, drainage systems, whirling round, eddying, rushing towards a centre but never reaching the centre, no horizon visible, barely any sky, no open spaces, nowhere, and the times of day were reduced to nothing but the hands of the clock and the seasons to window dressing. In summer it was very hot, and the air-conditioning sang, and there was little fabric on bodies. And in winter it was very cold, and the heating systems pumped, and the bodies were packaged up. But everything between the two was lost.

Summer, yawning, determined to go, was still in the doorway, as autumn was already looking in at the window. The nights were getting longer, for two or three days the sea was warmer than the air, till their temperatures matched up. Now the mist did not disperse till early afternoon, and the breeze became a steady wind that crept through the cracks into the house. He took to wearing a pullover and stopped swimming. The beach darkened and became moist, the sand no longer filled in his footprints behind him. Traces remained, and were only occasionally erased by the night wind.

He put the piece of paper in his wallet. It was something he could take back to mark these three years, more than the memory of sand sculptures, but less as well, a piece of paper on which there had once been words. He would look for an apartment, take up his new job right on time, perhaps phone Lisa and arrange to meet her for a meal. She could have changed in these years. He would tell her about New York, Coney Island and Bay Head. He would show her the piece of paper, which would be hanging framed over his bed.

Along the boardwalk at Point Pleasant strolled autumn. The ice cream parlour was closed, the food smells from the stalls and kiosks were stale.

A black girl approached him. Very young, definitely under twenty, perhaps no more than fifteen. The combination of childlike naivety and calculated lasciviousness excited him immediately, although he meant to turn her away, and she took his arm. The sound of her red high-heeled shoes on the wooden boards. His soundless footfall. She tried to talk him into taking her home with him, but he turned down the suggestion brusquely. His neighbour saw everything. At Bay Head, she had once said, trying to make a joke, there were a lot of blacks, and, savouring his questioning expression as she paused longer than necessary, before adding her 'punchline': black Cadillacs.

They got into his car. Routinely she directed him a few miles inland to a small pine wood. Along the edges of a sandy woodland path, thrown-away drink cans and cigarette packs.

Here, she said, and asked how he wanted it.

He shrugged and wondered if he wanted anything at all.

She named the prices for various services. The radio was playing an old Rolling Stones track, you could almost taste the hot dogs, French fries they sell. Under the boardwalk, down by the sea, on a blanket with my baby . . . He tapped out the rhythm on the steering wheel, nodding to the music or to her offers, reached for his wallet, gave her some money.

He was funny, she said, perhaps afraid of his silence. She pulled her acid green t-shirt over her head, adjusted her seat to the recline position, slipped off her short black skirt, on a blanket with my baby, red panties underneath, hot dogs french fries they sell.

So, she said. What's doing?

He shrugged again, licked his dry lips, felt for a cigarette.

She unzipped his trousers, which he let her do without response, and rubbed his genitals. He felt nothing. Not even resistance, nor revulsion either, not even at himself. He felt nothing, under the boardwalk, down by the sea.

Stop it, he said softly. It was a misunderstanding.

She looked at him uncomprehendingly and tried to draw his hand to her little breast. He put the key in the ignition, started up the engine.

No problem, she said. Don't worry about it. These things happen.

She pulled her clothes on as he was turning the car, and he drove her back to the boardwalk. She did not turn to look after him but vanished quickly behind a fast food stand.

At home he lay on the bed and masturbated, imagining the black girl standing before him with her legs apart and himself licking her clitoris, but with an empty, transparent bottle on his tongue like a rigid condom.

When darkness fell he packed his cases. He felt secure because he no longer needed security, drank nothing, and slept deeply.

At dawn the cry of a gull on the roof woke him. The cry went straight to the pit of his stomach, he almost started bolt upright, but then he listened, the cry still in his ears, and felt contented to have been woken in that way.

He locked the house, left the cases on the steps, and handed the keys over to the neighbour. Fetching the luggage, he knocked the metal case into the post by the steps. It swayed, hesitated, then broke off sideways with a rotten sigh. From the crumbling stump poured forth a startled, panic-stricken mass that ran black and higgledy-piggledy in every direction. The wood gave off a cloying, sweetish smell that pursued him as far as the railway station.

At Point Pleasant he pulled down the compartment window and leaned out. No one got off the train, some people got on. On the platform were the mother and her two children from the ice cream parlour. He was disappointed that the boy was not wearing the Panama hat, and mildly jealous to see the woman embracing a man. Then she got into the carriage in front of his own. The man handed up the pushchair. The boy remained on the platform holding the man's hand.

He cast about for something in his memory. He knew he had already found it once. It brushed past his head like a gull at the beach, he felt the air from its wingbeat, almost a touch. The search provoked a sweetish, almost unbearable excitement in him, like sexual excitement just before ejaculation. And suddenly he had it. He took out his wallet and went through it. The piece of paper was missing. It must have fallen out when he gave the girl the money. Or it had stuck to the banknote and the girl was now carrying it about with her. Or she had thrown it away.

He smiled and looked forward to the moment at the airport in Germany when the luggage would rise from the depths and everyone would reach for what belonged to him.

For Hilde Frye

Irina Liebmann

Did You Use the Night?
(after Cibber)

Did you use the night? Hard to get into it. Burrowed into the darkness face first, it was hard to make anything out, faces, averted, were there, indignant, you weren't among them. Maybe this isn't the right way for this night, I was thinking, when the phone rang. A woman was speaking, voice smooth as plastic cable, claiming to be my friend Hermine Voss, beyond the ocean, and wanting to hear my laugh. Laughing, nothing to it, but while I was laughing I was thinking how shameful it would be if it was a trick being played from the next room. Because how can a voice come so loud halfway round the earth and say I'm the second living person in the world, in this night. I did wear my hair up, said the plastic cable, but it's always coming down, then I tore it off, fell in the water, splash, down to the bottom, splash go the waves, the light goes on above them, gets brighter, maybe it's sun over the Atlantic, what's going to happen now, Hermine, here, in the darkness.

But by day they are gilding the cross on the church tower opposite the supermarket where the trams go past, always on time, and green vegetables are expected. Daily, say the shop assistants. In the night you were standing at my door. Open up you cried, I want to tell you something. And when you were inside you said, I want to give you something. What do you want to give me, I asked. Everything I own, you said, because I'm getting out. But the country's borders are closed to everyone, I said. That's new, you said and wanted us to talk about your death. If I remember correctly we talked about it all night, and when it grew light I saw you lying asleep on my bed.

But by day they are gilding the cross on the church tower opposite the supermarket where the trams go past, always on time, and it is getting warmer from day to day. In the grocers', green vegetables are expected. Daily, say the shop assistants. All the people in the trams are dressed in bright things, freshly washed. This year, with white skirts, the women are wearing black stockings and black shoes, and the boys wear partings in their black dyed hair. Some of them have only a little bush of hair on the crest of their scalps, others shave crosses into their hair or smear red paint on their foreheads as if they've been wounded. But they all stand silently around the tram-stops, and all get quietly in when their tram comes.

Did you use the night? It didn't grow quiet. The gas-pipes in my room clicked, I also heard zips clicking on the street and men wanting petrol. Click and they were gone. Click I switched on the television, sound off, there were planes flying over the sea, silent, silent over the Atlantic, where Hermine's plastic wire has been rocking, for days, silently, to the rocky shores of the Mediterranean, over houses that shine bright at night because they are white to the tent-city of the Bedouins, where brown eyed palace guards stand. Silently the bombs fell through the air and burst tents into flowers, everything flew up towards the still falling bombs, everything flew up and back over the sea to England, the aeroplanes sank down to the cold ground, only what came from the tent circles in the air. It's the latest news. The palace is on fire.

But by day they are gilding the cross on the church tower opposite the supermarket where the trams go past, always on time, and it is growing warmer from day to day. In the grocers', green vegetables are expected. Daily, say the shop assistants.

All the people in the trams are dressed in bright things,

freshly washed. This year, with white skirts, women are wearing black stockings and black shoes, and the boys have partings in their black dyed hair. Some of them only have a little bush of hair on the crest of their scalps, others shave crosses into their hair or smear red paint on their foreheads as if they've been wounded. But they all stand silently around the tram-stops, and all get quietly in when their tram comes.

Pass along, says a voice in my direction, Pass along, you can see someone else wants to get on. Someone with a patch of paint on his forehead puts his right foot, hobnail booted, on the step and comes up to join us. He looks around, all the people present lower their eyes and we're moving, all together.

That night it took me a long time to get away. Drifting off under my blanket I saw the edge of a small town in August, evening sun shining, bushes in meadows. When did you come? I'd rather you didn't go, I said to you. I want to see you from the other side, you said, then I only remember us turning away at the same time, in our sleep.

But by day they are gilding the cross on the church tower opposite the supermarket where the trams go past, always on time, and it is growing warmer from day to day. In the grocers', green vegetables are expected. Daily, say the shop assistants.

All the people on the tram are dressed in bright things, freshly washed. This year, with white skirts, women are wearing black stockings and black shoes, and the boys have partings in their black dyed hair, but they all stand silently around the tram-stops, and all get quietly in when their tram comes.

Pass along, says a voice in my direction, Pass along, you can see someone else wants to get on. Someone with a patch of paint on his forehead puts his right foot, hobnail booted, on the step and comes up to join us. He looks around, all the people present lower their eyes and we're moving. Under the railway bridge it grows dark for a moment. For eight months of the year the light before and after the bridge is just as murky as it is under the bridge, but not today and not for days. The row of houses to the left, which we are about to see, will be bright, I'm about to see your window in the sun.

That night you were standing at my door again. Open up you must take everything, you said, and I won't die either. I'll explain everything in detail. And why don't you need it all any more, I asked. Because I'm getting out you said, and you were in my apartment again. I'd just like to know where you're heading, I said, and you pointed your finger at the television, where the palace was still burning. A doctor was bending over the youngest princess, she took up only a foot and a half of the military hospital bed. She was dead. The doctor stood up and said: Her father hasn't come.

But by day they are gilding the cross on the church tower opposite the supermarket where the trams go past, always on time, and it grows warmer from day to day. In the grocers', green vegetables are expected. Daily, say the shop assistants.

All the people on the tram are dressed in bright things, freshly washed. This year, with white skirts, women are wearing black stockings and black shoes, and the boys have partings in their black dyed hair. Some of them only have a little bush of hair on the crest of their scalps, others shave crosses into their hair or smear red paint on their foreheads as if they've been wounded. But they all stand silently around the tram-stops, and all get quietly in when their tram comes. Pass along, says a voice in my direction, Pass along, you can see someone else wants to get on. Someone with a patch of paint on his forehead puts his right foot, hobnail booted, on the step and comes up to join us. He looks around, all the people present lower their eyes and we're moving.

Under the railway bridge it grows dark for a moment. For eight months of the year the light before and after the bridge is just as murky as it is under the bridge, but not today and not for days. The row of houses to the left, which we are about to see, will be bright, I'm about to see your window in the sun. Now a man pushes me away from the window by opening today's paper. There's enough room for people to spread out their papers and now for some minutes the bottom two floors of all the houses on the left side of the street are hidden by paper with printed words, big and small, the names of the countries around the Mediterranean swarm around a photograph, this page is turned towards me, the photograph shows a child standing in the rubble with arms dangling, and now we're driving past your window.

Did you use the night? I was in an empty apartment. I turned the gas and the light off and looked at the street. Opposite, people came out of the cinema and looked up at me. Then I pulled the curtains closed, put the key to the flat on the windowsill and ran into the stairway. At home I tested the lock on the door of my flat and opened a window. The air outside was warm and smelled of petrol.

But by day they are gilding the cross on the church tower opposite the supermarket where the trams go past, always on time, and it grows warmer from day to day. In the grocers', green vegetables are expected, daily, say the shop assistants. All the people in the trams are dressed in bright things, freshly washed. This year, with white skirts, the women are wearing black stockings and black shoes, and the boys have partings in their black dyed hair. Some of them only have a little bush of hair on the crest of their scalps, others shave crosses into their hair or smear red paint on their foreheads as if they've been wounded. But they all stand silently around the tram-stops, and all get quietly in when their tram comes.

Pass along, says a voice in my direction, Pass along, you can see someone else wants to get on. Someone with a patch of paint on his forehead puts his right foot, hobnail booted, on the step and comes up to join us. He looks around, all the people present lower their eyes and we're moving. Under the railway bridge it grows dark for a moment. Now a man pushes me away from the window by opening today's newspaper, there's enough room for people to spread out their newspapers and now for minutes the bottom two floors of all the houses on the left side of the street are hidden by paper with printed words, big and small, the names of the countries around the Mediterranean swarm around a photograph, this page is turned towards me, the photograph shows a child standing in the rubble with arms dangling, and now we're driving past your window. The curtains are drawn. The cinema opposite is showing a film whose name is painted on the boards around the entrance. STAR TREK A SPACE-SHIP HEADS BACK TO EARTH AFTER 300 YEARS. A space-ship that set off when the Great Elector died, I think, and look down the tram compartment, where a man is towering above everyone else. A girl clutches his shirt and goes on talking while he looks around the compartment, to me and past me, he wears his hair long and there's something about his eyes. Now the tram stops, corner of Dimitroffstrasse, where nobody can get in or out. That can take three or even four minutes. Of the cars outside I can see only curved metal roofs and in each a left hand on the wheel. The boy with the patch of paint on his forehead lights a cigarette. That is not allowed, so everyone looks into our corner, including the tall guy.

At night the telephone was broken. I tried to phone you but every time I heard two women talking about their biorhythms. On the eleventh I'm back out of the minus range, a voice said. Congratulations, I said and tried your number again, while a picture came on the television. An American in a flowery dress opened her mouth wide, nothing more came from the receiver, not even a sign, everything where we are is fine, says the American, and I thought when it's light I'll throw you the television over the wall.

But by day they are gilding the cross on the church tower opposite the supermarket where the trams go past, always on time, and it grows warmer from day to day. In the grocers', green vegetables are expected. Daily, say the shop assistants.

All the people in the trams are dressed in bright things, freshly washed. This year, with white skirts, the women are wearing black stockings and black shoes, and the boys have partings in their black dyed hair. Some of them only have a little bush of hair on the crest of their scalps, others shave crosses into their hair or smear red paint on their foreheads as if they've been wounded, but they all stand silently around the tram-stops, and all get quietly in when their tram comes.

Pass along, says a voice in my direction, Pass along, you can see someone else wants to get on. Someone with a patch of paint on his forehead puts his right foot, hobnail booted, on the step and comes up to join us. He looks around, all the people present lower their eyes and we're moving, all together.

Under the railway bridge it grows dark for a moment. For eight months of the year the light before and after the bridge is just as murky as it is under the bridge, but not today and not for days. The row of houses to the left, which we are about to see, will be bright, I'm about to see your window in the sun. Now a man pushes me away from the window by opening today's paper, there's enough room for people to spread out their papers and now for minutes the bottom two floors of all the houses on the left side of the street are hidden by paper with big and small printed words, the names of the countries around the Mediterranean swarm around a photograph, this page is turned towards me, the photograph shows a child standing in the rubble with arms dangling, and now we're driving past your window. The curtains are drawn.

The cinema opposite is showing a film whose name is painted on the boards around the entrance. STAR TREK A SPACE-SHIP HEADS BACK TO EARTH AFTER 300 YEARS. A space-ship that set off when the Great Elector died, I think, and look down the tram compartment, where a man is towering above everyone else, a girl clutches his shirt and goes on talking while he looks around the compartment, to me and past me, he wears his hair long and there's something about his eyes. Now the tram stops, corner of Dimitroffstrasse, where nobody can get in or out.

That can take three or even four minutes. Of the cars outside I can see only curved metal roofs and in each a left hand on the wheel. The boy with the patch of paint on his forehead lights a cigarette. That is not allowed, so everyone looks into our corner, including the tall guy. Now I know: your eyes are in his head. So that's how you get here in daytime, I think, and it makes me laugh. Then you smile too. We still haven't started again.

The boy with the cigarette blows his smoke at the windows, behind which the cars are now edging forward, and your eyes are still on me. Once we've gone over the crossing a lot of people will get out, at the next stop the tram will be empty, then we could get closer, but now the driver gets out.

He walks past us all back down the street, there's another tram behind us and a third, we can't see more than that in the closed compartment.

Open the door, says somebody, and the boy with the cigarette in his mouth beats with his fist on the plastic window above the door and pulls it open. Slowly everybody gets out on to the road. The air outside is warm and smells of petrol.

The girl is still holding on with one hand to the shirt of the long-haired guy, who has your eyes and stands next to me.

What shall we do now, I ask you. Let's take the underground, you say, and we look over to the station across the street, but the people coming from there only want to get on the tram and now the first has got to our group. It's a woman with glittering earrings. She says: the underground is on fire.

Christoph Hein

Night Drive and Early Morning

The car, an old Opel, belonged to Max's father and was a rattling, mauve enamelled vehicle, a misshapen technical cube with a snout. The windscreen could be opened and raised, and that, together with the two ashtrays in the back of the car, was the Opel's only luxury. It had a stick gear lever, an iron rod, almost a yard long, with a plastic ball on the end, which protruded between the two front seats. On the road the driver had to place his hand on the black sphere to prevent the lever jumping out of gear. Max drove the car whenever he got the chance, and now and then he suggested that I come with him. Then, when we came to deserted country roads, he let me drive for a few miles, although I did not have a driving licence. Each time I gripped the steering wheel with both hands and sweated; Max held the gear lever tight and nervously encouraged me.

Max called me on Friday. After work he was to drive a teacher, an acquaintance of his father, to L. and bring him back to Berlin the same night. He asked me if I wanted to come with him, and I said yes. Then Max said that it was a three hundred and seventy-five mile round trip, and he only had eight hours to do it in, so there could be no question of letting me take a turn at the wheel. I replied that I would come anyway.

When I arrived at his place in the afternoon, he had already driven the car out of the garage. His father was standing on the pavement and talking to an unusually thin man with a careworn face. The man seemed to be only a few years older than Max and really looked dreadfully skinny. He got into the car and sat down awkwardly on the edge of the back seat.

When we reached the motorway, Max leant back. We talked quietly, the teacher behind us stared nervously out of the window. Later we sang songs, hymns and hits.

We left the motorway as night began to fall. Just before L. the teacher asked us whether we were informed about everything. I said that I didn't know anything, and Max said we weren't interested, he would take him and his family to Berlin and didn't want to know about anything else.

I was confused and somehow unsettled and looked at Max, but he only stared straight ahead and didn't respond.

Then the teacher said, 'I think I should tell you. I believe it's more honest. I am going to go over the border in Berlin tonight. With my wife and daughter.'

Astonished, I turned round to him. 'How? How are you going to get across?'

'Through the sewers. There are eleven of us altogether. A man from the waterworks is taking us. I met him at lunchtime today.' The man spoke in a singsong, plaintive voice. I looked at Max and at the same moment realised that he had known earlier only not wanted to tell me. I was disappointed. I was hurt because he lied to me. I wanted him to trust me in order to prove to him that I was his friend, even if I was only sixteen and he was eight years older.

The teacher went on talking. 'My wife and my daughter are coming with me. Our guide knows the sewers like the back of his hand. He's already taken a lot of people over to the other side. He's employed by the waterworks, but I already told you that. There are eleven of us, but I don't know the others.' He spoke very quietly and paused briefly after every sentence. 'That's important. So that we don't put each other at risk, you know. The man made a good impression on me. I think he can be trusted.'

'You shouldn't tell us that,' Max interrupted him.

The teacher persisted, 'I think it's fair, if you know where you stand with me.'

Max turned round as he was driving, 'But we're not interested.'

The teacher was silent now. I leant against the door and scowled at Max. I didn't want to talk to him, but I hoped he would notice that I was angry. He lied to you, I told myself, he doesn't trust you.

In L. the teacher's wife was waiting for us, a young, blonde woman, hardly more than a girl. She invited us to have coffee. Max declined, he had to be back in Berlin at midnight, and if there were any problems with the car on the way we might regret the coffee break. The packed cases and two rucksacks stood in the hall. When Max saw them he laughed.

'It's only the bare essentials,' said the woman. She had turned red when Max laughed and looked at her.

'Then you'll have to hire a bus.'

'And how much can we take with us?'

'Three suitcases, more won't fit in.'

The woman looked despairingly at the luggage, at Max, then at her husband.

The teacher moaned, 'I told you from the start . . .'

'We'll take the rucksacks on our knees,' decided the woman.

'Of course,' Max snapped, 'just to let them know at the checkpoint what you're up to!' He went outside, I followed him. The teacher brought two suitcases and a rucksack, which we stowed away in the boot. We got into the car. The teacher remained standing nervously beside the car and waited, his hands didn't stop fidgeting.

Then the woman appeared. She was carrying her perhaps two-year-old daughter in her arms, the teacher took the child from his wife and asked her something. She nodded, and both of them turned round and looked at their house for a moment.

When they got in, the woman said to Max, 'I made some coffee for you.' She held out a metal thermos flask to him, but Max started the car and only said impatiently, 'Wasn't necessary.'

'Later perhaps,' I said and took the flask from her. As

long as we were driving through L., the teacher talked insistently to his wife. I couldn't hear anything. Later the teacher asked how we rated the chances of crossing the border through the sewers. Max told him neither of us had an opinion about that. Intimidated, the teacher made an effort to get a conversation going. He asked about our jobs, about the situation in Berlin. Max replied tersely and I did likewise.

When we reached the motorway it was pitch dark. The child woke up and began to cry. Irritated, Max told the woman to soothe the child, he was tired and nervous and had to concentrate on the road and the motorway signs. The teacher's wife whispered intently to the child and rocked her back and forward on her lap.

When Max lit a cigarette, she asked him not to smoke because of the child. Max looked round at me astonished before he threw the cigarette out of the window. I felt sorry for the woman, and I wanted to ask Max why he was being so spiteful. I didn't do it. A few hundred yards further on Max stopped the car by the embankment. The teacher started, and asked if something was wrong. Max shook his head, he only wanted to smoke a cigarette. We got out and walked up and down. It was cold. I warmed my fingers from the glow of the cigarette. Then I drank coffee from the thermos flask and gave it to Max, who grudgingly took it.

In the car the teacher's wife handed us an already opened bar of chocolate, which felt soft and warm through the wrapper, sticky. We gave it back and said that we didn't eat chocolate.

When we reached the outskirts of Berlin, I called the teacher's attention to the imminent identity check.* I advised the couple to pretend to sleep and to appear to let themselves be wakened. The teacher thanked me several times for the advice. A few minutes later I regretted my suggestion, because when the border guard stopped us and wanted to

---

* Before August 1961 and the building of the Wall, there were border controls not only between East Germany and West Berlin but also between East Germany proper and East Berlin *(trans.)*.

see our identity papers, the teacher acted his supposed awakening with such exaggeration that I was afraid the officer would become suspicious. The teacher yawned without stopping, rubbed his eyes, acted as if he didn't know what he was doing, while the border guard looked at him indifferently. Finally Max snapped at him to show his pass. The guard tapped his cap with two fingers and let us continue.

Without speaking we drove into the night-time silence of Berlin. It was quarter past twelve and very cold as the Opel had no heater. Max stopped the car, took off his jacket and gave it to the woman. She should put it on, he said curtly. The woman thanked him with an odd, gentle smile. Then we drove on.

When Max stopped among some ruins close to the Spittelmarkt and let everyone get out, the child woke up and whimpered. We handed out the luggage and quickly took our leave. The teacher took Max aside, but the two of them soon joined us again. We pointed out the direction which they had to take. Then we got into the car.

I asked what the teacher had wanted from Max. 'He offered me money for the trip. Twenty marks,' said Max, 'I didn't take it.' We then twice drove past the supposed meeting place, but not a soul was to be seen. I wondered how the teacher and his wife could disappear so quickly.

As arranged, I slept the night at Max's house on a foldout couch. In bed we smoked and drank beer and I hoped he would talk to me. But he said nothing and only stared at the ceiling, and so I was silent too.

The next morning we ate breakfast together. Max boiled eggs and made coffee. Tired, we sat in the kitchen and listened lethargically to the radio. When the door opened, Max didn't turn round. He probably assumed that it was his mother. Only when the teacher's wife said good morning did he jump. I laughed awkwardly and said something like: It can't be. The woman stood at the door wearing a dressing gown, she did not seem to have slept well and looked very beautiful. She told us that the man from the waterworks had not come. The other people had not turned up either, possibly the attempt had been called off at short notice. She did not know.

Max struck the table angrily with his fist and said, 'Shit. All this running away is shit.'

The woman smiled sadly. Then she continued. She had come here during the night, Max's father had opened the door. Her husband had gone back to L. by train, to teach in his school the next day.

'Do you want coffee?' asked Max. The woman shook her head

I looked at her the whole time. Her appearance at our breakfast table after such a night seemed absurd and comical to me and I wondered if it was embarrassing for her, simply to show up here again.

Max sat at the table without saying a word.

Abruptly the woman asked, 'Why do you hate my husband?'

I was astonished when Max replied, 'Because he's a loser. Because he doesn't leave you in peace. All he's good for is running away.' He said it in a quiet, gentle voice, as if he were talking about someone who was dead. And I did not understand him, I did not grasp why he despised and hated the teacher. It was cool in the kitchen. Water bubbled in the kettle, a tram rattled by outside the house, and I thought about the teacher who was now probably in L. again and getting ready for lessons. Max stirred his coffee, I looked at the woman. Her eyes had grown moist, tears came, they ran slowly down her cheeks and gathered in the corners of her mouth. Then her dressing gown opened. The belt loop had loosened and the two overlapping sides of the towelling coat separated with the woman's quick breathing. Only the nipples were covered for just a second, then they too were exposed. I now saw her breasts, her white stomach, her thighs. Her navel and pubic hair were hidden by the wide backrest of a kitchen chair. And while I tried to discover whether she was wearing panties, or rather whether she wasn't wearing any, and was at the same time trying to avoid every movement, so as not to call her attention to my interest, I wondered in amazement whether she did not notice her nakedness or whether she was really such a scheming tart.

I very much wanted to stroke her, touch her breasts and yet hardly dared breathe. My mouth seemed to have dried up, I had to swallow several times. And then I realised that she didn't notice me at all. I was invisible to her, as invisible as a child. And suddenly I understood why Max spoke to her with such hate, and I was shocked by his fierce, uncontrolled love.

Max stood up without looking at her, and went out of the kitchen. The woman tied her dressing gown tight around her and walked over to the window. She pressed her face against the pane, her shoulders trembled.

I cleared my throat and stood up likewise. She didn't respond.

A couple of minutes later I left for work with Max, he was silent and looked out of the tramcar window. And again and again on that Saturday, as I stood at the press and put the wet metal sheets into it, I tried to remember as exactly as I could the night drive during which Max and the teacher's wife had fallen in love with each other. And I tried to grasp why I didn't understand it.

Bodo Kirchhoff

In the Opera Café

In the more carefree circles of the intelligentsia the talk was of a man who was forever turning up in the Opera Café. Ladies of a certain age would sit down next to him, their faces motionless, listening to stories delivered in such a quiet voice that nothing was audible even at the next table; accompanied by a few relaxed gestures, this gentle murmur obviously had effects that only those who took no notice could escape.

A number of weeks passed before, with the suddenness that sometimes follows the hesitant consideration of an action, I sat down beside the whisperer, as he was known by now to the young urban professionals who used this café as their stage. Another word about my hesitancy: I am not a lady of a certain age, I am a man in his early thirties. In the past I wanted to be an actor, and today I go to the Opera Café. I always appear there in new outfits, often people barely recognise me. With a bold hairstyle, artfully made up, dressed all in silk and with lacquer on my nails, I sat down beside the whisperer, purely from curiosity, resolving only to shake or nod my head.

I ate a slice of cake and drank a cup of tea and looked in the mirror on the opposite wall. I saw myself in it, and thought the lady was good enough to die for, and I saw him. He could have been fifty, and he might have been taken for a literary critic—as everyone knows, they look the way the public imagines writers look. After a while our eyes met in the mirror and he began to whisper. 'Are you answering my advertisement?'

I gently shook my head.

'On somebody's recommendation, then.'

I nodded, and turned slightly, so that I could see his profile. He was gaunt, without being the gaunt type; he was a man in a new role, it seemed to me. 'Let's get business out of the way first,' he said, barely moving his lips to speak. I took a big bite of cake so that I wouldn't have to reply; he ordered a glass of mineral water. Until it was brought not another word was spoken. He took a drink and turned his face to me, and a pattern of little wrinkles appeared on his cheeks. 'So you wish me to tell you something.' I nodded again, and he opened a daily newspaper that lay on the table in front of him. A contract was revealed. 'Sign it, if you agree. Your initials will suffice. It is a private arrangement.' And I glanced through the few lines.

The contract obliged one to remain silent about everything that was whispered, and to transfer a certain sum of money to a named account within ten days. Any breach of the agreement and further contact would be broken; one could be sure of being treated as though one didn't exist. That struck me, in the circumstances, as restrained, and I signed my initials at the bottom. The whisperer laid a hand on the paper. As skilfully as a pickpocket he spirited it into his much too large suit, and with his other hand he offered me a card—it bore nothing but a bank account number. I put it in my pocket. I was gripped by an excitement like that which precedes the act of love . . . It was in starkest contrast to the solidity surrounding me. It was the quietest time in the Opera Café, which was not flooded with the more light-hearted members of the intelligentsia until the lights went out in the advertising agencies and financial institutions. The waiters were leaning idly on the bar, glancing over in our direction. They didn't recognise me, I hardly recognised myself. The whisperer ran his middle finger along the rim of his glass, without any ambition to produce a sound. I took a pen from my handbag and wrote on the edge of the newspaper: 'What now?'

'I shall tell you about lust.'

I must have looked sceptical at that, because he said: 'Or do you wish to hear something else?' I shook my head and began to knead the end of the tablecloth. Finally I glanced at him and he ran his finger along the rim again, this time producing a note.

'Why are you looking like that?' he asked. 'No man has ever been looked at like that before . . .'

I looked elsewhere. He had been grossly exaggerating, but I was flattered; the first of my many acquaintances made their dramatic entry. They were long-legged owners of fashion shops and other salons, dressed in the most expensive, shimmering materials, who liked to laugh at my little jokes. Successful women with leathery necks and cobblestone knees who, for all the fragrances they emanated, could still take away my taste for the opposite sex; perhaps they felt the same way about me, and perhaps that was why we were acquaintances. I smiled in their direction, while the whisperer, without any words of introduction, told of a room to which we would have withdrawn. It was on the first floor of an old hotel, street noises could be heard. 'But your breathing soon drowns out the hubbub of passing voices. You are exhaling in short bursts, little pearls of sweat are appearing on your forehead . . .' I finished eating the cake, and tried not to be affected by the whispers. My acquaintances were now standing at the bar trying to look cosmopolitan: it was a funny sight; the whisperer went on unflustered.

'You hollow your back, I hold your hot face. My hands are cool. You would like to speak, but you can't. I take your arms and lay them beneath your head, I kiss your armpits. With my lips I write the word happiness on your skin. Soon it reaches from your shoulders to your knees. I smooth your drenched hair. You look at me as if you were heading towards an abyss, you keep saying, "No". Then I straighten up and break your resistance.' I felt myself blushing. Almost voiceless, I breathed, 'What with?'

'With my greater age.'

I dabbed my lips and looked at him. The man was wreathed in an aura of gravitas. He was an orderly creature, unlike everyone else in the Opera Café—whether it was the advertising men in their linen suits or the car salesmen with their pinstriped suits and hankies, the hairdressers' assistants with bow-ties: they all made fools of themselves (I was their head fool). I was thinking about that as he went on with his story. 'We both know there will be no second attempt. Together we must pass through a needle's eye too small for each on our own, so great is our desire. Only if we risk everything for one moment, then we may do it. I am still keeping myself under control, and thus giving you time; this is also part of the superiority granted by my age. But I am also making you feel that I could forget myself at any time. I am keeping you in this state of suspense, your whole body has been gleaming now for a long time. Now and again we talk quietly. Each of our words is like an additional, skilful touch. We avoid any nicknames for my member. We call it Cock. Our bellies part and cleave together again, producing noises that make us laugh. You grab blindly at my face. Your nails tear my back. You tear your mouth open, and I cover it gently. From the street rises the cry of a beggar; our hotel is in a decaying capital city. You stiffen for a moment, and I hold my breath too. Then a single faint movement is enough, and I feel your fingers clench. A tram goes past below, shaking the floor. Your teeth close on my hand. I suppress your cry . . .'

He looked at me and ran his thumb along the tablecloth. He understood the art of the pause. I wanted to ask him who he was, but I couldn't find the words. It was as if he had all the words and I had all the speechlessness. He went on. A stream of quiet, musical sentences entered my ear. I closed my eyes. I forgot the contract, I forgot a man was talking to me. As if it was all coming from the mouth of an enchanting woman, that's how much it was confusing me. A loud, unmistakable laugh from one of my acquaintances— he works in stocks and shares—echoed as if in the distance.

I was somewhere quite different, in that hotel, almost breathless . . . 'You're gasping for air, I stroke your hair. We have the whole afternoon ahead of us. We pant in silence. You have that upturned gaze of someone refusing to relinquish their dream. You are dreaming of perfect lust, of sinking into it. I touch your knees, you murmur nonsense words; pillows and blankets have long ago fallen on the floor. The skin on your breasts is taut as a drumskin. There are bright little flecks of foam on your lips. You emit a raw, almost male sound. And I embrace you with all my power. On the pavement, lottery-ticket sellers are calling out their numbers. It is oppressively hot in the room. You arch your back. For five, six, seven heartbeats you are no more than a creature dissolving. I look at you now with a certain detachment. I can see you forgetting yourself. Then a tremor runs through all your muscles, and you go limp. A pallor crosses your face, and it takes on a childish expression. You are beginning to feel cold, so exhausted is your body; you ask my name. I whisper it, and you repeat it quietly. Shortly after that comes monotony. Nothing heralds it, it is suddenly there. And you turn to the wall while I dry my face and hands. My eye falls on the folds in the curtain. What time can it be, I wonder. To fight against my fatigue I talk to you about your feelings. I would like to know what you feel for me. And to the wall you answer: nothing . . .'

'I would never say that.'

These words had slipped from me, not in a deep voice, admittedly, but not in the tone of a woman either. The whisperer looked at me. His face bore traces of sleeplessness, it now struck me. 'Are you telling this story, or am I?' he asked abruptly, and at the same time I felt something warm. His hand was resting on my arm: there had been nothing about that in the contract. He smiled for a moment, and the way his lids grew heavy and gave his expression a broken quality told me that he could only pursue this curious trade because women meant nothing to him, or had stopped meaning anything to him. He seemed to despise them all, after loving one in vain. He pushed back his white shirt sleeve with the tip of his finger. It was an ingrained movement. He wasn't wearing a watch, but you could see a lighter strip of skin around his wrist. He must have pawned it, the idea occurred to me: he's completely finished, all he was able to save was his language.

'Is the story over?' I asked gently.

He looked into my eyes and I closed them. I could clearly see the hotel room in front of me. I hardly heard his first words. Then he raised his voice as if we were alone. 'It has grown dark, and I'm ordering a meal for us. Sea-food and a bowl of fruit, freshly squeezed orange juice, two consommés. A young waiter brings it to the room, he comes and goes silently. We eat in bed. Then we sink into a light slumber. The noise of the night-time traffic wakes us up. The air is above us. I reach around your hips, and in a matter of seconds we are united. We are no longer speaking now. Your "Now" mingles with the beggar's cries, which have grown louder . . . I hold you until it fades away. We are lying side by side. Let's go out into the night, I suggest.' He drained his glass, and I nodded. My sole desire was to set off with him and go into the night, coming back to the hotel at some point. Until I opened my eyes, until I asked him, 'Who are you?'

'This isn't the place.'

He smiled again, and that smile was meant for the man in me; just like me, he didn't seem to be acting any more, and suddenly his face struck me as familiar. I was burning with the conviction that I was sitting beside a famous person who had changed his skin. The hand on my arm grew heavier.

'Were you pleased with my story?'

I waved to the waiter. Once more I tried to gain some time. My answer would have to be well considered. For I was more than pleased. I was in love. And the whisperer certainly felt my weakness for him, but gave no sign that he did. He had tact, and that too distinguished him from everyone else in the Opera Café. He now looked to me like someone gazing calmly on the failed construction of his life. The waiter came to the table. I ordered a dry white wine. We were offered the evening paper. Headlines spoke of countless dead, it left me cold: neither he nor I was among them, I thought. I looked over to the bar. A strange quiet reigned in the Opera Café, as if the conversation at each of the tables had broken off. Shameless looks came from the women with the leathery necks. I wasn't close to any of them, but each of them bragged of their familiarity with me—although they found me half repellent. But such is life. I aped them, inspecting the wildness of my hair-do; they were all constantly worked up about their daring hair-dos.

'Your story,' I said, 'was very beautiful.'

'It's over.'

'I don't think it's even started. I'd like to know who you are. Trust me.'

'Would you come home with me?'

The waiter brought me the wine. I took a drink, I said yes. And the whisperer clasped his hands behind his neck and told me his name.

I put the glass down. Again I was burning, aware this time of having made a tremendous discovery. He was the enigmatic character whose major private bank had burst like a soap-bubble some three years previously, after he had, simply by using his eloquence and having a ridiculously hypnotic effect on the otherwise rational members of his profession, taken its balance sheet to dizzying heights—it had been the talk of the Opera Café. He had served a two-year sentence, and now no one recognised him. The slippery power-broker of those days had become a fine-tuned teller of stories about powerlessness in the face of physical pleasure; he seemed to have kept nothing but his lucid language. I asked him what had brought him to this quiet new trade.

He had one talent only, he answered: creating something from nothing with nothing but words. He had been prohibited, for as long as he lived, from using this talent to make money multiply. So he no longer used it in the pursuit of symbolic pleasure, but of immediate pleasure alone. And it paid its way. But it was time to go now. It was too full here already.

'You must go on with your story . . .'

'It's finished.'

'Then think of a sequel.'

'All stories end, if you continue them too long, with death. I'd rather not.'

I doubted his motives. I thought that he might be remaining silent for reasons of taste. For how could he bring what he had said already to a higher pitch, if not with something disgusting? I asked him whether he told all ladies the same thing.

'There are variations. But they all end in the same place. That must have something to do with my experience of life . . .'

'Didn't you have a very charming wife?'

'She divorced me.'

'Why?'

His hand on my arm grew a little heavier again. I didn't delve any further. 'And now you live alone?'

'In a *pension*. But it's better if you don't go there with me. All I really have left is my talent. The best thing would be not to come with me at all; it wasn't a good idea on my part. Forget all about it.'

I said nothing, and he added that he had not yet built up the armour to cope with the perils of a relationship. After his release he had immediately gone in search of a new marriage, in the hope that his apathetic view of the world, acquired in prison, would vanish quite naturally at the side of a wife. At first, he said, single ladies had listened to him on the basis of a carefully worded lonely-heart advertisement; his stories, the product of prison fantasies, were merely a test of their approachability; indiscretion and word of mouth had turned this into a source of income. And, a last contact with the opposite sex. But the whole business had been a source of ennui for some time now.

Why was that? I asked. Because it had grown so easy, he replied. He now had the right words for every situation; sadly pleasure was based only on repetition. He longed for something new . . .

'Imagine we're together in your *pension.*'

'It's a very cheap *pension . . .*'

'Make it a bit more elegant. Big, soft beds, heavy curtains; stucco.'

'A nice idea.'

'And we've been lying side by side for hours.'

He laughed abruptly, tonelessly, and I noticed that he had a tendency to weep when he laughed; he wiped the moisture from his eyelids with his little fingers. Then he asked: 'Where had we got to?' and I answered: 'To monotony.' Whereupon he closed his eyes and folded his hands and moved his lips before he spoke.

'Or let's say fatigue. We'd got as far as fatigue; it's night-time. You are lying on your belly, your brow deep in the pillow, I'm sitting beside you and breathing in the scent of your skin. Although we've made love twice, we still haven't consolidated our intimacy. We're not yet on informal terms. I kiss your back. You sigh . . .' And he gave me a quick look and I sighed—I couldn't help it. Then he took our contract out of his suit and slowly crushed it, while he went on in a raised voice. He was now the only person talking in the Opera Café. I took a napkin and wiped the red from my lips, I selected the smile that brings me the most success with people; I combed my hair out of my forehead. Faces stiffened. They were starting to recognise me, me and him too. The craftiest of my acquaintances suddenly stood there open-mouthed. They couldn't believe it. My new friend was now addressing everyone. He was signing off, everyone could tell.

'The small of your back,' he cried, 'grows hollow. You reach behind you and our hands touch, you open yourself to me. I kiss you where no one has ever kissed you . . .' He paused, and the café held its breath. 'But you can kiss *my* arse,' he concluded, and began to laugh in such a way that any chance of re-establishing social contact was impossible. He was almost barking, and I joined in, we were dogs on the loose.

And what then, you would like to know—what happened then? Well, our audience was practically paralysed. The young urban success stories were lost for words. I looked into blank, wooden eyes and gradually came to my senses. It was so quiet that you could hear people walking past outside. Still breathless, my face hot, I was still taking in every detail—the wandering Adam's apples in the leathery necks, the calloused hands, the delicate jingle of jewellery, the goose-bumps beneath the chains. Spat on by an ex-banker and a fool like me, they stood and crouched there, shocked in a very, very ordinary way. I could see only oppressive stupidity, the scattered fragments of a more care-free intelligentsia. My friend put money on the table and rose. He offered me his arm and we walked past the bar. Nobody said a word, not a hand moved, everyone avoided my eyes. Only at the door, in the open air, did I think I heard voices—a wave of fury that chimed wonderfully with my own arousal. We walked without speaking; he in the old school, on my right, I, in a womanly fashion, on his arm; now and again we laughed, but very quietly.

The *pension* was near the station. At the door we solemnly shook hands. 'Farewell,' I said, and darted sideways. I practically fled. I imagined his room small and damp; on the pillow there might be a little bar of chocolate that we would certainly have shared. I felt no sadness in myself, no, that was fine. The only rather idiotic thing was this state of arousal. It simply refused to fade.

Katja Behrens

Love

I didn't want that. I can't understand how things managed to go that far. It was just a glance. It started with him looking at me, not fleetingly and not with curiosity either. He looked at me as no man had looked at me for years. I had left the windows open, and he had simply climbed in.

I had woken, in the dark room, from a dream, thought something was tapping around in my dream, but I could still hear a quiet movement in the house, didn't want to believe there was somebody there, after all the years when there was nothing, wanted to go on sleeping but got up without turning the light on, went barefoot down the stairs.

Downstairs in the corridor I felt for the light switch. Suddenly it was light and a man stood in the living-room doorway, stood there blinking in the light. I wanted to scream. Then I saw that he was very young, and wasn't afraid any more, walked up to him, talked, I don't know what, something. He didn't move and said nothing, looked at me suspiciously, and when I was standing before him he grabbed me hard by the arm. His mouth twitched, and I knew, one false move and he'll hit me, but there was nothing violent about his eyes, rather something questioning. And something astonished.

I'll make some tea, I said, and he let go and put his hand in his trouser pocket, and I turned around, felt my back, the back of my neck, the back of my head, if he has a knife, if it went in my back. I went into the kitchen, saw myself as he saw me from behind, in my nightdress, barefoot, my hair pressed flat. He followed hesitantly and then stopped in the middle of the room. Sit down, I said, while I opened the kitchen cupboard and took out the tea and got cups ready and again—Sit down, because he didn't move. I pulled one of the ever-empty chairs from the table, saw him out of the corner of my eyes sitting sulkily embarrassed, on the edge of the chair, and busied myself cheerfully in the kitchen, when suddenly the crockery flew from the table and shattered in the night-time silence on the floor. I bent down and picked up the fragments one after the other, and tried to remember the number of the flying squad, and thought, with the sharp fragments in my hand and a handle on my little finger, I should run away, out of the house, to my neighbours, took the fragments to the bin without looking at him, and put two new cups on the table and said: Please, I don't have too much crockery, and poured the boiling water over the tea while he looked at me with his arms folded in front of his chest.

If I can't recall the moment from which there was no return, I do know precisely when I first heard his voice and what he said. He said, he said it matter-of-factly: Don't think for a minute about calling the police. And I had pulled myself together so completely that I was able to ask in astonishment: Why should I call the police?

Up to that point everything is clear to me. A thief had broken into my house, he was young, and I was holding him in check with the composure that comes with age. Suddenly it was so silent in the kitchen that I could hear the quiet murmur of the motorway in the distance. We both looked into our cups without saying a word. I could still feel the pressure of his hand on my arm, my uncombed hair, my unprepossessing nightdress made me embarrassed, I lost my sense of security, I couldn't look up, look at him, felt my mouth growing dry and then looked up, straight into his eyes, which were looking at me as if he was now seeing me for the first time, with a tenderness that left me defenceless. I forgot how he had come, his shirt was open, and outside it was light, the first bird was beginning to sing.

When he asked me if I lived alone I should have said, no, my husband's sleeping upstairs, and I'd have been safe. He would have drunk his tea and gone. I would have opened the front door for him and said goodbye to him as one would to a visitor, and then I would have turned the key twice and closed the living-room window, and maybe I would even have called the police. But I nodded, without looking at him, knew that I could now stand up and go into the bathroom to comb my hair, thought into the mirror, you're mad, if only, why didn't you, had to hurry back to the kitchen. You have to tell him now he must go.

When I came back he had stood up, had folded his arms in front of his chest again, and I thought, you don't have to say to him, didn't dare ask whether he wanted more tea, the neighbours would soon be getting up, it was fine, if now, as long as no one saw. But he didn't go, looked out of the window into the dawning day, then turned to me, and I forgot the neighbours and let him draw me towards him, felt his young body in the middle of the kitchen, in the middle between the white kitchen furniture for a moment I was small and sheltered. But then I looked up to him in the light of the kitchen lamp, and I remembered the wrinkles in my face, while he kissed me with lips as careful as an animal's muzzle. I remember I thought he would go when he immediately, almost roughly, let go, but he didn't go, looked suddenly helpless, so I stroked his hair, his black hair, out of his forehead, sat down again, poured tea, confused.

I can clearly remember the terrible afternoon when he left, with a brief embrace in the open front door. I thought I had grown quieter in the past few years, had been so sure of myself. But even when I was clearing up the kitchen I felt the first signs. The house was emptier than it had been for ages. I sat at the table and smoked, one cigarette and another, everything was motionless. It was raining. Only those drops running down the window-pane, the sky grey, the garden comfortless. I crept into bed and tried to sleep. Why did you, could be your son, my son. His hands, so slender and powerful. I got up and stripped the bed. The smell remained. And the shame. Don't think about it, forget it, don't pick up the phone, don't see him again. And when I actually did manage, over the next few days, to let the phone ring, I thought, you've learned. But I didn't feel like doing anything, wandered around the flat, slumped at the kitchen table and smoked, lay in bed and smoked, and sometimes I remembered how he had stretched out his arm so that I could lie down in his armpit, the sharp smell of his warm, sweat-moist shoulders.

I shouldn't have weakened. But the house was so empty it would have driven you mad. If I put on a record the music made me nervous, and if I took it off the silence made me even more nervous. It rained, it rained for days, and the sky was gloomy, as gloomy as my sensibleness. Then I gave up, I don't know when, at some point I went to the phone.

I could barely hear what he was saying, I just listened to his voice, and it was as if I was lying next to him, with my eyes closed, sated and heavy. I answered, without knowing what, and only came to myself again when I had hung up and accepted the invitation. And immediately I thought, of course you don't go, under no circumstances do you go. No one would think mother and son. Don't think about it. Life as before. And I went across to my neighbour, ready to tell a lie if she asked me about the young man who had recently left the house. Just a few words, but no justification, and everything as it had been, as if this shaming story had never been.

I can't remember why I went. I just remember that the night before, shortly before I went to sleep, for a moment I had smelt the heavy scent of his sleepy body, but in the morning I had woken sober and utterly sensible. I was probably getting cocky because I felt so secure, and perhaps I thought, you can't simply stand the boy up. At any rate I caught myself changing, although I hadn't even decided to go. I still remember exactly how I sat in the car, disgruntled because I was too early, wondering what are you doing here, toying with the notion of driving home again.

He looked quite different from what I remembered. Even younger, but beautiful, too beautiful, and far too casual. I went up to his table and wondered how I would ever get through this evening, ashamed that I'd come.

I don't like thinking about how I greeted him with my outstretched hand and, hardly having sat down began fumbling for cigarettes in my bag. He held out his pack to me and said something or other, I just remember being astonished and that I sat dignified in my chair, exhaling smoke, and that I was confused when he asked me what I wanted to eat. I stared at the menu, I'd have preferred not to eat anything at all. Now I know he was embarrassed too and talked because I was looking at him and not listening. A candle burned on the table and I looked at his hand moving slowly under his open shirt, over the skin to his shoulder, coming to rest where it's smooth and round and solid, and when I was listening again an old lady was sitting bolt upright in bed with her hair in a mess screeching Thieves Murderers, still screaming when he had turned around long ago, fled, out the window, down the drainpipe, above him this squealing Thieves Murderers and he had gone down the street quickly but not too quickly, behind him Thieves Murderers getting slowly quieter. And he ate and laughed, and I laughed too and thought my God I hope nobody's listening. He looked at me a little mockingly and after the meal he lit two cigarettes, handed me one and touched my hand quite gently, and suddenly we both grinned as if we'd stolen cherries and were now hiding under a wall spitting out the stones.

I remember convincing myself for a while, must stop, making a fool of yourself, need a man, I need a man and not a child. How foolish to imagine I had made a decision, a firm decision, to bring this story to an end, once and for all, the minute he phoned again. He didn't phone. At first I was worried, then furious, and finally I was filled with longing and waited and waited and listened for the phone that wouldn't ring, and cursed him and couldn't sleep and thought perhaps they've caught him and was startled whenever I saw police in the street. Once a police car drove past the house with two young policemen who looked me over shamelessly. Then I was sure that they'd caught him and couldn't believe it when he was standing at the door the next day, in the rain, laughing, with a dripping, fragrant bouquet.

I can't forget how he pulled me into the rain. The drops fell warmly into our faces, and he introduced me to the trees in the pinewood where I always went walking alone, von Innstetten,* he said, a man with principles, deadly dull, and drips fell from the branches of a venerable old pine, the smell of pine-needles and the ground soft, and when we came out of the wood it had stopped raining. The sun was shining, the hilly country before us, meadows, the grass wasn't high yet, the green still fresh, and beneath it, still visible, the voluptuous curves of the earth. We clambered over a fence by a field and climbed a hill, and at the top I felt the cracked wood of a tree trunk behind me, pressed against the tree, the scratching bark, his body, his hands, and I thought, you're too old for this. We slid down into the damp grass. I saw the sky up above, no longer grey. I looked into a little blue lake in the clouds, and the grass smelled fresh and a bit sharp.

The memory comes and goes. Sometimes when I'm thinking about something completely different it's suddenly there, and however hard I try to shake it off there's nothing to be done. Then again, if I'm like a stone for days and prefer to bear the pain, it withdraws and I've forgotten everything, I'm like a door nailed shut. But when I've finally found my way back to everyday life and no longer want to know anything, then that boy is suddenly lying there again, saying: I don't want to function. Don't want to be roped in. Don't want to get used to things.

I felt superior. If everybody thought like, if we all? And

* Baron Geert von Instetten, the unbendingly principled husband in Theodor Fontane's novel *Effi Briest (trans.)*.

the people he steals from are supposed to do all the work? Did I really imagine I was cured? But yes, I thought, now or never, and tried to separate myself from him. And I didn't wait, not for the first few days.

This was a time when everyone told me I was looking good, and I didn't look into the mirror with resignation, but smiled to myself as if something had been left by time and my resolution. And then I realised I was waiting. I realised from the way I dashed to the phone when it rang, the way I listened when a car parked in front of the house. And when he stood at the door a few weeks later, he was there and the house was lived in again. I leaned against him, looked out the window into the overgrown, sunlit garden.

Was it that moment? From time to time I wander about in my memory searching for the one moment. If I should ever find myself in court, they'll be able to define it precisely. The minute you said you were ready, the jewellery. But I don't think it was the day he brought the chains and bracelets and we argued for the first time. He had put the jewellery on the table and asked: Can you look after this for me for a while? It wasn't that the things were stolen. I was beyond that by then. But that I was thinking, he's using me, he wants to abuse me.

I made tea in silence. He smoked in silence, I laid the table, while he held his arms folded over his chest, cigarette in the corner of his mouth, his eyes screwed up against the smoke. I was looking at the pattern on the tablecloth, the white and blue flowers, surrounded by white and blue rectangles, and a tea-stain, damp beside his cup. When I glanced up he was expressionless.

There's a hole in my cellar, I said. We can hide it there. And I took one of the chains in my hand and thought, now you're part of it. For a few days I was disturbed. But that soon went. And I know exactly when. It was when he helped me close the holdall. And I still can't explain it, that feeling of security at the sight of his arm. I only know that I came to terms with the jewellery in the cellar when I saw him carrying my bag.

Maybe it was on the trip, the very first day, when we took off our shoes and clambered over the rocks. He put his arm around my hips and we waded into the water. Then he let go, to swim. Maybe it was the moment when he emerged laughing from the water, wiped his wet hair from his face, and the sea smelled of salt and fish. Or else it was the night on the beach when we sat in the water, listening to the waves, just a thin moon, and the unchanging back and forth with no beginning and no end. But maybe it was quite different, and I was like the traveller who enters a house where nothing is familiar to him, not his host, not the bed, not the smell of his room. And just as the traveller, although unaware of it, grows a little more accustomed to the strange house each day, he may have become my home, that impetuous man running from his fears, running towards them, this hater of the everyday using himself up in the Sundays he made for himself.

I wasn't there when they caught him. He didn't want me to come.

Not this time. It's too risky. That was the last thing he said. First I was hurt, then I was furious, then I started to get worried, and then suddenly I was suspicious. And if he hasn't in the slightest, if he's met a girl, a young girl, and with the suspicion came the fear, the fear of losing him to this girl, a girl with firm breasts and a young body and already I was wondering what her name was and how long he had known her, I was already quite sure he had lied to me otherwise he'd have taken me with him, and all I could think of was that girl with the young face. I tried to console myself with the idea that she might be stupid and ordinary, and I still felt inferior because she was free of suspicion, of melancholy, stupid but not used up, and I couldn't even hold it against him, she suited him better. I lay in bed until morning, waiting, and when it grew light and he still hadn't come I got up and got dressed. I didn't need to look into the mirror to know I had my old face back.

I waited all day. By evening I couldn't take it any more. I

looked in cafés and pubs and bars, and every time I opened a door, the hope, he'll be here, if I saw a young man in the distance, I thought, it's him. I looked into all the faces and didn't see any and thought maybe they're still in bed.

When a police car drove slowly past me I turned round to go home. Still in my coat, I started drinking. I waited and drank and waited and listened. Just before I woke up, for a moment I had the crazy hope that he had come in the night and was now lying next to me. I kept my eyes closed for a while, almost happy, almost certain that he was there and I had only to reach out my arm to touch him. I resolved not to reproach him with anything, and although I knew very well he wasn't there, I felt around in the bed.

I remember opening the paper and reading the sentence: *He led a life that kicked us all in the face.* I remember standing up and opening the window, opening it wide.

Robert Gernhardt

The Empire of the Senses and the World of Words

The couple making love on the narrow bed had got problems.

'Not so much tongue!' he said. This startled her so much that she stopped using her tongue altogether. He wasn't happy with that either: 'A bit more tongue!' he said.

She thought how simple things once had been. Meanwhile, he was inspecting his erection. It really did seem pretty good. Now he wanted something in return. She could be wetter, he thought, and remembered how wet she always used to get. Or was he already beginning to idealise the past?

'Yes,' he said, 'come!' But he could feel her slipping further and further away from him. Where on earth had she got to? He propped himself up and looked down her body to where his penis kept disappearing into her. 'Vigorous' was a word that came to mind, 'monotony' another. The vigorous monotony of it was beginning to get on his nerves. She moaned softly. Aha! Now I've got her, he thought, and accelerated his thrusts. But she'd only moaned because he had lost her. What had happened to that wonderful talent of his for finding her out, running her to ground, carrying her away? Or maybe she was the one who had waylaid him and taken him with her? She wished she could tell him where she really was, and where she wanted to go, but then she would have to spend so much time explaining; and anyway, now it was their bodies' turn to do the talking. Why did neither of them say anything? She tried to think of a way of extracting herself from the affair without losing face. She moaned, this time in the hope of deluding him.

Flattered, he bit her ear. Now I've really got her, he thought, and he was glad she seemed so ignorant of how little she had him. He had his erection after all—and that was quite enough to be going on with. Now he was going to give her what she wanted. Cheerfully, he bit her ear again.

'Ouch!' she exclaimed unthinkingly, and immediately reproached herself for doing so. In a state of rapture one does not say 'ouch'. She wondered whether there was any chance of her cancelling, or at least neutralising, the 'ouch' by sighing in sensual abandon. But she knew all too well that it was too late for that.

'Did I hurt you?' he enquired, alarmed. So we really are going to have to talk it through, she thought. Appalled at the prospect, she raised her head just enough to lick his neck. She felt guilty, and thought she could only make amends now with a passionate love-bite. Her 'ouch' still rang in his ear, but now the sensation of her tongue at his neck was annoying him. 'What are you doing?' he asked under his breath. Instantly, he regretted it, for wasn't it a passionate woman's right to be sucking at the neck of a virile male without bothering about bruises, cover-up attempts, knowing comments? But then again—does a woman in ecstasy say 'ouch'?

She was not about to let up. She wanted to get it over and done with and hoped to take him by storm, to drag him along with her to orgasm. Or rather, to his orgasm, for she had long since given up the thought of having one. If only he could keep on believing in his! She sucked harder.

'Ouch!' he said. She let her head fall back limply on the pillow and opened her eyes. They gazed searchingly at one another while down below the pushing and pulling continued unabated, for that had almost ceased to have anything to do with them.

To look into another's eyes is always to engage in a test of strength. Eventually, one pair of eyes must avert its gaze—under any normal circumstances. During normal sexual intercourse, however, one of the participants will usually close his or her eyes. In so doing, he or she intimates to the other that they know where they are going and how to get there. Thus a single shutting of the eyelids may often contain more lies than any number of words.

Meanwhile, the couple are still looking into one another's eyes. Each knows that they cannot allow themselves to fail at sexual intercourse. They've never failed at sexual inter- course—a fact which has always given them the strength and sense of purpose to go on sleeping together. Because actually, wasn't sexual intercourse the most unnatural thing you could think of? It might just be possible for two completely differ- ent people to coordinate their bodily energies and juices, but that, on its own, amounted to little more than having intercourse at cross-purposes. Wasn't it equally important that the fantasies, the daydreams and nightdreams, indeed the entire unmentionable dregs in the depths of each person- ality should converse with those of the other in a process of dynamic interchange? And all that, if you pleased, without saying a word? They looked at each other in silence.

They both felt responsible. Neither had been able to pro- vide and experience the required pleasure. Or at least, nei- ther had done so unambiguously enough. Pleasure and pain make good bedfellows, but pleasure and 'ouch' are mutually exclusive. Both knew they had come to a crossroads. But which way should they turn?

Whenever intercourse threatens to go wrong, the very proximity of the participants' bodies ensures an ever greater divergence of their feelings. She feels disappointed; he's in a huff. Is he not in possession of a very serviceable erection? Though for how long? After all, he's no saint. The devil takes the best of erections sooner or later if a woman isn't prepared to show it the appreciation it deserves. Although the man has some knowledge of the physical and psychologi- cal complexities of female desire, he nevertheless considers the constellation of forces required to induce arousal in a man like himself to be of an altogether more complicated nature. The bells should be ringing out for a surefire erection like this; instead she's making life difficult. He feels instantly ashamed of having had this thought—but he's offended none the less. Somewhere deep down inside him flickers the vague notion of a woman who, without voicing the slightest protest, would be only too happy, indeed would consider herself privileged to celebrate an erection like his. He remembers that the woman under him has, until now, been quite capable of fulfilling these requirements—a reflection which wrenches his thoughts back painfully to the crossroads. But where is he supposed to go? He scrutinises the woman's face. Disappointed, she closes her eyes.

She isn't disappointed because of him. She wants the man on top of her to like her; she would prefer to spare him disappointment of any kind, including that of having disappointed her. She would like to share the pleasure he feels at his erection, and regards it as her own failing that she cannot. She used to feel that she could take the credit for his pleasure. Gradually, however, his reliability, the sheer mechanical quality of his physical responses, had begun to upset her. For what did all these erections really have to do with her? Were they not ultimately stimulated by all those characteristics she shared with every other woman? On one occasion he had been turned on by the hair on her legs, a thick fleece which she'd always found rather embarrassing. But the fact that he had loved it had made her love him all the more that afternoon, and since they couldn't make love very often, for she was married, she had always retained a fond memory of that meeting. But that was long ago. She began to form the obscure image in her mind of a man whose response to her was not triggered by the functions she shared with those of her sex, but who loved her for, and inseparably from, everything that was unmistakably unique about her. The earth didn't have to move for her; all she wanted was the feeling of a tongue tenderly setting the hairs of her leg on edge. Why didn't the man on top of her just do that? Why did he have to go to such exhausting lengths? Why was it so impossible for him to accept the tiniest little bit of help? Disappointed, she closed her eyes.

The man, who had seen doubt expressed in the woman's

open eyes, or perhaps even rejection, saw in her closed eyes a sign of success. She had yielded, so he thought. He could now close his eyes again too and accelerate his thrusts. All would be well! Things had always gone well in the past! He shut his eyes and felt her arms close around his neck. She drew his head abruptly down towards hers. He opened his mouth, expecting it to meet hers. But suddenly remembering her unwanted tongue, she moved her head aside at the last second. His tongue met with the pillow. This was so unexpected that he opened his eyes in consternation—without, it must be added, seeing very much. The woman's arms were pressing him face down into the darkness of the pillow. Annoyed, he closed his mouth. How had he come to be licking a pillow? He wanted to return to the light, but her folded arms behind his neck prevented him. A scuffle ensued which neither of them was rightly able to interpret. Having, for her part, decided to stand aside and let him have his way, she saw his jolting and jostling as proof that he, at least, had managed to get himself back on the rails and was now writhing in the grip of lust. She tightened her grip in sympathy. He, in turn, read this as a sign that she had now entered a realm of self-centred gratification where he could not follow. He found this flattering, but was also rapidly running out of air. In order to breathe, he turned his head to one side. It now lay back to back with hers. This panting, Janus-faced head, whose sighs no longer had anything at all to do with carnal desire, belonged to two quite separate bodies, and each of these bodies was intent upon giving the other pleasure. One of them constantly penetrated the other, a motion which the second duly accommodated. For each body had received strict instructions from its respective head to provide the other body with everything that head thought the other body desired and the other head longed for. This eventually grew boring.

There's no going back, though. They are both going to have to stick it out, however unfortunate their position. In fact, they'll have to go through with it even if they change their position. But actually, neither feels up to it. Each of them is hoping for a sign from the other. If only one of them could get across the finishing line, that would at least be worth something. But since each of them is interested solely in the other reaching their goal, nothing moves. Except their bodies, of course, whose dynamics are becoming increasingly absurd. At the same time, they both still think they can keep their knowledge of this absurdity to themselves. They still have their eyes tightly shut, aware that even a glance would reveal all. And thus they remain, each desperately hoping to elicit from the other a tell-tale sigh, a signal that deliverance is nigh. They are—in a nutshell—doomed.

After this had been going on for some time, or rather for much too long, they decided—almost simultaneously—at least to simulate successful arrival. They accelerated their movements and increased the intensity of their sighing and moaning. This unexpectedly harmonious turn of events so much surprised the man and the woman that they opened their eyes wide and turned incredulously to face each other. It simply could not be true that after all their toing and froing they should arrive at their destination together. Looking into each other's eyes, they saw how untrue it was. In fact, it was such a complete and utter lie that the effect of its discovery was to make them promptly shut their eyes again. But now that they had seen through each other, there could be no hope of rescue. They disentangled themselves from one another and opened their eyes, this time only to avoid each other's gaze. She felt for her watch, which she had left on the floor somewhere. There!

'I really must go,' she said, 'Herbert's coming home early today.'

What an insult! Herbert never came home early on a Wednesday. Why had he decided to come home early today, of all days? Offended, he sat up. Attempting to console him, she let her hand run gently down his back. As she did so, her forefinger stopped to investigate a spot on his skin. She scratched at it without thinking. 'Stop that!' he said. Now she was offended, too.

After that, neither of them spoke. They got up, got dressed and went to the bus-stop.

They had to wait for a bus; it would be a while before they could go their separate ways. Eventually she broke the silence: 'You going out anywhere then?'

'No, going back to the flat. Got work to do.'

'Don't overdo it, will you?' She had meant this affectionately, but he couldn't help hearing in it an implied criticism of his sexual performance. Hadn't he done his best? She'd been the let-down!

'Never mind, you'll soon be back with Herbert,' he said.

'What's that supposed to mean?'

'Just what it says.'

'And what does it say?'

'Just what it means.'

She glowered at him. He couldn't help smiling. What was 'say' supposed to mean? What was 'mean' supposed to say? They were nothing but words, signs whose value wasn't fixed and never would be, copulating continually to beget the most beautiful and useful ambiguities. It was enough to vary the tone of your voice! Just my element! he thought. Wasn't it strange to contrast this with what his body had managed to cobble together such a short time ago! What a restricted code body language was! It consisted entirely of true or untrue statements—or rather only true ones, since lies were immediately obvious. The whole relationship—he had been seeing her now for almost two years—suddenly seemed incredible. Unbearable! Bodies were so direct! What they said was always so straightforward. They were only capable of exclamatory statements: I desire you! I want you! That is, when they weren't giving commands of the most basic sort: Yes! Now! Come! They were incapable of forming a subjunctive, these bodies. Figurative language was entirely beyond them. Was there ever such a thing as an ironic erection? An ironic orgasm? What these bodies had to say to each other was about as subtle as a sledgehammer. Or worse even. Me Tarzan, you Jane—wasn't that what their sweat-drenched dialogues on the narrow bed boiled down to?

Again, he had to smile.

'What are you thinking?' she asked. Instead of giving her an answer, he pummelled his chest with his fists and let out a Tarzan-like cry, which, because of the bystanders, was somewhat subdued, if not almost soundless: Uaahuahiohuu!

'Herbert really is coming home earlier today,' she said, mistaking his almost whispered Tarzan-cry as a form of humorously voiced protest. Almost as though she were trying to squeeze out of him some sort of consent, or jolt him into seeing her side of things, she leant her arms on his chest and gave his shoulders a firm shake: 'Hey, you!'

'Me Tarzan,' he said, 'you Jane?'

'Be serious for once!'

As if he hadn't been doing exactly that all afternoon! No, longer, for the best part of two years! He had taken everything seriously: her, Herbert, how endangered her marriage was, how dangerous their love was—and more than anything else he had taken their pleasure seriously, since that was the only thing which justified putting her wedded bliss and the peace of mind of both of them continually at risk. He had gone astray in a stony desert of emotional and carnal seriousness, and now he felt an overpowering desire to seek his salvation as quickly as possible in the nearest swamp where the ground was continually shifting and actions and words had no consequences; actions because they had no effect, words because they had no meaning.

'What's on your mind?' she enquired again.

He couldn't possibly have told her. He knew she wanted to hear a clear expression of patent emotional commitment— 'something she could live with,' was the way she had once put it. The problem was that his train of thought was carrying him deeper and deeper into a region of non-committal vagueness. He had left Tarzan and Jane far behind him and was emerging from a dark tunnel where it had gradually dawned on him that people had been demanding seriousness of him all his life: first priests, then teachers, and finally women. He had escaped with impunity from the gravity of the Creed and the grindstone of the school textbook, only to let himself get caught up in the earnestness of carnal desire. Initially, he had seen every decent act of illicit sex as a kick in the pants of those very forces that had once done their best to impose their idea of decency on him. But didn't these apparent adversaries ultimately share the same interests? Wasn't their credo ultimately the same: 'Get down to the essentials'? And yet he had always felt so inessential. He had always had to pretend in order to keep up appearances: first unshakable faith, then diligence at school, and this afternoon—physical desire. Today hadn't been the first time, either. But who was he making all these sacrifices for?

'Tell me what you're thinking, for heaven's sake?' she asked. Wasn't it more of a command this time?

Thought control! Hadn't that always been the declared intention of all these totalitarian powers—these priests, teachers and women? Now he was really going over the top, and enjoying it too.

Finding one's way in life was difficult enough without signposts like 'truth' and 'lies' pointing you in all the wrong directions. Hadn't humanity survived only because a part of it at least had managed to dodge these signposts rather than following them blindly? He felt his mind churning out one thought after another; and as if wishing to apologise, he took her in his arms. She searched his eyes for an explanation. A bus came. It was the wrong one. They turned once again to each other. He felt he had to do something; against his better judgement he tried to give himself a meaningful, slightly pained look. Perhaps that would do the trick.

'Say something!' she implored.

He turned on the pain a little bit more and allowed himself to be carried away on the voluptuous current of his thoughts. A black GI with a huge ghetto-blaster had joined the bus queue, and he was reminded of something a friend had said to him the day before about why a common acquaintance had suddenly packed up and emigrated to the USA: 'He used to have all those girlfriends, didn't he.' So what? 'Well, about six months ago he got to know this black woman.' Oh, really? 'Yeah, and black-sweetie-pie chased all his other honey-pies away,' and then he had gone back to the States with her . . . But he had lost any interest in what his friend was telling him. What had caught his imagination was black-sweetie-pie and all the other honey-pies, the conversion of grey, ashen fact into shining revelation, the glorious transub-stantiation of material into spirit, reality into fancy—

'Say something! Please!'

Reality back again! 'Sweetie-pie,' he said beseechingly.

'What?' She took a step backwards. He was about to explain to her what had made him choose a term of affection which neither of them had ever used for each other before, when her bus came. The moment had come which, until today, had meant temporary separation, mutual reassurance, kept promises to see each other again. But today they hesi-tated. 'Hey!' she pleaded, one foot already on the bus. 'Black-sweetie-pie!' he replied, unable to suppress his laughter.

'You idiot!' She got into the bus without looking back. She kept her eyes to the front as the bus left, remaining in that position while it disappeared into the distance.

Wounded, he followed the bus out of sight. Actually, 'idiot' was quite an ambiguous word. Hadn't it originally meant someone who kept themselves out of the public sphere, a person of private means? Had it not taken centuries to degenerate into a synonym of fool, jester, madman? And didn't both meanings apply to him?

'Me idiot,' he thought, and he liked the words so much that he repeated them to himself under his breath.

He had a dictionary of foreign words back in the flat. When he got home he would look up what an idiot really was. He turned to go. 'I'm an idiot,' he said to himself, eager not to forget what it was he wanted to do: 'I'm an idiot!'

Botho Strauss

from *Congress*

The scene is the study and adjacent salon of Professor Tithonus (actually: ALBIN SCHERRER), an emeritus oceanologist and ardent autograph collector. His fourth-floor flat in an old building is spacious and tranquil, and the windows and balcony face on to a green courtyard, the tiled perimeter walk of which is shaded by young chestnut trees and jasmine bushes.

The interior is on the ornate side, but not overdone or cluttered. Against the walls, bookcases alternate with glass cabinets containing mementoes of field trips, exotic art and artefacts, masks and votive figures, or valuable manuscripts and incunabula. To the rear there is a closed grand piano, on it a framed black-and-white photograph of the Vatican Euterpe—muse of lyric poetry and music.

To the fore of the salon, seated in a semi-circle at a low glass table with orientally voluted edges and feet, are the following people: FRIEDRICH AMINGHAUS, the reader. Across from him, separated by the length of the table: HERMETIA, the Professor's young wife. Beside and more or less between the two of them: CZECH, a friend of Tithonus and his colleague of many years' standing, an elderly but not aged man with a low, wrinkled forehead, reddened eyelids and ashen cheeks. It is a warm autumn evening—doubtless the very same evening of 16 September when Friedrich was originally to have given his lecture at the TIME FOR THOUGHT Congress. Through the open door of the balcony the footfall of the Professor can be heard from time to time pacing the courtyard below. From the open

*window of a ground floor apartment issue the unfeeling synch-
ronized voices of the perpetual TV film, which the* CONCIERGE
is watching, doing crossword puzzles at the same time.

HERMETIA	*(reclining in her broad armchair, she looks up from her book and kicks restlessly under the edge of the carpet with the toe of her shoe)* What is he up to? How much longer? He's been walking up and down the courtyard all evening—the old fellow.
CZECH	Please, don't refer to him as 'the old fellow'. He's your husband, after all.
HERMETIA	What do you think? Will he let me go? What will his decision be?
CZECH	I don't know.
HERMETIA	You've known him so much longer, you know him much better than I do. Surely he must see reason at last.
CZECH	Here you both are, with eyes for each other only, and it keeps getting harder to keep you apart. And down below is my oldest friend. And what about me? Am I a go-between? Am I here to prevent you from getting together? What am I still in a position to make or mar?
HERMETIA	He can't keep walking up and down for ever!
CZECH	He! You talk as if he were a stranger! Till not so long ago, till this happy young man put in an appearance, he was yours, yours.
HERMETIA	*leaps to her feet* I'm going to check if he's started shuffling or groaning or muttering yet.
HERMETIA	*crosses to the balcony, the open book in her hand, and leans over the railing*
CZECH	How did you get into this sealed-up world, anyway?
FRIEDRICH	I was returning a valuable edition of Kammerer's *Law of Series* to the old man. It was still among my father's books when he died. He

	asked after it shortly before I left to attend the congress here.
CZECH	You call him the old man—but he wasn't that old, not before you crossed his threshold. It was a real heyday in this home. That marvellous man and that carefree girl lived a life that was magical: I saw it with my own eyes. Now it has all crumbled to dust—and you cannot imagine what it was like.
FRIEDRICH	We have no power over the passing moment.
HERMETIA	*cries out softly on the balcony, returns to the room*
HERMETIA	My book. I dropped my book into the courtyard!
FRIEDRICH	How nice. How lovely!
CZECH	And what did he do?
HERMETIA	He picked it up and popped it in his pocket. Now I don't know what page I was on.
CZECH	Sit back down, precious—you'll have time enough to read the book straight through from cover to cover again.
HERMETIA	Do you suppose he looked up—even once? He just walks up and down, pops the book in his pocket—he'll never decide.
FRIEDRICH	My beloved, sweet sovereign. All that counts is that we are not discouraged. It cannot take longer than this one night. We shall ... what's the matter? What's wrong? ... Have pity: I have to go to her. I have to soothe her!
CZECH	Patience, Aminghaus.
FRIEDRICH	But just look at her hands. She's beside herself!
HERMETIA	My book's gone, my book ... (*to* CZECH) Will you get my book back for me, my dear, good friend?
CZECH	He'll want to give it back to you himself.
HERMETIA	You're so heartless, so cold! You're on his side!
CZECH	You're hurting him the most!
FRIEDRICH	*agitated*

We're hurting him the most! You are too—hurting *us*!

CZECH I am obliged, I am condemned, to remain in my place till he returns. It is not a task that can possibly be free of inner conflict and injustice ...

HERMETIA Tell us a story, Friedrich! You can see the old man's out to wear us down and sap our energy with his everlasting thinking-it-over. I beg you both, don't let me dry up here in my own heat as if I'd been poked with an incubus's fork. Either we manage to keep each other going with candid stories, and raise our desire and attraction so high that mastering them earns us extra dividends of lust ... or else something utterly unreasonable, something that breaks all the rules and everything we agreed on, will happen right this very second!

The two men, elder and younger alike, were now witnesses as Hermetia, as if the loss of her book had deprived her of a drug she was addicted to, began to tremble all over, hugging both arms tight to herself. They also saw a cold, feverish gleam come into her graphite-coloured eyes, giving her sensuous face a wretched, almost wily expression for a moment. Friedrich, at all events, saw at once that the condition of the woman he desired, to whom he had repeatedly revealed his feelings but whom he had never touched more intimately than with a firm clasp of the hands, was worrying, and that she needed prompt help and care. Without preamble, therefore, and without more ado, he began to improvise a story that came to him from out of the penumbra of the closing days of the congress and which he now refined somewhat for Hermetia, half inventing it and half re-telling.

'A middle-aged man whose health was in a critical state had travelled to a town in which he was a stranger, to attend a conference. He had gone out to lunch and was sitting outside a small restaurant with a glass of mineral water, waiting for

the waiter to take his order. There were only a handful of
tables and chairs outside in the square, which was closed to
traffic, and was like an air well, hemmed about by a backdrop
of office blocks, bank headquarters and insurance companies.
The man was watching a muffled figure busy rubbing and
fluffing at a gilded banister railing under a lofty portal. This
person was wearing a parka with the hood over his head,
and under it some kind of tracksuit which also had a hood,
which he had pulled far down over his forehead.

"Aren't you the *Schwanendreher?*" he had wanted to ask,
at first, thinking of the old song, of Hindemith's music. Only
the sick or the half insane go about so warmly clothed in
summer, he thought.

"Aren't you the railing cleaner?"

It was very hot, and, though he was sitting in the shade,
the sweat was running into the man's clothes. The waiter
came out, rubbed out the menu on the blackboard, and
wrote up a new day's special, at a reduced price.

"I have been mute for so long. Why don't I go over to
the railing cleaner and ask him something?" The man was
trembling badly as he rose; the fever had left him weak, and
he had to hold on to the arm rest as everything went black
for a moment.

The muffled cleaner made an altogether sensible reply—
grinning slightly, it is true, and revealing his rotten teeth and
the gaps between them. He was not, however, someone who
rebuffed approaches. He said: "The railing goes up a very
long way. You can't see the end of it, and I've been cleaning
it for more than a lifetime."

"The railing is very high. Gilded, too—or rather, with a
brass covering . . ."

"Yes, it *is* high, and if I'm to carry on cleaning it higher
up I'll be needing a long ladder pretty soon."

"But whoever could hold on to that railing? And where
are the steps that ought to be coming down between the two
railings?"

"They don't need any steps to get down. They find their
own way."

"Who? Who comes down here?"

"The giants. This will be the last point where they hold the railing before they set foot on the earth and the earth bends under their weight."

The man returned to his table, sat down, and drank some of the water. The waiter came out, rubbed out the menu on the blackboard once again, and again wrote up a new one, at a further reduced price.

The man thought: "It must be my illness and tiredness that have brought me to this part of town. That must be why I am seeing things unclearly. Deep within myself, where I am healthy and not yet gnawed away by the illness, I do not believe in the things I see. But it may also be that, in this central but none the less most remote part of town, reality itself is like a mixing box, leaving out some of its components as it chooses and artificially adding others, and so creating an area that has been destabilised in various ways, a place where it is not possible to take one's bearings in the usual sense. And even if the phenomena one sees are not entirely unfamiliar, but still have a known quality to them, it may be because this technique is capable of achieving infinite interchange between things that did really exist at some earlier date and things that exist now, forging a single improbable entity out of them. At least it is not my own mechanisms, my own memory, that are making up things like this. I have never seen the likes of it in my life, never dreamed or thought up anything of the kind. It is the sleep of the outside world—not mine! No, it's not mine!"

It was now almost midday, and the sun was behind one of the office blocks, leaving the city centre square quiet and round in the shade. A girl came by, wearing a short, tattered dress and carrying a neon letter under her arm. She sat down at one of the unoccupied tables and began to fondle the letter *O*.

"Don't you agree," she asked the sick man, "that once the garland of all your experiences is woven and complete your self disappears into its hollow, inner circle, into its hollow?

When something completes a circle, it embraces a hollow or vacancy in the centre."

"Yes," said the man, "you're right. What is alive in us is only the edge, the garland, the *ronde* of events. The periphery of what has happened to us. The chain of humiliations. It is the outer ring that closes. The ring road around our city centre, with the traffic of people and events circulating on it. Only the arrow of time pierces the heart."

"The letter still glows in the dark as it always did," said the grown-up girl, "a friend of mine had the nerve to detach it from the roof of a bank and steal it. By the way, it's the first letter of my name. I'm Oda."

"Your ring, your initial, is like the earth's atmosphere, repelling the impacts from without, the great events of the world that are plunging along the track to your heart, the great deaths and disasters. They sheer off and shatter, dispersing into the band of dust made of countless little rotating events. Only words reach your heart. The great deaths will never make it that far. They will never touch you."

He was already very ill, but he said: all my wounds are outside of me.

He went up to the dark room above the restaurant with the girl, and there she crouched before him on her elbows and knees with the *O* about her hips. She raised her ample softness up through the glowing initial, and the man, with all due care so as not to break the glass, and yet with all the liberties he pleased to take, was now able to enjoy her body.'

Hermetia had to smile when she had heard this little fantasy. It was only too transparent that she herself was meant to be the one who filled the ring. Her condition had noticeably improved as Friedrich told his tale. Now she was cheerful again, and wanted to see herself more boldly mirrored in the reader's eyes, and to hear more twilight transactions of the same kind.

'I have not told you yet,' continued Friedrich, 'that after

our first meeting in this apartment I came across you twice in the next day or so, in town, quite by chance, without your noticing or recognising me. No doubt you remember that afternoon when I brought the old man that book he already supposed to be pretty much lost forever. We sat in his study, and he talked about happy days of close friendship with my father, till in the end some trifle prompted a row and they went their separate ways, for good. While he was relishing his memories, I could hear the short sharp tapping of high heels on the parquet floor beyond the half-open sliding door, accompanied by the muted rattle of crockery, and before long I saw the back, the long hair and the slender body of a young woman stretching up on tiptoe, her thighs against the edge of the dresser and her short, knee-length skirt taut on her graceful, well-made body, reaching up a naked arm to the topmost shelf to fetch down a tea set and a vase. As I listened absent-mindedly to the old man, I began to wonder who the beautiful creature might be. Who was the woman walking to and fro out there? When would she come in to join us at last? When would she be standing before me, where I could look at her? At long last the tea arrived, and there you were, putting the tray on this table. I stood up, taking a good look, and the old man told you who I was and introduced you as—his wife! I must have blushed to the roots. I know that I instantly let go again of the soft, warm hand you gave me. To be confronted with your brightness and ease completely threw me, and I felt apprehensive—just as one is hesitant before a conquest, when one senses and gauges the entire audacity and gravity of it, and is tempted to quickly turn on one's heels. But it was already too late. Your smile, welcoming and with the promise of danger, revealed that you felt no differently than I did. As we said hello, you had crossed to me, and at that moment you were the most threatened of people I could imagine, equally far from the familiarity of home and the enormity of the unknown. You had set the cups down before us and poured out the tea, and had promptly turned your back on our talk once again and begun to pick dead leaves off the plants at the far side of the room, by the grand piano. Now I was on the alert for any opportunity to turn and look at you unobtrusively, to catch your earnest, unprotected gaze. Presumably the old man realised fairly soon that he had only half my attention, because suddenly he broke off and looked at you with a strange, ambivalent smile, and with what seemed to me the improper pride of an owner, as if you were the finest in his collection of exquisite foreign treasures. "Strictly speaking, my dear," he said to you, checking out of the corner of his eye to see if I was catching his learned allusion, "strictly speaking I ought to compare you to the goddess Eos, the goddess of the dawn, eternally fresh and youthful. For there can be no doubt, can there, that I myself am your old Tithonus, unable to die?"

For a moment I did not know who he meant or what myth he was referring to.'

'Professor Tithonus! Ah! Professor Tithonus!' groaned Hermetia, facetious and playful.

'Absolutely!' the reader remarked, aping the old man— 'professor of marine studies, known for his research into sea monsters'—and he too indulged in disrespectful and affected witticisms.

Czech, the old friend, warned them both not to make fun of the old man, the injured husband, and urged them at least to spare him the sound of their laughter from above as he paced his heavy rounds of the courtyard below.

'Very well,' resumed Friedrich, his smirk a little more subdued: 'Tithonus, as the poor old man was called, though immortal, was nevertheless becoming old and childish, for Eos, eternally young, had made the wretched mistake of forgetting to ask Zeus to grant Tithonus perpetual youth. So, although he was cared for and fed by his beloved, he was kept hidden away in a dark room, on account of his terrible appearance, and there he grew gradually shrunken and wasted. It was to him that the old man was alluding, and he was still referring to the myth, toying with it in a manner heavy with significance, as he finished by admonishing you, his young wife: "If one can wish for things, one ought not to forget half the wish. Wishes have to be complete too. This presupposes that the person making a wish already has a part in the world that is wished for, and above all the world that it is possible to wish for."

Before the professor, still half turned to me, doled out his amusing lecture to you, you had already sat down beside us and were leaning back quietly in your armchair. It now struck me that you repeated one particular physical gesture: you liked raising your arms behind your head, elbows out, to loosen the hair out of the nape of your neck. It seemed an uncalled-for movement, and to me, therefore, who as I read the very first pages, registering every signal and lure of an enthralling stranger, it appeared an invitation, both unconscious and deliberate, to view freely your upstretched body, and your raised breasts straining under a thin, dark red blouse. To my way of reading, this is the "bared armpit" position adopted by scantily clad odalisques on divans in countless paintings. It is the well-known trope of complaisant welcome. It is apparent through any kind of clothing, and universally seems the most willing of the attitudes a clothed woman can decently strike. Given this loaded beginning, you will perhaps understand how greatly it dazzled and terrified me, even drove me away, when I happened to see you the following day, quite by chance, down at the lakeside where people go swimming. You had been sailing, and were guilelessly unpeeling your black rubber suit in full view of the other bathers, till it hung like a cut-away second skin about your naked hips. Your moist, warm breasts, my inmost secret, were now revealed and visible to all, bared with the indifference that goes with sport. How shamelessly chaste ... how innocent of intent, how uninhibited! There you stood exposed on the grass, oblivious of desire to the very depths of your sex, *neutral*, without any image of yourself. I closed my eyes in alarm: even so young and unconstrained a woman must surely know that something so choice, extremity of the tree, fulfilment and fruit, can never mean as little to another person as it does to herself when she happens to be exhausted and is simply getting her breath back ...

It was a comfort to me, and a sensual relief, when that same evening at the Lord Mayor's reception I met a woman dressed both stylishly and sinuously. She was wearing a broad-brimmed carmine-red hat which she never took off despite the fuggy air in the packed, low hall where the congress participants were having their drinks. There, Hermetia, perhaps for the first time in my life, I managed to take my delight in pure temptation, in the layers that clothe the body, and savoured it to the full. Don't undress me! that indolent creature seemed to warn me. You can only have me in my clothes; all I have is this clothed state; only dressed can I cast shame to the wind. And was it not so? How often a woman's negligent, or simply accidental, or utterly ingenuous exposure had stunned my senses and robbed me of all my strength. Not till this woman, without removing her hat, amiably put her ultimate nakedness, her vitalising skin on show through the tight, soft wrap of her clothing, did I experience the pleasure one can take in a body in all its true and sinuous grace. In the semi-concealment of a bay window, not quite withdrawn from the gathering, we clung and touched more deeply than the naked ever can. It was not long before the violence and earnest of our desire overpowered us. Her firm features dissolved into astonished tears that coursed down her clothing, while I marked her with a visible stain. Her obsessive craving for intimacy and for the most private of pleasures ran as high and strong as mine, and seemed insatiable.

Nevertheless, I could not put your image out of my mind. The impact of seeing you *thus*, without meeting you again, continued to afflict me. But when it happened a second time, and you appeared before me once again by chance, out of nowhere, the experience became a more painful, almost unbearable test. You must realise that for a long time my physical spirit had not come across anything quite as contemptible as the coarseness of the young, careless woman who shoved past me at the cinema, clutching her travel bag and Coke bottle and pressing her round soft buttocks into my privates as I rose politely from my seat. She leaned forward to say something that couldn't wait to a friend two rows down, without in the slightest realising what intimate bodily contact she was making. And that friend addressed across the rows of heads was none other than you, my beloved Hermetia. You half turned and raised your head, and it was you I saw beyond that coarse, unfeeling back, you whose eye I tried despairingly to catch and constantly failed, while all the time your friend was so flush against me that I imagined I could feel her vocal chords tensing right down to the backs of her thighs. Or rather, I did not feel it, it was my humiliated sex. And if my sex had done as it was plainly inclined, and had suddenly gone its own way and pushed on ahead into that perfect, heedless voluptuousness clad only in some thin, flimsy fabric—I am sure the woman, utterly bereft of the physical spirit as she was, would have thought that too was merely an accident, or else she would have pushed the insignificant resistance aside, so eagerly was she leaning forward to you, so thoughtlessly was she leaning her back against the pilaster relief of a human being.'

As Friedrich came to a close, Hermetia was restlessly shifting her position in the broad armchair, and he asked her concernedly whether he had said anything wrong or anything she found unpleasant. She denied it and affirmed she had been hearing precisely what she desired to hear—though of course her desire was forever needing to be controlled afresh. 'I do not know where to put my feet. I perch them on the armchair and sit on my calves. I put them on the floor and they take on a life of their own, wanting to wander over to you . . . I clasp my arms around my knees, so they don't— dear Czech!' (and here she turned abruptly to the old friend) 'I'm afraid I shall have to go out for a minute and freshen up.'

'Dear Hermetia,' replied the distressed chaperon, 'I have been expressly requested not to order or forbid you to do anything. Even so, I should like to ask if you could possibly bring yourself to stay with us, and so not endanger further this fragile group we now constitute. Only as long as each one of us three remains in view of the others is there still a certain guarantee that any excitements that might arise will ebb away again, be balanced, and not get out of control. For this reason I should now like to put in a little story of my own, which I hope will calm you down somewhat. It may not have a very soothing ending, true, but still it should serve as an example to return us to the level-headed patience we need up here if we are to handle this difficult interval with any skill. So now imagine a spacious ante-room, almost a salon, on the executive floor of a modern business enterprise. The architectural design is friendly and graceful, and the room is furnished with cool, soft pieces. The marble panels, green plants and splashing fountains make waiting there a pleasant thing. In this case, the people in the room, meeting there for the first time, are the old friend and the new-found lover of the man sitting in the director's room to the rear, behind a closed door, apparently occupied with business that cannot wait. The friend has travelled here from abroad expressly because a grim and all too clear dream had recurred more than once. In it, the director of the company, once his patron and benefactor, was facing a lethal threat which he himself was unaware of. The friend has made his long journey purely in order to warn the man, and to see for himself that he is well—to warn him against the very person now sitting on the salmon-red leather seat beside him. For she was the one, unmistakably, that he had seen as the harbinger of doom in his dream. It is hardly possible to imagine the initial horror that overcame him when he saw her again, in person, right outside the door of the threatened victim. Yet to his amazement it soon emerged that this beautiful suspect—cheerful, modest and complaisant as she was—did not match the pallid dream image at all. There, though her appearance was the same, she had been aflame with intricate pride, and had been instantly recognisable as a herald of damnation. But in reality the person sitting beside him was ingenuous and warm-hearted, and he was already beginning to have serious doubts about the meaning of his nocturnal visions and to feel that he had essentially made his journey in vain—except, of course, that he would be glad to see his friend again in a moment, and to congratulate him in all sincerity on his happy choice in love.

Meanwhile, the businessman and designer was sitting in the solitary refuge of his office, by no means busy with urgent business but rather staring idly into space, as if crippled by his unappeasable suspicion. That alone was the reason why he was keeping the two people who were so close to him waiting as if they were strangers come to petition him, and a nuisance. He suspected them both, in different ways. When he was told of his friend's sudden arrival, his first and only thought was that he had come just to collect an old debt, the embarrassing remainder of a demand one would have thought long since settled, dating back to a take-over the two of them had once launched together and in the course of which they had both lost a great deal of money.

He was loath to let his new lover in, on the other hand, because he himself had had a dream the previous night, in which he had been persecuted by her and humiliated in the cheapest of ways. He had discovered that from the very start she had been deceiving him. Indeed, he had seen her in the very act of committing her infidelity (though without being able to identify her lover) and had seen her, magnified and all too close, with a palpable immediacy that is given to dreamers alone when they see what has not (yet?) happened but can no longer be averted once they have seen it. And so he felt incapable of facing her that morning, until the dream had been completely deleted in his blood.

Meanwhile, the two suspects waiting outside were becoming more relaxed and easy with each other, plainly finding each other pleasant company as they talked. At length they came to the conclusion that, in the office, one item of business must be leading to the next, and that they would not be called in for the foreseeable future.

So they decided to go out for the time being, and have a light lunch somewhere nearby, then perhaps go for a stroll about town. Later, they decided, when office hours were almost done for the day, they would return to that drearily stylish ante-room.

When they emerged on to the street and were trying to cross over, the woman, who was revelling in a free morning with nothing to do as a schoolgirl might, flung caution to the wind and skipped quickly and nimbly through the heavy, roaring traffic. The man, in every bit as good spirits, was not about to be left behind, and dashed after her without looking right or left. But at one point he hesitated for just a fraction of a second, and stepped into the path of a thundering articulated lorry as it was overtaking. He was flung aside by the impact, into the squealing traffic, and instantly killed as another vehicle ran him over.'

It was scarcely to be expected that this story would find favour with its audience, nor did it. Neither did it calm the two others who were waiting; rather, it robbed them of courage, and clouded their mood. Hermetia was especially reproachful, finding that the old friend had made too make-shift a job of encoding his anecdote. 'So you think that for one of us three this night-watch will end in death? Is that what you're saying? Well, it can only be me. I am sure to be the target when he suddenly stops walking round the court-yard getting nowhere, loses his head, and puts a violent end to a situation that has grown too tense.'

The reader, however, whose spirits had likewise been depressed, murmured: 'I am the intruder, I must be the friend in the story who has come in a hurry and is caught by fate, by the disaster that has been foreseen and which shifts abruptly from the one to the other of them.'

'But,' objected Czech, 'if anyone should be seeing himself in this little story, it must be me. Only I can be this wretched fellow who ends up paying for every injury—I am the one who has not given his best friend the loyal and exclusive support he needed!'

Hermetia had now sat up in her armchair and cut him off, determining in a tone of casual yet cruel relief: 'He will kill himself. I have no doubt about it. As soon as he grasps that our relationship can no longer be broken off or stopped . . .'

Friedrich, flinching palpably on hearing this quiet but forceful blast of hardness and coldness from the mouth of his beloved, was now at pains to distract himself and the others from morose thoughts of this kind; so he pressed on with a more sensual tale, in which, he explained, a dream also acted as a kind of carrier, infecting day with night's contagion and making reality uncertain with visions.

'The little incident that follows, which can hardly claim to be a story, is also governed by the arrangement that keeps Hermetia and myself apart here. Its terms alone decide our words at present, and are making us talk of desire to each other in ways that, if we could only act, would never occur to us or cross our lips. But now let us see whether *talk*— shallow and empty though it has become—might not prove once more, in our distinct case, its power over the physical spirit, and thus ultimately over the body too.'

'Recently I had a dream in which I was in a marquee in the country. Unemployed artistes, and others who could only perform a single number and could find no circus that wanted them to do it, were showing off their bizarre tricks, which generally took only a short time to perform. As the climax, the one and only genuine acrobat of Death was announced. Two awkward characters made their appearance, a man and a woman, both dressed in the same grey, the woman (who was only the assistant) wearing a rough blouse that was boldly open. They took up positions beneath a kind of horizontal bar on which an immense roller that looked like a steel press was mounted. The acrobat now demonstrated that, when a motor was switched on, the bar revolved, and anyone who might be balancing on it would almost inevitably be caught in the roller (which was also turning), first by the trouser leg and then entire, bit by bit, as the unstoppable crusher pulped him completely. He showed this by pushing empty wastepaper baskets along the bar. They were caught up in the steel rollers, cracked and splintered, and were flattened.

The audience grumbled from the very start and expressed their doubts that anything sensational or really daring could be performed on that low bar with its excessive machinery. Even before his act, they struck up a debate with the artiste, who for his part—before he had given his performance!— repeatedly assured them that anyone on the bar would indeed be in guaranteed mortal danger. Several members of his Czech artiste family had already fallen victim to the murderous contraption, he said. The audience retorted that the risk was not really palpable; it had to be apparent if people were to be thrilled. There would not be much to see, would there, if someone balanced on a moving bar and *wasn't* caught by the roller? It wouldn't be much of a show, would it? Apart from simply averting the one disaster, the stunt involved no prowess at all, and, in any case, on that low bar the act could never be breathtaking, no matter how skilful. The deadly machine was unusual but superfluous. Unlike a performance on the high wire, it could hardly touch human fears, nor could it aesthetically ennoble and redeem the audience's greed for sensation. The image of the contraption was unimaginable. They did not even want to see the act. The audience refused so much as to see a brief demonstration of the death acrobat's skill, considering that, whatever the nature of that skill, he was putting it to the wrong ends, in their opinion—to ends that ran counter to people's hunger for a spectacle, and were alien to the world of circus. They chased the artiste and his assistant, who looked as if she might be his sister, out of the big top.

After the show, I came across the two of them by their car, busy tying down their pieces of equipment on the luggage rack. I talked to them, making it clear that I did not share the audience's ungenerous attitude and honestly regretting that I had not been able to see their act. But they did not seem particularly interested. In fact, I was astonished to see how little the wretched incident had apparently affected them. They simply carried on packing up their things

and chatting to me. It turned out that, appearances notwith-
standing, they were a married couple, not brother and sister,
and normally they worked as caretakers in a factory owner's
country villa which was unoccupied most of the time. Even
so, their features were of almost identical cut. The eyes of
both were dark and rather narrow, almost slits, and their
bodies were of the same muscular kind that suggested farm-
ing backgrounds. The woman's figure, in particular, possessed
a powerful sexual expressiveness. Her body was tough,
earthy, firmed-up from use, and accustomed (as my dream
revealed to me repeatedly) to being there for her husband's
pleasure at any interval during the day's work, in the shed
or the garden, anywhere at all, rough and ready, in the
darkness under the hall stairs or on the washboards in
the cellar—anywhere rather than in bed of a weary evening.
There she stood, casually, her blouse still open as it had been
when she defencelessly offered her charms to the audience,
her bare flat breasts visible from the side and the little bolts
of her nipples rubbed stiff against the rough material of the
blouse. They talked about leaving Czechoslovakia, and about
the many circus shows they had performed there, with great
success—always, though, with their children, too, who had
always been better at putting on a show on the bar than they
themselves were. As the woman reached up with both arms
to the car roof to tie something down, her blouse rode up
and her skirt slipped below her navel. With the great clarity
only possible in hypnosis I could see the thick hair of her
shadows curling over the waistband. I asked if they were not
afraid of reprisals against their children whom they had left
behind at home, but she said no and smiled a crooked,
trickster smile: "Our official reason for being here is to look
after refugees."

Immediately I knew what they were hinting. In everything
they did, they were in fact acting for an eastern secret service.
Their sole task—camouflaged by a multitude of pretexts—
was to track down fellow-countrymen who had fled, spy on
them, and perhaps recruit or blackmail them.

At the word "refugees", the two of them vanished, and

with them the entire setting of the dream. In what followed—
in accordance with the anarchic logic of dreams—I was
involved in dangerous chases, till in the end I seemed about
to be cut apart by the razor-sharp steel rims of Mercedes
steering wheels.

A morning or two later, as I went down to the street to
go to the newsstand as I do every day, I could hardly believe
my eyes when suddenly the selfsame woman with the somewhat Asiatic face, the woman I had had such intimate
glimpses of in my dream, was there before me, standing in
the doorway of the next building, sheltering from the rain.
Once my initial confusion had subsided, I felt a great urge
to talk to her. I found it quite impossible to think of her as
a total stranger. She for her part cast me a wary glance as I
mounted the steps towards her and asked if I might tell her
my dream. I had not spoken more than a few sentences
when I realised that she did not find what I was telling her
particularly strange. She nodded a number of times, as if she
could confirm everything I said and did not need to correct
anything. In disbelief I asked if there could really be something to my nocturnal imaginings, and if I might really have
hatched out the whole thing after simply happening to see
her in the crowd somewhere and registering her unusual
face.

No, she said, nodding more violently, it was exactly as I
had dreamed it, or more or less. That was how things were
with her, with her and her husband. And—she fell silent
for a moment—and the "political" matter was correct too.
Roughly speaking, it was true that they were both in the
employ of their fatherland, though their every movement
and activity was not governed with the fantastic rigour I had
imagined.

The question I now faced was whether my nighttime con-
sciousness was a place of transit for other people's realities,
or whether I was not merely being fooled by a delusion, and
this young woman was taking her cues from what I said
and was really no more than a wily street girl capitalising on
my confusion to lure me up to her room?

I decided not to believe a word she said. She pushed open the front door behind her, and we entered a cool stairwell in semi-darkness, where a lit-up lift was just going up past the mezzanine floor. Without my saying a word, she undid her clothing, and I saw the same firm body I had seen in my dream.

"Yes," I said, much as an agricultural inspector might when he examines a grain sample or a farm's accounts. "Yes," she said too, in a tone of resignation to her fate, and she buttoned up her clothes again, everything now having been confirmed in the most solemn of ways.

She asked if she had been wearing her green skirt or her beige, slashed skirt in my dream. She also asked, with a ghost of her crooked smile, how I had felt about her, given that I had watched her several times in the brief, breathless embrace of her husband in between household chores. She wanted to know if I had liked the way they "did it" or whether I had been revolted by it. She also wanted to know which washboards I had seen in the cellar, since she couldn't for the life of her remember any. In any case, he only "had" her twice in the cellar, three times at most. She could hardly contain her questions, and wanted to know every detail: how she had "performed" on the various occasions I had witnessed in my dream, and what effect she had had on me. The questions came thick and fast, and I was hard put to describe everything in the detail she demanded.

It was almost as if she were taking my account as a way of meticulously checking her own future behaviour, and correcting it here and there. It was as if she were establishing an improved, more accurate image of herself that she would be aware of at all times and could refer to as actors do.

Was she not in fact obsessed with the need to acquire an impenetrable exterior, so that, even in her most intimate moments (before the all-seeing eye of central headquarters), she would cut a perfect figure?

I must confess that at first I had great difficulty controlling myself, since describing all the shameless facts I knew concerning her, even in the most minute and sober of fashions, had aroused my own desire intensely. At points my desire did indeed seem to get out of control, and I think we were both on the topmost ridge of excitement, where only a single step or chance touch would have been enough to have us tumble unseeing into the lift and devour each other to the very mouths. And all that transparent talk, all that unrestrained restraint, would have been torn down by the violence of our passion. But I crossed the ridge unhurt, my dearest Hermetia, and wore myself out giving precise descriptions of her secret moments, as she urged and demanded—and, as I did so, the cloud, the heavy scent of desire, gradually dissolved into tiny traces and particles, and my lust itself, as it resolved into fine constituents, had soon completely disappeared. In the end, as a result, I saw the woman in the most dreamless and neutral of states that any female creature has ever been seen in by a man's eye.

We said goodbye in a perfectly formal manner, as if we had merely been obeying, with meticulous discretion and to the satisfaction of both parties, the instructions of some faraway secret service that had brought us together just one single time in our lives.'

Anna Rheinsberg

Fay

He's whispering. (It's hard to make out what!) 'Naked,' he whispers, and almost chokes. *Shame.* And he turns dark red. He bursts into laughter. A child's laugh, high and wild. Startled, his hand darts to his mouth. Loud, too loud. 'Naked,' he whispers, 'naked, naked.' He trembles, he laughs.

He cowers at the foot of the bed. Bed? More like a metal grate, a narrow iron frame, askew, worn-out. On it a dirty mattress, full of holes.

A bed in the middle of the squalid room, bleak, poor. A sad, a wretched place. It's hot. Hot pale, transparent backdrop, muggy air, flies thudding against the window. Apart from the bed and a bucket, filled to the brim with green, cloudy water, the room is empty.

'Naked?' he asks.

He's wearing a torn shirt with almost all the buttons undone. He's sweating. His hollow, gaunt ribcage sticks out oddly. His arms are short and powerful, his shoulders fat, moist, his trousers down round his knees.

His arse is pathetically white and small; the delicate, bony arse of a child.

He's young, smooth, healthy, and nasty.

He's hoarse, in pain: his throat's sore, he's still trembling. 'Naked?' he asks.

'Smile!' he says now. He says it coldly, nastily. The buzzing flies make him impatient.

He looks at her.

He's full of shame, shame and silent rage. She's kneeling awkwardly in front of him, her face to the window, expressionless, mute and evidently tired.

'Costs more,' she says.

'*Smile*,' he says, and hits her in the face.

She wipes the blood away with the back of her hand. She bends over him, she smiles. Fay.

She lowers her gaze, an eye mirrored in the windowpane.

She sees—nothing, she spits.

A fly walks across her skin; it tickles. Lying down, she stares into a fog.

Pain (in the head). She's cold; she shivers.

'Naked, it costs . . .' But she stops herself. No, *she*'s not going to say that word.

Fay. Fay crouching in the bushes. It's evening and the trees are in full bloom. Fragrance, passing shadows, laughter, arms weighed down by cherry blossom. Birds! The moon.

Fay has a flower in her hair, she's deaf. She's plugged her ears with last year's rose hips! She crouches, she doesn't move. Stiff, she holds her breath, breathless.

Fay looks down at the small animal. Dead. The stone feels light in her hand. The animal's head is a lumpy pulp of brains and blood. Skin. They're calling her.

Loud, shrill voices. Shouting. Fay, Fay, they call. Her mother's crying. Fay can hear her.

Where are you? they call. *He*'s not with them.

Fay dips a finger in the bloody mass.

The voices recede . . . grow softer . . . Soft where-are-yous swallowed by the wind, hardly more than a breeze, a breath of air. Then all's quiet.

Fay climbs nimbly, fleet of foot, over the hedges. Barely visible, a mere dot (on the horizon), skipping—a leap.

And it's dark.

Now it's night.

When she remembers—remembers him—he's just an eye. Pale, grey, shadowed by a stumpy fringe of colourless eyelashes. Small, narrow, expressionless eyes, devoted, faithful. During the day he says little. During the day, Fay feels his shy, innocent gaze on her; tired, dull, strange.

He works hard enough for two. He's big, strong—he's washing his feet (in the basin). She watches him, he has such graceful, dainty feet for a man!

He shows great care, too, caressing, stroking the backs of his feet, his insteps and ankles with a peculiarly gentle, bashful pleasure.

He sighs.

He keeps a mute distance from Fay . . . Never lets her out of his sight, not by day. And by night—

She gives him double portions at mealtimes. 'Serve your brother!' her mother says.

Fatty pieces of meat make him feel sick.

She knows which bits to give him. His stomach heaves.

During the day he sometimes stands at one of the windows. The windows are always closed. Big, bathed in sweat, quivering. She stands behind him then. But she doesn't touch him. Never.

He smells . . . She breathes greedily and fearfully and it turns her stomach. He has such mean, alert eyes!

During the daytime he doesn't speak to her, never, not a word.

He works. He spits in front of her. Good-for-nothing.

Dreamer. Feeble-minded! Where did he pick up that expression?

At night she's a glass. He hurls the glass against the wall, over and over again.

At night she sings.

At night the words lie in wait . . . Nasty words, waiting for a chance to get out, out through her throat, out through her mouth, out.

Dirty words, swearwords.

The words hurt her. Silly, mean words. Someone says them. Fay can hear them.

Someone's whispering to her, rough, nasty. She doesn't know where it's coming from. She's deaf.

So she sings.

Loudly. Until someone bangs on her door. Quiet! Shut your mouth!

She lies with her arms around her knees. It's so dark in the room. The words sit on her chest, in her throat, a fever, dirt. She forces her hand into her mouth. If she speaks, he'll beat her.

Where oh where are they from . . . these words. She wishes she could be dumb, just be a hand, a foot, work. Say nothing. Be a hand and a foot like him. An eye.

At night she puts a chair against the door.

The faraway smell of burning in the morning, early. In the window the sky's just a patch of white. Like hot milk. Dry milk. He's breathing softly. Her hands are sore, her hands and feet. She doesn't move. Soon the sun will be out, glaringly bright, hard, just like every day.

Soon he'll . . . awake. Then he'll untie her hands and feet.

He nestles up to her (he's still asleep!), his sweat and the clamminess of his body make her skin itch.

She never cries—never! She looks at the sky, her small breast is red/swollen, her back stiff, twisted, the ropes cut into her flesh.

She starts. He's opened an eye.

He looks at her.

She strikes. The child under her shrieks, its mouth a torn O; it thrashes desperately, roars.

The scream rings in her ears, her blows rain down mercilessly, hitting, beating it with the coathanger, until skin tears, skin splits open like a yellow fruit.

She stops for a moment, exhausted.

What are you going to pay me?

Listless, tired. She's bored. Oh he saw all right! He's smart.
He knows how much.

'Smile!' he commands, and he becomes angry, his naked bit
of flesh trembling, going limp.

He's ashamed. Now he's ashamed! He's shaking with rage.
His mouth narrows, a mouth like a fishbone, hard. He bites
his lip, sucks. Fool. So that's how she thanks him.

'Play with me!'

He's crying, walking up and down, in a panic, like the fly,
his white shirt flapping round his knees. He stumbles. Rubs
his chest with his arms.

'No.'

A foreign word. Unknown to him. No. Strange. 'What?'
She holds out her hand. Come on.

He hesitates, his breathing fast and hard. The suggestion of
a smile, unsuspecting. *He's smiling.*

The smile goes wrong.

She ties the rope around his wrist, gives him a push, gently,
guiding him forward. The room is bright.

'Come on,' she says, tenderly, whispering, stroking his spine.
How gentle she is. Fay. Bend over.

And she pushes his head in, into the cloudy water, forces
him under, quickly, unwaveringly, a firm, painful grip. He's
a fish, and she laughs and the word comes into her head
again, oh, her headache ... how sore it is, sore, sore, mean
and rough. Death.

Katja Lange-Müller

Sometimes Death Comes Wearing Slippers

Schizo-grannies and senile dementoids, sometime of female gender, wander in a sleepy stupor, in well-worn slippers or barefoot if they can't find them, down the long dark corridors of the isolated women's gero-psychiatric ward, to the toilet. Past the bathroom, where—behind the door left ajar, between the bathtub and the washing machine, clothes-horses, buckets, nail clippers in slipper boxes, cock-roach-infested cupboards—the wheeled stretcher waits, with a fresh laundry-marked sheet. Fear of wetting themselves again shoos them out of their beds, which are close together. Room by room, in a straggling gaggle, groping with the awkwardness of the blind for walls rubbed raw or the hem of a friendly nightie, they set off, nothing but the urgent awareness of a full bladder in their drug-addled heads. Torn-off dreams hang from their tangled plaits like drunken train-bearers.

Outside the bathroom they abruptly pause for a moment, because the electric light falling through the slightly open doorway dazzles. But then they lurch on, in their out-at-heel slippers, like vanquished naval forces cruising on in the desolate battleships that still remain. Barely one of them will succeed in wearing out her last pair completely. Most will have to pass them on to their successors.

The slippers are the property of the hospital, and, when someone no longer has any need of the pair she was given to wear, they are handed on to the next candidate for death. Once one of these pairs of size 40 yellow and brown checked slippers have stood six or seven times beside the bed from which none arises in health, it is withdrawn from circulation. Then the woman most recently admitted gets a pair of standard issue size 40 yellow and brown checked slippers brand new as from the factory.

Whenever someone else has died, the slippers of all the patients are re-allocated in the described manner. The deaths are not frequent enough for the business of exchange to interfere in any material way with the normal routine of the ward.

That's the way it is. They find the toilet, and if it is already engaged they use the chamber pot as an alternative, sit down, and listen as well as they are able to the flow of events: the light is on in the next room, but it is deathly quiet, the cockroaches are warily biding their time in the corners of the cupboards. It is not hard to imagine what lies ahead yet again: a sign of the cross, it isn't oneself. They make it back to their nests faster, though now they no longer urgently have to pee, and with a more assured step. 'Comes the spring with April's showers, comes a year of happy hours,' it says on a wooden plaque on the wall, which Sannchen poker-worked with a glowing knitting needle in craft therapy once. The words are the chorus of a song that used to be her favourite.

Sannchen, Susanna-Magdalena Dombrowski, from somewhere by the Vistula in Poland, the schizophrenic, highly-dosed old washerwoman, formerly a laundress, made up rhyming adages, collected dead flies, hit out at the nurses, dismissed doctors, and claimed to have a twin brother in America, a bridge-building engineer who had gone missing and who bank-rolled the whole hospital and everything else beside—Sannchen died, at the age of eighty-four, unattended, with a bedsore as big as a fist in the small of her back, of acute cardiac failure, as the women were taking their midnight leaks.

The night nurse, a woman of many years' service who had hit upon the four geriatric Ps—Pottering, Picking, Pooping, Pissing—did not notice the exact moment of her passing. At the time it must have happened, she was just heaving a veritable dream of a granny out of her wet nappies, setting her on the commode, and, through her gap teeth, whistling 'See if you can manage something' in her north German accent.

Now there she stood, looking down and rather taken aback to be seeing a corpse. Only at eleven o'clock she had coaxed half a cup of cold coffee into poor Sannchen, and now there the creature lay, dead.

'Heaven knows if she still heard the wee nightingale singing. It's singing like crazy again tonight.'

Dreamily the bird-loving night nurse, Bärbel, listens past Grandma Bauer's unceasing 'ye-es, Daddykins, ye-es, Daddykins' and blind Traudi's 'my mother said, she said, you're not going there, my mother said' and all the other snoring, groaning and fantasising to the sweet sounds of the fluting nightingale. Now she can define the time at which the threshold was crossed, from dying to being dead and at peace, as precisely ten minutes past midnight.

'Dead is dead, and it doesn't matter to the one who dies how long she's been dead. Funny, most of them become angels at night. I suppose because they stand out so nicely against the black sky, the wee white souls. They take their bearings from the stars, like the seafarers of old. They have an easier journey of it at night. And the fisherman, St Peter, the sad man with the great key round his neck, not so young either, can see them better, the poor thin wee souls, who always fly up, as if they're nothing but air, when I'm on duty, at night. You're through with suffering, our Sannchen.'

Oblivious, Bärbel stares at Sannchen's last, left eye, which looks up to her silverly from the depths of its deep, tear-filled hollow like a coin in a bucket.

The night nurse does not really feel like bursting into tears. Snuffling in a restrained fashion, she confides the most emotion she can muster to her handkerchief: 'Every night it's the same wee carry-on.'

With soft but busy steps she goes into the office. She now has to notify the duty doctor in order that he may set a legitimate seal on the self-evident fact of death and ascertain the immediate cause. Then she has to put out the medical history, a death certificate, stethoscope, spatula, all of it tidily arranged on a laminated tray which, in accordance with the nature of the situation, she will hold in silent, submissive readiness in front of her, just as the chocolate girl on the wall in the nurses' room holds her daft, forgotten, useless china cup before her.

In the folder with the death certificates there is also a copy of the *Guidelines for Supply Nurses and Off-Ward Personnel in Case of Medically Ascertained Death*. Night nurse Bärbel has nothing else to do now but wait for some sleepy-eyed doctor in a wrongly buttoned uniform to come strolling over to the ward. So for what may be the hundredth time she reads through the guidelines which the ward sister drew up, which she herself wrote out in a fair copy years ago, and which the late Grandma Amanda bound in a plastic binder:

'Preparing a corpse.

'First, wet squares of cellulose should be placed on the eyelids. The lids should be closed immediately after decease as this can no longer be done in a natural way at a later time. In one's own interests, however, strict care should be taken to ensure that the hands of the person who does this have no injuries of any kind. If there is even the slightest break in the skin, the wearing of rubber gloves is strongly recommended.

'Whilst the necessary measures are being taken, all emotional involvement is to be avoided. If this cannot be achieved owing to inexperience or other reasons, then it should at least be borne in mind that such involvement should not unnecessarily delay the speedy completion of the work.

'Where the cosmetically important binding-up of the chin is concerned, young or inexperienced staff are particularly prone to use insufficient force. Chin ties that are too gently knotted rarely withstand rigor mortis, with the result that the usually toothless mouth is soon gaping wide open again.

'All parts of the corpse, particularly any that may have

been soiled during decease, should now be washed thoroughly with lukewarm water.

'Once all of this has been done in the prescribed sequence, it only remains to put a fresh nightgown, open at the back, on the body and then transfer it to a trolley.

'The death certificate, once completed (preferably by the doctor), should not be tied with string to one of the big toes, as is often done elsewhere, but should be attached to the right shin with a plaster.

'Finally, the corpse is covered head to toe with a further fresh sheet, and placed in as cool and quiet a place as possible (such as the bathroom) till morning.

'Everything else is the responsibility of the morning shift.'

Night nurse Bärbel has fixed up the corpse nicely. She looks just as she did in life: her hair as it always was, her hands folded, and dressed all in white. Now the nurse folds the two quarters of the sheet that she has pulled out from under the mattress over poor Sannchen and picks her up carefully. Her caution is a reflex conditioned by use of the pot. Because they always wail so fearfully, these threadworn flyweights, if when you carry them you have to crook them a little to fit them on the bucket.

But Sannchen, as thin as a rake, is far heavier now than she was when alive, and lies on Nurse Bärbel's fleshy forearms as stiff as the Virgin ascending. 'This perpetual fear of dropping them, on account of that sly saying, "Those who pray badly, lie badly." They used to use threats like that to drill nursing qualities into us in training.'

Nurse Bärbel manoeuvres stiff, heavy Sannchen neatly into the middle of the trolley, rolls her out of the old sheet on to her left side, smooths the two tips of the open nightie over her bottom, and lets her flop on her back again. 'Bye-bye, then, duckie,' she says, before she spreads out the second, fresh sheet over the dead woman, her nose and toes holding it up taut like two tent-poles. She was a forceful personality.

'That trendy doctor on stand-by earlier on, nowadays they all think they're psychiatrists, out to hypnotise their blonde girlfriends—he screwed up those two nostrils of his snub nose like two tiny arseholes, as if this place smelled like a puma's cage. They all sniff so short-winded and disgusted whenever they take a wrong turn and end up here, or have to come because it's their turn. They'd be better thanking their old mothers for bringing creatures such as them into the world at all, them and their noses, the moustached perfumy so-and-sos.'

Poor Sannchen is ready, and Nurse Bärbel is finished too. She manhandles Sannchen for the last time. 'We really ought to get a schnapps for this at the hospital's or God knows who else's expense. A good clear double. The people who laid out corpses for a living in the old days always used to get a drink, mostly more than one. But then, maybe the bodies tended to be much older.'

Nurse Bärbel has rolled the trolley back to the bathroom. Now she can open the windows, switch off the light, wash her hands a few times in ethanol and once with soap, and then finally put on a large helping of the potato soup that was kept for her from lunch, to warm.

She has to hurry. In just an hour she will wake the girls, three idiot women of about fifty who do simple chores and cleaning about the ward. The girls have from half past till four to wash and dress. In the mean time, Nurse Bärbel handles the last toilet session for her tour of duty. After that, the four of them begin washing the patients who cannot do it themselves any more. At the moment, that means thirty-two out of the forty-six.

Hungrily Nurse Bärbel spoons the soup from the saucepan. In her left hand, a cigarette burns down. The cockroaches in the bathroom can scuff about again at last and eat toilet paper, for two or three hours at the outside, till the night is over.

The morning starts a Thursday. It is the day the cake comes. The three helpers—who have a little crocheting to keep them occupied in the hospital sewing room—and the girls are allowed to take a bath today and change into fresh knickers.

'Our Sannchen's died,' says the early morning shift nurse as she doles out one wurst sandwich and one of jam each. They chew in silence. To most of them it is not news. They had guessed as much, before midnight, in a dream, as they were peeing. Even so, it is almost a miracle, since Sannchen was only the third oldest among them. But then, why *not* her. She always was that way, headstrong.

They really are very quiet at breakfast this morning, they don't moan, don't poke each other. Some of the ones who normally avoid looking at each other do so now.

Before the helpers and girls take their baths, the music therapist comes by with his accordion, perfectly timed for coffee and cake. He plays for three-quarters of an hour; he gets paid for a whole hour. He rattles off his tried and tested repertoire: 'Men are deceivers all', 'In the greenest valley', 'Why are you weeping, dear lady?', 'The flea waltz', 'The grassy bank by my parents' grave' and, for the last half hour, nothing but the for-she's-a-jolly-good-fellow anthem 'Hoch soll sie leben'. That gets them singing again. Too slow, too fast, out of key, and, of course, loudly. As the therapist is already packing up, the morning shift nurse whispers to him: 'Last night one of our girls died.' The therapist consults his watch, puts on a patronising air, straps on the accordion once more, and plays something by Lehár. They all enjoy the encore and, paying no attention to the change of tune, keep on singing their favourite song, 'Hoch soll sie leben'.

They love birthdays. A birthday means weak real coffee at an unscheduled time, laid on by the one whose birthday it is. It means that the selfsame one beams, because all you can do is be happy if there's nothing else you can do. It's a pleasure to see something so nice, a happy birthday girl. It gives you hope, and courage in the struggle, the competition to see who will live longest. Birthdays count. No one collects deaths. What counts, counts. What doesn't count, doesn't: eighty-seven springs to one winter.

'Comes the spring with April's showers, comes a year of

happy hours.' The most scandalous thing of all is when someone has no appetite. It is the only thing that sets them telling
tales. 'Nurse, she isn't eating her soup.'

The music therapist has long since left and still they are
singing, singing Sannchen's death to death. 'Hoch soll sie
leben.'

Things like that heal quickly. If they break a thigh or leg,
it doesn't heal. Not with them, not any more. The penalty of
clumsiness is that if you fall, you lie down. And those who
lie fall into the very thing that falls on them once they lie
down below. But the loveliest song on earth covers everything over: 'Hoch soll sie leben.'

After four p.m. the ward sister clears out the bedside
cupboard by the bed that used to be Sannchen's. She won't
have time to do it tomorrow; tomorrow is Friday, she wants
to knock off earlier. And anyway, they may have to move
about today. Who will have to go where is something the
ward sister cannot decide till she knows what the newcomer
is like. It's either straight into the infirmary with her or
everyone changes beds. You have to be prepared for sur-
prises. Some of them hardly survive the day they arrive.

Sannchen's effects consisted of a pocket mirror in a blue
frame, a pony-tail grown matt and thin as a mouse's tail
from years of lying about, three photographs, and a chemise
sequinned with glass beads in a pattern that is no longer
identifiable. The soft muslin on which the ruined pattern was
embroidered must have been eaten up by moths. All that is
left to hold the crumb-sized black beads together is a tangled
confusion of matted metal threads. Who knows, all these
things may never have originally belonged to Susanna at all.
They may only have been presents from some patients or
other, who in turn had received the one or other of these
objects as a gift. They are always very generous in their gifts
to fellow-patients on the ward once they realise the end is
near. From time to time one of them is mistaken about that,
and recovers. In such cases she can do what she likes but
the presents are lost for good. No one steals in here, but they

all keep a close guard on their belongings. Neither insanity nor forgetfulness can change that.

Sannchen's personal property goes to the girls. They have hardly any use for any of it, but they are pleased all the same, and show their thanks by working hard. The girls are needed, so let them help themselves. The rest of what is in the bedside cupboard is property of the state: a pullover, a skirt, a pinafore, underwear, stockings, and the oldest pair of ward slippers. An untouched sample tub of Nivea cream that a trainee nurse brought Susanna, for the dry skin lichen in her face, goes to the office.

'These are finished,' says the thrifty ward sister, pushing a hand through the hole in the left slipper. 'You needn't bother mending these. The new one can have a new pair. Goodbye.'

At five p.m. there's a ring at the wired-glass door. The late shift nurse opens up, surrounded by the girls, all curiosity. The rest are indifferent to the new arrival. Whenever a bed becomes free on the ward, it is taken the same day.

The newcomer looks like Rumpelstiltskin did when he had just given his name away. The two ambulance men are holding her arms crooked in theirs, as if they were about to dance off together to a waltz.

'Fine, now come on over here, easy does it. No need to be afraid, we're just going to have a little bath.'

The nurse sits the newcomer down on the oilcloth-covered chair used for examinations in the office, takes off her clothes, and drapes a bath towel across her shoulders. So that she does not feel too naked: old women are so bashful.

WARD REGISTER: ARRIVALS
Schneider, Hildegard
Born 3.7.1900 at Ottendorf-Okrilla
Prelim. diagnosis: senile dementia
Personal effects on arrival:
1 summer coat
1 dress (cotton, green)
1 blouse
1 pair of underpants

1 pair of tights
1 pair of shoes (worn)
Identity card
3 photographs
1 silver ring (without stone)
1 pocket mirror
1 letter opener (real tortoiseshell)
1 artificial leather handbag (worn)

The nurse puts the woman's belongings in a cambric bag, sticks a strip of plaster on it, writes 'Schneider, Hildegard' on the elastoplast strip, and strikes off the same name from a list headed 'Patients to be taken on to ward as soon as possible: doctors' recommendations'. 'Schneider, Hildegard' did not appear till the second row from the top, but the name was marked with a red stamp meaning 'urgent'. By now the tub has run half full. 'Lift your leg up. Don't be afraid—it's all right, I'm holding on to you. Now come on and just relax a bit. Just a splash of rose oil and that'll be lovely.' The oil is a liquid disinfectant. The newcomer is shaking but she can wash herself. A good sign.

'The girls will show you your bed. It's in room four, the sixth bed in the row on the left. The one by the window.'

The girls stand giggling behind the nurse. They are still delighted at the inheritance they have just received.

'Run up to the loft, will you, and put this stuff with the other bags? You can leave Hilde to sort it into the right place, at least she has some idea of the alphabet. Right, now these are your things to wear.' The nurse counts the usual items into the newcomer's lap: knickers, blouse, stockings, garters, skirt, pullover, pinafore. But the woman's gaze remains firmly fixed on the floor. Down where the yellow and brown checked slippers are. She stares at them speechless, for a long time, as a kindergarten pupil might stare at a leather-bound edition of Goethe that she had won in a prize draw, till at length she stretches out her still wet toes to nudge one of the two teddybear-yellow bobbles. 'Mine?' she asks. 'Hm—we'll have to be clipping those claws of yours, won't we?' the nurse replies, and eases the awkward, trembling feet deformed by Parkinson's into the pair of slippers that are—for the time being—hers.

Christoph Wackernagel

The Gap

I

The first appearance of the two accused, Franz T. and Eberhard M., drew an astonished reaction from the public gallery. It was not intellectuals with a hint of the office worker about them who stood before the court, which was to pass judgement on their supposed responsibility for the disappearance of twelve million marks from a casino, but rather respectable, almost timid members of the lower middle class. Nor did the start of the proceedings conform to expectations:

At the very beginning, when they were being asked about their personal circumstances, former tax consultant Eberhard M.—with the agreement of Franz T., seated next to him, whose other jobs had included temporary waiter, windsurfing teacher, film extra and electronic engineer—stressed that the information in the documents had to remain provisional, since these might not have been their only careers—although point for point they matched the facts in every detail.

That was 'not the only truth', shouted Franz T. when the indictment had been read to the court—although he was unable to provide any further explanation of this, being interrupted by the presiding judge who attached a great deal of importance to the idea that there was only one truth, and that it could only be determined after the end of the main hearing.

Thus, only the statements of the accused could provide a clear idea of their view of what had happened:

'It is not our intention,' Eberhard M. began, 'to contradict the version of events proposed by the public prosecutors. Everything may have occurred as they suggest, but—and we think that the question of criminal responsibility currently under discussion has an importance that goes far beyond our individual case—the truly remarkable thing in relation to the disappearance of the twelve million—about whose location we are sadly, as prisoners, unable to provide any information—is not the fact of its unnoticed removal from the safe, but the possible discovery of different, really existing realities connected with it.'

A whisper passed through the court, the court reporter took notes with a frown, the lawyers laughed with a shake of their heads—not without a flicker of uncertainty in their faces.

'There may even,' the accused continued, 'be several true realities in different periods of time; we were unable to find that out. As to the question of the vanished money, however, that is of secondary importance; what is crucial is that the longer we are prevented from trying to get it back, the more likely it is that it will be spent by someone else who may get hold of it in another reality. Incidentally, this suggests that traditional legal ideas need to be revolutionised: is it right, for example, that the individual involved in that case will not be subject to criminal proceedings, while we, as we have been informed, face a sentence of five to ten years? At this point we might also remark that—'

The rest of his words were drowned in a loud murmur from the public; according to his lawyers, Eberhard M. stressed that the sentencing and imprisonment of the two accused would put the seal on the disappearance of the twelve million once and for all.

An intervention from the public prosecutor was rejected on procedural grounds—he had demanded that a stop be put to 'this nonsense', but was informed that the accused were talking about the case at hand, and that it was thus the court's responsibility to decide what was sense and what was nonsense—after this interruption on behalf of the prosecution, it was Franz T.'s turn to provide move detailed explanations:

'The whole business started when we got bored at work. There we were sitting at our monitors day in, day out, and we had nothing else to do. The pictures from the gaming rooms were the most interesting ones, but during working hours they were the least important, because of course they were manned by plain-clothed guards. The pictures from the entrance and the lifts were hardly any more varied—there was a certain excitement in the fact that we had to make a preliminary check on them; but even here we practically never had to go into action, and watching the same pictures on the screens with the necessary concentration was becoming more and more of an effort. Most disagreeable were the screens showing the street, the underground car park and the various staircases. They were empty most of the time, and every time a person appeared we had the same reflex reaction: "Was that something?—Does it mean something?—Are we supposed to react in some way?"—all questions that could be answered immediately with a blunt "No", and we found ourselves thrown back into a state of dull, listless brooding. All sense of time threatens to vanish, there's nothing to talk about, soon you can't tell whether you're awake or dreaming—and we might remark in passing that those pictures pursue you into your dreams—you think you're hallucinating and you can't tell whether or not you've just seen something, and you've long since given up trying to see the sense in looking at something when you know what it's going to be. But your resistance to the slow process of seeing your own person, your identity and, finally, your intelligence, overpowered, breaks down under the relentlessness of this deadly, farcical repetition, and in your few lucid moments you find yourself thinking, "If things go on like this, I'm going to turn into an animal." '

'I'—Eberhard M. picked up the thread—'of course felt much the same. I must, however, confess that my reaction was rather fatalistic, and I tried as best I could to get through the working day, although I sometimes came close to wasting away with apathy.

'If the court takes all these circumstances into account, it will surely understand my astonishment when, one night, at that dead time between two and three, suddenly, on the screen, I saw my colleague going up the stairs. I rubbed my eyes, I pinched myself, I grabbed his arm: he was sitting next to me, flesh and blood, and at the same time he was going up the stairs; it was crazy, I thought, I'm going mad, my sense organs have given out on me, particularly since my colleague went on acting as if everything was normal, and paid no attention to my excitement. Finally he disappeared from the picture, and I decided I must have been hallucinating—when he appeared again down at the bottom! I slowly grasped that I was having my leg pulled, and I calmed down. When I saw that Franz could no longer keep from grinning, I asked him how he'd done it.'

'It was quite easy, of course,' said Franz T., 'once I'd realised things couldn't go on like that I thought, well, then, make your own programme. Or a different one, at least. Right, so what I had to do was get hold of a recorder, do a bit of rewiring and find a chance to do a recording. It went like a dream. I only wish I'd thought of recording his face as it switched from dull and dozy to staring, gaping like a halfwit—that was a sight, priceless, and something I'll never forget as long as I live.'

'It may well be that it was highly amusing for my colleague to see me like that. And his need for diversion may have been satisfied for the time being. My own, on the other hand, had just been awakened, and I suggested continuing the game, but with a few variations.'

II

'First of all,' Eberhard M. began to explain, 'I wanted to be filmed too. The games rooms, free at that time of day, were best suited to the purpose. As we were playing back the tape on a different monitor, we were able to see simultaneously what we had just recorded and the usual view of the games room next to it.'

Franz T. continued: 'I asked him to go back downstairs, so that I could see him both live and on tape, side by side. Please don't ask me why.' With these last words he turned to the presiding judge as if awaiting a reply. The judge smiled and nodded.

'We agreed,' Eberhard M. continued, 'that I would take up exactly the same position and, if possible, say something without moving my mouth—he was to guess which was the real and which the recorded image.'

'Having arrived downstairs,' Franz T. picked up the thread, 'he did assume the agreed position, but called to me to come down, because the door to the safe was unlocked, and hardly had he finished speaking than he vanished from the screen so quickly I thought his real image was the one on the tape, and that it had come to an end.

'But I didn't give it another thought, and ran downstairs.

'He was nowhere to be seen. At first I thought it was a bad joke and called out to him. No reply. I looked around the rooms. No Eberhard anywhere. I tried the door to the safe. It really wasn't locked. But he couldn't be in there either, as the cameras set off an alarm the minute someone walks into the picture. I stood in the games room without a notion of what I should do.'

'Exactly the same thing happened to me. When I thought Franz was on his way down to me I walked back to the unlocked safe door and thought about what I should do. But Franz didn't come. I called up to him once more. No reply. Was he playing a trick on me again? I got annoyed and went upstairs.

'But there was no Franz up there either.'

'We couldn't have missed each other,' Franz went on, 'because there was only one way to get from the gaming hall to the surveillance room. So this time I was the one whose leg was being pulled. I decided to go back upstairs.

'In the meantime the tape had run out. Snow flickered on the monitor. I began to feel uneasy.'

'I felt the same in that respect,' Eberhard M. confirmed. 'Had something happened the moment we used the monitor for something else? A robbery? And was Franz working with the thieves? I considered phoning the relevant section of the police, where we had a special number. But when I got my wallet out of my jacket I started having doubts: if I did that, it would come out that we'd been manipulating the surveillance system. On the other hand, Franz might be in danger!'

'I thought much the same, but I was understandably more hesitant about getting help, given that it was me who had started the whole thing off. I looked thoughtfully at the empty picture showing the gaming hall. Eberhard had been in it only a moment before. Mechanically, with no precise purpose in mind, I ran back the tape on which I'd recorded him. Perhaps I wanted to console myself with a reproduction of him.'

'I, meanwhile, had decided to have another look downstairs. But once again there was no one to be seen, and I made one last attempt to get Franz on the intercom.'

'And I thought,' Franz T. broke in, 'there was something wrong with my eyes. Hardly had the tape started up again when, just as suddenly as he had vanished, Eberhard reappeared on the live screen! At exactly the same moment I heard him calling to me, sounding upset. I answered him, and once he had stormed back upstairs we got into an argument. He claimed he had been upstairs and had left his wallet behind and accused me of stealing it because it was, of course, nowhere to be found.'

'It was a while before we calmed down again and managed to listen to each other's stories. Unlikely as Franz's story sounded, neither could I imagine him stealing my wallet, and if he had been having me on he'd have given it back then and there.'

'First of all,' Franz began to explain the further course of events, 'in an attempt at reconstruction, we looked again at the tape we had recorded. But we couldn't see anything out of the ordinary.

'But then I remembered the speed with which he had vanished and reappeared. In fact, he said, he hadn't moved with particular speed at any point. And if I recalled correctly, he was, both when he vanished and when he reappeared, in the same position on both screens, the position we'd originally agreed upon.

'Maybe it was a kind of short circuit resulting from the fact that both screens showed identical images? Eberhard said no: the same picture often appeared on several screens, but it never produced a short circuit. My objection: these are all reproductions, while here you have a match between the reproduction of reality and reality itself, the man-made image of reality and that same reality. Could it bear that? Eberhard asked which?, and asked the difference:

'Only in purely technical, logically arrestable reality would a short circuit have meant an instrument breakdown. But the instruments went on working!'

'Might the disturbance of reality that we have perceived,' Eberhard M. interrupted excitedly, 'be attributed to a breakdown in our own heads? A short circuit of reason, so to speak? And a short circuit both simultaneous and simultaneously perceived?'

'Both of us knew, however,' Franz T. objected, 'that we hadn't lost our reason. The "short circuit" therefore had to take in the whole of reality in some form as yet unknown to us.

'And we had a clue to that: Eberhard's vanished wallet.'

'The problem could not be solved,' Eberhard M. concluded, 'with logic and reasoning alone. We had to proceed in experimental fashion. So I proposed that we repeat the whole sequence of events using the same tape. Working on the premise that the congruence of reality and its reproduction was the crux of our dilemma, we worked out a number of situations in which I would assume exactly the same position as I had in the recording, and a number in which I assumed a different one.'

It was Franz T.'s turn to speak. 'Now everything started happening very quickly. In fact the process repeated itself as we suspected it would: at the moment when both positions matched, he vanished from the live screen, and contact was broken.'

'And hardly had I taken the position up again,' added Eberhard M., 'when our contact was re-established.

'We timed our experiment, and once we'd observed that our measurements agreed to the second, I decided to test our premise and go and get the wallet back.'

'To avoid taking any risks we established not only the exact time at which tape and reality were to match, but also established, down to the smallest detail, every hand movement, every body posture, even gestures and facial expressions: he took up his position, vanished from the screen—and reappeared after the agreed time. Laughing, he took his wallet out of his jacket.'

'Laughing with relief, however,' Eberhard M. hastened to add, 'at being freed from uncertainty: I had been in familiar, all too familiar surroundings, and yet were they somehow different? Nothing had changed, except that contact with Franz had broken off, and yet it suddenly seemed strange and uncanny. I secretly hoped, during my last steps towards the control room, that it would all turn out to be a joke, and Franz would be waiting for me, laughing—but that's not how it was. The room was empty, the wallet was still where I had inadvertently left it. I quickly picked it up and hurried back to the agreed place.'

Franz T. summed things up. 'So we seemed to have proven that the perfect identity between a recorded and an actual reality led to the breakdown of the latter, to a cellular division, a kind of cloning of reality, you might say, the constitution of a precisely identical reality, in which everything is duplicated, apart, perhaps, from human beings.'

Once again, his face bright red, the prosecution lawyer interrupted. Controlling his voice with some effort he demanded that 'this impudence' be brought to an end. He was rebuked by the judge. It was disagreeable to have to remind the prosecution that forbidding the accused to speak could constitute grounds for appeal.

Franz T. continued, 'Only gradually did we realise that we might have made a discovery which could have utterly unpredictable ramifications. Either we had been dreaming or we had gone mad—or else we had discovered something that could revolutionise man's view of the world more completely than the discoveries of Galileo or Einstein; a discovery, then, for which we would go down in history.

'Rather than concentrating on this historical dimension, however, we had—and with the best will in the world we can't say which of us had it first—quite a different idea: the money in the safe.'

III

Eberhard M. cleared his throat. 'The source of all this excitement—and I should like to make this perfectly clear—was the fact that the door to the safe was unlocked. So it was only because we were fulfilling our duties so conscientiously that our thoughts in this confusing situation immediately turned to the money in the safe. In view of the fact, of course, that we had just made the discovery that reality existed twice over, we couldn't help thinking that the money would also have to exist in duplicate.'

'And not only twice,' said Franz T. quietly, 'if we assume that the duplicated reality must also be subject to duplication—something that we could easily verify—the twelve million must also exist twice, three times, four times—an infinite number of times.'

'So it was primarily a problem of transport,' Eberhard M. continued, but was immediately interrupted by the judge: 'Am I given to understand that you intended to transfer money?'

'I thank you for this question, your honour,' said Eberhard M., 'for my statement naturally requires some clarification. We intended to transfer the money from this second reality—

which we had discovered and towards which we therefore felt we had certain rights of ownership—into our own, in which we probably are at this very moment, and not, for instance, the other way round! This must be acknowledged as the actual intention behind our action! All further actions were, in fact, only ways and means of realising that intention—although it might initially seem either otherwise or even the other way round!'

'Our problem was, in fact,' Franz T. hastened to explain, 'that we didn't know whether the other reality was purely material, or whether people existed in it as well. We hadn't met with ourselves there, so we did not need to assume, for example, that there was a police station there, or more precisely, a manned police station where someone might object to our intention of removing the money from the safe in the second reality.'

'So,' the public prosecutor was heard to say, his voice raised in fury, 'the conditions of ownership were not entirely straightforward!'

'Seen from over there, of course not,' Eberhard M. answered quickly, 'but from here, they certainly were. No legal provision has hitherto been made for goods from another reality.'

The public prosecutor shook his head and bent over his papers.

Franz T. spoke again. 'That was not the only reason we had to avoid any risks. Could it not be that realities were constantly being duplicated somewhere or other, since the invention of film and television? Could it be that some people didn't even notice that they were suddenly in a different identical world? Could this be the cause of the disappearance of fifty thousand people a year in this country, whom no one has been able to find despite watertight surveillance and the introduction of new ID cards? Wasn't a crashed light aircraft recently found with no one in it? Could this have led to the failure of the authorities in the face of political violence? Could it be that people were being duplicated without being aware of it? Are we all in real reality, or have we been in the second or third or the who-knows-which reality for heaven knows how long? As regards these proceedings, might we not also ask ourselves whether they are actually happening in the reality in which we imagine them to be happening? And those are only a few examples of the questions we had to ask ourselves.'

'Anyway, they compelled us,' Eberhard M. summed up, 'first of all to carry out an experiment in the first reality, as we might call it for purposes of convenience, that might make it easier to transfer the money from the second.'

'We can't really talk of compulsion here,' protested the visibly enraged state prosecutor, who seemed to be on the verge of losing his temper altogether, 'it is an outrage to use such formulations in this context; I ask the court to reprimand the accused.'

The judge frowned.

'The court has noted the formulation used—and also the public prosecutor's intervention. Further counsel will be required before we can arrive at an opinion on the matter. It is the right of the accused in all cases to present his own version of events.' Turning to Eberhard M., he said, 'Please continue!'

'Thank you very much!' said Eberhard M. 'Whichever way one looks at it, the risk involved in bringing the money back from the safe in the second reality was, given the many imponderables, too great—so the obvious thing to do was to borrow the money from the safe in the first reality, place it near the transfer area, transfer it to the other reality, and then to fetch the duplicate from there.'

Since it was becoming clear that they needed to provide a technical explanation of how the removal of the money was to be effected despite all the safety precautions they had undertaken, Franz T. spoke.

'That was quite simple, of course, it worked according to the same principle which we had already been following the whole time. We made a fairly lengthy recording with the surveillance camera of the room next to the safe. Then we fed our recording back into the camera and were able to walk into the anteroom without setting off the alarm.

'As we knew the combination of the safe for professional reasons, we were able to get the money out in only a few minutes.'

'That is a confession!' cried the public prosecutor, his voice tremulous with triumph.

Seriously irritated, the judge turned to the prosecutor. 'I must call you to order,' he said, 'this is an explanation of the matter at hand, which only the court is allowed to interrupt. The court is, as I have already stressed a number of times, in a position to form an opinion itself. Even the defence strategy employed by the accused, unorthodox as it may be, cannot be grounds for the instruments of the law to behave in a similarly unorthodox manner.'

Now Eberhard M. picked up the thread. 'As I already knew of the alternation of the realities from my own experience, my intention was to fetch over the money that was, we presumed, already in the second reality. I only mention the fact that we naturally intended to return the original money simply to complete the picture, because we never for a second dreamed of keeping it for ourselves.'

'The way we imagined it, we wouldn't have needed it anyway,' added Franz T., 'once we were in possession of twelve million things would really get going: because these would be duplicated again, and the resulting twenty-four would turn into forty-eight—and so on and so on. The possibility of switching from the second to the third, and from the third to the fourth, and collecting the money in each— that was excluded for the time being. We didn't have a great deal of time to carry out our experiments.'

'Experiments,' the prosecutor murmured.

Eberhard M. went on: 'So we put the money on the roulette table near the camera, made a recording a few minutes long, and after making a final check to see that everything was OK, Franz ran the picture. Shortly afterwards the connection was broken—so I was in the second reality.

'Was I really going to find the money? And would it be

equally easy to bring it back? Would I, thanks to these inexplicable and indisputable events, be a millionaire, or would I face a rude awakening?

'My heart beating madly, I turned around:

'There it was!

'I quickly grabbed the money and assumed my position.

'I waited impatiently for contact to be re-established.

'We'd finally done it!'

'But at that moment we saw something astonishing,' Franz T. continued. 'Hardly had Eberhard reappeared on the control monitor, than we noticed that the money had vanished from the roulette table!'

A loud whisper in the public gallery; a gasp of excitement even escaped the public prosecutor, before he started muttering to his colleagues.

'Silence in court,' shouted the judge. Even he seemed to have grown nervous.

'Anyway,' Eberhard hastened to say, 'I still had the money from the second reality on me!

'After Franz had hurried downstairs, we stood around for a bit, wondering how we could recover from our disappointment.'

'You don't,' Franz T. interjected, 'throw away the chance of being a millionaire as easily as that.'

'So I suggested,' Eberhard M. continued, 'returning to the status quo ante. According to the laws of logic which—in spite of the experiments we had just undertaken, which tended to contradict them—we still thought we could apply to these phenomena, if the duplicate that we had brought back could be returned to the second reality, the original money from the first reality would reappear.

'No sooner said than done. I took the money, assumed my position, waited until the contact broke—'

'—but no money appeared when Eberhard vanished,' Franz T. concluded his explanation. 'I waited with feverish excitement to see what would happen now, whether Eberhard would bring it back, or whether it would only reappear when he came back—but there was no sign of it. I wondered briefly whether Eberhard might be taking me for a ride, so that he could have the twelve million all to himself, but that was nonsense, because the twelve million were only going to be the basis of our plan.'

'I wondered that as well,' said Eberhard M., 'but as I saw it there was the additional problem that Franz couldn't have got downstairs as quickly as that.

'Obviously, we concluded, the duplicate had assumed the properties of the original after it had caused the original to vanish, and now possessed the attribute of presumably real reality. Therefore, if anything was as it should be, it must be possible to bring the money, like the wallet, back from the second reality.

'So we made a new recording, and with the greatest excitement I waited for the contact to break, my heart was thumping its way into my throat, I turned around:

'No money.

'At that very moment everything was clear to me in a flash.

'Because we had made a new recording, this second reality could only be a duplicate of the first one: hence one without the twelve million.

'It seemed an age before I came back.'

'In the meantime I'd noticed it as well,' Franz T. said sadly, 'and I'd also been struck by something else: the original of the recording, made when the twelve million was still there, had been wiped when we taped over it.'

'This idiot,' said Eberhard M., 'has effectively wiped the twelve million.'

There was a moment of unease in the court.

'Which doesn't mean,' Franz T. remarked, 'that the money has actually been wiped! How do we know that the second reality, once it has been created, doesn't exist for ever? Might we not just have to find a way into it again? How do we know which reality we're in at the moment, for example?

'But we would not answer such questions that night. Day was already dawning, and, more or less apathetically, we let events take their course.'

'However,' said Eberhard M., 'the chances of getting the money back will diminish with the passing of each day that we—if we are sentenced—are forced to sit in jail instead of being allowed to go in search of the lost reality.'

The petition on the part of the defence that the court should decide which was the real reality was rejected as inadmissible.

The second petition to test the statements of the accused with an experimental demonstration, so as to ascertain its truth component, was granted. The presiding judge then added the following procedural constraints: first of all that the public should be excluded, and secondly, that the process should be followed via the court's surveillance camera.

The court official who, following Franz T.'s instructions, matched the recording with the picture in the courtroom, later reported:

'Suddenly they were all gone.'

Daniel Grolle

Murder

Big John screws up his eyes against the light. 'Damned sun!' He spits. A small thread of glistening spittle hangs at the corner of his mouth. He wipes it away, lifts the cellar key to his lips between the tips of two fingers and, with a pained look on his face, inhales. Masterfully, he blows the smoke out again without taking his eye off the street.

It's three o'clock in the afternoon. The last two lessons have been cancelled so now he's behind the rubbish skips by the cellar door, his Colt stuck in his belt. He's already blasted three goddam redskins' brains out. You don't get many coming down Henriettenstrasse at three o'clock, but Big John's a damned good shot, feared throughout the west, cold as ice. He lets them get just past him on the pavement, about nine feet away from the rubbish skips. That gives him long enough to get bead and notch lined up and smack one into the back of their heads. He's pretty sure of a bulls-eye too, and if the pedestrians turn he can take cover in the cellar quick as a flash. You won't get no redskin finding him there. He knows his way about—even knows the secret passage behind the boiler. It's a sure thing!

Hasn't been a damned redskin come by here for a quarter of an hour now. It gets boring sometimes. But a cowboy's got to be patient. He knows that. Big John stays cool. Kneeling down between the two rubbish skips, he can keep the street well covered. He's almost finished smoking that cellar key for the third time. He stubs it out on the stones. 'Damned smoking! Ought to stop. Ah, well . . .' He lights up the next.

Sucking smoke deeply into his lungs, he looks down at his revolver. It's a genuine Douglas Colt. Only ten of them in the whole wide west and you can bet your bottom dollar them goddam redskins want to get their hands on all of them. It's a real Colt, with a revolving drum and a round, seven-shot magazine. They're much louder than caps and much better. And anyway, a real flame comes out the end. So quick you can hardly see it.

The last redskin he gunned down was a granny from the old people's block at the end of the street. He took really good aim, focusing pretend crosshairs right on the back of the granny's head, then training the bead of his revolver exactly on the intersection of the cross. A clean job! And when he squeezed the trigger he really did see a flame shoot out the end. It was only for a fraction of a second, but it went straight towards the back of the granny's head. And in front of the flame was a real bullet. A normal cowboy wouldn't have seen it. But the granny felt it all right. She touched the exact spot with her hand and wheeled round, startled. He shot off like the blazes into the cellar and hid behind the boiler. It's a really great hiding-place! Especially when he flattens himself against the tank of the boiler.

Big John pulls back the catch to open the magazine of his Colt and lets the drum fall out into the palm of his hand. He presses out a red ring of cartridges. The smell of sulphur rises to his nostrils. It's plain enough: five cartridges really have been used. Only two left. It's scary and makes him feel important all at once.

His uncle Theo gave him the Colt for Christmas. The weapon was wrapped in polystyrene and was really heavy; not light like the stupid thing Big John had before. At Christmas he'd practised on the newsreader first. He was quite a good target to start with because he didn't move much.

Big John's come a long way since those days. He knows it, too. Carefully, he puts his gun back together, inserting a new ring of cartridges. Better safe than sorry! He holds it up to his ear, gives the drum a spin and sniggers. He clicks the drum back into the firing position and lets his eagle eye take in the whole street. Another damned redskin coming! And look at the way he's sitting in that saddle!

Michael is twenty-two, it's springtime, and he wants to fall in love. We'll see, we'll see! Sometimes you've got to chance your arm in life! He laughs to himself as he cycles down Henriettenstrasse. In his jacket pocket is a bottle of tomato ketchup which he has to take back to the Arpsens' place. Still some distance away, he sees the boy between the rubbish skips. He also sees the pistol pointing at him. Ha! Just you wait!

Big John spits. This time the spittle leaves no thread. It's going be a ticklish job this time. Dangerous, too. This brave's young—Big John knows these damned swine! Nearly got caught by one the other day. Managed to slam the cellar door in his face at the last minute! Got to get that bastard with the first shot or things could get hot.

Just before he reaches the skips Michael rides his bike up on the pavement. Big John screws up his eyes and takes aim with superhuman precision. The stomach this time! Lone braves on horseback are real hard to hit! Gripping his pistol in both hands, he keeps it trained on his target's stomach. Right opposite him, the rider turns and grins. The shock sends a spasm through Big John. Looking into the rider's grinning eyes he pulls the trigger—feels the recoil—sees the flame—hears the bullet thud into the redskin's back. The rider screams and—with a horrible racket—bites the dust.

Big John freezes. He waits till all is quiet. The only movement is the back wheel of the bike, spinning. Then it stops too. Tentatively, Big John comes out on the pavement from between the skips, ready if need be to make a dash for the cellar. But there's no need to run away. The brave's stretched out on the ground, motionless. Big John takes a step towards him. Then he sees thick blood oozing out from under the jacket.

He's never seen so much blood. Shite! Horrified, he dives for the cellar and slams the door shut behind him, then slams the wooden door of the corridor, too, but the banging frightens him, so he closes the steel door of the boiler room as carefully and quietly as he can. He hears his breath booming despite the noise of the machines. He tries to breathe more quietly, only it's terribly difficult and gives him the hiccups, and that's even louder.

With his hiccups, knocking knees and stomach cramps Big John cowers against the dusty wall behind the tank in the boiler room. But before it's too late he manages to get his gunbelt undone and pull down his trousers. Immediately it spurts out of him against a hot pipe. He feels a sharp pain in his tummy. Big John knows he's going to have an awfully sore bum. But what's a sore bum when you've just shot someone dead? His legs are shaking even worse now, his teeth chattering. And it stinks.

He's got to get out.

He pulls himself together. With his Colt firmly gripped in his hand, he rushes out of the cellar into the stairwell, past the door of his parents' flat and up all five flights till he's at the top of the house. As quietly as he can he takes the attic key from the box outside the caretaker's flat. Suddenly, the door opens and the caretaker's standing there glowering at him. But Big John's got the key and darts to the attic door. Quickly, he unlocks it, then locks it behind him again. The caretaker doesn't know what's hit him. Could be he knows about Big John's Colt. Or perhaps he's seen the damned redskin's dead. But Big John can't go shooting the caretaker too.

Now he's really shaking. The caretaker's started banging at the attic door. 'Hey, what the hell are you doing up there?' he shouts. 'Come on, open up!'

But Big John's got other plans. Rushing to his parents' section, he clambers up on an old table, shoves open the skylight and heaves himself up on the roof. He's never dared do that before. The roof slopes so steeply, and anyway, there's nowhere to go up here. For a moment he hears the sound of a police siren down in the street, but then it goes quiet again. The police do that on purpose so the murderer doesn't know they've arrived.

Suddenly, Big John loses his balance and slithers down the

roof. A few slates follow him down. A broad-backed chimney stops him falling over the edge. He clings to it and looks down. There's no police car down on the street, but the redskin's back on his feet.

Michael had lain next to his bicycle for some time without moving. Eventually, a pensioner had come along with her dog. The dog had tried to lick up the ketchup. Pulling it away, its mistress had minced quickly past him up the street. After that, nothing else happened. In the end Michael got up, laughing and feeling pleased with himself. 'That was quite something—what I call chancing your arm! And it won't be long till I fall in love, either!' He grins and gets back on his bike. The front mudguard's rubbing on the tyre because of the fall, and he's going to have to wash his shirt and jacket, too.

Big John watches from above. His Colt, forgotten now, slips from his hand, slides down the roof and tumbles over the gutter. Falling five floors to the garage entrance, it killed one of Hamburg's last ladybirds.

Peter Glaser

END

Excuse me for speaking to you like this in a café, but I love you.

There's nothing to explain. You walked down the street in the evening light, I saw you, and now I love you.

I don't wish to frighten you. You are wonderful, I love you. These things happen.

No, thank you, I don't wish to sit. I want you to see my body. Here. My body must convince you. Don't misunderstand me, please.

Oh, what eyes you have! As dark as any night has ever been. And that evening light in which you arrived. You know, I was going to leave four weeks ago. The light has kept me here in Marabá. It fascinated me, until I saw you.

I must go now. I'll be in Hotel Colón at nine. I'll be waiting for you in the bar. Please come, I'll be waiting for you. Hotel Colón. It's here. On the map. *Totalmente Reformado. Conforto e Higiene Absoluta.*

You may well laugh. You are an American. I'm not from here, either. May I kiss your hand, Señorita?

YOU ARE WEARING A DIFFERENT DRESS. It is a little more sophisticated than the dress you were wearing in the café. Unfortunately, the light is so bad in here. When we leave we'll stand under the streetlight by the hotel and I shall look at you in your new dress.

You are wonderful, even here in the smoke and bad light.

Would you like another coffee. I can recommend something. *Eduardo, two infernales.*

One must take care not to drink too much of this.

DO YOU SEE THOSE TWO MEN playing cards over there. At the red table. Their names are Zé and Juan. They are *pistoleiros*. You can go to them and give them one hundred and fifty dollars and they will kill me for it. Perhaps they'll want fifty dollars more because I am a foreigner. The value of every life can be expressed in an exact sum of money. I also find it quite astonishing. Insurance premiums, or the fee of a killer.

I've often played cards with them. I've always lost. I don't think they would kill me immediately if I won.

I am glad you have such a black sense of humour.

I lived for some time in Germany. The people there do not understand how one can laugh about such things. They don't laugh about love, either. Feelings are always a kind of work to them. I'm not German, oh no.

LOOK HOW LITTLE THERE IS IN OUR GLASSES. I shall put my hands on the table.

Look.

This is my heart. I love you. Give Zé the hundred and fifty dollars later. I mean it seriously.

WHY SHOULD *I* STAND UNDER THE STREETLAMP?

Over here. Imagine the light is warm water and you are taking a shower in it. You are radiant. You are all aglow. You don't need to stand under the streetlight at all. You are a shining light.

It's a little hard to be romantic when rats keep scuttling over the pavement. Don't let it worry you.

BRAZILIANS WOULD NOT HAVE DONE THAT.

Brazilians would have kissed in the dark. Nearly all of them are Catholics.

Do you have a God? Because you kiss so sinfully.

I sometimes think of God, and feel nothing but myself. I know I am insignificant beneath the stars. I am a cold breath from eternity.

But you are a whole sky full of radiant stars.

Let us leave here. Otherwise they may yet christen us, or marry us, or have us cremated.

THAT'S MY ROOM UP THERE, yes. And you were going to show me your dress. No, I have no gun under my pillow. *Higiena Absoluta.*

I HAVE BEEN UP FOR TWO HOURS SITTING AT THE WINDOW. Good morning, beauty.

I've been watching Eduardo. He's slaughtered a pig. I saw the blood and the red of the dawn sky and your red mouth and the red glow of my cigarette.

To be lying in bed with you is like a dream. I no longer need to sleep. I have dreamt everything I need dream. *Eduardo, coffee.*

SO YOU WORK FOR *TIME* MAGAZINE. If the way you make love is anything to go by then you must write great stories. *No, don't.*

Ah well, now the pillow's gone flying out of the window. There it is, lying down there in the blood. I'm going to shave.

There ought to be a blade in that drawer. I slipped it between the pages as a bookmark. No idea what the book is. I don't understand Spanish. The Bible? Thought it might be. It makes no difference, I might as well read it all the same. I don't understand a thing, but the words sound like music.

I'm going to shave now.

DO YOU SEE THAT GREEN AEROPLANE. That is Hernandez. He runs supplies to the gold-mining camp in the north.

There are hundreds of them up there, all digging shoulder

to shoulder. The slopes of the riverbanks look like a gigantic beehive. I was there two months ago.

They kill themselves, or each other. The shafts are unsafe and keep on collapsing. They shoot each other by day, and at night they stab each other. Hernandez sells them beans, beer and shovels for their gold.

There was another man with a plane in Marabá. He wanted to fly a second supply line to the camp. His plane went up in flames in its hangar and he burned to death with it. Apparently, Hernandez stank of petrol like an Esso tiger that day. Hernandez does good business.

I'M GLAD I hadn't met you before. I would have gone looking for gold if I had.

With gold next to your skin you must be dangerously beautiful.

You are a shining light, and gold will glow on you with all its rich, wild radiance. I can see it now.

Your aura seems to scream, it is so loud.

YOU MUST BE VERY CAREFUL if you intend to write about the big landowners.

You know, the *fazendeiros* are nervous. The government wants to carry out a land reform. Many of the landowners have extremely dubious title deeds on their land, and there are thousands of small peasants who have no land at all. They have taken to the jungle, which also belongs to the landowners.

The *fazendeiros* have armed their own people. You realise, of course, that you cannot move about quite as freely here as in Milwaukee.

A *pistoleiro* will demand a million *cruzeiros* for a dead peasant, or for someone like myself. That's a hundred and fifty dollars. I don't know how much he'd want for a journalist.

YOU EAT ONLY THE HEART OF THE BREAD.

Do you always leave the crust?

GOOD VEHICLE. It has high axles. The Transamazonica is in dreadful condition.

Stop over there by that fat lady with the pipe. I'll buy two of those fruits from her. They look so good. I don't know what they're called.

I've got a headache, too.

Use your knife to scoop out the stone.

It's so damned close today.

The flesh of the fruit is the same pink as the lips of your vulva. Feel it. Yes, of course that's why I bought them. Look, my hands are wet with the juice. I have gloves of glass. And you have a glass chin.

IT MUST BE SUNDAY. The bells have been ringing all morning. I caught a frog over by the saw-mill. I've put it in that tin.

What I was doing at the goldmines? I'm interested in poisons.

There are some indios who live in the jungle near the goldminers' camp. They make a drug called *yaaqui* which they get by boiling a certain liana. The indios there also have one or two other things I need.

Perhaps I'll tell you about it some time.

IT WASN'T ANYONE KNOCKING. It was the frog.

It wasn't the frog after all?

What does Eduardo say?

That it isn't Sunday after all.

A grave found. Fifteen people, yes. *Pistoleiros*, yes, fifteen peasants. Shot, of course. Ask him who the Fazenda Quiloce belongs to.

Go if you want. I must stay here. That funny medicine-man of mine, that's right.

I won't talk to Zé and Juan.

Eduardo, coffee.

HAVE YOU BEEN TO THE CINEMA IN MARABÁ

YET? It's amazing. It's like being in an aeroplane during a storm.

This is the first time I have been to South America. For three months.

It's blood. No, not from shaving. It was a sharp leaf. I was in the jungle. The medicine-man showed me the *Place of the Wet Spirits*.

He isn't really a medicine-man. He's a warrior. An indio, of course. Oh yes, he's a sly fox all right. No, not an Inca.

THERE'S A RESTAURANT OVER THERE IN THAT BLUE BUILDING. I've ordered ham and bananas. The wood of the table smells so good I could eat it. You smell of dust and that perfume you wear. It's wonderful. But one cannot eat a scented woman.

I LIKE FILMS. I often used to go to the cinema in Europe. A lot of television, too.

It's another of those days. Blue, blue, blue, and not a cloud in sight. The air is so transparent you'd think it wasn't there.

Do you think you could explain to a child why the sky is blue? The thing that's always silly in films is death. I mean the way people die in films.

They lie on their backs, say something, and then their heads loll over to one side.

If it hits them standing up it's usually because they've been shot. They clutch their wounds for a moment, their faces contorted, then fall over.

Or they fall over a cliff. Very effective. A stunt. Exploding cars. Hernandez setting fire to an aeroplane. There are only two or three standard types of death in the cinema. Pathetic.

THE FILM WAS CALLED *WOYZECK*. A jealous soldier stabs his lover at the edge of a small lake. That was a really good film-death.

You could see her body jerking and twitching, and the spasms in her face.

Quite impressive for a film. Klaus Kinski played the soldier. I can't remember the woman's name.

YOU SAY I've never called you by your name. You're right. You are the woman in the evening light, and the woman who makes gold become radiant.

YOUR TYPEWRITER IS COLD. It was in the car all night. The paper's cold, too. Perhaps it's better that way. With the things you write. You're always smoking black tobacco. Now your hands are cold, too. I've asked Eduardo to bring us a paraffin lamp. The medicine-man took the frog. You have to put the frog on a hotplate and get it to sweat. There's poison in the sweat. It's called *bufotenin*. The witches in Europe rubbed it into their skin when they wanted to fly. No, I'm not going to start a magic airline. Hernandez is much too nasty for my liking.

You shouldn't let your long hair get so close to the lamp.

I DON'T WEAR A WATCH. It's probably around four. Can you pass me the Coke on your bedside table.

Shooting stars, really? I told you I didn't need any sleep. I didn't see any.

I'm never bored. This is a simple, whitewashed room. It's very pleasant. In Europe they stuff their rooms too full of objects and pictures and music.

You've made a wish, I suppose.

I thought so.

YOU ARE RIGHT, I'm not really in the poisons business. I merely earn my living that way.

I kill.

Well, how else can I put it. I kill people.

No, nobody pays me to do it. I have to find other means of obtaining money. I work as a self-employed killer, but nobody hires my services. Or to be a little more precise, I work independently doing away with people. It is like being an artist. If you don't market your art you get into financial difficulties.

No, no political motives. No emotional ones either. I'm not the type who saws up women and stuffs the pieces in plastic bags, if that's what you mean.

I AM A STYLIST. Perhaps it would be more correct to say that I am a stylist of perfect unscrupulousness. I have never had a conscience.

By the time I was nine I had developed an industrial aptitude for killing. I have never hated anyone and I don't eat meat.

I have certain friends, and I do love you, *but I am the one who loves changing from nothing to one.** I am a cold breath from eternity.

I don't wish to frighten you.

You wanted me to tell you.

Close the window if you're lighting the lamp or the mosquitoes will get in.

Do you want to see my face, or shall I see yours?

IT'S LIKE A DIVINING-ROD. I have a finely developed sense of—well, what shall I call it?

A sense of what is ultimately evil.

Some people carry it inside themselves as a future truth. This man will one day destroy everything around him. He will destroy every human being he can find. When I meet someone like that I can feel this force. I see the ultimate evil in his future.

Of course I don't expect you to believe me. I'm just telling you. That's all.

SOMETIMES IT ARISES OUT OF A TINY GESTURE, sometimes from a fleeting odour of the skin or clothes. Sometimes it comes shooting up from the very depths of a person's voice like something rising from a bottomless pit miles under

* *original italics in English*

the surface of the ocean. And then I can feel it, and I know beyond any doubt whatsoever that this person is destined to destroy.

Whenever I come upon a person like that I kill them. I never kill with metal.

I have no reason. Only the certain knowledge that this person will destroy, and that I can do something to prevent him.

I COULD SAY: of course I'm mad.

But then there is no society whose order means anything to me. I'm a murderer.

I'm telling you my truth. You believe that I love you. I believe that I can see a person's destiny. What is the difference?

It is a much keener sense of conviction than a feeling. It is the only thing I am really good at.

HELLO.

I've been sitting out here on the patio all day.

Nothing. I haven't been doing anything at all. The sun's been shining. I've been letting the soles of my feet brush over the sand on the concrete. Sometimes I beat a rhythm on the metal table. Sometimes I stare at the foam on my coffee.

Let's sit inside. It's about to start raining.

You've been doing some more writing. You're so curious about everything.

THAT STONE I left lying outside on the table, I found it at the *Place of the Wet Spirits*. Leave it in the rain for a while.

No idea when the rainy season starts here. You Americans aren't the only people in the world who are uneducated. Here, take this leather belt. It suits you. It's so slim and supple and tough.

I'll get the stone for you. It's only a piece of quartz, but try smelling it. Yes, when it's wet it smells of wild flowers.

It's a very special stone.
It's for you. Take it.
Yes, it's astonishing, isn't it.

I HAVE NEVER LEARNED HOW TO DANCE. But perhaps I can do it anyway. I'll just pretend I'm fucking you standing up, okay. That's what tango is after all.

I know the guitarist. He's a radio ham.

ALL RIGHT, I'll show you the *Place of the Wet Spirits*. I can probably find the way, but only if we go at night.

You must dress up for the occasion. It's a very holy place. You must put on make-up. I'll be wearing a tie.

What do you mean nonsense. I was there with that sly fox of an indio, wasn't I? It won't work if we don't dress up for it.

Okay, now let's go to the cinema.

THAT IS A SATELLITE, not an aeroplane. There are another three hours till sunrise. No jet flies so high that it could be reflecting the sunlight already.

It doesn't matter if the car radio isn't working. Would you like me to sing something? It's an Austrian folksong. It has to be sung this loud so that it can be heard up in the mountains when someone sings it in the valley, or the other way around.

Drive in there between the tobacco plants so nobody can see the car from the road. We'll walk the rest.

Where on earth did you manage to drum up that red evening dress? Brought it just in case. Aha.

No, there's nothing in your eye. Turn off the headlamps.

THIS IS THE PLACE.

Of course it feels a bit weird walking through the jungle in a suit at night.

We have to wait until sunrise. Then you can see the rainbow over the waterfalls, and the spirits.

We've got to get down under that precipice. It's about a

hundred and fifty feet down to the basin. That's the actual place.

I feel quite dizzy, too. It's still dark after all. What a noise these animals are making.

I'M OVER HERE.

That isn't pollen in your eyes. It's the mascara. There's *coraya* in your mascara. A poison that only begins to work in sunlight. Now you are blind.

You saw the rainbow. Don't move around so much on that ledge. You'll fall.

No, the *coraya* isn't because of the spirits. This isn't the *Place of the Wet Spirits* at all. This place is your grave.

I TOLD YOU ABOUT GOLD NEXT TO YOUR SKIN. I didn't tell you everything.

I have seen all of your beauty. It is the kind of beauty that kills and destroys.

I have to go.

Rainald Goetz

Inspected

Dead people must be real dead people, the dead brain spattered against the wall must be real dead brain, the blood that spurts from the body on to the grass, must be real pale red blood, and the neck on the rope must be no swan chopped to death, but must be an earlier not yet dead and now dead hanged real person. The dead who have so absolutely, definitively, violently been made dead, must have been murdered by murderers who regard their life as a mission to carry through without adulteration in reality by every possible means the cause of their ideal, to which they owe their position in the real. A human life does not weigh nothing, but normally approximately between nine and twenty stone. Its ideal value can be calculated, inestimable is only the old aria of idiocy, which prefers to estimate everything instead of calculating. In the middle of the living person himself the ideal value of life has the precisely determinable value of zero. In that place there is only an ideal value called death. In the vicinity of the living person, on the other hand, the non-ideal real life of his body draws a high ideal value to it, sometimes so-called love. From the outside, this high ideal value looks like feeble-mindedness, and consequently in the next room it has sunk almost to zero again. If things really were any different, then the burden of sorrow, which the dead person imposes on his surroundings and which is in reality apportioned there among many, so that it may tolerably be borne, would now fall upon each individual quite alone, who would have to bear the whole burden of all the dead alone, and mass suicide would be rational, but things are precisely not like that, but are as they are. The high ideal value of the murder of Schleier is founded on the fact that at the conclusion of calm and rational calculations the state chooses the ritual human sacrifice, which it demands from itself, so as to be freed from its own history by history. The non-Fascists, however, three policemen and Herr Heinz, the chauffeur, who are not calculatedly sacrificed by the state, but executed by the revolution, become sacrifices in their function as men of the people, and out of the locus of this function the highest ideal value aligns itself with them. The revolution has made this value visible in murder and murder makes visible the decisive mistake in the calculations of revolution, and so the revolution shatters on precisely this ideal value of the life of four men of the people. No calculation by a thinking machine, no matter how intelligent, would have been able to simulate this computation. Real people had to really act in reality, because only real, non-ideal, sensually material matter can draw all ideals to itself and so create what was previously neither there in reality, nor conceivable in it. That all ideals look so hideously old, the state altar dripping with Fascist blood and the revolutionary consistency which ends in suicide, means celebration of a better and non-ideal reality, which consequently draws better and less ideal more real ideals to it, and transfers the computation of the consequences to its time, which is instantaneously there. It can very well happen that history itself, which knows no comfort in forgetting and must go on dragging the burdens of all times in itself with itself, and sometimes no longer can and no longer wants to do so and would on the spot make any sacrifice to every friend Skeletor, since old decaying Charon no longer pokes his skiff across the black River Styx, if only the black lord of darkness would at last take all of time itself and its maid history over into the final realm of the three-fold night of the total death of everything. But whoever is weary may rest, and sleep comes to comfort him. And the seas turn, and the earth breathes pale blue air, and the stars look down.

At daybreak we were on our feet again, loaded everything into the canoes and we were up and away. Landscapes shot past, hills, woods, small villages, sometimes we went skimming over shallow, stormy reaches, lake smell, a broad river, huge cities at times, and then fields, meadows, smell of burning again. It was autumn, the maize was still standing but otherwise the fields were dark, already neatly made ready for winter, and in the morning haze ragged individual wisps of thin, pale smoke slanted down into the smouldering piles of old leaves on the ground. Without a helmet the chase across the land of rapid changes was cold, cool and very cold in the face, where there were forests the air was an icy wall, punched through by the road. If the road crossed other roads with houses it was warmer, and sometimes there was a trace of the smell of bread in the air. There was thick fog in the valleys and the water of the rivers flowed invisibly downstream into larger rivers. There were also lakes beyond Potsdam and red Brandenburg sand. Finally at Wannsee it was winter, and the solid glass ceiling of firmly frozen ice, many tons in weight, really was borne by the water below, and covered by crystalline white powder above. Snow also covered the shore and the old villa, and sleep twitched in the turret. When the sun had risen, the leaves had blazed golden and red, broad-leaved trees full of colours in every colour, but time was short and left no time for rest. Apparently a flight, on the best machines of course, heavy bikes, and black leather jackets kept the infernal eagle warm. Through the beautiful morning silver death's heads raced ahead of the throttle on the middle and index fingers of each right hand. Today was Sunday and there were no wrong questions. So the flight was a flight from answers which filled one with fear, pursued till one was finally weary, exhausted of course, and yet still rushing on in exhilarating escape. If angels came towards the infernal eagles, the left fist was raised aloft from the handlebars in careless greeting. Raspe woke up and knew immediately that he had once more dreamt yesterday's television programme, forty years ago today. He looked at his watch, it was seven twenty-four, no, it was later. Someone said, he's still alive, and Raspe wanted to explain that he had somehow eaten and played in the Acheron thirty-three years ago here in Berlin, in the broken dark dead stumps of the remains by the rough edges of the old walls, to the howl of the sirens and the thunder of the stuff being hurled down, where, he doesn't know, tired sparrows sang something, he fell over, why, he doesn't know any more, more because of tiredness and it would all be very pleasant now, there on the high seas, at last to sink down, gone under, in the darkness, down to the marine plants in the depths, and again he started up and had to laugh, because, rather more likely, he really had spent half the night here on the floor among the mountains of his poor newspapers, it seemed to him now, waking and pretty much in command of his senses, and he stood up. Rust in every bone announced unmistakably that this body had slept here. Raspe stood at the window and looked down at the calm white lake. He blinked and suddenly saw that, seen this way, the bare skull now looked at him quite differently from before, strangely enough with the other eye. If one let the image dissolve, the threateningly isolated very dead hysterical pupil turned into a very much alive human eye, which gazed out of the dead skull, heavily and very tiredly, but shocked wide-awake, at whoever was looking down. Raspe nodded, it was Sunday, the time between the years had been overcome again. The snow lay there, fallen truly masterfully. A crystal of spherical shape, repeatedly grooved inside by five cornered stars, firmly gripped at the edge by a reversed spherical crown with nine merlons, additionally held by twenty-four small short thorns, each one pointing right into the centre of the crystal, which seems comprehensible, how beautiful the whole thing appears, when one looks at it on TV through the electron scan microscope. Afterwards Jan Hofer, those were the closing news headlines, good-night from all of us. The national anthem strikes up.

It was Monday, seventeenth October, and the end had come. Into the hands of the revolutionaries time had placed the weapon of a defined location, with which the offensive, exhausted by itself, could bring itself to a conclusion together with the whole seven years' war. The steely bounds of the aircraft brought to an end the time of open time, which had dictated to the actors the complicated deed of non-action. Under the pressure of limited time, the logic of speed of immediate force now takes the place of negotiations, whose subject was the announcement of the time-destroying and therefore not pointless information that negotiations were going on. Precisely for that reason the unmediated dialogue between revolution and state repeatedly demanded by Stammheim can also at last take place, an illusion of course, but consequently pure incarnation of history. On this last afternoon the representative of the Federal Chancellor, instructed by the Chancellor to talk to Baader, really does sit opposite the not yet dead Baader for seventy minutes in the visitors' cell on the seventh floor in Stammheim. The state acknowledges the revolution as an enemy who belongs to it, and so destroys the enemy inside itself. Both sides of the ideal axis Social Democracy and Red Army Faction thereby put their signatures to the unconditional capitulation before the strength of the allied powers of contemporary German reality of the war inherited from the German war. Acting unambiguously, the victorious side seals this document of Stammheim in its own way. Since the early hours of morning, when Flight Captain Schumann, who had been shot in Aden, was thrown out of the aircraft down the Schmidt emergency chute into the desert sand at Mogadishu, the machine has been standing ready there, waiting for the attack by the German anti-terror unit, which is entrusted by the cabinet with the liquidation of the revolutionaries and the liberation of the hostages. Five years ago, the liberation of nine Israeli Olympic competitors taken hostage on the fifth of September seventy-two by a Black September Commando had cost the lives of all the Israeli hostages in the Munich massacre at Fürstenfeldbruck military airfield. Here, however, the seventh week to the day since the fifth of September had begun, and the difference to that other fifth of September runs via the Palestinian commando which the German commando makes use of, to the abyss of an identity, which history cannot confront without going crazy. So history closes its eyes and must, worst torture of all, wait. Meanwhile, on board a special Lufthansa aircraft without lights and under protection of the darkness of nightfall, the anti-terrorist unit has landed unnoticed at its destination. The last ultimatums expire, and the very last ultimatums are again and again postponed. The control tower is in constant radio contact with the pilots' cabin at the front of the machine. Highly sensitive listening devices are attached to the fuselage of the aircraft, rigidly immobile on the ground, to monitor every movement. But breath is not enough to raise an aircraft into the air, and the fear holds. Of course speed is the decisive factor. Operation Fire Magic is in position. Time pauses, waits, it is two minutes past midnight. The control tower talks, the cabin replies, and the tower replies again. So it goes back and forward, and time moves on again after all, beat by beat. If the last moment is given, because it sees itself given, it comes to pass, and everything else complies with it. Whether a shattered brain, spattered against a cabin wall, still sees a dazzle grenade is not known. The deed puts its hands over its eyes, and the one who was dazzled is dead. No one sees any more great brightness than he can bear. Blindly therefore time finishes off the work of all.

Raspe saw himself at the window as clearly as if he was dreaming, and he stood up and completely broken dragged himself to it. He pushed the glass of the skylight, large as a sheet of paper, out into the morning, and pale, cold autumn rushed into the room. Close opposite was the windowless high rock of the next building, and behind that the stubby visible parts of the two distant but uninhabited towers poked into a tiny bit of sky, which grew and became ever larger, the more his forehead leaned out into the brightness. To the left the roof canyon was open towards the east, and from that direction the day came marching up towards him, as a many helmeted front of cloud crests behind clouds, a formation reaching down to the earth, where, sharp as a cleaver blade, a last colourless thread lay, glittering as furthest brightest heavenly cleft of light. Invisible reports and programmes radiated noiselessly through all these heavens, so fast and so rich in communication of images and words, that the poor dead gods, were they not dead, would envy the human beings, who had invented practical things in order not only to fly through the air in a cramped aircraft, when time was getting short, but also to be permanently present with their spirit there in those spaces without borders. Unfortunately problems also arose. For under these heavenly spaces, criss-crossed on many frequencies, lay ragged amid its seas the heavy and ancient solid land of Europe, which already had such huge mountains of dead corpses lying in it, that sometimes in autumn, it itself felt like lying down with them on its own terrible earth with the hard old burnt leaves, which in the end too were allowed to die on the ground, so as at last to go under completely and be but a floor to the oceans. Against that it was convenient that real humans, who sensibly lived together in masses in the cities, were not thrown out of the earth but on to it, out of the not yet dead humans, and thereby normally knew ways of adequately getting through life until it's finished. So for example the Oktoberfest drunk, as he lay in the puddle of beer, to softly mumble and hum songs to the earth which earlier had been roared out very loud and in chorus in the beer tent and although this corpse-like heaviness could not of course understand even live is life, it nevertheless felt a strange whiff of something at its outermost edge, which held and enclosed it. So it came to pass, that no one wanted to go too far away from the tuning fork of the really human voice, neither dark down into the depths of deadly nature, nor too high up into the all too high ideal ether, otherwise something went wrong with the thoughts in the brain. Without tuning, however, thinking knows exactly one clear unique thought, that is death. If the forces, which separate what is separate, are weak, then death would best of all like to leave thought behind and interfere in life in the deed of self-murder. Suicide, however, and the Wannsee self-murderer, now on day two hundred, proves the nonsense, not the opposite, was and is the idiocy, as repeatedly reported here, bong. Good morning, here is Deutschlandfunk at eight a.m. with the news. Raspe threw himself from the window to the table and switched off the death-bringing radio. In Stammheim the revolutionaries had not survived the massacre of the liberation in the desert. Baader was dead, Raspe lay dying. The revolution has accepted the sentence of the people and carried it out on itself. The wretched, crooked desk was completely covered by pieces of paper into which writing had been hammered, weighing them down with real words. On the floor was a light-coloured trainer, there the old chair without arms, here the stone, beside it spherically the orb of the coloured globe, properly separated by white space from the counter-sphere of naked skull, and between them the face. One hand hung at the neck and the head was of granite. The matter was a matter of time. The numbers counted themselves, the colours blazed out of themselves, so history flared up and had told itself. If the fire is extinguished, the cold at last visibly becomes a piece of world. I went over to the desk and packed everything up. It was a little after eight, no, a minute past eight. I remember very well the darkness of that day. I stood at the window, paralysed, and looked into nothing. Dust behind the bony forehead, desolate images, shredded by anger, and revenge wanted to think, but the dazzled eyes saw nothing. I breathed in. Throbbing, my pulses charged the blood towards the brain. It was dark and infinitely chaotically benighted there. Further out, however, at the edges, where alone matter is firmly bounded and it itself comes properly to an end, everything was strained to the utmost, towards the world, certainly in possession of the senses.

On 5 September 1977, Hanns Martin Schleyer (not Schleier as in the text), the president of the German Employers Federation (and a wartime member of the SS), was seized in an ambush by the Red Army Faction in Cologne. Schleyer's chauffeur and three policemen were killed. The RAF demanded the freeing of eleven prisoners in return for Schleyer. The German government, whose chancellor was Helmut Schmidt of the SPD, refused to give in. On 13 October, the crisis was given a further twist when a joint RAF/Palestinian commando hijacked a German passenger plane flying from Majorca. The airliner finally landed at Mogadishu in Somalia, where on the night of 17/18 October a German anti-terrorist unit stormed the plane and rescued passengers and crew. Early on the morning of the 18th, in Stammheim Prison, Andreas Baader, Gudrun Ensslin and Jan-Carl Raspe, all founder members of the RAF, committed suicide. Irmgard Möller survived an attempted suicide. On the evening of the same day Schleyer's body was found in the boot of a car in Mulhouse in France. (*trans.*)

Adolf Endler

From the Proceedings of the COBLACO

An Invitation

... and the COBLACO, dear Consistory Councillor, the COMMISSION FOR THE CONSERVATION AND DEVELOPMENT OF THE BLAZESAK COLLECTION, has been active for some time. The purpose of our meetings, held every Friday from 7.30 p.m. in the back room of the GAMBRINUS, an establishment located in the so-called 'Chansonette' quarter of Berlin/GDR, is gradually to obtain a satisfactory overview of the BLACO, the BLAZESAK COLLECTION, with a view to its possible future function in determining the character of a MUSEUM OF EVERYDAY LIFE of our country. Friday after Friday after Friday the COBLACO devotes its attention to one of the more notable items from the estate of the CASANOVA OF CENTRAL DISTRICT; generally, these are the so-called SOUVENIRS which Bobby-boy Blazesak kept (usually with his name stamped on them) to assist recollection of certain serious 'affairs' should need arise, usually whenever—as he put it—it 'overcame' him ... To speak plainly: the week before the week before the week before last found us discussing three marzipan pigs from Stralsund which, grown rock-hard over the years, were described as 'one hundred per cent emotionally disturbed' by 'cracked'—Dr Nachtfalter; the week before the week before last, our debate centred upon that deadly, gnarled walking-staff from the border regions of Germany, a souvenir of the '1st Pan-German Rambling Day, 14th July

1939'; the week before last saw us rise to the challenge of a woefully isolated, red pubic hair displayed in a small, padded metal box from Nieder-Brunnst ('In league with the devil,/ Red hair and freckles'); last week we worked at a Transcaucasian pencil-sharpener in the form of a tiny book (*THE MAN IN THE PANTHER'S SKIN* by Shota Rustaveli), with which Bobby-boy Blazesak had once tried to sharpen his pencil (*goaded* by the very sight of the pencil-sharpener, he had hoped to compose his memoirs). What trials and tribulations might have been spared the COBLACO research teams, had Bobby-boy Blazesak really managed to get his pencil sharpened! We daren't think of it . . .

As a HISTORIAN OF MENTALITY (or to be more precise: a HISTORIAN OF MENTALITIES), as they call us these days, as well as the unanimously elected Secretary of our Friday evening sessions, permit me to forward to you and yours, my dear Superintendent, a first, modest sample of my minutes, which, as you will see, will occasionally venture beyond mere proceedings in what are commonly understood to be the interests of a future, voluminous CHRONICLE OF THE BLACO AND COBLACO, which the present author already expects to win a place in world literature alongside Boccaccio and the DECAMERON (and no, he has never been a 'modernist' in the true sense of the word). I trust that you will find your own way to the GAMBRINUS, and that you will allow these wonderful lines by Johannes R. Becher to accompany you as you amble through Central district: 'Let us once again go rambling/In gentle meadows and by mountain spring;/You, whose distant peaks rise gleaming,/You, our lovely German land, I sing!'

A Work of Art Rediscovered

The 43rd session of the COBLACO was initially devoted to the COBLACO itself, or rather to the threat, arising from the enormous popularity of its meetings, to its 'politico-martial unity' (as defined by the old Stalinist and superpimp,

Grandpa Poensgen), before finally moving on to a more important matter: namely, the solemn and devout contemplation of that small, but moving work of art which, during the course of some recent excavation in the shed belonging to the second-hand dealer Tute Tengelmann, had emerged glistening from oblivion, so to speak. Indeed, the small body of researchers and excavators was quite dazzled (as an extant photographic record of the momentous event reveals): for here, recovered at long last, though regrettably deprived of much of its silver coating, was that legendary and masterful replica of Robert 'Bobby-boy' Blazesak's fleshy, sensitive right hand, a gem of early sixties GDR-sculpture which has every chance of becoming the preferred (perhaps even 'miraculous') relic of followers of the rapidly growing, Bobby-boy-Blazesak cult.

Yes, there it was, with its little finger maliciously set apart from its fellows, and the thumb curling slightly inward (as if reaching out for something very, very delicate—like a banana, a band-fish, a bandoneon, or a balustrade), while its three middle fingers, a trio of resolute, and yet hesitant prehensile instruments of extreme sensitivity, were displayed in the very act of 'apprehension' (here, for once, the word is used in its proper context and actually does make some sense); thus, and not otherwise, it 'stood'; severed some four centimetres above the wrist, surrounded, on the oval table in the back room of the GAMBRINUS, by an impenetrable thicket of beer and schnapps glasses, it pointed heavenward, or rather indicated in an apparently monitory or criminatory manner the advanced state of crumbling disrepair into which the plafond of the historic room had fallen . . . According to COBLACO historians of art, the creatrix of the work, one Daisy Erkrath, may have taken her inspiration from the hands of Jean Cocteau, which, cast in solid silver, had been immortalised in similar fashion during his lifetime and portrayed in the West German *FILM-REVUE* of 12.5.59 on the occasion of the visit of the West German film star Sabine Sesselmann to Paris (vain as peacocks, these art-critic types—never miss a chance to show off what they know!);

portrayed, in fact, alongside the owner of the Cocteau hands, a melancholy Jean Marais, known to his friends as 'Jeannot' and shown ruminating over the hands in a manner at once French, sonorous and ponderous—as entirely befits the extremities of such a mercurial master; for these were hands that had performed not a few miracles—that much was clear from the outset; and in this respect, at least, they were practically on a par with those of Bobby-boy Blazesak himself . . .

One thing is certain, though: Daisy Erkrath, an artist who had only recently escaped from West to East—sadly, we were to lose track of her completely in later years—and who, though no longer very young, was a star pupil of Arno Breker, as well as a notorious glove-fetishist, had evidently been transfixed by the sight of the Blazesakian right hand (according to Bobby-boy's own account of events); as a belletrist, one has occasionally experienced similar phenomena oneself—'I *must*, I simply *must* turn that into art, even if it costs me half a day's hard labour'—were the thoughts probably buzzing and bubbling inside her: 'At least grant me this one last favour in life—this extraordinary, masculine extremity with its soupçon of the womanly! Such a *revelation*! . . .' And it may very well have been the last of her twenty-three GDR-hands (among them, the left—no, not the right—of the present author), for the extravagant artist subsequently vanished without trace, indeed possibly forever, in the caustic, early-morning haze of Berlin—an occurrence for which there may be more than one possible explanation. We, for our part, are fortunate enough to have inherited—beside several less striking, indeed rather hastily executed and merely bronzed hands from Daisy Erkrath's studio—a work whose survival and rediscovery must surely be put down to an awesome stroke of luck: the SINGLE HAND OF A FIGURE KNEELING IN PRAYER AT A WHITE BAROQUE ALTAR , which COBLACO art critics increasingly refer to in professional circles as the lady's last (?) work.

The 'crazy old bag's' advances towards our hero, described by Bobby-boy Blazesak in a number of strongly divergent accounts, were not only ultimately successful, as evidenced by the Blazesakian hand now firmly in the hands of the COBLACO, but—as Bobby-boy himself pointed out—extraordinarily direct, conducted in a state of extreme agitation and open to two, if not three, possible interpretations—not least in respect of an assault that was tantamount to rhetorical rape, and which verged on the Marinist, if not the Gongorist. Struggling to resist her steadily intensifying state of ecstatic transport—and I refer here to minutes compiled by myself during the Ulbricht era with assiduous attention to nuance—the pale blonde had been engaged for some time in protracted observation of the prompt, and yet 'circumspect' action of the Blazesakian hand in lifting a first, a seventh, a twenty-third glass of beer to his tenderly glistening lips in an establishment by the name of OLLE MOLLE, or TOLLE KNOLLE, when all of a sudden she had lost her self-control and let rip, allowing the full force of her pent-up feelings to come down on the CASANOVA OF CENTRAL DISTRICT *like a ton of bricks*, to employ the parlance of the man-in-the-street, or the 'man of praxis' (Gert Neumann): 'O my God! How long have I been searching for a hand like this! It feels like centuries,' Bobby-boy Blazesak heard the rather plump, blonde artist rave, 'This is a hand I'd like to get to know much, much better . . . Is it the hand of some daring gambler, some hashish-crazed hammer-thrower, the hard and heavy right hand of some happy-go-lucky Hadshi Halef Omar, a hand that's both harp and harrow? Just look at that hooked hare-lip in the hollow between the lifeline and line of fate—oh, it's driving me mad!'

Now, it would be wrong to assume that Bobby-boy Blazesak's certainly rather favourably developed hand had not frequently been exposed to fervent fondling and sucking, indeed had attracted the most eloquent of panegyrics! For all their smouldering intensity, however, these relatively reticent expressions of feeling had been accompanied, if at all, by the kind of activity one might attribute to an ardour of the stiller sort: preludes to relaxed smiles and a lingering 'buena notte', 'good-bye', or 'sleep well'. This bore no comparison whatsoever to the tension between Frau Erkrath (and who cares whether she was really a glove fetishist, or just a common-or-garden hand fetishist?) and Bobby-boy Blazesak's well-formed extremity (how Bobby-boy would have liked to remove it from the table and bury it between his legs!): for Daisy Erkrath had been aroused to a *positively unique* pitch of almost religious frenzy by Bobby-boy's increasingly restless right hand, whose coyness could not have been more excruciating had it reckoned with imminent defloration, or been some innocent little animal awaiting immolation at the sultry saturnalia of some horribly sensualist sect, whereby neither scenario was entirely mistaken as to the reality of its situation. For it seemed that to the artist, who had probably had good reason to flee from the West, Bobby-boy Blazesak's entire one metre seventy-two centimetres (O, at least)—this actually peeved our hero, unlike the alarmed public of the OLLE MOLLE—and the great wealth of his manifold attractions were reduced to the dimensions of a mere garden gnome, to nothing more, in other words, than a thirteen-or-fourteen-centimetre hand to which her metaphorical advances were becoming wilder and more dissipated the greater her courage grew, although (according to Bobby-boy) it was unthinkable that she should have drunk more than the 'owner' of the object of her desires: 'Oh, what a hand, what a hand! I can already see it in bronze, or hung with Christmas-tree baubles, or squeezed into a tightly-fitting silver glove, or gauntlet . . . *Man, you've got one humdinger of a mitt there!*' Thanks to his own reports, we know that these ravenous attempts to take verbal possession of Bobby-boy Blazesak's right hand had made him feel 'uncommonly anxious', giving him the shivers 'from top to toe'. But it was not until Daisy Erkrath had finally launched into a speech packed with pathos and pathology and addressed 'to my fellow Berliners'—'BEHOLD THE HAND!'—a speech to a *very mixed* audience at the OLLE MOLLE—not until Bobby-boy Blazesak and his hand had finally realised that not only Berlin, but 'a considerable proportion of humanity' had been persuaded to stare in the most obnoxiously brazen manner at his (or its) untrained (for once) fingernails, that they began to show signs of wanting to make a break for it 'long before closing time', a phenomenon no less foreign to his hand than to Bobby-boy Blazesak as a whole . . . 'Behold the hand,' Daisy Erkrath repeated; and it was not only humanity alone, but the entire rest of the universe—the blinking eyes of millions of stars—which, overwhelmed by the sculptress's powerful spate of words, insisted on observing the tormented contortions of Bobby-boy's right hand, a hand that hardly dared approach a beer glass (never mind the safety rope of a montgolfier), a hand at the end of its tether, whose twitching and tugging eventually left Bobby-boy Blazesak with no choice but to stagger to his feet and leave the OLLE MOLLE, listing heavily . . . This was later to be referred to as a 'hasty retreat', though Bobby-boy's manner of departure was actually more of a roll than a spurt, followed, needless to say, by an already triumphant sculptress—'So you're from the West, are you?' was the last Bobby-boy heard himself ask; and then . . .

Then, as we all know, Creativity must have its due; and the product stands before us now, just as the COBLACO team investigating Tute Tengelmann's junk-shed first encountered it in the discarded bedside table of a certain Heide Schnack, with a greasy newspaper cutting—to which a later session of the COBLACO may be devoted—skewered on its index finger; thus it must have seemed to the delighted finder that Bobby-boy Blazesak himself were proffering him a recipe for SERBIAN STUFFED CABBAGE, taken from the German-language supplement of the Czech magazine *ZENA & MODA* (10/82), a recipe—mon dieu!—concocted for the COBLACO cosmos, heaven-sent, so it seemed, for inclusion in the Bobby-boy Blazesak galaxy—SERBIAN STUFFED CABBAGE: why don't you give it a try yourself! The present writer, verily no master of the culinary art, has hitherto shirked putting *ZENA & MODA*'s proposals into practice: 'Remove the outer leaves from the cabbage top, cut out the stump and blanch the head till leaves loosen. Then take the head out and drain. Wipe the meat, put through the mincer and sauté with onions in fat. Then add salt, pepper and one egg. Strip the leaves from the head and beat the ribs a little to ease rolling. Use the larger leaves 2 at a time. Finely chop remaining leaves and add to the meat filling. Divide the meat filling among the prepared leaves and roll, taking care to shut in the stuffing from all sides. Grease the pan with remaining fat, add a rasher of bacon and allow to stew slowly in a pre-heated oven. Finally, beat sour cream with an egg, pour over the stuffed leaves and bake until golden...'—A token of friendship that! But where on earth had it come from, and to whom on earth was it addressed? It was undoubtedly the sort of gesture of which Bobby-boy Blazesak would have approved—but then whom to thank? Daisy Erkrath herself? The practically unknown bedside-table owner, Heide Schnack? As briefly indicated above, we have decided to postpone a thorough-going examination of these matters until a later date, largely because the capricious junk-dealer Tute Tengelmann has nothing but a hurtful, and unproductive sneer for the Commission's investigators... We won't forget that in a hurry, Tengelmann! You will have to do without our waste paper in future—and it looks as if there'll be quite a lot of it, too! Get the picture?

The Razor-blade with Spider's Legs

How often we must have argued over the coat-of-arms and letterhead of the COBLACO! As if there were not more pressing BLACO matters for us to discuss! At the beginning of the 64th session, reserved for Bobby-boy Blazesak's shocking RAZOR-BLADE ON SPIDER'S LEGS, the author believed the tiresome COAT-OF-ARMS DEBATE to be a thing of the past; at the conclusion of the session, however, he is astonished to find it has been stirred up again by admirers of a BOHEMIAN BEER-TANKARD which, due to a mechanism as yet insufficiently researched, plays the polka tune ROSAMUNDE whenever it is raised to the mouth and tilted to a drinking position (my God, who *are* these people!). Though very little is known of the origins of the Czechoslovakian beer-tankard, COBLACO members ought to be acquainted with the fact that the razor-blade was a matter of acute importance to the CASANOVA OF CENTRAL DISTRICT (especially in view of his strict weekly timetable); this, after all, is the legendary WEDNESDAY GILLETTE, and Bobby-boy's Wednesdays contained something very special: the only day of the week, at least in German, whose name (MITTWOCH) contains a very short, and highly characteristic 'i'—shrewd observation, eh?

Bobby-boy Blazesak: 'Business considerations alone dictate that certain Wednesday appointments are rock solid. On Wednesdays it's my livelihood that's at stake!' Certainly, the harrowing ordeals of a Monday, which usually involved having to deal—in more senses than one—with Wiebke Mewissen, are not the worst way I happen to know of spending such a difficult day of the week—and if that sounds like a threat, it's quite intentional! Nor were the artificial paradises of a Friday to be sneezed at, initiated by the incessantly and mirthlessly giggling police-boot fetishist, Welta Hackensack-Dau; but Wednesday evenings were simply 'a cut above the rest', with their crowning, so-called 'midnight display of sports and gymnastics' held under the electrifying sceptre of Satanic bombshell Dr Veronika Klarmatz, also known as 'missus 120 volts', or as 'the female *Turnvater* Jahn'. Whether or not one is ultimately in favour of the defilement of this most sinless of weekdays, Bobby-boy and his mates of the 'light-metal underground'—'drainpipe-mafia' would actually be a more fitting description of the gang's activities—had to attend Wednesday evening meetings, which were disguised as casual skat sessions, 'come what may'; for these dubious gatherings high up in the Weinbergsweg took place, as pointed out above, under the regimen of none other than

Miss Veronika Klarmatz, Doctor of Sciences, who held in her hand all the strings, even the shadiest, of what was—at best—a one-eighth-legal drainpipe enterprise with dealings so complex, not even her most intimate business partners could make head or tail of them. Nobody would have dared address Doc Klarmatz, married and divorced eight times, as 'Matz'; 'I'll have you lot as mats all right!' would undoubtedly have been her riposte (according to Bobby-boy anyway, who occasionally attributed daemonic—but never diabolical—powers to the female sex); the response, in other words, of a being who seemed sprung from the darkest of Romantic hearts, or brains . . .

In a word, it was a real she-devil who got her hands on Bobby-boy and his mates every Wednesday; blue-haired, purple-lipped and shod in bright green, she would dab behind her earlobes and upon her torpedo-shaped bosoms a perfume at once repulsive and enthralling, a scent which exuded the unmistakably sweet aroma of ripe cadaver; it was called OPTIMIST—naturally, and was only available on the black market. (So cultivated was she that her inexplicable penchant for the folksy, for the 'distinctive solidity' and fanciful rusticity of folk-art, seemed, by contrast, quite perverse. Did it all come down to her Nazi family and her early devotion to the ripe, firm, full-blooded ideals of German maidenhood? Although evidently from Oranienburg rather than Upper Bavaria, she would adopt a Bavarian accent and subsume her relatively large team of partners under the crudely collective 'my boys'—a form of address, incidentally, which shocked them into temporary paralysis.) But there was one thing even the lowliest member of the 'inner circle' knew: by the witching hour, when 'forfeits' began, a game to which Veronika, with great sensitivity and an enormous repertoire of obscene jokes, never failed to transform even the most gripping round of skat (no sooner had you called 'full house' than you were reduced to your underclothes), all her 'boys' had to be present, or else they'd *got something coming* to them, and it wouldn't be brass, or tin . . . Yes, just imagine! Every single one of her boys, including Bobby-boy, every one of these highly respected businessmen from Prenzlauer Berg district, was obliged to sit at the card table 'one hundred per cent naked' while Veronique ignited her thirteen (!) weirdly stalacticious, folk-craft candles from the Erz Mountains, one for each of her very variously proportioned naughty boys, and 'two hundred per cent naked' when she produced the anxiously-awaited, super-sharp RAZOR-BLADE WITH SPIDER'S LEGS and passed it round for inspection among the ostentatiously shuddering company (critical sampling of the joys of Gillette by the hirsute backs of twenty-six male hands: unanimously okayed).

Then came the moment when our 'lady Doctor' took the magically gleaming razor-blade with its welded-on spider's legs and let it flash, zig-zag, to the whitest and softest flesh of her thigh, cutting a sizeable gash a few millimetres under, or to the side of, her so-called labia; blood gushed forth, inspiring delirious applause interspersed with interjectionary references to Professor Sauerbruch, which Veronika, with icy resolve and torrid magniloquence, brought to an abrupt end: 'Forever ... secret is ... the gate/To my dark and ... enchanted ... bower/Where *words of stillness* wait:/Sweet honey ... of the coyest flower/*And* nettle words ... of ... burning fragrance ... /How I long ... for ... the balmy incense/Of the garden ... that fades ... and then is gone/At every ... movement ... that turns *against me,*/A garden *I alone* can find,/*In myself only* ... and ... so *rarely,*/A shock ... a sudden scent ... *all-engulfing:*/Life's bitter ... lack of relief ... /Morning has broken! ... *I burst, singing*/ A weeping heart, untouched by grief ...'—Thirteen bodies, frozen in gestures of admiration and quiet awe, possibly a pretence: 'She speaks in tongues!' (One of them even started composing a disgusting little review: 'A poet at last who does not shun the bard's ancient ways—one who *puts her ear to the ground* and heeds the beat of our hearts!') Of course, very few realised they were enjoying the privilege of attending a POETRY READING with new, indeed the very latest poetry (no, it wasn't by Ulla Hahn)—the kind of poetry we were now and then presented with until well into the eighties, in *NEUE DEUTSCHE LITERATUR* for example, the magazine of the GDR Writers' Association. (I beg your forgiveness, dear ladies, dearest readers, but this type of thing actually does happen now and again behind certain closed doors in the GDR; not that often perhaps, but not infrequently enough for even the present, relatively chaste and tired-out author to have avoided becoming deeply shocked *as a human being* involved in such excesses, at least partly, I'm terribly sorry . . .)

Now that Veronika Klarmatz was stomping up and down with bleeding thigh—the shadowy imitation of a low-key Passion wobbling in the background—her words came in ever more vehement gasps: 'And . . . southern winds . . . blossom . . . with the word/And bring me . . . perfumes . . . on the summer breeze,/Undone . . . is the spell, . . . I arise like a bird,/Released . . . from my exile . . . in lands . . . that freeze./The liberty I have . . . *gained in terror*/Is *inner* . . . freedom, . . . *from* . . . *self* unbound./Overcome . . . is self-hatred's . . . fatal error,/In *word* . . . and *time* . . . forbearance . . . found . . .'

Etceteraetceteraetceteraetcetera.—Meanwhile, Veronika's recitation had left poetry fan Bobby-boy Blazesak feeling anything but mellow; nor did he feel particularly inclined to forbear with the lady and her undoubtedly exceptionally sensual satanism: behold the blood, the blood of Klarmatz, *a fluid of a special type*, tinged with the light grey of cement, or rat poison, *it's hard to believe one's own eyes*; like a trail of gunpowder, it trickles from the soft, white flesh of her thigh on to the Persian carpet; a single match would probably suffice to blow up the whole place . . . One or two of our thirteen drainpipe-heroes may secretly have harboured plans of this sort—in which Veronika's own blood could be used to put an abrupt end to her commercial and artistic terror.

One might ask—and the author, *who also writes poetry*, knows what he's talking about—whether it was not the *poet-*

essa's real intention during these Wednesday meetings to counter a diminishing interest in the lyric art with certain new and admittedly rather idiosyncratic methods; she may thus have hoped to render poetry somewhat more 'palatable' for her audience, even if the latter was restricted to the small and élite circle of her 'boys', and though the means at her disposal were little more than the bluntest forms of coercion and the shrillest of shock-tactics. If so, then Veronika Klarmatz failed dismally, though she was probably unaware of it herself; for even Bobby-boy Blazesak, usually the most open-minded of sorts, was absolutely not prepared to accept this interpretation of events; the lyrical intermezzo by 'the Satanic bombshell of the Weinbergsweg' had been 'Nothing but sheer malice! Nothing but mean, clever tricks!', while the partly hypnotic power (according to Bobby-boy) of her razor-blade had pursued our hero even into his dreams, at least on those rare occasions when he had dared skip the WEDNESDAY SESSION 'partly because of the sleet, partly because of flu'. Bobby-boy Blazesak, who possessed several books about dreams, was extremely reluctant to talk about his razor-blade dreams, several of which might easily have led people to suspect that the Casanova of Central district doubted his own 'virility'; and it really is more than unpleasant to imagine a Gillette-blade rushing towards one at full tilt on countless spider's legs a yard tall, slashing one's increasingly empty loins again and again, or even snipping with unflagging zeal at one's so-called glans, the shrieking glans of a desperately plunging member ... 'Better to go to Veronika Klarmatz every Wednesday!'—Seriously though, my dear associates—after all, the COBLACO was founded by none other than the author himself—you cannot seriously be considering resolving our tiresome coat-of-arms debate by rejecting such a splendid spider-legged razor-blade in favour of a mere gimmick like the beer tankard from Prague, however loud and dilettantish its version of *ROSAMUNDE* when one takes a sip (which some people have probably been doing too often recently ...).

Robert Gernhardt

The Riace Bronzes

Hermann Marquardt, a writer, looked thoughtfully down at his desk. He had just completed a story which seethed with hatred for his wife. He counted the pages—there were twelve—and wondered what to do with the manuscript. The writing itself was good, with long passages of infectious prose that positively burned up the page. Publication, however, was out of the question; his wife was bound to recognise herself in the story and exact some sort of revenge. And his wife's revenge . . . Marquardt gave a sudden start and listened. All quiet in the corridor and kitchen—not a sound to be heard through the firmly shut door of the study. For a moment he had to smile at his own fear. How could his wife be back so soon? She had only left an hour ago to meet her friend and could hardly be expected to return for another two hours at least. He hoped she would return alone, rather than with her friend. Unfortunately, however, the less preferable alternative was also more likely.

The story Marquardt had just finished was also about a woman and her friend—and about a writer whom the two women had persuaded to accompany them on a trip to Florence. The writer wanted to go to Florence to see the Riace bronzes, which had been restored there and were being shown before going on to their final destination, the Museo Nazionale at Reggio di Calabria, a town in the very south of Italy.

The writer had read in the newspaper about the discovery of the two bronzes on the bed of the Ionian Sea. His curiosity had been further aroused by photo stories in magazines; before long, the exhibition in Florence of the two Greek, early Classical figures of warriors had quite fired his imagination. Although the exhibition had been extended once already, and the closing date was approaching fast, first one, then the other of the two women managed to think of some trifle they couldn't postpone. Eventually, they had arrived in Florence on the day before the exhibition was due to close. The following day, however, which was definitely the last, the two women pointed out that they had a long day before them and insisted not only on taking their time over breakfast, but on setting out afterwards to purchase shoes, bags and scarves. They then demanded lunch in a restaurant that was difficult to find, but which, according to a friend well versed in things Italian, was an absolute must.

Of course, the writer had not neglected to emphasise with increasing vigour that time was passing, if not going to waste, for whereas it would be quite possible to finish the shopping tomorrow, today was their last chance to see the bronzes. After lunch, however, things got worse. Suddenly, the women complained that the shoes they had bought didn't fit, and that certain scarves and bags they had bought didn't match, and that it was essential to go back and exchange them before their receipts became invalid. What was more, the writer himself was expected to escort them to the various shops without delay; for was not he the only one who could speak Italian? As for his reminder that the exhibition was due to close at six, both assured him that the hotel reception had given them quite different information; the exhibition was due to remain open on the day of its closure until eight o'clock, for which reason they would be obliged if he would kindly refrain from shitting his pants.

Despite his misgivings, he allowed their assurances to mollify him; and in spite of his attempts to hurry them on, their exchange of unwanted articles and purchase of new ones continued unabated; and although they assured him that they had plenty of time left, he began to implore them with growing urgency to set off at last with him to the Museum of Archaeology, where the bronzes were being shown. By the time the ladies finally condescended to leave, however, it was too late; the exhibition really did close at six. They arrived at the museum five minutes before closing, and it was due only to the verbal torrent of the writer and the pity taken upon them by one of the attendants that they were permitted even a brief and distant view of the heroes. Quite unperturbed by the mass of visitors pushing—or rather, being driven—hurriedly past them, the statues were tranquillity itself. Miraculous messengers, risen from the depths of a lost era in which artists had been able to lend a lasting value to existence and a meaning to life itself.

An almost savage desire to get to the bottom of the mystery of these quite palpable apparitions by approaching them as closely as possible made the writer press forward through the throng of oncoming visitors. However, the sympathetic attendant, now wholly without sympathy, had immediately recalled him, urging him to be reasonable: it was time to close, why hadn't he come earlier. The two women expressed equal impatience. What on earth did he want? It was perfectly possible, they insisted, to see everything from the entrance; indeed, they had already seen everything, without even paying:

'Two large, naked and astonishingly green men.'

'Yes, with astonishingly small peckers.'

The events thus related represented an abridged version of the contents of the writer's twelve-page story, but they did not capture its essence. For while Marquardt had borrowed the plot more or less (in fact, exclusively) from reality, his actual theme had been the sharp contrast between the two women, slaves of time who hurried from one fashionable boutique to another, and the two men, discovered by chance after waiting almost two and a half thousand years at the bottom of the sea. The latter had something to say to us today precisely because they didn't say it at all: they were it.

Naturally, Marquardt had done everything he could to cover, or rather wholly erase, his tracks. He had turned his decidedly slim wife, who was of average height, into a decidedly stout type of outsized proportions. He had changed her friend's age and looks, too. Above all, he had given them entirely different names; and yet while this subterfuge might throw strangers off the scent, or distant acquaintances at the very most, the couple's close friends would see through these ruses immediately. As for his wife, there was no doubt that she would grasp everything after the first couple of sentences.

Instead, he felt his own doubts growing. Had he really given them such different names? Marquardt's wife, whose real name was Carla, had featured in the story as Anna; her friend Gisela, meanwhile, had become Irmela. Dismayed, he realised how similar were the syllables and vowels of their true and invented names. On a separate piece of paper he briefly jotted down a list of other women's names, but these all ended up with two or three syllables too: Helma and Claudia, Vera and Ingeborg, Clara and Griseldis. What a waste of time! And anyway, even well chosen names, less compulsive in their snug approximation to the facts, would be quite unable in themselves to eradicate the basic flaw of the text: its transparency.

Marquardt was enough of an artist to interpret his predicament as a challenge. He knew that great poetry had always taken nourishment from the crudest of realities, but that in so doing it had also digested reality according to the rules of art, before excreting it in highly concentrated form. The recently recorded outpourings of his soul had shown but a superficial and transient layer of his experience with two women. At the heart of the matter had lain questions of a quite different order, questions of temporality and timelessness, of longing and of life's fleeting moments lost: in the broadest possible sense, therefore, questions of life and death. But couldn't such questions be presented in vastly different attire? Fully determined, the writer proceeded to scrutinise the contents of the imaginative wardrobe to which each and every artist has access. He would soon show his wife what inventiveness and an artistic sensibility could come up with! He would write something in which she would find herself not so much portrayed as put on the spot. Caught unawares, her sense of exposure would deprive her of the appropriate means of retaliation. Keeping her mouth shut would then be the only guarantee that what she knew about herself would remain private. Or rather, what they knew. For somebody else would be in the know, too: he would! Rubbing his hands in glee, Marquardt sat down to rewrite his story.

This, of course, was easier said than done. To begin with, the writer found even thinking about it difficult. A change of scenery perhaps? He considered having the man and two women visit some other exhibition in some other place. What about the Etruscan exhibition at Arezzo? No, too near Florence. The Egyptian exhibition at Hildesheim? He hadn't seen that one. The Frans Hals exhibition at Amsterdam? That was too long ago, and anyway, the wonderfully apt contrast between the temporal women and timeless men would be entirely lost; lost, too, would be the final, longing gaze of the women's companion, as the newly resurrected warriors inexorably sank below the horizon. It was a highly symbolic situation, impossible to transpose to a room full of portraits of Dutch merchants who had no more been lost than they had risen from the dead in the first place.

Marquardt, a man of quick perceptions, soon noticed that a change of location would do nothing whatsoever to help his story along. Would a change of period solve the problem?

In his thoughts, he dressed up his trio in a series of very different costumes. He transported them to England during the middle of the previous century and had them miss an exhibition of the Elgin Marbles, robbed by Lord Elgin from the Acropolis. He wondered, too, about setting the same plot against a Berlin background during a turn-of-the-century exhibition of the Pergamon Altar, assembled fragments of which had been shipped from Turkey. But no sooner had he considered these possibilities than he discarded them again. After all, when had the Elgin Marbles first been shown in London? And had there ever been a first showing of the Pergamon Altar? Hadn't the bits and pieces immediately become the property of the museums at Berlin? Marquardt, a writer who felt that the facts should be allowed not only a normative, but also a creative role, saw himself getting bogged down in research so complicated that its results would be unlikely to repay his effort. The story was still about two superficial women preventing a man of profundity from enjoying a particular aesthetic and spiritual experience. There was still a danger that somebody, perhaps his wife's friend, would recognise the plot and demand retribution. In short, it simply wouldn't do.

But Marquardt was not about to give up. He had not yet tried altering the characters themselves, a proposition whose feasibility he now set about putting to the test. What if he simply reversed their roles? A woman wishes to visit the exhibition of the Riace bronzes, her husband and his friend decide to accompany her, but fritter away the time with their shopping—the writer stopped himself short. What was he going to have the two men buy in Florence? And how was he supposed to counter a reading of the plot which inappropriately emphasised its sexual bias? Two men, the veritable slaves of fashion, prevent a woman from seeing two naked men—now that really had very little indeed to do with the story he had in mind. Not a trace of the temporal and eternal; no question of his wife secretly feeling exposed. She wasn't stupid, after all. His simple reversal of the facts would be just as obvious to her as the cowardice that had given rise to it in the first place. But then he would look stupid. But no, he wasn't stupid, and nor was he cowardly. He was bold and cunning. His wife would soon find out! Cowardly, eh? Stupid, eh? He'd show her all right! He was a writer, wasn't he? He had more than one string to his bow. Parables, fables, fairy-tales, for example: venerable, yet ageless narrative forms that had always done good service in pointing to the essential in what might otherwise have appeared incidental, and had always done so in a way that granted the apparently incidental addressee an insight, indeed granted him little choice but to see just how essential was the error of his ways! Thus it was that the writer Hermann Marquardt thought of the story of the three bears.

It went something like this: two she-bears and a he-bear had arranged to meet on St Irmela's Day in order to climb Mount Lawrence, for they wanted to see the sun set over Lake Spinach. Of course, they had a very good reason to choose St Irmela's Day for their expedition, for it was on that day alone that the sun set exactly between two huge, red, sandstone rocks, traditionally known—nobody knew why—as 'Bronco I' and 'Bronco II'. Every year on the same day since time immemorial the 'burning Broncos of Lake Spinach', as one poet had christened this natural wonder, had been attracting onlookers to Mount Lawrence, where it was generally considered that the most advantageous view of the marvel could be had. It was said that the spectacle had the power to make secret wishes come true. Whatever, there was one thing about which everybody agreed: no spectator could afford to be late, for the sun set extremely quickly in that part of the world. No sooner had the indescribably beautiful glow of the lake and rocks faded, than they were plunged into total darkness. For this reason, visitors were always advised to bring torches to light their way home.

Once he had constructed this somewhat unwieldy setting, the rest of the story seemed to flow from his hand effortlessly: the he-bear urging the she-bears to set off, the she-bears finding a meadow full of bilberries on the way up, time passing endlessly while they tucked into the berries and ignored the he-bear's warnings, then all three of them arriving at the summit of Mount Lawrence with the last, weak rays of sunlight setting the horizon over Lake Spinach faintly aglow, the two 'Broncos' themselves barely standing out against the night sky, the homeward journey of the disappointed and somewhat frightened she-bears only avoiding disaster because the he-bear had taken the precaution of bringing three torches, whereas, naturally, the she-bears had forgotten theirs. The moral of the story was self-evident. After fully admitting the reprehensibility of their dawdling, the two she-bears went on to express intense gratitude to the he-bear, whose prescience had brought a life-saving light to the darkness of their mortal night ... The writer could not suppress a smile. While this deviated somewhat from the facts, the ending of his story none the less gave symbolic weight to the truth.

He retained his smile while rereading what he had written—now reduced to four pages. How subtly interwoven were his allusions: Lawrence—Florence, Spinach—Riace, Broncos—bronzes; yet how eloquently they would speak to his wife! Couching his main theme in the form of a parable might make it more abstract, but did not detract from it. On the contrary! How apt, how unforced was the combination of entertainment and instruction! Marquardt leant back and looked up from his desk. Now he was actually looking forward to his wife's return. Let her come back with her friend! What did it matter to him? All the better, in fact!

Both women turned up half an hour later. They did not make their way straight to his study as Marquardt had initially feared and as he now hoped, but dilly-dallied first in the corridor and then in the bedroom, probably in front of the mirror, thought the writer; and indeed, that was exactly where they were. Eventually, however, they remembered yet another mirror: him. His door practically flew open, and there they were standing in his room: what did he think of the combination of last year's wraparound skirt and these brand-new calf-length boots?

It was some time before Marquardt got round to telling them of his new creation. His chance came with his wife's question: 'And what have you been up to all day then?' He practically forced his four-page manuscript upon her, insisting she at least have a look through it, and didn't leave her in peace until she finally agreed to read it out. On tenterhooks, the writer leant forward to listen. This was it.

It wasn't quite what he expected. His wife's tone while she read out his four pages could almost be described as a drone, interrupted only now and then as she threw long-suffering glances at her friend, or made dismissive remarks about the plot and, especially, the names of the locations: 'Lake Spinach? What weird ideas you have! Who has ever heard of a rock being called Bronco?' Finally, she handed him back his manuscript, adding: 'You and your bears! Try writing about people for a change!'

This was the cue for his wife's friend, whose face, until that moment, had remained quite expressionless. Declaring she was as hungry as a bear, she asked the others what they thought about nipping over to the Italian restaurant.

While his wife's words had filled the writer with a wild desire to reveal the whole truth, the mere sound of the word 'Italian' was enough to make him want to pull open the drawer of his desk and disclose, before the two women's very eyes, the safely hidden original manuscript. However, a sudden thought prevented him from doing so. Was it not tantamount to self-betrayal for a writer whose theme was the contrast between timelessness and temporality to covet such short-lived triumph in the here and now? Should not he, of all people, trust in the retributive justice of time? Was not time the proven ally of all true artists, and would it not, sooner or later, bring to light what was hidden in the depths of his desk—not only this text, but many, many others whose hour also had not yet come?

'Are you coming with us or not?' asked his wife.

'I really must get something down me,' said her friend.

'Just coming,' said the writer, and locked the drawer of his desk.

About the Authors

Katja Behrens was born in Berlin in 1942. From 1960 she worked as a freelance translator. Between 1973 and 1978 she was a publisher's reader, after which she travelled extensively.

She has been a full-time writer since 1978 and has received several literary awards, including the Ingeborg Bachmann Prize. She lives near Darmstadt. Her most recent publication is *Salomo und die anderen. Jüdische Geschichten* (1993).

Thomas Brasch was born in Yorkshire, England, in 1945. In 1948 he moved to the GDR with his parents. He was not allowed to finish a journalism course for political reasons and had to get by with casual jobs; later he was expelled from film school and sentenced to two years and three months in prison. Subsequently he did casual work again, before finally being given permission to go to West Berlin, where he still lives today as author and playwright. Recent published work includes the plays *Lovely Rita. Rotter. Lieber Georg* (1989) and *Frauen—Krieg—Lustspiele* (1987) and the story 'Mädchenmörder Brunke' (1995).

Clemens Eich was born in Rosenheim in 1954. Trained at the Zürich Drama School, he has acted in many theatres and now lives and works in Vienna. He has received the literature prize of the city of Mannheim. In 1980 he published a volume of poetry *Aufstehn und gehn*, and in 1984 the play *So*.

Adolf Endler was born in Düsseldorf in 1930. In 1955 he moved to the GDR, had numerous jobs, including transport worker and crane driver. He studied literature for two years and lives, as a writer, in Berlin. In 1990 he was awarded the Heinrich Mann Prize (GDR). In 1987 he published *Schichtenflotz. Papiere aus dem Seesack eines Hundertjährigen. Prosa*, in 1991 *Citatteria & Zackendullst*, and in 1994 *Tarzan am Prenzlauer Berg*.

Ludwig Fels was born in Treuchtlingen in 1946, and was a brewery worker, labourer, machine operator, press worker and packer. Since 1973 he has lived from writing and in 1983 he moved to Vienna. He has published numerous volumes of prose, poetry and drama, including *Der Anfang der Vergangenheit* (poems, 1984), *Die Eroberung der Liebe, Heimatbilder* (1985), *Rosen für Afrika* (novel,

1987), *Blaue Allee, versprengte Tataren* (poems, 1988), 'Der Himmel war eine grosse Gegenwart' (story, 1990), *Bleeding Heart* (novel, 1993), the plays *Heldenleben* and *Ich küsse Ihren Hund, Madam* (both 1985).

Robert Gernhardt was born in 1937 in Estonia and studied painting and German in Stuttgart and Berlin. He is one of the editors of the satirical magazine *Titanic* and a member of the German Artists' Association. He lives in Frankfurt am Main. His most recent publications are *Glück-Glanz-Ruhm. Erzählung-Betrachtung-Bericht* (1990) and *Lug und Trug. Drei exemplarische Erzählungen* (1991), *Die Falle. Eine Weihnachtsgeschichte* (1993) and a volume of poetry *Weiche Ziele* (1994).

Peter Glaser was born in Graz, Upper Austria in 1957. After various jobs such as night security guard, surveyor and assembly line worker, he has lived as a full-time author in Hamburg since 1983. He writes for the weekly newspaper *Die Zeit*, for the magazines *Pflasterstrand, Tempo* and *Lui* and is a regular contributor to *Datenschleuder*, the magazine of the Chaos Computer Club, Hamburg. His publications are *Schönheit in Waffen. Stories* (1985), *Vorliebe, Journal einer erotischen Arbeit* (1986), *Glasers heile Welt. Peter Glaser über neues im Westen* (1988) and the play *Die Osiris Legende* (1988).

Rainald Goetz, born 1954, completed a Ph.D in history and a medical degree (he has worked in psychiatric hospitals). He is a contributor, as cultural commentator, to the magazines *Der Spiegel, Transatlantik, Konkret, Merkur* and *Kursbuch*. In 1993 he was awarded the Mülheim Drama Prize for the second time. His first novel *Irre* (1983) caused a considerable stir. *Krieg* (plays) and *Hirn* (stories) appeared in 1986, followed by the novels *Kontrolliert* (1988) and *Die Festung* (1993).

Daniel Grolle was born in Giessen in 1963, he now lives in Hamburg. First published at the age of twelve, later texts appeared in anthologies, *Nicht mit dir und nicht ohne dich* (1983), *Schule über Leben* (1983), *Frühreif. Texte aus der Plastiktüte* (1984), *Ein Lied, das jeder kennt* (1985).

Christoph Hein was born in Silesia in 1944, grew up near Leipzig and attended grammar school in West Berlin, but moved back to East Berlin in 1960. He was a waiter, bookseller, assembly line worker, journalist, assistant stage director, then studied philosophy and became dramaturg and writer at the Volksbühne in Berlin. He has received several prizes, including, in 1990, the Erich Fried Prize. His most recent publications include *Öffentlich arbeiten. Essays und Gespräche* (1987), *Der Tangospieler* (novel, 1989), *Die fünfte Grundrechenart. Aufsätze und Reden 1986–89* (1990), as well as the plays *Die wahre Geschichte des Ah Q* (1983), *Passage* (1987), *Die Ritter der Tafelrunde* (1989) and the novel *Napoleonspiel* (1993). Several of Christoph Hein's novels have been translated into English.

Bodo Kirchhoff was born in Hamburg in 1948. After two years military service and a long stay in the USA, he studied education, gaining his Ph.D in 1978. He has been writing plays and prose since he was at school. From 1982 Kirchhoff began to write reports for the periodical *Transatlantik* and travelled extensively. Out of his travel experiences developed his first novel *Zwiefalten* (1983), the play *Glücklich ist, wer vergisst*, the *Mexikanische Novelle* (1984), several books of short stories and in 1990 the novel *Infanta* (which was translated into English). The novel *Der Sandmann* appeared in 1992, his novella *Gegen die Laufrichtung* in 1993.

Gerhard Köpf was born in Allgäu (Bavaria) in 1948, studied German, took a doctorate and taught at various universities. He lives in Munich. His most recent publications are the novella *Borges gibt es nicht* (1991), *Piranesis Traum. Roman einer Autobiographie* (1992) and *Papas Koffer* (1993).

Brigitte Kronauer was born in Essen in 1940. She studied education and was a teacher. Since 1971 she has lived in Hamburg as a full-time writer. Her most recent books are the novel *Die Frau in den Kissen* (1990), *Schnurrer. Geschichten* (1992) and *Hin- und herbrausende Züge. Erzählungen* (1993), and *Das Taschentuch* (1994), a novel.

Katja Lange-Müller was born in Berlin (GDR) and worked as copy editor, picture editor and compositor and was for five years an auxiliary nurse in Berlin hospitals. From 1979 to 1982 she studied at the Johannes R. Becher Institute of Literature in Leipzig. She lived in the People's Republic of Mongolia for a year before being employed as a publisher's reader. In November 1984 she moved to West Berlin and in 1986 she was awarded the Ingeborg Bachmann

Prize. In 1988 she published *Kaspar Mauser—Die Feigheit vorm Freund*.

Irina Liebmann was born in Moscow in 1943. She studied Sinology in Leipzig. Since 1975 she has lived in Berlin. In 1981 her first book *Berliner Mietshaus* was published in the then GDR. It was followed by reportages and plays for the radio and the stage. In 1987 she was awarded the Ernst Willner Prize in Klagenfurt, since when she has published several novels.

Klaus Modick was born in Oldenburg in 1951. He studied German, philosophy and history and has worked as a waiter, advertising copywriter and editor. Since 1982 he has lived in Wiefelsfelde as freelance writer, critic and translator. He has published four novels, *Das Grau der Karolinen* (1986), *Ins Blaue* (1987), *Das Licht in den Steinen* (1992) and *Der Flügel* (1994).

Hanns-Josef Ortheil was born in Cologne in 1951. He studied music, German, philosophy and comparative literature. After his doctorate he was an assistant lecturer at the University of Mainz. He has been a full-time writer since 1988 and lives in Stuttgart. His most recent novels are *Agenten* (1989), *Fermer* (1991), *Abschied von den Kriegsteilnehmern* (1992) and he has also published a volume of essays *Das Element des Elephants. Wie mein Schreiben begann* (1994).

Karin Reschke was born in Kraków in 1940 and grew up in Berlin. She worked for a number of magazines and since 1975 has been writing reportages, prose and reviews. Her second book *Verfolgte des Glücks—Findbuch der Henriette Vogel* (1982) was awarded the literature prize of the *Frankfurter Allgemeine Zeitung*. In 1987 she published *Margarete*, in 1993 the novel *Das Lachen im Wald*, and in 1994 a further novel *Asphaltvenus*.

Anna Rheinsberg was born in Berlin in 1956 and studied German and ethnology. She was co-editor of the Marburger Frauenliteratur-zeitung. Her most recent publications are *Herzlos. Kerlsgeschichten* (1988), *Kriegs/Läufe. Namen. Schrift. Über Emmy Hennings, Claire Goll und Else Rüthel* (essays, 1989) and *Narcisse Noir* (poems, 1990).

Jochen Schimmang was born in Northeim in 1948 and grew up in East Friesland. He studied in West Berlin and has lived in Cologne since 1978. Further publications are the novel *Die Geistesgegenwart* (1990), *Carmen. Eine Geschichte* (1992) and *Königswege* (1995).

Botho Strauss was born in Naumburg in 1944. He studied German, theatre history and sociology. He acted in amateur productions, was an editor and critic of the periodical *Theater heute* and dramaturg at the Schaubühne theatre in Berlin, where he lives. Strauss' plays have made him famous. He has been awarded the Georg Büchner Prize (1989) and the Berlin Theatre prize (1991). His most recent publications include *Theaterstücke* (2 vols, 1991), *Angelas Kleider. Nachtstück in zwei Teilen* (1991), *Beginnlosigkeit. Reflexionen* (1992), *Das Gleichgewicht. Stück in drei Akten* (1993) and *Wohnen-DämmernLügen* (1994).

Christoph Wackernagel, born 1951, actor and printer, member of the Red Army Faction, served 15 years in prison. After his release he dissociated himself from the RAF. In 1986 he published *Nadja. Erzählungen und Fragmente.*

Johanna Walser was born in Ulm in 1957, studied German and philosophy in Berlin and lives and writes by Lake Constance. In 1986 she published the novel *Die Unterwerfung* and in 1991 *Wetterleuchten. Erzählungen.*

Permissions

Katja Behrens, 'Liebe' from *Die weisse Frau. Erzählungen,,* © Suhrkamp Verlag, Frankfurt am Main 1978.

Thomas Brasch, 'Fliegen im Gesicht' from *Vor den Vätern sterben die Söhne,* © Rotbuch Verlag, Berlin 1977.

Clemens Eich, 'Gegenlicht im Zwischenraum' from *Zwanzig nach drei. Erzählungen,* © S. Fischer Verlag, Frankfurt am Main 1987.

Adolf Endler, 'Vorbildlich schleimlösend/Notizen' and 'Aus der Arbeit der KOSABLA' both from *Vorbildlich schleimlösend,* © Rotbuch Verlag, Berlin 1990.

Ludwig Fels, 'Jemand aus der Familie' from *Kanakenfauna. Fünfzehn Berichte,* which was published in 1982 by Hermann Luchterhand Verlag, GmbH & Co. KG, Darmstadt and Neuwied., © 1993 by Ludwig Fels.

Robert Gernhardt, 'Reich der Sinne, Welt der Wörter' and 'Die Bronzen von Riace', both in *Kippfigur. Erzählungen,* © Haffmanns Verlag AG, Zürich 1986.

Peter Glaser, 'AUS' from *aus. Mord Stories.* Edited by Herbert Winkels, © Verlag Kiepenheuer and Witsch, Köln 1986.

Rainald Goetz, 'Was ist ein Klassiker' from *Hirn. Geschichten,* © Suhrkamp Verlag, Frankfurt am Main 1986. 'Kontrolliert' from *Kontrolliert* (pp 288–296), © Suhrkamp Verlag, Frankfurt am Main 1988.

Daniel Grolle, 'Da ist was da unten' and 'Mord' both from *Keinen Schritt weiter. Erzählungen,* © Hermann Luchterhand Verlag GmbH & Co. KG, Darmstadt and Neuwied 1986.

Christoph Hein, 'Leb wohl, mein Freund, es ist schwer zu sterben' and 'Nachtfahrt und früher Morgen' both from *Nachtfahrt und früher Morgen. Prosa,* © Aufbau Verlag, Berlin and Weimar 1980.

Bodo Kirchhoff, 'Im Operncafé' from *Ferne Frauen. Erzählungen,* © Suhrkamp Verlag, Frankfurt am Main 1987.

Gerhard Köpf, 'Fahrenheit' from *Innerfern. Novel.* Published 1983 by S. Fischer Verlag, Frankfurt am Main., © Luchterhand Literaturverlag, Hamburg 1993.

Brigitte Kronauer, 'Die Frau in den Kissen' from *Enten und Knäckbrot. Sieben Erzählungen,* © Ernst Klett Verlage GmbH und Co. KG, Stuttgart 1988.

Katja Lange-Müller, 'Die grosse Reise' and 'Manchmal kommt der Dot auf Latschen' both from *Wehleid—Wie im Leben. Erzählungen,* © S. Fischer Verlag GmbH, Frankfurt am Main 1986.